THE CASE RUNNER

THE CASE RUNNER

Carlos Cisneros

Arte Público Press
Houston, Texas

The Case Runner is made possible through grants from the City of Houston through the Houston Arts Alliance and the Exemplar Program, a program of Americans for the Arts in collaboration with the LarsonAllen Public Services Group, funded by the Ford Foundation.

Recovering the past, creating the future

Arte Público Press
University of Houston
452 Cullen Performance Hall
Houston, Texas 77204-2004

Illustration by Manuel Meza
Cover design by Exact Type

Cisneros, Carlos
    The Case Runner / by Carlos Cisneros.
        p.   cm.
    ISBN 978-1-55885-510-6 (alk. paper)
    1. Mexican-American Border Region—Fiction. 2. Texas—Fiction. I. Title.
PS3603.I86C37 2008
813'.6—dc22

2007047292
CIP

♾ The paper used in this publication meets the requirements of the American National Standard for Information Sciences—Permanence of Paper for Printed Library Materials, ANSI Z39.48-1984.

8 9 0 1 2 3 4 5 6 7   10 9 8 7 6 5 4 3 2 1

This book is dedicated to my parents, Mere & Chabe,
and to my wife, Lynda, and the kids,
Carlitos, Alex, and Annie.

Disclaimer

This is a work of fiction. All similarity to people, places, events and situations is purely coincidental

Acknowledgments

A special thanks to the wonderful folks at Arte Público Press and to Bill and Martha Greenleaf. Thanks for believing.

Prologue

Rio Grande Valley, near the Texas-Mexico border, April 2003

THE YOUNG MOTHER STRUGGLED to move her legs but had no sensation in either of them. She lay pinned down between the soil and the flattened roof of the passenger van, barely breathing, her hip bones crushed to pieces. In the darkness, she could smell her gasoline-soaked clothes. With great effort, she freed one arm and ran her hand over her face. She was caked in blood and mud. Although her left arm was dislocated at the shoulder, her left hand still clutched a brown teddy bear.

"*Mi hijo, mi hijo*," she cried out in a raspy whisper, her jaw bone broken in two places. "My son." There was no answer. All she could hear was the agonized moaning of another victim dying inside the van. She felt herself drifting in and out of consciousness. "*Por el amor de Dios*," she sighed one more time, "*¿dónde está mi bebé?*"

Struggling to stay awake, she was now shivering and going into shock. She thought of her husband back in Mexico and how much she missed him. She wondered if this was the end for her and her baby boy.

When she came to again, two figures were working on her legs. "*Por favor, ¡encuentren a mi bebé!*" she wept desperately. "*¡Por favor!*"

She tried to pull herself up and get their attention. To her horror, both her legs were missing. That's when she felt the knife like pain from the tourniquets.

"No!" she screamed in agony. Seconds later, one of the figures reached over and gave her a shot of morphine. The pain was gone, and so was she.

The tire blow out that had sent the passenger van flying off the South Texas highway—ejecting most of its passengers to their death—was caused by a poorly constructed Firelazer XP All-weather Radial Tire. When the 911 call came, Emergency Medical Services and law enforcement personnel were dispatched from the nearby cities of Raymondville and Harlingen.

The Valley Methodist Star Flight helicopter and crew were also summoned and put on standby. For State Trooper Tom Martinez—an accident reconstruction specialist with the Texas Department of Public Safety responding to the call that muggy Saturday morning—the bloody carnage smelled of payday.

"What do we have?" Martinez asked one of several Emergency Medical Services technicians working frantically on the victims.

"You don't want to know," said Peterson, a paramedic at the scene. He was fuming. "If you ask me, it appears like a bunch of illegal aliens being smuggled up north."

"Doesn't surprise me," Martinez said, sounding disgusted. "How many fatalities?" He was wearing the standard-issue gray uniform, black boots, and black windbreaker with the words *DPS FORENSICS* across the back in white.

"Don't know yet . . . still counting, maybe eight. Wait! Make it nine, if the amputee over there doesn't make it." He pointed out a female lying next to the overturned van. "She's in bad shape."

"What are her chances?" Martinez asked.

"Not good."

"Man, what a mess!" Martinez uttered as he photographed and measured the scene. He was having difficulty negotiating his way around the muddy sorghum field, twisted metal, debris, and dead bodies.

"I hear you," agreed Peterson, "It's been a few years since we've had a rollover with so many fatalities."

"Any ID on the victims?"

"Yes, I think Sheriff Deputy Guerra has that info," replied Peterson as he pointed the deputy out in the distance. Deputy Guerra could be heard a few feet away communicating with headquarters as he exchanged information regarding the victims and the company that owned the passenger van. Another deputy was sitting in a patrol car parked on the road's shoulder, writing his reports.

"Hey, Deputy Guerra," yelled Martinez, "come take a look." The trooper was kneeling down near the crumpled front end of the van.

"What is it?"

"Have you had a chance to see this tire?" he asked.

"No. Why?"

"Here's the cause of the accident," Martinez said matter-of-factly. "The left front tire's treads came apart, causing the driver to lose control. Add to the mix the van's high center of gravity and speed . . . and nine times out of ten you'll end up with this, a deadly combination."

"Yes, you're right," said Guerra. "And look here. The van flipped at least four times, tossing its occupants like puppets . . . some as far as seventy feet." He was pointing out the places within the twenty-acre sorghum field where he'd found some of the bodies.

Martinez fixed his hat and, pointing to the horizon, added, "I found pieces of the tire's treads, about two hundred feet that way from the point of impact with the cattle fence. Judging by the weight of the van, the distance between the rim's prints on the asphalt and the final resting point . . . I would say the van plowed through the fence at eighty miles per hour. Not even Jeff Gordon would've been able to bring the van under control at such speed."

"They must have been flying," the sheriff deputy replied as he scratched his head in amazement.

While pretending to continue to canvass the scene's large area, the state trooper walked away from the rest of the emergency personnel and placed a call on his cell phone.

"Hello?" answered the man at the end of the line.

"Jeff," Martinez said quietly, "Jeff Chordelli, is that you?"

"Yes," the man said, "this is Jeff. What can I do for you, Tom?"

"Hey, Jeff," Martinez said as he struggled with the cell phone on his shoulder and tried to light up a cigarette at the same time. "I didn't recognize your voice." His back was facing the others, and he was trying not to speak too loudly.

"What is it?" Chordelli asked.

"I got a case for you and Willy."

"Oh yeah? I'm all ears."

"Here's what I got so far," Martinez replied, blowing a cloud of cigarette smoke. "Rollover accident outside Raymondville, middle of nowhere. Defective left front tire. Fifteen-passenger van. So far, there are eight fatalities, including a young boy, three survivors with serious, life-threatening injuries."

"It smells like big money. With that many fatalities, we should be able to squeeze the defendants for at least twenty million, possibly more."

"You want Willy to take over?" asked Martinez.

"Yes," ordered Chordelli, "tell him we need all of the relatives signed up, ASAP. Wives, husbands, parents, everyone with a potential claim, I want all of them on board. There's no time to waste."

"All right. I'll have him get on it right away."

"Bye."

Click.

The investigation into the rollover accident later revealed that all victims had boarded the fifteen-passenger van in Brownsville, Texas at 4:30 a.m. that foggy Saturday morning. They had been on the road a little over an hour when the rollover occurred. Most had been headed to Houston.

Two were headed to Gary, Indiana, where they worked at the IBP meat plant. They had been visiting relatives in Mexico. Wives and children awaited their return back in Gary.

One young female, en route to Florida, worked in Orlando as a housekeeper in one of Disney's properties, the Floridian Hotel. She shared an apartment with two friends from El Salvador.

Five young men, all in their twenties and single, worked together on an oil rig off the coast of Houston. They were from the Mexican Gulf cities of Tampico and Veracruz.

The only other female passenger and her young son were believed to be from a place near Puebla in Central Mexico. Their origins were not exactly clear.

Chapter 1

THE LAW OFFICE OF ALEJANDRO DEL FUERTE was scheduled to open for business sometime in the late summer or early fall of 2004. For three months, prior to hanging his shingle, the twenty-five-year-old had been busy making plans to move back home and embark on his professional career. That summer in Houston, while waiting for his Bar results, he'd started making plans for his return to Brownsville. He'd sold his worldly possessions in a garage sale, netting about one thousand bucks, and sank about two hundred dollars into his old beat-up MG Midget to fix the brakes and tune it for the trip. And he'd spent the week before he left visiting old friends before the big send-off celebration at Elvia's Jazz Cantina on Westheimer Boulevard.

As a baby lawyer, he'd managed to score a small office across from the Cameron County courthouse. He had convinced the landlord of the old, decrepit office building to agree to an oral lease for two hundred dollars a month. The deal had been done over the phone. They had exchanged the one-hundred-dollar deposit and office keys through the mail. The newly licensed attorney was ready and anxious to hang his shingle and start making money to pay off his student loans.

Saturday morning, Alejandro del Fuerte landed in downtown Brownsville and headed to his office to get ready for Monday. He'd driven through the empty streets in and around downtown with the car's top down, enjoying the South Texas morning. Alex, as his friends and law professors knew him, had yet to step into a courtroom, lock horns with opposing counsel over a contested hearing, argue a simple motion or even make an announcement. He was a baby lawyer, plain and simple. Even the time spent as a child working at his grandfather's Notaria Pública No. 44 in Mexico had not prepared him for the real practice of law, with real clients and real judges, in the real world.

The young attorney was in the process of unloading boxes from the trunk of his car when, out of the corner of his eye, he noticed an old man sitting on the curb across the street. The old man seemed to be talking to himself, oblivious to what was going on around him and puffing away on a cigarette. The man was deep in thought and never noticed Alex walking briskly up to him.

"Are you okay?" asked Alex. "*¿Estás bien?*"

Startled, the old man jumped to his feet and looked the young man over, glancing at his South Texas College of Law T-shirt, worn jeans, and tennis shoes. But he said nothing.

Alex pressed him for an answer. "*Buenos días,*" he extended his hand to greet the old man.

Trembling, the man took his hat off, pulled it close to his chest, looked down meekly, and said, "*Buenos días, señor.*" He would not shake hands with the young attorney.

"Are you okay? *¿Le puedo ayudar en algo?*" asked Alex, both in Spanish and English.

"I don't know, *señor* . . . I come look . . . for my *familia,*" replied the old man in broken English. "I need help. Lost, *perdido. ¿Me puede ayudar usted?*" He was clutching his hat over his heart with one hand and with the other making signals as he tried to explain his words.

"Let's talk in my office," Alex shot back in Spanish as he grabbed the old man by the arm and led him toward the small building in the middle of the city block, across the street. The old man struggled to follow Alex. He made it into the building and followed him down a dark, narrow corridor.

"*Qué bueno que habla español,*" he said as he gave thanks to the *Virgen de Guadalupe* for enabling him to meet someone who spoke Spanish.

"I also speak English," added Alex.

"*Qué ventaja,*" the old man marveled. It was such an advantage to speak both languages, and speak them well.

"It can be," Alex acknowledged.

They walked through a door with the words *Alejandro del Fuerte—Abogado, Criminal Law, Personal Injury, and Family Law* on it.

"Here, take a seat," said Alex, pointing to a fold-out chair placed in front of a small desk. They were both now talking in Spanish, just like two long-lost friends who had not seen each other in years.

"*Gracias.*"

"I'm sorry for the way my office looks," explained Alex as he gestured at the boxes of books on the floor. "I'm barely starting out. I hope you will excuse the appearance. *Disculpe el tiradero.*"

"It reminds me of my home, back in my mountain village," said the old man. "We have very little furniture."

"Oh, yeah?"

"*Sí.*" The old man looked toward the boxes scattered throughout the office. "We lead simple lives. . . . We even sit and sleep on *petates* on the floor. It is a humble home, with dirt floors and twigs for a roof."

"I see."

"How long have you had your office?"

"Just started. I'll be open for business on Monday."

"May I have some water?" asked the old man tentatively, seeming embarrassed to be a pest.

"*Seguro.* Let me get it for you." Alex got up from the desk and walked to another room in the back. He rummaged through a box looking for an old coffee mug from law school. The sound of the running water faucet filled both empty rooms. Seconds later, Alex returned to his place behind the desk and handed the cup to the old man. "Here you go. What's your name?"

The old man took a big swig, put the mug down on the desk, and said, "Porfirio Medina, *Señor Licenciado*. But my friends back at the village call me Pilo . . . P-i-l-o." He took another drink out of the cup.

"Please call me Alex, and forget the *Señor Licenciado* stuff. Did you just cross the river?" Alex asked as he looked the man's clothes over. They were muddy, wet, and covered with grass stains.

"Yes. There was a heavy fog as I waded across the river. I vaguely remembered the area from over thirty years ago when I came to the States looking for work."

"So, you got here this morning?" Alex peeked at his watch. It was only 8:00 a.m.

"Yes. It took about two weeks to hitchhike from my village in Central Mexico to Matamoros. I crossed the river two or three hours ago, when the fog was thickest."

"So that was around four or five in the morning? Any problems?"

"I almost went down," explained Pilo, "but managed to elude the agents. The two parked under a large *huisache* tree were asleep. The agents on bikes were another story. They gave pursuit, but the fog was thick, and I lost them. I hid under a bridge at a nearby golf course."

"*Ah, sí*, I know the area," said Alex, "it's called the Fort Brown Golf Course, right on the river levee." It was an area with heavy traffic that was flanked on one side by the campus of the University of Texas at Brownsville and on the other side by the downtown area. "Well, I'm surprised you didn't get caught," Alex added, sounding amazed. "The agents even harass the golfers who go down there to play."

"Even guys like you?"

"Even guys like me. It's a hassle. Let me tell you, one time a rookie even detained a Texas state official by accident."

"So, what happened?"

"They let the senator go, but he raised hell, and the rookie got transferred to Alaska," said Alex with a grin.

"I guess I got lucky, then."

"Yep, you did. You must have a pretty strong reason to risk getting arrested and maybe even going to prison, especially at your age."

Pilo stopped for a moment and took another drink. "I'm searching for my wife Rosario and my three-year-old son, Juan José. It has been almost a year, and I haven't had any news of them."

"How often would you hear from them before?"

"My wife would wire me some *pesitos* every month. She would drop me a line every other month or so."

"So, the money and the letters stopped coming altogether?"

"Yes," Pilo replied.

"Where were they supposed to have been staying?"

"*Aquí mismo, en Brownsville.* The last letter I received from my wife had a Brownsville return address." Pilo pulled a crumpled envelope from a brown paper sack covered in oil stains and handed it to the attorney. "That's why I'm here. I hope they're okay." The old man was now staring down at the worn, stained carpet that covered the floor. His eyes were watery.

"So, you got worried and came looking for them?"

"*Sí, señor*, that's it."

Alex took the envelope. The return address read:

> Rosario Medina
> 49 Shadow Brook Lane
> Brownsville, Texas 78520

It was addressed to:

> Sr. Porfirio Medina
> Callejón de Palmas 36
> Tepantitlán, Edo. de Puebla
> México, C.P. 213789

Alex examined the envelope carefully. He recognized the residential area listed on the return address but did not recognize the area in Mexico.

"Where is Tepantitlán?"

"It's a little village on the outskirts of Teotihuacán in Central Mexico," Pilo explained. "Have you heard of the Pyramids of Teotihuacán?"

"Yes, I've always wanted to go. Maybe I'll get to see them someday."

"We live nearby. There's not much there. The villagers take their chances and travel to *El Norte*. Some die at the hands of *co-*

yotes, others drown or die of dehydration. I got lucky and made it, but not before getting robbed by highway robbers and beaten to a pulp by the *federales,* who were trying to extort a bribe."

"Is that the reason for the black eye and scratches on your forehead?" Alex asked, probing a bit.

"*Sí.*" Now Pilo was also pointing to his teeth.

"They knocked out your front teeth, too?" asked Alex, eyes wide open. He felt terrible for the old man. Even his own teeth started hurting.

"This is nothing," explained Pilo, shrugging his shoulders. "I have heard of others that get arrested by *la Migra* and spend years in prison. My wife and son got lucky and managed to sneak across in the spring of 2002. They were to stay with a relative until my wife could find work as a live-in maid somewhere."

Alex interrupted. "Do you have the relative's name?"

"Her name is Aurora López, she's my wife's aunt. I have a phone number." Pilo pulled a folded piece of paper with scribbling on it from a crumpled paper sack.

"Did you try calling her?"

"No. I could never figure out how to call the States."

"I see. When was the last time you heard from them?"

"That letter was the last thing I received. It was around March of 2003."

"I see the envelope. But where's the letter?"

"I only brought the envelope. The letters are back home, buried in a box. I thought all I needed was the address. Why, do you need the letter?"

"No. I was just wondering."

"All the letters had the same return address. That's where they had been staying in Brownsville."

"Well, I guess the address can point you in the right direction," Alex said. "At least that's a starting point."

"You know, I heard all these horror stories of things that happen to the *mojados*, so when my family found a job, a place to live, I thought they would be safe. But now I don't know what to think. For her not to write, to not send money is very strange. That was not like my Rosario. It's killing me."

"I know what you mean," Alex replied as he looked at Pilo. The old man was having a hard time containing the tears.

"I prayed to God every day and gave him thanks because they were okay," Pilo said between sobs. "At least Rosario had not fallen prey to a slave ring. Rumor had it there was a sex ring in McAllen, across from Reynosa. Did you hear about that?"

"What was that?" asked Alex, dumbfounded.

"Smugglers that keep the women as sex slaves."

"No, I never heard that. But I read somewhere that the organizations kept the children for ransom."

"Really?" blurted out Pilo in shock, eyebrows raised. It was obvious he'd never considered that possibility.

"That's what I heard. So, you're lucky that Rosario and Juanito made it to Brownsville okay." Alex glimpsed at the calendar on the desk and realized that it was now almost the end of August 2004. The letter was postmarked Brownsville, March 17, 2003.

"I hope they're safe. On my way over here, I kept thinking the problem was the mail. Mexico has the slowest mail, and Tepantitlán is in the middle of nowhere. That's what I wanted to believe. I don't mind dying, as long as I know that they are fine. That's all I want. Can you help me?"

The toothless *indio* looked like he was ready to croak of sorrow and affliction. He was clutching his hat and the paper bag close to his chest as he blew his nose into a rag. He turned away as he struggled to contain his tears. Alex could relate. He'd been raised, single-handedly, by his grandfather. His parents had died when he was in the fourth grade. He missed them every day, probably the same way the old man missed his wife and baby.

"I see," Alex added nervously. "Let me think." He played with the envelope in his hands. Yes, he felt terrible for Pilo, but the whole thing also made him uncomfortable. Having the old man sitting in front of him opened the door to all these sad and distant memories. Maybe it was better not to get involved.

"*Ayúdeme* . . ." Pilo begged with sad eyes.

"So how are you going to find your family?" Alex asked, trying to ignore the old man's request.

"That I don't know. I guess the *Virgen de Guadalupe* will show me the way. She kept me from dying on the side of the highway. And how do you explain the fog this morning? And not getting nabbed by the Border Patrol? My faith will get me to my family. She put you in my path. Please help me find them."

"I don't do this kind of work, but I can show you how to find the address on the envelope on a Brownsville map."

What Alex, the recent law school grad, needed was paying clients. Clients with big fat cash retainers. And from what he could gather, the decrepit old man probably didn't have even a hundred dollars to his name.

"*Por favor, señor*, help me find my family. It shouldn't be too hard."

"You don't understand. I don't have the time or the resources. What's worse, I don't even know if an attorney can help an illegal alien. As we sit here, for all I know I might be breaking some shitty federal law somewhere. And I just got licensed. I don't want to lose my license right off the bat because it turns out I was helping a person in your situation. Besides, do you have any money?"

"I have *trescientos pesos*."

"Thirty dollars?"

"*Sí, señor*. Those are my last *pesitos* I managed to hide from the highway robbers. You can have them."

"I can't take your last thirty dollars. It's not worth it. Besides, what's going to happen to you?"

"I'll be fine. I can eat from the garbage cans and find a place to hide in the meantime. It won't kill me."

"I don't think I can take your last three hundred pesos," replied Alex, all the while thinking of the fifty- and one-hundred-thousand-dollar retainers his criminal trial advocacy professor would flaunt in class. Hell! Professor D'Guerlain had shared with the class the story about the rich millionaire accused of murder who paid a million-dollar retainer. That was what Alex needed. Clients with cash. With *billetes, lana, feria!* Not some poor, undocumented wetback asking for a handout.

"*¿Por favor?*" begged Pilo with sad eyes.

"I just can't do it," Alex explained. "It's not right. I would feel terrible taking your last three hundred pesos and then forcing you to eat out of a dumpster or something like that." Truth be told, the young man didn't have the guts to tell the old man that thirty dollars just was not going to cut it. What kind of retainer was that? If D'Guerlain ever found out, he would die laughing.

"I see," Pilo muttered in anguish.

"Why don't you go seek help at the Mexican Consulate here in Brownsville? It's not far from here."

"*Ta bueno*, I guess I'll be going, then. Sorry to have bothered you. I didn't mean to take your time."

Alex felt terrible, but he needed to be firm. This was a business, and he needed paying clients. Professor Lawton had said that was the hardest part of the job: having to say no.

"*Mira*," Alex interjected, "I'm sure the Mexican Consulate can help you. They're very good about helping all the Mexican nationals that end up in trouble over here."

"Do you really think they will want to help a Tlahuica Indian like me?"

"I don't see why not. They're there to help. That's their job."

"Well, then, can you tell me how to get there?" Pilo asked. "I don't want to waste any more of your time."

"We're on Harrison and Eighth. Go to Sixth Street, two blocks up, and left until you see Elizabeth Street," said Alex, pointing the way. But right then and there, Alex stopped cold in his tracks. He remembered seeing agents on bikes always casing the consulate. He was sending the old man to the vultures. It was one thing to need paying clients and quite another to hand the old man over to the feds.

"*Espera*," said Alex, "maybe that's not such a hot idea. I don't think you should walk to the consulate. Not now, anyway. I don't think you should walk around downtown looking like that. You'll stick out like a sore thumb."

"Eh?" the old man muttered. He stood there, looking confused. He seemed to be struggling with the grim prospect of having to leave the safety of Alejandro del Fuerte's law office.

"Damn it!" mumbled Alex quietly under his breath. It looked like he was stuck with the old man. Certainly he couldn't let him walk out of the office in plain daylight.

Why me? thought Alex. *I didn't sign up for this. I need clients that can pay big chingón honorarios—fat, juicy retainers! I don't need this crap right now! Please God, help me figure out what to do. Someday down the road, I'll do my pro bono work, but not right now. My student loans will be due any day now. I need paying clients, please, for the love of God!*

"*Ándele, Mr. del Fuerte, écheme la mano,*" interrupted the pesky old man. "Lend me a hand. I'm almost sixty years of age, and I don't have much time. *Diosito* will repay you. Not knowing what happened to my family is killing me."

"Sixty, is that it?" Alex said, annoyed by the whole situation. "I thought you were older."

"*Bueno,*" Pilo said, the comment having gone right over his head. "I labored all my life in the fields, under the hot sun. As you can see, the hard work and hard life have taken their toll."

They stared at each other in silence, Alex watching Pilo across the desk: two different worlds brought together by chance, just like that. The old man looked as if the American Dream had chewed him up and spit him out; the baby lawyer stood at the Dream's starting gate.

The attorney was deep in thought, shaking his head, looking at the ceiling. Would he end up like the old man, he wondered? Hungry and decrepit, his spirit broken? And if his girlfriend, Paloma, found out he was helping *mojados,* would she approve, especially after the last break up? Hadn't he promised that after the Bar, he would buy her the biggest engagement ring this side of Mexico? But the timing wasn't right, not while he was setting up shop. Surely the moment she found out he was representing an illegal alien with no money, she would hit the roof. Especially when her father, the most powerful figure in the Texas legislature, had offered to call his friends and land him whatever job he wanted, as long as he was serious about marrying his daughter.

Did he want to be the youngest administrative judge the State of Texas had ever seen? Or did he prefer a job as an assistant attorney general, or clerk for the chief justice of the Texas Supreme

Court? Maybe he was cut out to be an insurance defense attorney? After all, several Austin firms had heard that Lieutenant Governor Yarrington had a *yerno* in law school. They had already advised the high-ranking politician that his future son-in-law could count on an excellent-paying job upon graduation. The truth was that those firms were not really interested in Yarrington's future son-in-law. Besides, who the hell was Alejandro del Fuerte? They had never heard of him! He didn't have a famous lawyer dad or famous mother judge. He had no distinguished judicial lineage. He was a nobody. *Who am I kidding?* he thought. *I don't even have the grades. I graduated at the bottom of my class. I barely finished "Summa Cum Difficulty."*

The firms, like all the major players and lobbyists, just wanted the lieutenant governor happy. And with good reason. Using his dominant position in the Texas legislature, Yarrington could pass laws that could either help or destroy a person. Laws that could put someone out of business or help line his or her pockets. Laws that could make a firm a ton of money when clients came knocking. It was about being on the right side of the fence. State agencies and public universities knew this. Daddy Yarrington controlled the purse strings: a $130 billion budget, a budget the size of the state of Texas.

And what if his future son-in-law had not wanted to practice insurance defense? With one phone call, Rene Yarrington had boasted, Alejandro del Fuerte could become an associate at Brace, Kemp, Liddell & Elkins, a plaintiffs' firm with Yarrington's seal of approval. As one of the Texas Five and a big campaign contributor, it was what people called "a firm with Austin and Washington connections." Just one call, and he would be guaranteed the partnership track.

All that is out the window now, thought Alex. *Especially if I choose to help Pilo. Once Paloma tells her daddy that I'm representing wetbacks, the backlash will be intolerable.* He could already hear the harsh words that would be said. This kind of dirt-poor client was a far cry from the lobbying jobs the lieutenant governor had in mind for his future son-in-law. After all, Paloma was used to a certain lifestyle. Time and again, Yarrington had made it perfectly clear that the man who married his little girl had to meet certain standards.

"All right," Alex snapped as he cursed his luck and reached, grudgingly, for a pen and a piece of paper. "Please, sit down. Tell me about Tepantitlán."

"It's a small place with three hundred inhabitants. Mostly Tlahuica Indians, except for the doctor and his wife. We all farm the land in order to survive. There are no jobs, really. The young ones leave to go to *El Norte*. However, it is a beautiful place surrounded by mountains. The beautiful río Caracol runs nearby."

As the old man rambled on about Tepantitlán and its portrait-perfect landscapes, Alex interrupted him. "Did you ever consider that maybe your wife and son moved somewhere else?"

"Yes, the thought crossed my mind. But she would not have just packed up and gone without telling me. That was not like my Rosario."

"Well, let me ask you this. What did she say in her last letter?"

"That they missed me and that she had been thinking about coming home for a while. She wanted to come visit for a few months, let the boy see his dad, and then return to the States. Maybe next time venture up to Houston."

"Really?"

"Yes, she was going to ask the *patrón* if she could go home in the summer and then return in the fall."

"So, after she mailed her last letter, you were expecting her and your son in June, thereabouts?"

"Yes, late May or early June, 2003."

"And they never arrived?"

"That's correct. Then, to make matters worse, I never heard from them again. So, all this time I've been agonizing. Do I go? Do I stay? What if I go search for them, and they show up back home and we miss each other?"

"In her letters, did Rosario describe the family she was working for?"

"No, not really. Only that they were very demanding, but that they loved Juanito. That anytime the couple's grandchildren came to visit, Juanito would play with them. The grandchildren really loved him. They were very nice to my boy."

As Pilo spoke of Juanito, Alex noticed a smile of joy appear on the old man's face. His eyes lit up. No doubt about it, it was clear to Alex that the old man loved and missed his baby boy. It was plain as daylight.

"Now," asked Alex, "during this period of time, when the mail stopped coming, was the mail still being delivered to others in your town?"

"Yes," said Pilo, "the man at the general store and others were getting their mail. Once or twice a month, but it was still coming."

"So, then nothing? No mail? No telegram or moneygram? You never received anything else from Rosario?"

"*Nada.*"

"So for the last eighteen months, you have not had any news, correct?" asked the young attorney as he scribbled notes on his yellow pad.

"Yes. That sounds about right."

"And you're sure that that was their last address at Shadow Brook, here in Brownsville?"

"That has been the same address in all the letters I ever received."

"All right," said Alex, "I'll tell you what I'll do."

"What's that?"

"On Monday," Alex started, "I'll track down the address and maybe call the house or even your wife's aunt Aurora, see if she's heard anything."

"I really appreciate it, Mr. del Fuerte. You don't know how happy you make me."

"So, have you thought about where you're going to stay in the meantime? You need to lay low, you understand that?" Alex pointed out.

"Yes, I will try to do that. I just hope I don't get picked up."

"I'll tell you what," Alex said, rubbing his chin, "go down to the Hotel San Carlos on Washington Street. It's two blocks down that way," said the young attorney as he pulled a couple of bills from his jeans pocket. "Take this sixty dollars and pay for two nights. I'll see you here on Monday after lunch. Maybe I'll have some news for you."

"*Gracias, gracias, señor,*" Pilo replied, barely able to hold back the tears.

"Don't thank me," snapped Alex. "You owe me that money! I had earmarked it for business cards. Believe me, not only am I broke like you, but I'm also eighty thousand dollars in the hole on student loans. If you think about it, that means you're eighty thousand dollars richer than me! How do you like that comparison?"

"You're kidding, right?"

"Am I laughing?" Alex asked in a firm tone. "If you have money left, use it for food, and if you can, go to Jim Jones' Ropa Usada and get other clothes."

"All right, then. I'll do as you say, Mr. del Fuerte."

"Very well. On Monday I'll try to track down the phone number for 49 Shadow Brook Lane and call. Who knows? Maybe Rosario and the boy are still there. Of course, that won't matter if you don't stay out of trouble. If I was a betting man, I'd say the Border Patrol will pick you up. I hope I'm wrong. Watch your back. There are a lot of agents hanging out in the downtown area. So, I wish you luck. Until Monday, you're on your own."

"I'll be careful, Mr. del Fuerte, I promise," Pilo replied. "I thank you with all my heart."

"I mean it, Mr. Medina!" Alex countered. "If you get busted, you'll go in front of Judge Politz. Then you'll serve prison time. Finally, the INS will deport you back to Mexico. To make matters worse, the deportation proceedings can take another year. So, in the meantime you'd be just rotting in jail. And there would be nothing I could do. So, don't get caught."

"I promise I'll watch my back."

"Just to show you how bad things have gotten, I can't even put you up for a night. I could be charged with harboring an illegal alien. And if I gave you a ride anywhere, I could also be charged with transporting an illegal alien. One can never be too careful now that we have Border Patrol agents coming out of our ears here in Brownsville."

"It is that bad, eh?" Pilo asked.

"Like Nazi Germany," replied Alex. "I'll see you Monday after lunch. I'll try to have some news for you."

Alex led Pilo out of the office and pointed the way to the Hotel San Carlos.

Chapter 2

AFTER THE MEETING WITH PILO MEDINA, Alex stayed in his office and got ready for Monday. He finished unloading his remaining belongings from the small trunk of his car and started making a list of supplies needed at the office. The encounter with Pilo had reminded him of his own grandfather. Grandpa lived alone across the border, in Matamoros, and the young attorney made a mental note to go see him in the next few days. Alex and his grandpa had enjoyed great times fishing for red fish and speckled trout in and around the shallow inlets of the Laguna Madre. After the death of his parents and up until the time Alex left to go to college and law school, the young attorney had lived with his grandfather in Matamoros, south of the Texas border.

Alex stopped dusting his old law books, put them down on his desk, and walked over to the only window in his small office. He was trying to find Pilo in the distance but had no luck. Across the street and past the Cameron County courthouse, in the skyline, he could make out the arches of the gateway bridge to Matamoros. He thought about his client and wondered if he'd made it to the safety of the Hotel San Carlos.

The meeting with Pilo had triggered all kinds of bittersweet childhood memories. He'd grown up in this cross-cultural vortex in which national boundary lines got blurred. Americans worked across the river in Matamoros. Mexicans from Matamoros shopped and studied in Brownsville. Both cultures flowed and merged back and forth. They grew, married, lived together, and both economies relied heavily on each other. Alex himself, the son of Mexican nationals, had been born in Brownsville and had graduated from St. Ignatius Catholic High School in Brownsville.

Smugglers' Alley—as the locals called the stretch of border from the Gulf of Mexico to Brownsville—had seen its share of trends. During the Civil War, the confederates smuggled cotton out from the Port of Bagdad at the mouth of the Rio Grande, in exchange for medicines and war supplies. At the turn of the century, guns and ammunition were smuggled into Mexico from Brownsville. During the Prohibition years, thousands flocked to Matamoros to drink. Even gasoline, cooking oil, American beef, chicken, pork, and other staples were continuously smuggled into Mexico by the food service and hospitality industries there.

In the 70s and 80s, American and Japanese electronics were smuggled into Mexico out of Brownsville's airport via small private airplanes. At that time, these rogue pilots started selling empty cargo space in their planes to the drug cartels and smuggled cocaine and marijuana back into the United States. Recently, the area had seen alien smuggling organizations spring up in record numbers. There were even organizations dedicated to smuggling drug profits out of the States.

Like a lot of other attorneys starting out, Alejandro del Fuerte had not gone to law school thinking that one day he would become a lawyer and start lending money to his clients. Much less did he think that his first client was going to be an undocumented alien, which, in itself, presented all kinds of problems. Alex had always dreamed of litigating big cases against corporate wrongdoers. Nothing would give him more pleasure than making a name for himself as the lawyer for the underdog and, ultimately, giving a bloody nose to corporate America in the form of big jury verdicts —headline grabbers, seven- and eight-figure verdicts.

But the reality of having graduated in the lower fifty percent of his class, with mountains of debt, and not wanting to use his girlfriend's dad's political connections, called for practicing what they called "door law." Alex was hanging his shingle because it wasn't as if the top firms were knocking at his door trying to recruit him.

Completing law school had been a major struggle. He'd waited tables and bartended to pay his way but still managed to rack up almost eighty thousand dollars in student loans. He couldn't afford an answering service, much less a receptionist. His office was bare, the only furniture being a beat-up desk, an old file cabinet, a typewriter, his computer from law school, and boxes of used law books and junk. What happened to the sign-on bonus and the litigator's job with the top firms? What about the firm retreats and the partnership track?

Well, this was it, solo practice. Not a month after passing the Bar and with less than a few hundred bucks to his name, he was lending money to his first client. Maybe Lieutenant Governor Yarrington had been right! Maybe it was time to let him make some calls for Alex, and so end the struggle. His future father-in-law could find him a real cushy job, with perks and a corner office overlooking Town Lake in Austin. Alex would be having lunch at the Headliner's Club on Seventh Street, enjoying the good life.

He looked for the notes of his meeting with Pilo. What did Rosario and the boy look like? he wondered. Was she really as pretty as Pilo claimed? Could it be that maybe she had simply fallen out of love and left the old man for a younger one?

He tried to picture the kind of family that would take in a live-in maid with a young boy. Were they rich? Middle class? Hispanic? Well, he was not going to spend a lot of time on this file. He was already losing money. He needed to hustle and bring in paying clients. Clients with real money, whether dollars or pesos. He could use them both. He needed to get on the ball. Monday would be the day to go introduce himself to the judges and beg for court appointments.

Chapter 3

THE ADDRESS ROSARIO HAD GIVEN PILO, 49 Shadow Brook, was in a tony Brownsville neighborhood called Hidden Meadows Professional Estates. Alex knew of the area because growing up he'd heard that this was where judges, lawyers, and doctors lived. The homes were palatial in size, sat on five-acre plots, and none was worth less than half a million.

The home was guarded by a tall brick fence, which made it almost impossible to peek inside. The mailbox outside the plantation-style mansion was empty. There were no names, nothing that could provide a clue as to who lived there. He'd seen the area before, but had never actually met anyone who lived there. The area reminded him of River Oaks in Houston.

With nothing else to go on and with no funds to hire a private investigator, he had no choice but to roll up his sleeves and dig through the trash bin in the alley behind the home. It was early enough that he could still go to the YMCA, shower, and change at his office, where he'd been staying, before heading to the court-house. It was 5:45 a.m. on Monday.

Sitting at the end of the alley behind 49 Shadow Brook was a large green trash bin. He drove to the alley, parked the old M.G. Midget close by, and walked to the trash bin. As he opened it, a putrid stench hit him dead in the face. He turned on his flashlight. There were numerous trash bags, and the bin was almost full. If Paloma could see him, certainly this would be the last straw. Nothing he could say could explain this. Well, no one could say that he didn't go to bat for his clients. Maybe some day, Paloma and Lieutenant Governor Yarrington would understand.

He held his breath as he reached in and pulled out a couple of trash bags. Going through them, one by one, he remembered some obscure case, *Greenwood v. California*, he'd read in criminal procedure class in school. Once anyone's trash made it past the curb of one's home, there was no expectation of privacy. The bags inside the bin were fair game.

From the fifth bag, Alex pulled out a utility bill. It was for 49 Shadow Brook and it was in the name of Walter Macallan. He put the utility stub in his pocket, returned the trash bags to the bin, and headed to the Y for a quick shower. It was still early. After a change of clothes back at the office, it would be time to hit the courthouse, make the rounds, and introduce himself to the judges and staff. Hopefully he could land a few appointments and generate some income. He was down to his last couple of hundred bucks and still needed to get supplies for the office and figure out what to do about his student loans.

Even though it was a short walk from his office down the street to the courthouse, Alex realized he was drenched in sweat. It was barely 8:00 a.m., and the temperature had already reached a sweltering eighty-five degrees. Of course, wearing a second-hand Salvation Army two-piece wool suit didn't help matters, either. But for now, the suit would have to do. Until his finances improved.

Alex went through the glass doors and was met by a couple of security guards running the metal detector machines. He emptied his pockets and walked past the metal detector. Once he recovered his belongings, he walked toward the shoeshine stand by the coffee cart near a corner of the lobby area. He decided to get a quick shine, take in the scene, and cool off. "How much?" asked Alex.

"Five bucks," said the person running the shoeshine stand.

"What's your name?"

"Louie," said the man.

"Is the property records section in this building?"

"That's in the administration building, next door," answered Louie in broken English. "Second floor. Looking for someone?"

"Yes, you could say that," Alex replied as thoughts of the name Walter Macallan came to him.

"Well, whoever you're looking for, if they own property or a business in Cameron County, they'll be listed in the property records," Louie added with confidence.

"What do you know about the judges?" Alex mumbled, trying to avoid looking like a smooth idiot right out of law school.

"Well, do you need to make a quick buck?" Louie could tell right away that the young attorney was going to need more than just a shoeshine.

"Yes," said Alex.

"Just starting out, right?"

"Why, was it so obvious?"

"Yep, but don't worry. A lot of the big shots around town started just like you. Guys like Frank James, Joe Costilla, Neto Oliveira, Dave Walsh, and others. They're legends around these parts, and they're still my clients. They tip pretty good, too."

"Well, that's good to know."

"By the way," added Louie, "here's my card. You can page me if you need a shine. If you work nearby, I'll come to your office."

"Oh, that sounds good, thanks."

"You can ask around, all the judges use me and even page me to chambers, even Judge Lynda Gonzalez. I shine her pumps. No problem. You can always find me here."

"Always?"

"Yes, unless the River Levee is overflowing with Border Patrol agents. Then it might take me a day or two to get back," Louie explained.

"Ah," said a surprised Alex, while at the same time thinking of his client, Pilo. He was beginning to get the picture. The undocumented aliens were everywhere, even working at the courthouse. Who would have guessed it?

"Go introduce yourself to Judge Damian Sanchez from County Court One," Louie recommended to Alex. "If you can be in his courtroom every day by 8:00 a.m., he will appoint you to lots of cases. They don't pay as much as the felonies, but misdemeanors are easier to get. Besides, you can't hurt a client too much if you screw up his misdemeanor case."

"And what do I say?"

"Just introduce yourself to Judy, his court coordinator. You'll see he's the hardest working judge around here and loves to move his docket. If you're really serious about making some quick cash, go see him. Oh, by the way, if you're bilingual, he'll really like that. You could probably start working right now."

"I see. . . . Hey, is the courthouse always this busy?"

"Jury Mondays. It's always like this."

It was almost 8:45 a.m., and droves of people were starting to report to the Central Jury Room. Armies of attorneys, with their staffs, were descending on the courthouse looking important and ready to pick a fight.

"How do I get to his chambers?" Alex asked.

"Elevator, second floor. Straight across the hall. One last thing," Louie added, "the district judges have their favorites. So, in order for you to get appointments out of those courts, which obviously pay better, you'll have to get in good with the judges' staff. But, just between you and me, watch out for Rosie with Judge Walter Macallan in the 148th. She's evil."

"So, Walter Macallan is a district judge, eh?" asked Alex with eyes wide open.

"Yep, the only Republican on the bench," Louie the political analyst replied.

Alex gave Louie a five, thanked him, and bolted for one of the elevators. He got in with a score of different people and pushed the second-floor button. In the elevator there were a couple of state troopers, a couple of defendants, one or two employees of the district clerk's office, and a couple of attorneys. The attorneys made small talk with each other and exchanged a few pleasantries. When the elevator opened on the second floor, Alex got out, followed by the troopers and another attorney. The rest were headed to the third floor where the district courts sat.

Alex saw the doors to County Court One. The courtroom was directly in front of the elevator doors, and he could see through the glass doors that the judge was already on the bench. The rows of seats behind counsel's table were full of people.

There was a mixed bag of defendants. It was easy to tell the ones who could afford hiring private counsel from those who were seeking a court-appointed lawyer. Similarly, there appeared to be different kinds of attorneys there to handle different kinds of cases.

Alex stood in the back near the entrance and paid attention. Judge Sanchez was going down his civil docket and calling out the cases. He expected all attorneys with cases on the docket to be present and make an announcement. The list was long. It would be a while before the judge took a break. Maybe at the break, Alex could go introduce himself and hit the judge for a handout.

While waiting for the right time to see Judge Sanchez, Alex left the courtroom, found a pay phone by the restrooms down the hallway, and called Information.

"Walter Macallan on Shadow Brook?" said Alex into the receiver.

"Let me check that for you."

There was a pause. Alex felt his heart racing.

"Here we go," said the operator, and she gave him the number. "Have a good day."

"Thanks," Alex mumbled as he scribbled the number on a piece of paper. He took fifty cents out of his pants pocket, dropped the coins into the pay phone, and dialed the number. The phone rang about six times before someone picked up.

"Judge Macallan's residence," said a pleasant female voice at the end of the line.

A bit surprised, Alex composed himself, gathered his thoughts, and mumbled a response. "Yes, ma'am, I'm looking for Rosario Medina and her son Juan José. Are they still working there with you?"

There was a long silence. Alex waited.

"Yes, hello?" Alex started again. "Are Rosario Medina and her son Juan José there. . . . Do they still live there?"

There was a click, and the phone went dead.

"Well, thank you very much!" said Alex, somewhat annoyed as he pulled out his wallet, looked for an old calling card, and got ready to call the number again. He was not going to stop until he got an answer. As he searched his wallet, he noticed the crumpled piece of paper that Pilo had given him with Aurora's number on it. He dialed that number. The phone rang about ten times. Finally, as he was about to give up and hang up the receiver, someone answered.

"*Bueno*," said an old man in a slow, trembling voice.

"*Este . . .* " said Alex, "*¿Está la señora Aurora?*"

"*Un momento*," replied the old man.

Alex waited as the man went to get Aurora. It must have been the longest two minutes, but now, after the last hang-up, he needed answers more than ever.

As Alex continued to hold, he wondered if Judge Sanchez had finished calling the docket. He still wanted to go and make his acquaintance and hopefully pick up an appointment or two.

Finally, somebody came on the phone. "*¿Sí?*" asked the lady on the other end.

"Aurora?" asked Alex.

"*¿Sí?*" answered the elderly lady taking the call. "Who's this?"

"I'm looking for your niece, Rosario Medina, and her son, Juan José. Do you know if they still work for Judge Macallan?" inquired Alex. "You see, Pilo is in town, and I'm trying to find them. He would really, really like to see them, if at all possible."

"No!" Aurora gasped. "That can't be!" she shouted across the telephone line. And with that, she started wailing.

"What's wrong?"

"*Ay, señor*," replied Aurora, still sobbing, "my niece and her son died in a horrible accident a year ago."

Alex's mind went blank, and he started feeling sick. *Did I just hear that they died? Did she mean both? How can I face Pilo now?*

"What?" asked Alex again. "What happened?"

"Look, I cannot talk to you on the phone," said Aurora in a cautious tone, "but I can meet you later this evening. Give me your address and number."

Alex did as she asked. "I'm across from the courthouse," he added. His mind was racing.

"Okay," she said and hung up.

He stood there like a zombie. "Damn it!" he murmured under his breath as he left the pay phone area and walked back to County Court One. He was going to have to lie to Pilo until he knew exactly what had happened. It was bad enough to lose a spouse, but to lose a son? Now that was a terrible blow. There was no way the old man could survive the news. Had they taught him this in law school, how to give a client bad news? He would keep quiet, at least for now.

County Court One was in recess by the time he got back. Alex spotted a group of attorneys who were being summoned over the intercom back to chambers. He followed them but was intercepted by a young lady.

"Can I help you?" she said. "I'm Judy Wilson, the court's coordinator."

"Yes," said Alex as he cleared his throat. He was still visibly shaken after the phone call with Aurora.

"Is everything all right?" continued Judy.

"Ah, yes . . . I'm just a little nervous. I've never done this before. I needed to meet Judge Sanchez and introduce myself. I just passed the Bar and moved back to town. I'd like to pick up some court appointments." Alex handed her a slip of paper with his address and a phone number, which she took and read.

"Well," she responded, "I'm the one who handles the appointments, really. The judge signs off on the payment vouchers and decides the amount to pay each attorney for the work done, but it's me who actually appoints the attorneys."

"I see."

"However," she went on, "the judge always likes to meet the attorneys being appointed to the cases. So come on back here and let me introduce you to the judge. Right now the judge is visiting with some attorneys, but I'll take you in there as soon as they're done."

"Thanks," Alex replied as he wiped the sweat beads from his forehead with a handkerchief. "I'll just wait out in the hallway."

"Go ahead," Judy said.

When the attorneys were done, Judy invited Alex to come to the back. She knocked on the door, and a voice inside directed her to come in.

"Judge," Judy said, "this is Alejandro del Fuerte." She read his name from the slip of paper. "He's a new attorney, just back in town and looking for appointments."

"Nice to meet you," said Judge Sanchez. The judge was thin, standing at about five feet, seven inches. He looked to be in his early forties and had a tiny amount of white hair on the sides of his head. He was wearing Dockers, a cotton Guayabera, and leather moccasins with no socks.

"It is an honor," said Alex.

"What school did you go to?" asked the judge.

"South Texas College of Law."

"That's a very good school. I hear Dean Prosser has an excellent advocacy program."

"Oh, yes," Alex concurred.

"The lawyers from that school can really try a case. So tell me, are you ready to pick up some appointments? Can you speak Spanish?"

"Yes, and yes," said Alex, excitedly. "I just hung my shingle across the street and will soon have to start repaying those student loans. You know how it is."

"Well, my boy, today is your lucky day. Judy will take care of you." Then he called to Judy in the office next door, "Right, Judy?"

"Sure," came the reply.

Within a moment, she returned to the judge's office.

"Judy," asked Judge Sanchez, "what do we have left over from the jail docket?"

"There's the misdemeanor possession of marijuana case, with Domingo Garza. He's the tough guy who says he's not guilty and wants to go to trial. The one who wrote you just last week that he was very dissatisfied with the last attorney you appointed him, Mr.

Harding. He ended up firing him right before we picked a jury last week, remember?"

"Oh yeah," growled the judge, seemingly fed up with the defendant.

"You want me to appoint Mr. del Fuerte?" asked Judy.

"Sure, I've had it with that guy!"

"Alex," said the judge reaching over to put his hand on Alex's right shoulder and look him straight in the eye. "I want you to try that case today. Don't worry, I'll help you. Do you think you can pick a jury at 11 a.m.?"

Alex looked at his watch. It was 10:00 a.m. He remembered something that he'd read in criminal procedure class about having ten days to prepare for trial. He was now feeling sick to his stomach and thought about asking the judge for his ten days. He felt like bailing out, except that the judge was giving him the opportunity of a lifetime. Hell, there were lawyers in mega-firms dying to try a case after putting in seven years, and here he was, first day on the job and being pushed to pick a jury.

The novice attorney wanted to decline. *But what if the judge gets offended?* thought Alex. *What if this was a test? What if I refuse and the judge doesn't want to appoint me to any other cases? This is too much for a first day!* He thought about Aurora and about Pilo. He was supposed to be in his office after lunch. When would he have time to prepare for trial? Jury selection was in an hour!

"You think I can handle it?" asked Alex, his voice cracking a bit.

"Yes," said Judge Sanchez, "you'll have fifteen minutes for *voir dire*, and so will the state. And you won't start putting on evidence today. I have another case going before yours, but it will be a short, one-day trial, too. For your case, we'll pick the jury at 11 and start the actual case on Wednesday at 1:30 p.m., after lunch. So you'll have time to talk to the assistant district attorney, look at the file, and talk to your client to prepare your case.

"Also," continued the judge with a wink, "from what I hear, I think the state has a bad search on its hands. I understand the way the car stop was conducted may have risen to the level of a pretext stop. So that's all I'm going to say about that. There might be a suppressible issue."

Alex thought to himself, *I'm* frito—*done! First the thing with Pilo's family, and now I'm supposed to pick a jury within one hour, and to top it all, I've been appointed to a difficult client.*

"Okay," he mumbled, "I guess if you think I can do it, Judge, then I'll jump on it. Where is Mr. Garza? Can I talk to my client?"

"Yes, of course." The judge seemed impressed with Alex's go-getter attitude.

"Judy," called the judge to his assistant, who had returned to her office, "page Joe and have him bring up Mr. Garza from the holding cell."

"I just did," was Judy's reply.

"Good. Why don't you go to the conference room down the hallway, and the bailiff will bring you Mr. Garza and the court's file so you can get acquainted with the case."

Judge Sanchez pointed Alex down the hallway to a conference room that double duty as a jury room and interview room for probation officers.

As Alex sat there waiting for his client, he opened the court's file. He flipped through some motions that had been filed by Mr. Harding, the previous attorney, but all he could think of was Rosario, the boy, and his client. *Why had no one notified Pilo?*

Chapter 4

THERE WAS A LOUD KNOCK ON THE DOOR. "Here's Mr. Garza," announced Joe the bailiff with a grin from ear to ear, "your client, Mr. del Fuerte." Short and wiry, Joe was wearing a two-tone brown uniform with his gun and rounds clipped on his large utility belt. He sported a thick moustache a la Pancho Villa, and his forearms were covered in tattoos.

"Ah," answered Alex, startled, "please come in and take a seat, Mr. Garza." He was still preoccupied with the upcoming meetings with Aurora and Pilo.

"Mr. Garza," said Alex, clearing his throat, "I've been appointed to represent you. And I'm happy to represent you. However, let me say this: Judge Sanchez wants us to go to trial today. Are you aware of that?"

"I'm ready to go to trial, Mr. del Fuerte. The dope was not mine, and I am not going to plead guilty to something I did not do!" the client said, fuming. The inmate was shackled at the legs and wrists, had a shaved head and goatee, and smelled like a high school locker room.

"All right, I hear you," the young attorney said as he loosened his tie. "Let me ask you, was the marijuana found inside the car's ashtray?"

"Yes."

"And it was a small amount?"

"Yes."

"And you were pulled over inside the HEB grocery store parking lot?"

"Yes! Yes! Yes! Where are you going with this?" barked the defendant. The veins on his neck were starting to show.

"I just need to check . . . a couple more questions. Did you consent to the search?"

"No."

"Were you told the reason you were pulled over?"

"No."

"All right. Let's switch gears here. Tell me a bit about yourself," demanded Alex.

"I came to the United States twenty years ago when I was a *mocoso*, barely fifteen. When I was twenty, I was arrested and deported. After I was deported, I reentered the United States and returned to Chicago. I married a girl from the Philippines who happened to be a resident alien. We have two children, both of them are U.S. citizens. She couldn't petition me because of my prior deportation. All this time, I've been working in a hotel in downtown Chicago doing room service and banquets. That's how I've supported my family for the last ten years. My wife also works at the hotel in housekeeping. But now," added Domingo, "I've got this misdemeanor charge, and I can't get back home."

"What were you doing back in Texas if all your family is in Chicago?" asked Alex.

"In late May, I received a call from Mexico that my mother was on her deathbed," explained Domingo. The tough guy's eyes got watery. "I needed to see her one last time. So I took the bus to El Paso, and from there I crossed to Juárez. I continued to León, Guanajuato, got home just in time, and said goodbye to my mother. She was buried the next day. After the funeral, I decided to come back and try crossing somewhere near Matamoros. I called my cousins who live in Brownsville to get a ride once I had crossed. I stayed with them a couple of days to figure out how to make it past the Sarita checkpoint up north. As luck would have it, that day my nephew lent me his car because he didn't have to go to work. I got pulled over as I was driving out of the HEB parking lot. I had no idea the kid had a *churro* in the ashtray, I swear."

"Okay, I think we have something we can work with. Let me go visit with the assistant district attorney. I'm going to ask Joe to take you back and have the jail let you put on your street clothes so we can go to trial. I'll see you back in the courtroom at 1:30 p.m. for jury selection."

"All right, then. See you after lunch," said the defendant.

Alex headed back to County Court One, walked in and headed toward counsel's table, where two prosecutors, one a man and the other a woman, already sat. "Good morning," said Alex, "can I see Domingo Garza's file?"

"Sure," said the male prosecutor.

"My name is Alejandro del Fuerte," continued Alex. "Looks like the judge just appointed me to this case, and he expects us to try it this morning."

"I know," interrupted the female prosecutor. "I'll be trying it. Let me give you the file. By the way, my name is Gisela Montemayor."

"*Mucho gusto*, it's a pleasure to meet you," responded Alex, trying to set the hook and force her to answer in Spanish, if at all possible.

"*El gusto es mío*," said Gisela in perfect Spanish. She smiled with pleasure and looked into Alex's green eyes as she sized him up. The prosecutor was wearing a smart navy blue business suit and black four-inch pumps. She had her hair pulled back in a bun.

"Please, call me Alex."

She reached out to shake his hand, and Alex instinctively shoved his hand into hers. Her hand was smooth and silky and felt incredibly fine. He had a hard time letting go but forced himself. One thing was for sure, though: not only was the assistant D.A. slender and beautiful, with sandy brown hair and gorgeous honey-colored eyes, she looked like she could easily hold her own in the courtroom. She could be real trouble in front of a mostly male jury.

In an instant, Alex's outlook changed. His worries about Pilo and Paloma went away, and Rosario and the boy were placed on the back-burner, temporarily. Even jury selection, something he had never done on his own and which scared him to death, seemed within his capabilities. He would just have to remember the exercise from his criminal trial advocacy class in law school and wing it. Funny how a woman's touch or smile could make everything seem all right.

Gisela's voice brought him back to earth. "Here's the file, Alex," she said.

"Oh, yes," said Alex as he took it. "I'll bring it right back."

"Sure," said the assistant D.A. as she looked him over. "By the way, please call me Gigi."

As he started walking back to the conference room in the back hallway, Alex realized he was in serious trouble. The D.A. had charm and brains and probably knew how to use both. He'd learned in law school that trials were lost and won not necessarily on the facts or truth of the case, but on emotion and perception. Juries, for the most part, followed their hearts. And if Gigi managed to get the case to the jury, chances were the jury would side with her. It looked like the assistant D.A. could persuade any jury, particularly a jury made up of all males. She would have them eating out of her hand, *sin problema*.

If, on the other hand, due to some technicality the judge had to decide some issues before the case got to the jury, then things could turn out differently. This was particularly true with judges who were pro-defense. Pro-defense judges were known to throw out cases if there was a bad search or arrest or anything remotely resembling a coerced confession. Criminal defense lawyers in the Valley called these judges *cojonudos* because they were not afraid to make the tough calls, even with a media-packed courtroom. They were tough *hombres*.

Back in the conference room, Alex was having a whirlwind of a day. But he felt alive and excited. Yes, he had errands to run and plans to meet Pilo and Aurora in the afternoon, but he liked the fact that he was busy. He was about to select his first jury and argue his first motion to suppress. No amount of studying in law school could have prepared him for this. This was the real world, and it was both terrifying and gratifying.

There was a knock at the door

"Yes?" asked the young attorney.

"It's me, Joe," said the bailiff, smiling. "Just wanted to tell you that the jailers will have your client back in the courtroom at 1:15, in case you need to talk to him before jury selection."

"Thanks," said Alex. "Hey, Joe, before you go, do you think the judge might take up the motion to suppress first, after jury selection? It might be dispositive of the whole case, and this way we wouldn't waste the court's time. What do you think?"

"Now you're thinking like a lawyer," responded Joe, and added, "I'd push it."

"Great," said Alex. "Oh, one more thing."

"What is it?"

"How come my client isn't out on bond? I mean, this is just a small possession of marijuana case. He had less than a joint."

"He has an INS detainer. Our jail cannot let him go because he's got a hold from the feds. Which means he's here illegally, and when he's finished with this case, he'll be deported back to Mexico," Joe explained, shrugging his shoulders.

"So why are we messing with this case? Why not just send the poor guy back to Mexico? He'll never come back. Why keep housing him, feeding him, and spending taxpayers' money on a stupid misdemeanor case?" Alex queried as he tried to figure out a way to dispose of the case without having to go to trial. Besides, he would rather figure out what happened to Rosario and the boy than be spanked and embarrassed by a talented prosecutor with beauty and brains. They were both in trouble, he and his client. One thing was certain: if the case got to the jury, it was pretty much over.

"That's a good question. Maybe you should ask the prosecutor. If Ms. Montemayor had her way, your client would be getting the needle," said Joe, chuckling.

"You mean the lethal injection?"

"Yes."

"She's that tough, eh?"

"Oh, yeah . . . and unreasonable!" remarked Joe as he walked away.

An hour later, at precisely 1:00 p.m., there was another knock on the door. It was the bailiff. In his right hand he held a stack of papers, juror questionnaires and jurors' personal information cards.

"Mr. del Fuerte?" asked Joe.

"Yes?" said Alex.

"I'm sorry to bother you. Your jury panel is lined up outside the courtroom in the hallway waiting to be seated inside. Do you want the list of names?"

"Yes, leave the list here with me, please," replied Alex, deep in thought as he tried to figure out how to play his cards.

"You didn't go to lunch?" Joe asked.

"No, I've been getting ready for the trial," Alex snapped. "Tell Judge Sanchez I'm going to move for a jury shuffle."

"The judge isn't going to like it," said Joe.

"That's too bad. I'm entitled to it."

Alex knew that a jury shuffle would force the court to send the panel back, and it would have to be rearranged. This could be beneficial, and it would buy him more time to prepare. Besides, he was entitled to it as a matter of law. After all, this stuff was still fresh in his mind since just a few months earlier he'd sat for the Bar exam.

Joe came back and escorted both Domingo and Alex back into the courtroom. Judge Sanchez was already on the bench, and two assistant D.A.s were at counsel's table.

Judge Sanchez was busy explaining to Mr. Morado, another defense attorney, how the court was going to handle two jury trials during the same week. The court expected to get through Mr. del Fuerte and Mr. Morado's cases by Thursday, even if it meant working through lunch.

"Mr. del Fuerte," barked Judge Sanchez, "are you ready to do jury selection?"

"Yes and no," came the reply from Alex.

"What do you mean?" the judge said, exasperated. He also tried to anticipate Alex's argument. "I don't like to waste time, Mr. del Fuerte, and the jury shuffle is a waste of time, in my opinion. Are you ready to try the case or not?"

"I have two concerns," Alex replied. "First, my client is still wearing his prisoner's uniform and that, I believe, is highly prejudicial and may constitute reversible error. Any potential jury member who sees him in his jumpsuit will think he looks like a criminal and therefore he must be a criminal and must have committed the crime he is accused of. Therefore, I object to the court entertaining jury selection while my client is in his prisoner's uniform.

"Secondly, even if the court forces me to select the jury this afternoon, I believe if we have a short hearing on the pending motion to suppress, that might be dispositive of the case and save the court time and effort. I would kindly suggest or ask of the court to allow us to have it at three o'clock this afternoon. That way, the D.A. will have sufficient time to get its witnesses down here in the afternoon. Plus, that would give me a little time to take care of a couple of things back at the office. I made an appointment for 1:30, not knowing that I would be involved in a trial, and I apologize for that."

Sounding impressed, Judge Sanchez said, "Mr. del Fuerte, the court can certainly understand why any half-decent defense attorney would not want to have a client dressed in a bright orange jumpsuit sitting there during jury selection. Particularly when our court of appeals has found that it is harmful error and prejudicial to have a defendant in his jumpsuit in the courtroom during his trial.

"Joe," barked the judge, "why isn't Mr. Garza wearing his street clothes?"

"Because," said Joe with a grin, "the laundry officer at the jail lost his clothes, and they're trying to locate them. They'll let us know if they find them. However, I don't see that happening any time today."

"Well, Mr. del Fuerte is right. I can't let Mr. Garza be paraded in his jumpsuit in front of the jury panel. That would not be good, and it's grounds for an appeal," reasoned the judge.

"Judge," interrupted Ms. Montemayor, "this is nothing more than a delay tactic by Mr. del Fuerte." She turned and smiled at

Alex as she spoke and continued to look his way as if to say, *I know what you're doing, but it won't work with me.*

"Well," said the judge, "Mr. del Fuerte is right. We cannot have his client sit here in his jumpsuit while we conduct jury selection. I'll tell you what we'll do. Let's give this jury panel to Mr. Morado, and later in the afternoon we'll entertain the motion to suppress with Mr. del Fuerte and Mr. Garza.

"Mr. del Fuerte," added the judge, "would you be interested in talking to your client about waiving a jury and just having the court decide his case? That way we don't have to request two jury panels, and if the motion to suppress is dispositive of all issues, then we won't even have to worry about a bench trial. What do you think?"

"Wait a minute!" interrupted Gigi. "The state firmly objects to waiving the jury. And there is no way that I can guarantee that the officers will be available to testify today at 3:00 p.m. I'll call border patrol and see if I can get the arresting officer to come in to testify."

"Well," countered Judge Sanchez, "he damn well better be available. You issued subpoenas, right?"

Alex could sense that any control the assistant D.A. had over the disposition of this particular criminal case was slipping away fast. He'd convinced Judge Sanchez to have the hearing on the motion to suppress. If he got lucky and the judge ruled that the stop was illegal, the case would be thrown out. That meant that the case would never get to the jury. That was probably something the D.A. did not want to happen. She had to be fuming inside, although outwardly she remained cool.

Alex had also managed to convince the judge to possibly not even entertain jury selection, which would mean no jury trial. Now he had the judge seriously thinking about just having a simple bench trial. Either way, it appeared that the likelihood of going toe-to-toe with the gorgeous honey-eyed beauty was slowly sneaking away. They would have to lock horns another day. For a young attorney fresh out of law school, Alex had held his ground pretty well.

"Yes, the subpoenas were issued last week for this week," Gisela explained, "but you know how it is, Judge. The officer might be hard to locate or might be away in training. I just don't know."

"All right then, we'll see what happens at three o'clock," said the judge in a stern voice.

Then, turning his attention to Alex, the judge said, "Mr. del Fuerte. We'll only have the suppression hearing today. Depending on what happens at the hearing, we might have a bench trial this week. Either way, we won't do jury selection today. So you won't have a jury trial this week. However, let's dispose of this case this week, one way or another. One last suggestion . . . I know about Mr. Garza's INS detainer, so think about a cold plea."

"Very well," responded Alex, "I'll talk to my client about your gracious suggestion. May I be excused?"

"Yes, see you at three o'clock," said the judge.

Chapter 5

ALEX WENT BACK TO HIS OFFICE across the street from the Cameron County Courthouse. What a Monday morning! Whew! He wondered whether Pilo would show up after lunch as agreed, or if he had managed to get arrested. It was 1:30 p.m., and he needed to get ready for the hearing in the afternoon. He was also starving, but coffee would have to do. It would be his breakfast . . . and lunch. *Ni modo.* He was too busy getting ready for the hearing, and the anticipation of having to look Pilo straight in the eyes and lie was not making things easier. Not to mention Ms. Montemayor. She looked like she could eat his lunch at any time. So he'd better be ready.

As he waited for the coffee to brew, the young attorney started digging through a stack of boxes containing his old law books and class notes. He found what he was looking for. It was the old textbook for criminal procedure class. He pulled it out and dusted it off as he reached for a cup of coffee. He took his cup and the textbook back to his desk and sat down. He was about to open the book when someone knocked on the front door. The noise startled him, but he got up and went to see who it was.

It was a young woman in her early thirties, looking somewhat distressed. *Now what?* he wondered.

"Yes?" grunted Alex.

"Are you an attorney?" asked the woman.

"Yes, what do you need?"

"Well," she said, "I need a divorce."

Oh, great! thought Alex in silence. *First Pilo, then Aurora, then a hearing to suppress, and now a divorce?*

"Can you come back tomorrow?"

"Look, I got money," said the woman. "I need to get this done. I won't take much of your time, I promise."

"It's not about the money, lady," snapped Alex. "I have a hearing in an hour, and I have to get ready for it."

"Just give me five, ten minutes, I beg of you. Please?"

"Okay," said Alex reluctantly. "Come on in." He sure could use a paying client, but he also needed to learn to say no.

They sat at the only desk. Alex looked for a pad and pen and thought of what to ask. He would have to pretend that he knew what he was doing. He had never before touched a divorce. The firm in Houston where he'd interned in the summer had only handled civil litigation and social security disability claims, not divorces. The one thing law school had taught him, though, was to ask questions. He could at least ask questions and try to appear somewhat competent.

"What's the name?" asked Alex impatiently as images of Ms. Montemayor prepping her officer swirled around his head.

"Linda Lawrence," came the reply. "I'm divorcing Clint Lawrence. I caught him cheating." She was pouting as she pulled out a brown envelope and took some photos from it. She laid them out in front of Alex on the desk. They showed a black Lincoln Navigator parked outside a room at the Motel 6 on Central Boulevard. Alex knew the motel.

"This doesn't mean anything," said Alex cautiously.

"You haven't seen the rest of the pictures," said Mrs. Lawrence as she pulled the remainder from the envelope.

"Here you go," she said as she tossed them his way. She started crying.

"May I get you some water?" asked Alex. "Or a tissue?"

"Please," she said between sobs.

Alex got up and went to the back room for the glass of water. As he filled the glass, he thought about Mrs. Lawrence. *Why would her husband cheat on her? She's attractive and looks classy, too.* He noticed that she was sporting a Lady Rolex and a tan Louie Vuitton purse. He'd also noticed her car keys on the desk. She drove a

Mercedes Benz. *She looks as if she could easily afford a board-certified attorney specializing in divorces.*

"Here's your water and some tissue," indicated Alex as he reached to pick up the remainder of the photos now on the desk.

The other photos painted a clearer picture. They showed a gray-haired Anglo male, probably in his late fifties, walking out of the room and escorting a young twenty-something woman to a car in the parking lot. The next picture showed the same man leaning into the driver's side of a red Miata convertible, kissing the woman.

Alex put the photos down. Looking at Mrs. Lawrence, he cleared his throat and asked, "How long have you been married?"

"Ten years."

"Any children?"

"No, we never had any. I have medical problems," confided Mrs. Lawrence.

"How about property?"

"We own a very successful import-export business. We started it when we married ten years ago. I don't want any part of it, but I would like to be cashed out . . . only what is rightfully mine. There are no debts. The cars and house are paid for, and we also own a condo at Frankie Plaza on South Padre Island. It's a three-bedroom on the tenth floor . . . probably worth about $450,000."

Alex started having doubts about his ability to handle such a divorce. He could already tell there were going to be some issues. How much was the business worth? Who would appraise it? Was it started with separate property funds from one of the parties? Did she also work in it? Or did she have an equitable interest in the business, and how much could that equitable interest be worth? Did the business owe any federal taxes? How much would he charge her? He had no idea!

"Mrs. Lawrence, I will be glad to take your case, but are you sure you want me to handle it? I mean, I just got back to town a couple of days ago. I . . . "

"Yes," she said, cutting him off. "Look," she continued, "my husband is from Brownsville and grew up in this area. I, on the other hand, am not. I was born and raised in Matamoros, just across the border. He knows all the judges and all the attorneys. No one really wants to represent me. I've already asked a couple of friends, and they all bowed out saying they would have a conflict because of their friendship with Clint. I need someone who will go to the mat for me, if needed."

Alex was still somewhat concerned. This was definitely not an uncontested divorce. It looked and sounded complicated. Professor Lawton's words came to mind: "Take the money, then figure it out." Yes, the money! Boy, he needed the money.

"I'll need some personal information from you and from him," continued Alex, "but more importantly, I need to know where to get him served, and whether you would like to serve him with a temporary restraining order in order to kick him out of the house while the divorce is pending."

"No," she said, "that won't be necessary. Our marriage has been on the rocks for quite some time now, and I've been living away from home in the condo out on the island. This all stems from my inability to bear him a son. When the business took off, he changed. Suddenly, he would drop hints that he wanted an heir. I can't blame him, really. Since he's much older than me, I guess he feels time is running out. I would have been perfectly happy adopting a child, but he would have none of it."

"I understand," Alex said compassionately. "Do you think he'll fight?" *Maybe the kid thing is just an excuse,* he thought. *Maybe this Clint character has had his share of affairs and is only now flaunting them.*

"I don't think so," said Mrs. Lawrence. "He's low-key and always hated attracting attention . . . making headlines."

"Is that so?" asked Alex. *That has to be a front,* thought the attorney. He also thought quickly about how to approach the subject of his retainer. At first, when she had come in, he thought the whole thing would be a simple divorce. But now, he couldn't take any chances. It looked like there was a lot of money at stake. It could get ugly and expensive.

"I would like to keep the pictures for the file," Alex pointed out as he reached for his cold cup of coffee.

"That won't be a problem. The investigator made doubles, and I've got the negatives," answered Mrs. Lawrence. "When do you think you can get started?"

"As soon as I'm retained," came the reply.

"What kind of retainer do you need?"

"Well," Alex hesitated, "I'll need two thousand, plus expenses. If we need to retain a professional business appraiser to value the business, that would be considered an expense. Maybe we'll also need a CPA or a forensic auditor to go through the books with the appraiser. It just depends."

"That sounds reasonable," muttered Mrs. Lawrence. "Can I write you a check?"

"That will be fine," Alex said with a nod. "I'll need you to sign a contract. However, maybe you can come back on Friday for that, since I'm not completely set up yet. Would that be okay? Oh, I'll also have a receipt for you. Sorry I'm out right now."

"That's all right," replied Mrs. Lawrence as she cut Alex a check for five thousand dollars.

"Wait," said Alex as he looked the check over. "The retainer is only two thousand."

"Yes, but I want to give you a bigger retainer," countered Mrs. Lawrence. "Is that so wrong? Besides, the money will come in handy. I can tell you're just starting out. Don't tell me you couldn't use new furniture and supplies?"

Alex was speechless. Five thousand dollars was a lot of dough. "Very well, Mrs. Lawrence, I'll have Mr. Lawrence served before the end of the week. At home, right?" He was in no position to argue with her.

"Yes, let's avoid humiliating the poor bastard. We'll get him on the division of assets," she declared as she made her exit.

Alex sat there taking it all in. He couldn't believe his luck. Just two days ago he'd been in the red. And now, after a whirlwind morning, he was in the black. It was unbelievable. And it felt good, too. He counted his blessings and gave thanks to St. Jude Thaddeus, patron saint of the downtrodden.

He opened his used book on criminal procedure and found the case of *Sitz v. Michigan*. He read it carefully, but it was not exactly on point. What kind of questions would he ask of the Border Patrol agent? How would he show the court that when the agent stopped his client, he was engaged in racial profiling? That was all this was! His gut instinct told him there had been no good reason to pull Domingo over.

He found an old notebook with class notes and started scribbling questions for the cross-examination. Would he put the defendant on the stand? Could he ask the D.A. to stipulate that Domingo's testimony be used only during the suppression hearing? Was that even permissible? He had no clue.

Maybe he would recommend to his client that he should take the stand and testify. The defendant had sounded pretty credible at the interview earlier. If the stop had gone down exactly the way Domingo said, and this was confirmed by the arresting officer, then there would be no harm in having the defendant take the stand.

Anyway, it looked like Judge Sanchez was leaning toward finding a way to punt the case. Alex just needed to get the officer to admit there had been no good reason to stop his client. Would the officer admit that? What if he was a pro at testifying in the courtroom? What if Alex couldn't make him budge during cross-examination, and it was he who ended up with cake on his face? Ms. Montemayor would have a field day! He had to figure out a way to convince the court that the stop had been done without probable cause and therefore was illegal. Then the judge would have no option but to throw out the case.

He took a swig of coffee and looked at his watch. It was getting late and was time to go. Man, the check in his pocket felt good. He couldn't wait to get to the bank to cash it. Maybe he could squeeze in one last cup of coffee. He would need it to get through the hearing; his stomach was growling. Yet there was much work to do. Work on the divorce, meet with Pilo and Aurora, and show that D.A. a thing or two.

He was about to get up for a last cup of coffee when someone knocked loudly on the door. Alex just about fell out of his chair.

"¡*Sanababiche!* Now what?" he mumbled under his breath. "Who is it?" he yelled, quite upset. He couldn't get any work done.

There was no response.

"*¿Quién es?*" repeated Alex in Spanish.

"*Soy yo,*" a man's voice said meekly.

Alex immediately recognized his visitor. "*Pásale,* come on in," he said and pulled open the door. He asked Pilo to come in and sit down.

Alex looked Pilo over and liked what he saw. The older man looked good. He was wearing a pair of jeans and a blue denim shirt with white tennis shoes. He wore no socks, but that was hardly noticeable. He was clean-shaven and was no longer wearing a hat. Instead, he was wearing a cap with some lettering on it. He looked rested and relaxed.

Funny, thought Alex, *now Pilo is looking comfortable and relaxed, and it's me, the attorney, who's stressing out.* He could tell Pilo was a little anxious and wanted to hear the news.

"Where did you get the cap?" asked Alex.

"I bought the whole outfit at Jim Jones' Ropa Usada for less than ten dollars," said Pilo, smiling and happy with his purchase.

"What does the cap say?" asked Alex as he reached out, expecting Pilo to let him see it.

"It says 'Rene Yarrington's Golf Classic, 1997.'" He handed over his cap. It was a white cap with the Lone Star flag embroidered on one side and blue letters on the other. On the top part of the brim were the small initials *R.Y.* It was slightly stained, but Pilo didn't seem to mind.

"Here's the skinny," said Alex, taking a deep breath. "I haven't found Rosario or your son, Juan José. But I've found the telephone number for 49 Shadow Brook Lane and have called it." He was lying to his client, but at this point he felt it was necessary.

"I also left a message with the person who answered the phone." This was also a lie, and he felt terrible . . . but maybe someday Pilo would understand. "I told the person that Rosario's husband was in town and wanted to visit. The woman would not divulge any information, saying only that she was going to give the message to the *patrón* and that he would call me, personally. However, the owner will not be back from his out-of-town trip until

Monday of next week. So that's all I know right now. We probably have to wait to know more . . . at least until next Monday."

"*Muy bien*," said Pilo, accepting the attorney's explanation.

"I assume you're out of money?" inquired Alex.

"I'm down to my last three dollars."

"I'll tell you what we'll do," explained Alex. "I got retained on a case today and have a little bit of money. I'm going to need you to come in tomorrow morning so you can pick up some money to get you through until Monday of next week. You think you can handle that? Come back in the morning without getting caught?"

"*Sí*," said Pilo. "I've been keeping to myself and, for the most part, have stayed inside my room. It has a TV, and I've been watching the Mexican soaps and the news. The only time I went out was Saturday, to get the clothes. I found a little restaurant right around the corner where I've been picking up tacos and bringing them back to my room. I've been eating inside my room, every day."

"Great work. You need to keep that up," said Alex. "Anyway, so it looks like we'll have more information about your family by next Monday, but right now I have to get back to court on another case. You can stay here or go back to your hotel, whatever you want."

"I'll head back to the hotel, but I'll see you tomorrow morning. Right?" asked Pilo.

"*¡Claro!*" said Alex with a sigh of relief. "Let's hook up in the morning and see how much money I can part with."

"*Ah, mira*," Pilo added as he made his way out the door, "look here, I want you to have these."

"What are they?"

"*Documentos importantes*," Pilo explained. "I can't afford to lose them. They're official documents. This is our Mexican marriage license or *acta matrimonial* signed by the ten witnesses required under Mexican law."

"Let me see," replied Alex as he took the *acta* from Pilo's hand. He examined it closely and read its contents. It stated that on the twenty-first of March of the year 1994, Porfirio Medina González, son of Juanita González de Medina and Ramiro Medina, and Rosario Martínez Meléndez, daughter of Rosalba Meléndez de

Martínez and Salvador Martínez, took the vows of holy matrimony at the office of the *registro civil* for the city of Puebla, Mexico.

The *acta* was signed by the presiding *juez del registro civil* and the requisite witnesses. It contained the official seal from the *registro,* and next to Porfirio and Rosario's names there were thumbprints.

"So, you guys got married in Puebla?" asked Alex.

"Yes, because there is no *registro civil* in our village," explained Pilo. "Everyone, including the witnesses, had to travel to Puebla. Once we were declared husband and wife, we all traveled back to Tepantitlán to celebrate."

"How far is Puebla from your village?"

"Four hours."

"All the witnesses alive?" asked Alex.

"Last time I checked," said Pilo in a sarcastic tone.

"What else do you have?"

"Wedding pictures. Pictures of us in our humble home and pictures of our baby, Juan José. Pictures of happy times . . . of days gone by," replied Pilo in a sad tone.

"Well, let me see them," demanded Alex.

There were about ten pictures in all. Some were from the *registro civil* in Puebla. Rosario and Pilo were holding hands and smiling, and the witnesses were lined up behind them. Rosario was pretty, with long black hair down to her waist. The pictures clearly showed an age difference, but it didn't appear to matter. The couple was happy; they were glowing and in love.

Other pictures showed the couple and the judge, the witnesses signing the register, and the party back at the village. It looked like the whole town had come to celebrate. Although there had been only ten official witnesses, for all intents and purposes, all the townsfolk had been witnesses, too. There was even a Mariachi band with only four musicians.

Alex looked at more of the pictures. One showed Rosario in her kitchen at home, kneeling down at the *comal* on the open flame, flipping tortillas. The last bunch of photos were of Rosario holding a small baby boy. There was also one with Rosario, the baby, and Pilo. They beamed with joy.

"Where did you get the camera?" asked Alex.

"They were disposable cameras that some witnesses bought on our trip to Puebla to the *registro*. When the doctor would travel to Puebla to load up on medicine for his clinic, he would take the film to the photo lab in the pharmacy. Then on another trip, he would bring it back. That is how we get our pictures. At that rate, it takes years to fill up a photo album."

Alex realized Pilo was right. The pharmacy he used to visit as a child in Matamoros had a photo lab inside. He'd even heard that mom-and-pop corner stores in Mexico City had photo labs á la Walgreen's.

"Oh! Look! Here is Juan José's birth certificate. It even has his two little footprints on the back," Pilo mumbled, trying to hold back the tears. He turned away from Alex, not wanting the attorney to see him in this state, and tried to wipe his tears.

Alex felt terrible for Pilo. It was hard to see a grown man cry.

Pilo sobbed quietly. The silence only served to magnify the sadness and the pain. Pilo finally got things under control, and he turned around and faced Alex. He looked him straight in the eyes and broke the uncomfortable silence. "I did not have these with me at our first meeting. I had stashed them away behind a dumpster in an alley as I was being chased by the Border Patrol the day I met you. I went back and recovered them. I figured they might be useful."

"Let me have the licenses and all of the pictures. I'll make copies for my file and give them back to you when we meet again next Monday. What do you say if we meet at 9:00 a.m.?"

"Okay," said Pilo. "Oh, one thing I forgot to mention. I have an older daughter from another relationship."

"What's her name?"

"María Luisa," said the old man. "She's married with children and lives in *la capital*. But we don't keep in touch."

"Where in Mexico City?" asked the attorney.

"Last I heard, she had a little booth and sold produce at a farmer's market, downtown."

"And her mother?"

"She died when María Luisa was twelve," explained the old man. "So I was a widower when I raised her, until she married and moved on."

"So Rosario is your second wife?"

"Yes. At my age, it's not good to be lonely."

"I see," replied the attorney. "*¿Algo más?*"

"No, that's all."

Alex walked Pilo out of the office and into the street. The wind was picking up, and the palm trees that lined Harrison Street were twisting in all directions. It might rain.

Alex was about to sit down at his desk again and finish getting ready for the suppression hearing when he heard a voice coming from out in the hallway.

"Hello, Mr. del Fuerte, are you in there?" called the voice.

"Who's there?" yelled Alex from the back office.

"Got a minute?" came the reply.

"Yes . . . ah, hold on," Alex shot back. "I'll be right there."

"Take your time," replied the man outside, waiting in the hallway.

Alex cracked the door open. On the other side stood a short man with a huge belly. He looked scruffy and not very well kept. He was wearing a green short-sleeved shirt that was way too short and too tight; his belly button was showing. The shirt, in Alex's view, was at least four inches off the pants. And the guy's stomach hung over the belt.

"What do you want?" Alex said, annoyed by the constant interruptions, which meant that he wasn't getting anything done.

"Alfonso Fernandez," said the guy, breathing hard as he pushed his hand into Alex's.

"Alejandro del Fuerte, *mucho gusto*," replied Alex as he looked the heavy man over. The man was having a hard time breathing and looked to be not in the best of health.

"I'm a bail bondsman and heard the buzz around the courthouse this morning. Apparently, you handled Judge Sanchez pretty well. Not too many attorneys get to do that."

"I see."

"I wanted to meet you. Actually, I wanted to be the first one to meet you, because other bondsmen will approach you for your business."

"What business? It's 2:45 p.m., and I need to be in court in fifteen minutes. Can't this wait?"

"Can we sit down?" asked Alfonso. "And by the way, call me Poncho."

"You got five minutes, make it fast!" snapped Alex.

"I'm here to offer you my services. Let me get straight to the point, since I only have five minutes. I can make sure you have an unlimited supply of criminal cases or clients. I think you could make a bunch of money, especially since you're starting out and need the clientele."

"I don't understand," said Alex.

"Look, when I'm bonding out someone who's landed in jail, for whatever reason, the first thing they ask is who would I recommend as an attorney. I guess what I'm offering is to steer them your way. I'll give them your name and number and your location. I'll also build you up, tell them things like 'this guy is hungry' or '*es un* pit bull!' You know, things they want to hear that will impress them."

"What's the catch?" asked Alex.

"Well, you charge them whatever you want, and if they do retain you, then you kick back thirty percent of your fee to me."

"I can't split my fees with non-attorneys. You know that."

"This business is mostly cash. Who's going to know?" Not getting any response from Alex, he added, "Look, everybody does it. I've helped every attorney who has made a name for himself in this town. They all started like you. Are you too good, or what? *¿Te crees mucho?*"

"Look, man," replied Alex in disgust, "I haven't had breakfast or lunch. I'm stressing out. I've got to be in court in the next five minutes. But let me get this straight. You barged into my office. You want an answer. On top of that you want me to pay you kickbacks for having you run cases and send them to me. In other words, you want me to break the rules of professional conduct, get disbarred, and never practice law again, right? That's what you're asking me?"

"Yes . . . eh . . . no."

"*¡Vete mucho a la chingada, pendejo!* Go to hell!" barked the attorney.

Alex reached for the door and started showing the bondsman the way out. He was in no mood to deal with anyone. Not now, anyway, when he was already late for court.

"Okay . . . okay," said the shyster. "I was just testing you. Look, it's no secret that everyone around here runs cases. It's a way of life. The little guys like me run the criminal stuff. I deliver fresh clients to the defense bar and get paid for it. Anybody can run cases. Sometimes it's a bondsman or a jailer. Hell, I've known cops and tow truck drivers that run car accidents, too. The chiropractors run cases. They buy the police reports and then send the clients to an attorney. The attorney has his practice next to the chiro's office. They scratch each other's backs. Hell, even nurses at emergency rooms have been known to run cases!"

"So, why should I care?" Alex demanded to know.

"Because this is something that will affect you one way or the other. So you might as well derive a benefit," explained Poncho.

"How's it going to benefit me when I find myself in front of the state Bar trying to explain my actions?" cried Alex.

"The guys on the disciplinary committees are in it, too!" countered Poncho. "And at the most, all you'll get is a slap on the wrist. Why do you think everyone runs cases? Because nothing gets done about it! When was the last time you heard of any attorney losing his license or going to jail because he was caught paying for cases or having someone deliver the cases for money? All they get is probation, pay a fine, *y ya! No es nada.*"

He was now giving Alex a look that said, *Are you that stupid?* "*Escucha,* brother," said Poncho as if he was about to run out of patience, "listen, if we don't run the cases ourselves down here, then some big firm from Corpus Christi or San Antonio will run the case and make the money. Do you know how much money is involved in the big cases? A wrongful death case against a car manufacturer or tire manufacturer can fetch five to ten million dollars."

Alex's ears perked up. "That much, eh?" the young attorney blurted out.

Poncho nodded.

"But, tell me, how does someone like you bring in the big cases?" asked Alex.

"Well, I just work the criminal end of it," Poncho explained. "So for the most part it's small stuff. However, if it's a big drug case at the federal level, it could bring in for the attorney, ah . . . let's say . . . a hundred-thousand-dollar retainer. So if I brought in that case to the attorney, my cut would be about thirty thousand dollars. *Pero* . . . those cases are few and far between. Drugs aren't moved through this county like in years past. The drug cases have dried up. Also, the federal public defender can get the mules the same deal a private attorney can. So the organizations got smart. Why hire a hot-shot lawyer for big bucks when the result is the same with the public defender? The sentencing guidelines are the sentencing guidelines. *Te toca lo que te toca.* There's no room to wiggle. I don't care if you're Rick D'Guerlain."

"Watch it, that guy was my professor!" complained Alex.

"I run lots of DUI's, assaults, small drug offenses, hot checks, unauthorized use of motor vehicles, welfare fraud, etcetera . . . Attorneys charge two to five thousand for these. I get my customary thirty percent referral fee for those. In cash."

Alex continued to listen as he looked at his watch. It was now 3:00 p.m. He wanted to slam the door in the bondsman's face, but the snake oil salesman had piqued his interest. He had to be honest: these were big numbers! For a guy who had practically sold Chiclets at the bridge while growing up in Mexico, the temptation of the mighty dollar was hard to resist.

"So do the math," added the bondsman. "I can send you five cases per week. Let's say that two sign up with your office, and you charge a reasonable five thousand for both. That could be twenty thousand in fees per month. In a year, you're looking at almost a quarter of a million dollars. Minus my thirty percent, you would be grossing around $150,000 a year. Not bad for a recent law school graduate. Besides, have you ever wondered why some attorneys house a bail bonding company in their office?"

"I was wondering about that. Anyway, I'm not interested in the little stuff," Alex interjected, trying to act like a hot shot. "Tell me about the big stuff—let's say a wrongful death case, something like that." He kept looking at his watch but was unable to move. The whole proposal sounded tempting.

"Those cases are typically handled by well-oiled organizations. Just so you understand, maybe this example will illustrate the point. It'll blow your mind. There was this attorney here in Brownsville who was contacted by an ex-client of his. This attorney was not a personal injury lawyer, but handled mostly immigration cases. The ex-client had used his services to obtain a visa for a spouse. Are you with me so far?"

"Yes."

"Turns out, the ex-client's nephew and a friend, both teenagers, had gone fishing in the ship channel at the port of Brownsville. They were fishing off an abandoned pier that once was used by the folks that owned Cummings Oil Transport Services."

"And then?" interrupted Alex, wanting him to hurry up and get to the point.

"Well, when Cummings closed its operations, they called the power company to come out and cut power to the lights that illuminated the working pier. The cables to the light posts ran on the pier, and the wear and tear, along with the salt water and air, had stripped the protective rubber coating down to almost nothing. Turns out there were some live wires left behind, and the boys stepped on them. They were both electrocuted."

"And then what happened?"

"So, the ex-client wants to enlist the services of the immigration attorney to come out and explain to the parents of the two kids what needs to be done next, whether he can take the case or whether they even have a case. The attorney knows it's a case worth at least five million, maybe more. He tells the ex-client that yes, he would love to help the family and will come by the parents' homes at 6:00 p.m. that same day. You follow?"

"Yes, go on. Hurry!"

"Before I continue, can I smoke in your office?" said Poncho as he pulled a box of Marlboro Reds from his pant pocket.

"*Ándale*, hurry up!" retorted Alex as he rolled his eyes. It appeared it was impossible to get rid of Poncho.

Poncho lit his cigarette and took three puffs in a row. Alex noticed for the first time the nicotine-stained fingernails on the guy's right hand.

"Okay, so the ex-client called the attorney at 1:00 p.m., just after the accident happened, right?" said Poncho.

"And?"

"By 4:45 that same afternoon, even before the immigration attorney could leave his office for the day, a firm from Corpus Christi had signed up the parents of both children and had filed suit on their behalf in the 148th District Court here in Cameron County. The same freakin' day!"

"You've got to be kidding me!" screamed Alex in amazement.

"I'm telling you. These folks don't play around. They'll do whatever it takes to get the case. I know the runner that signed up both sets of parents in the electrocution case. A guy named Willy. And do you know how he got the job done?"

"I have no idea. Do tell."

"He gave each family twenty-five thousand dollars to cover any funeral expenses or any other unforeseen expenses. Then he flipped it to a firm from Corpus Christi for one hundred thousand and five percent off the attorney's fees on the back end. So, tell me what incentive would a family like that have to sign up with the immigration attorney or someone like you? None! You can't play in the big leagues. At least, not yet. Maybe in a couple of years you might."

"But how can somebody show up in a moment like that and sign up the parents? That takes guts, no?" Alex noted.

"And more! But I'm telling you, you wave that kind of money in front of folks that have nothing, folks who make six, eight, or ten thousand dollars a year, max? Come on! To them that's a lot of money, and then they're told there's going to be more. I don't care who it is, they sign up . . . trust me."

"And the guy running the case? Did he use his money to sign them up, or was that the firm's?" asked Alex.

"It can be worked either way. Some independents sign up the case and just flip it. They'll sell it for double the amount they paid out of their own pocket. Others want a percentage of whatever the case brings on the back end. Others are just employees of the firm, such as investigators or 'consultants.' These folks are paid a salary to roam the countryside with scanners looking for cases. They're expected to work in conjunction with tow truck drivers and law enforcement officials to hone in on the good cases. Everybody is on the payroll. Law enforcement or the wrecker drivers tip them when an accident looks like it has potential."

"I had no idea any of this was going on," said Alex in an incredulous tone. "Certainly, they don't teach you anything about that in law school."

"Yes, I know," said Poncho, grinning. He took another deep puff, then blew smoke straight into the attorney's face. "And they also don't teach you that even if you have signed up the case, it can still be taken away from you."

"Wait a minute! What do you mean . . . even with a valid, signed contract?"

"Sure! Usually when the runner shows up with the money, he explains to them that it's perfectly legal to call the first attorney, if they've signed with someone else, and advise him that they've decided to retain somebody else. The standard contract has clauses in it where either party can terminate the contract at any time and get out. It only gets sticky if the first attorney has already done work on the case or has filed the lawsuit. But if it's a fresh new case, where the ink is barely dry, then a call is all it takes to tell the first attorney bye-bye. *Hasta la vista*, baby. *Ni modo*, it happens," said Poncho, smiling. He was beginning to see that Alex was finally catching on. "What do you think? Interested?"

Alex sat there in silence. He felt confused and somewhat disgusted. What was all that stuff he learned in law school for? All that stuff about honor and ethics? Why take the professional responsibility course? Wasn't that what everybody complained about—lawyers being vultures?

Poncho could see that Alex was deep in thought and struggling with the information he'd just received. "So, when do I send you your first case?" the bondsman asked.

"I'm not quite convinced that I'll be interested."

"Have you ever tried fried gar fish, *chicharrones de catán*?" Poncho demanded to know, quickly changing his approach.

"What does food have to do with anything?" Alex asked.

"Well, maybe we can go out to lunch sometime and let you sample our fine local cuisine. And we can talk business."

"I've had *catán* before," said Alex, somewhat indignant. This was a complete lie. He had never even seen an alligator gar fish in his life. He had fished the gulf waters before, but he'd never seen a *catán*.

"Okay, then let's go to the Blue Marlin on Billy Mitchell Boulevard. Let's make it Thursday. I'll come by your office and get you. Then we'll talk," concluded Poncho.

"Call first. I may not be available," came the reply.

With that, Poncho exited the office. Alex sat there, uncertain as to whether he had or had not agreed to go to lunch with this scum bucket. Well, it was done. Judge Sanchez was waiting.

Chapter 6

THE COURTROOM WAS EMPTY when the young attorney walked in. Alex took his place at counsel's table and put down his books. He looked at his watch. It was 3:15 p.m. Was he ready? Did he know what he was doing? This was it . . . flying solo! This was the real world. There was no Mr. Lassiter around, his mentor at the Houston firm, to hold his hand. No fake law school exercise. This time it was a real client in a real case with real agents and a really dangerous prosecutor.

He started reviewing his notes and the questions he'd prepared earlier. At that moment, the prosecutor walked in and sat down at the other table. She had an Anglo Border Patrol agent in tow. The agent, who looked to be in his late twenties or early thirties, was wearing his green uniform and carrying a manila file.

As Alex was taking it all in, Joe walked into the courtroom.

"Judge is on his way," announced Joe. "He's stuck in traffic, outside the Vermillion restaurant. He'll be here in a few minutes."

"Where's my client?" asked Alex of Joe.

"They're bringing him up from the holding tank. He's on his way," confirmed Joe.

About ten minutes went by before Domingo finally appeared, led by a young jailer with "Tavansky" on his name tag. Tavansky had Domingo sit next to Alex at counsel's table, exchanged a few words with Joe, who was sitting at his small desk off to one side, and exited the courtroom.

Alex and his client were talking strategy when Joe announced that everyone should rise and that the court was now in session.

The judge took his place on the bench, picked up a file, and read from it into the record.

"This is case number 2004-09-120-A, *The State of Texas v. Domingo Garza*. What says the state?"

"The state is present and ready, Judge," said Gisela.

"The defense is ready," countered Alex nervously. He continued, "We would invoke the rule, and my client is going to need an interpreter, Your Honor."

"Joe, please call Interpreter Solis and have him come and sit by Mr. Garza's side," ordered the judge.

"Right away," Joe replied.

"The rule has been invoked," explained the judge. "Any witnesses who will testify in this matter please stand up and take your oath."

The border patrol agent stood up and was asked to raise his right hand. He swore to tell the truth.

Judge Sanchez added on the record, "If there are other witnesses placed under the rule, the court will ask that they wait outside the courtroom. While waiting outside to come in and testify, they're prohibited from discussing any aspect of this case among themselves or with any third parties, except that they may talk with the attorneys in the case."

The judge looked over at the assistant D.A. and said, "Call your first witness."

"We call agent Richard Snyder, Your Honor."

"Officer, please come up and take the witness stand. You have already been administered the oath," the judge reminded him.

"State your name for the record, please," asked Ms. Montemayor without wasting a single second.

"Richard J. Snyder," said the officer.

"And tell us, Officer, how long have you been a Border Patrol agent?"

"Five years."

"Were you on duty on July fourth of this year?"

"Yes."

"Tell the court how it was that you crossed paths with Domingo Garza on that day," said the assistant D.A. without missing a beat.

"I was coming out of Luby's by the HEB on Paredes Line Road and Boca Chica Boulevard. I had been on my lunch break and was getting ready to get in my marked patrol unit."

"And then what happened?" asked the D.A.

"Well, as I was getting ready to leave the parking lot, I noticed this car with tinted windows drive by at a slow pace."

"Okay, go on," prodded the D.A.

"Objection, Your Honor," declared Alex, trying to break her rhythm. "This is turning into a narrative. Where is the question?"

"Sustained," ruled the court.

Gisela gave Alex a dirty look. Turning back to the witness, she asked, "What did you see next?"

"Well, I noticed that the car that drove by, a red Ford Crown Victoria, was going too slow . . . and it's well known that this type of vehicle is a favorite with drug smugglers and alien traffickers," replied the officer.

"So what did you do next?"

"I couldn't see inside because of the dark tint on the windows, so I figured the driver was hiding something, or maybe he was even an alien," said the agent.

"Objection!" cried Alex. "Calls for speculation. How could this officer know anything about the driver of the car?"

"Sustained," ruled the judge.

"What was your basis for thinking that there was an illegal alien in the car, Officer?" Gisela asked.

"These types of cars are always involved in drug trafficking or alien smuggling, and, based on the fact that the car appeared weighed down in the trunk and was driving real slow, I decided to conduct an investigatory stop," answered Agent Snyder.

As Alex sat there listening to the officer's testimony, he soon realized that his client had done nothing wrong. The officer had decided to stop the car on a bad hunch or racial profiling, nothing else. At least not enough to reach probable cause, which is what the officer would have needed to pull the car over. The officer would have needed either a traffic violation or some strong indication that the driver was an illegal alien in order to legally pull him over. So far, there was nothing.

"What happened after you pulled the car over?" asked the prosecutor with another rapid-fire question.

"I approached the driver's side window and asked the driver for his Texas driver's license or other type of identification."

"Did he produce either?"

"No, he said that everything . . . or that all his IDs were at home . . . something like that. So I asked him his name and whether he was a U.S. citizen, and he started getting nervous."

"Did you ever get any information out of him?"

"Yes. Finally he said his name was Domingo J. Garza and that his date of birth was September 18, 1970. So I ran his info on our database, and it came back that he had been previously deported. Then I asked him if he had any documentation that would have allowed him to be back in the States, and he couldn't answer."

"So you arrested him?"

"Yes, and proceeded to impound the car. When I was inventorying its contents, I discovered that there was what appeared to be a small roach or 'half-smoked joint' in the car's ashtray."

"And then what happened?"

"Well, I called Brownsville PD to come out and do whatever they do with the evidence in the ashtray, and I guess they decided to charge Mr. Garza with possession of marijuana."

"Is this the person you arrested that day?" asked Gisela, pointing toward where Mr. Garza was sitting.

"Yes, that is the defendant, Mr. Garza."

"Did you arrest him here in Cameron County, Texas?" followed up Gisela.

"Yes."

"And is this the marijuana that you found in the ashtray?"

"Looks that way, although I did not take possession of it that day. I believe BPD would have picked it up, tested it, and kept it in evidence."

"Judge," interrupted Alex, jumping up from his seat. "I would object to the officer testifying whether or not this is the marijuana.

Obviously, chain of custody has not been proven, and unless the D.A. has the custodian of evidence from BPD testify that this is the same joint that was picked up that day, then this witness has no personal knowledge as to whether or not this is that marijuana."

"Sustained," snapped the judge.

"Judge," responded the young D.A., "for purposes of this hearing, we know that the admissibility of the marijuana has no relevance. However, it should still be admitted, because whether or not this is the marijuana, that goes only to the weight of the evidence."

"Ms. Montemayor," said the judge. He had decided to throw her a bone. "Ask him if he recognizes that to be marijuana. But I won't let you introduce it unless you have the custodian of evidence from BPD."

"Agent Snyder," continued Gisela, "what is Exhibit 1? Do you recognize it?"

"Based on my experience and training, I would have to say that that is marijuana."

Alex sat there, taking it all in. He knew that whether or not the marijuana was admitted into evidence probably had no relevance to the issue at hand. What he needed to do was attack the officer's reasons for stopping the car.

"Pass the witness," said the assistant D.A., and with that, Alex was on.

"Officer, what traffic violation did my client commit on the day in question?" he asked without giving the agent an opportunity to catch his breath.

"I don't understand," replied Agent Snyder, a little perturbed.

"Is there a minimum or maximum speed limit inside the HEB parking lot?"

"Well . . . no . . . I don't think so," said the agent.

"So it's not against the law, is it, to drive slowly in a private parking lot, correct?"

"No."

"And you did not see my client, Domingo, drive into other vehicles, did you?"

"No."

"And you did not see Domingo drinking any beers while driving, did you?"

"Well, no, the dark tint would not have allowed me to see inside," said the officer.

"Did he use his turn signal as he was exiting the HEB parking lot?"

"Yes."

"Was the car weaving in and out of traffic?"

"No."

"So, you decided to stop this car because of the tinted windows and the make and model of the vehicle, correct?"

"Well, no . . . I mean there was more to it than that."

"Okay, what was it?"

"The car's trunk looked weighed down, and possibly there could have been illegal aliens hiding in the trunk."

"Come on!" shot back Alex, amazed at the officer's incredible responses. "You mean to tell me that every time you see a low rider driving down the street with its trunk down, you stop them?"

As Alex waited to see what far-fetched response the officer would come up with next, he looked over at the D.A. He could tell that she knew that the officer was in trouble and that the judge was getting impatient with the ridiculous answers the agent was providing.

"Well, no, I don't stop every vehicle whose rear is lower than the front."

"Well, tell the court what crime you say the driver of this vehicle committed before your very own eyes?" demanded Alex.

The officer was now visibly shaken and was beginning to squirm in the witness chair. Small beads of sweat were forming on his forehead, and Alex was quick to build on his advantage.

"So, tell me," continued Alex, "did you check to see if this car was registered to my client?"

"No . . . I did not."

"Did you ask him if this was his car?"

"Eh . . . no."

"Did he smell of marijuana?"

"No, not really."

"Did he have bloodshot eyes?"

"No."

"Was he incoherent?"

"Well, no . . . he was nervous."

"Did his clothes smell of marijuana?"

"I can't remember," said the agent.

"Well, did he look stoned?" asked Alex in amazement.

"No."

"Was the joint lit, as if he had been smoking it?" Alex demanded to know.

"No."

"Did you find marijuana on his person?"

"No."

"Did you find drug paraphernalia on his person?"

"What's paraphernalia?" asked the agent with a blank look on his face.

Alex, Gisela, and the judge rolled their eyes at the same time. Even Joe, sitting off to one side, and the court interpreter and the court reporter started chuckling. They were having a hard time keeping the giggling to themselves.

Judge Sanchez saw this and decided to cut Alex off right there and then. The damage had been done, and he wanted to save the rookie officer any more embarrassment and damage to his reputation. Even though the judge was known to lean toward the defense, he still respected officers who were out there trying to do their job. The judge knew that "probable cause" was a fluid concept that even seasoned criminal defense attorneys, including judges, sometimes did not completely understand. Alex, on the other hand, apparently had it down pretty well.

"I've heard enough," announced the judge, "and I'm ready to rule on the defendant's motion to suppress. The court finds that Officer Snyder lacked even reasonable suspicion, much less probable cause, to conduct this traffic stop. Therefore, since we have an invalid stop, the evidence seized from this wrongful and arbitrary traffic stop must be suppressed. It is fruit of the poisonous tree." After a pause, he added, "State, do you have an announcement?"

"Yes, Your Honor," said Gisela, shaking her head in a disappointed manner. "The state moves to dismiss the charges against Mr. Domingo Garza."

"Very well, the record will so reflect," concluded the judge and instructed Joe to advise INS of Mr. Garza's status.

"This court will be in recess," said the judge. "Mr. del Fuerte, please tell your client the good news and come see me in chambers when you're done."

"Will do," responded Alex with a grin on his face. He could now breathe a sigh of relief.

Chapter 7

THE JUDGE'S CHAMBER WAS A CAVERNOUS ROOM. Alex noticed the plush alpaca rugs scattered throughout the office, the rich hand-carved furniture, and the picture frames and diplomas adorning the walls. Also hanging from the walls, in elaborate, antique frames, were original T. Smith paintings of nature scenes. Each canvas was covered with peaceful and tranquil scenes of the New Mexico desert, the Texas hill country, the waters of the Gulf of Mexico, and the West Texas mountains, including the Mexican Sierra Madre.

"Alejandro," said the judge in a congratulatory manner, "may I call you Alejandro?" He was no longer wearing his robe and seemed genuinely happy and excited for the young attorney. He appeared full of energy, excited, in a boyish kind of way.

"Call me Alex," said the young attorney.

"Okay," said the judge, "I've got to tell you . . . that was very good for a young attorney fresh out of the gate. You remind me of myself when I first started practicing law."

"Thanks," replied Alex.

"Of course," Judge Sanchez continued, "in this instance it was easy to see that the agent was simply trying to find an excuse to stop the vehicle. Other cases are never going to be this simple. Domingo should feel very proud of you. You were right on the money. You asked the right questions and kept it simple and to the point. That was good. The courts always appreciate that."

"Thank you," said Alex, again.

"You know," continued the judge, "it's sad to see that Domingo is not out of the woods, yet."

"What do you mean?"

"He's going to be prosecuted for entering illegally after being deported and will probably end up being sentenced six to twelve months in federal prison."

"Is that so?" asked Alex, not quite understanding why the feds would be so harsh.

"Then to top it all off, when he finishes serving his sentence he will be sent to an INS detention center. Have you ever been to such a center?"

"No," confessed Alex. He didn't even know such places existed.

"They're like concentration camps, but the public has no clue. There are individuals in there who have been in limbo for five years, and they can't be returned to their countries, either because of political retaliation or persecution, and they can't be let out, either. So they just sit there. No one knows what to do with them. It's pretty sad, especially when this is America and these things are happening in our own backyard. You'd never think such things happened here in the States."

"I see," mumbled Alex.

"Then, to make matters worse," added the judge, "Domingo will end up spending several additional months at the INS detention camp, but hopefully he'll know enough to ask for a voluntary departure. A lot of detainees think they can stop the deportation process by refusing to ask for a voluntary departure, and they end up spending an additional eight months in confinement and still get deported."

"Really, they have to serve all that time?"

"Yes. And you know what the worst part is?" the judge asked.

"No," answered Alex as he stared at his old and weathered Ironman watch. It was almost five o'clock, and he needed to get back to the office to wait for Aurora.

"The families left behind," the judge answered. "Mothers, fathers, and children. They have to fend for themselves. Some end up on welfare, others fall between the cracks."

"I never thought of that," said Alex.

"Take Domingo, for example," the judge said. "When he was young, he got in trouble and got deported. Then he came back and straightened his ways. Ultimately, he became a responsible member of society. Now he leaves a wife and children behind."

"And a good job," Alex interjected.

"Exactly," cried Judge Sanchez, "a job that he's had for well over ten years. All that is gone, poof! Just like that."

"And what will a person like Domingo do back in Mexico," asked Alex, "with no job prospects, no family, and no future?"

"I don't know." Judge Sanchez was nodding his head, looking at the floor. "Probably die trying to get back to his family . . . back to Chicago."

Alex thought of Pilo. If only Judge Sanchez knew he was trying to help a client in almost the same predicament. Except in Pilo's case, the client had come into the States to look for his family and take them back to Mexico.

"And," the judge continued, "those now behind bars will tell you that they will risk life and limb trying to get back to their families. Risk everything—dying, being deported, or even going to prison. So the jails are full of these folks."

A picture began to form in Alex's head as the judge explained the fate that probably awaited Domingo.

"So what's going to happen to Domingo's family back in Chicago?" Alex asked.

"The family will be split forever."

"I can't even begin to imagine what that would do to the kids. That's horrible!"

"Alex, it goes on every day. It's a fact of life here at the border," said Judge Sanchez. "You shouldn't be surprised. INS has even deported mothers to the Middle East because of allegations they participated in antigovernment protests while in college. Think of the madness. A parent deported thousands of miles away, while the other parent and the children are allowed to remain here in America."

"*¡Qué bárbaro!* I don't know what's worse—not being able to see your wife and children or being a foreigner in your own country. Take my client. He's been living in the United States since he was about fifteen. He doesn't have any family left back in Mexico. No one really to go back to. There are no jobs. And then, he probably doesn't even have any Mexican papers either, since he's been living in the States forever. So he's in limbo, purgatory."

"I could tell you stories from my days in private practice," interjected the judge, "but they're too sad. And right now, we're celebrating. You outdid yourself. Good job defending your client. You will go far, Alejandro, I can tell."

"Thanks, Judge. I'm humbled," said Alex.

"All right then. Alex, make sure you present your payment voucher to the court's administrator for today's work. That way the county can cut you a check for your representation of Mr. Garza. I would imagine since you just started, you probably need the money, correct?"

"Yes, sir, I could use the money," Alex agreed. "Judge, I hate to cut the visit short, but I have to meet someone at my office. I promised her I'd be there by five o'clock."

"Well, then, you'd better go. It's almost five."

"Thanks for everything," added Alex in a pleasant tone.

"My pleasure . . . and please come back and get more appointments . . . any time."

Alex got up and picked up his coat that had been hanging from the chair. As he was walking out, he briefly stopped before opening the door and turned around to ask the judge one last question.

"Judge," mumbled Alex, "can I ask you something?"

"*Claro, con confianza*," said the judge. "Please feel at ease. What is it?"

"What can you tell me about Judge Walter Macallan?" asked Alex. "How did he come to be on the bench?"

The judge gave Alex a look of disgust, as if to say, *Why would anyone want to know anything about that man?*

"Well ∴ . ." the judge said, and hesitated. "You just got to town. What could you possibly want to know about him?"

Alex didn't want to reveal too much, so he quickly thought of something to say.

"You see, Judge, Joe, your bailiff, praised all of the judges, except Macallan, and before I go seeking appointments from that court, I just wanted to know if you had any tips or suggestions."

"I'd stay away from that S.O.B.," the judge said. "But if you must know, let me tell you a little about him, and then you can draw your own conclusions.

"Walter Macallan's father, Taylor Macallan, was a wealthy landowner here in the Valley. Old man Macallan had made his fortune in cotton during the forties and fifties. When cotton went belly-up, he switched to growing sorghum, sugar cane, and watermelons. The operation consisted of ten thousand acres. However, by the mid-sixties, old man Macallan had also sold exploration leases to major oil companies. One of these companies struck oil, and this increased old man Macallan's wealth. He received enormous royalty checks every month from the oil company. This new affluence allowed him to make huge contributions to the Republican Party and other conservative causes.

"Soon thereafter, his sons received appointments to governmental boards and cabinets. The last one to get an appointment had been Judge Walter. In the mid-nineties, while George W. Bush was governor of Texas, Walter Macallan was appointed judge of the 148th Judicial District Court for Cameron County, Texas. The bench had been left vacant when the district judge, Judge Terry Ransome, had run for the position of chief justice for the Thirteenth Court of Appeals. George W. himself saw that Walter Macallan would get the appointment as a 'thank you' to old man Macallan for having been a staunch supporter of the Republican Party."

Alex listened carefully, and in his mind a picture of Judge Macallan began to emerge.

"Walter Macallan's grandfather, Sergeant Travis Macallan," the judge continued, "had been a Texas Ranger from 1890 until 1915 or so. It was rumored that he'd acquired the family's lands by forcing numerous Mexican and Spanish settlers out. Having migrated from the north, he'd quickly realized that the settlers had no formal documents to show that they owned the vast tracts of land that they laid claim to. So he recorded in the county records false deeds making himself the grantee of the land already occupied by the Mexicans. He would then show up and explain to them that they had no rights to the land because he had the deeds. They were then ordered to leave. Those who opposed him soon found themselves incarcerated, tortured, or dead. The Macallans always lived by the sword.

"But you see, the problem with Travis's sneaky plan was that he forgot one small legal detail. His false deeds never fully described who owned the mineral rights to those lands. Thus, some argued that the Macallan family only owned the surface rights. When oil was discovered on those lands, a group of remote descendants from the previous owners filed suit against the Macallan family. Unfortunately, this was the late sixties, and the Macallan family wielded great influence over all the Anglo judges of Cameron County. Of course, in the sixties it was all male Anglo judges in the district and county courts. It wasn't until the late seventies that we first elected a Hispanic county judge. So those poor bastards got their claims and their lawsuit thrown out by a judge who was friends with old man Macallan.

"Anyway, Walter Macallan has been the only Republican judge on the bench in Cameron County in the last ten years. He's not very well liked, except by big business, doctors, and the insurance industry.

"Oh, also, I don't know if this matters or not, but when Walter Macallan was fourteen years of age, he murdered one of the family's Mexican maids when she refused his sexual advances. The girl was about seventeen or eighteen. Macallan felt scorned and humiliated, so he reached for a .22 Colt revolver and shot her in the heart. The maid left behind a one-year-old. Now, understand that to the Macallan children this was not entirely unusual, for they had seen old man Macallan shoot farmhands that he suspected were stealing from him. The family covered up the murder of the maid so well that very few people actually knew about it. This happened several decades ago, and it didn't even make the news. Old man Macallan buried the body somewhere on his farm. I know this because a great uncle of mine was a foreman for the Macallans. And since everyone was deathly afraid of them, no one ever brought it to light. Yet it was part of the family stories we heard when we were growing up."

"You know," said Alex, "something like that happened in Mexico, too. The Mexican papers wrote about an ex-president having shot one of the maids. The guy was a teenager when it happened. Years later, when he got into politics, his rivals discovered the cover-up and publicized the whole episode."

Alex looked at his watch and realized it was now past five o'clock. "Well, I appreciate you taking the time to tell me about Macallan and his family."

"Come back anytime," replied the judge.

"I will," answered Alex, and with that he walked out of chambers and headed to his office. The weather outside was changing, and the southern sky was now covered in dark clouds.

Chapter 8

ON THE WAY BACK TO HIS OFFICE ACROSS THE STREET, Alex thought about Judge Macallan. Even though he still had to meet the man, he felt a certain level of disgust and disdain toward him. It just so happened that Rosario and the boy were dead—and they had lived with Judge Macallan, too. From what Aurora said, however, it sounded like they may have been involved in a car accident. But did Macallan have something to do with it? What he'd just heard about the Macallan family, certainly made them capable of committing murder, but there was no way that a district court judge would be so reckless and get his hands dirty like that. Would a district judge be so dumb and risk going to prison?

Alex pulled his big key ring out of his right pant pocket and opened the office door. He set down the books he'd taken to court and checked his pocket for Mrs. Lawrence's check. He sure needed it and would hate to lose it. It had been an incredibly hectic first day. He reviewed everything that had happened and was amazed that he was still standing.

His stomach was growling. The only thing keeping him going was the adrenaline from having been in the courtroom on the motion to suppress. He wondered if Aurora had already stopped by and whether he might have missed her.

As he was standing there looking over his desk, he loosened his tie and thought about his new client, Mrs. Lawrence. He needed to draft the petition for divorce and get Clint served ASAP. After all, the client had paid him good money to take her case, and she probably expected a report by the weekend.

His thoughts were interrupted by a gentle knock at the front door.

"Who is it?" yelled Alex.

"*La señora Aurora*," came the response.

"*Ah, sí*," replied Alex from his office in the back. There was relief in his voice. "*Ya*, just a minute."

Alex opened the door and invited the woman to come in. They walked to the back office, and Alex asked Aurora to take her place in one of the two client chairs available.

"How are you?" Alex asked as he played with his tie and rolled up his sleeves.

"*Pasándola*, Mr. del Fuerte," Aurora replied.

"I have so many questions, I don't even know where to start," the young attorney explained. "Can I get you some water? I can make some coffee, if it's okay with you. I could use some, too. Can I interest you in a cup of coffee?"

"I don't have much time, *señor licenciado*," said Aurora.

"My name is Alejandro, but please just call me Alex. What's your last name? Please sit down."

"López. Aurora López."

"How are you related to Porfirio or Rosario Medina?"

"I'm related to Porfirio. He's my mother's first cousin. His mother and my grandmother were sisters."

"Oh, I see," said Alex.

"My mother and father were migrant workers and left Tepantitlán, Mexico, in the late sixties. We used to come up, go work in the fields up north, and then return to Mexico. Then, in the early seventies my parents settled down here in Brownsville. I've lived here since my early twenties, but my family had been traveling into the United States under the Bracero Program since the late fifties or early sixties. Some of my first memories as a child were of my whole family picking strawberries in the fields of Minnesota."

Alex didn't dare ask her age, but from her story, he calculated that she was in her mid-fifties. However, just like Pilo, she looked somewhat older.

"Who knows you're here?" asked Alex.

"My husband is waiting for me outside in the car," replied Aurora. "He's the gentleman who answered the phone when you first called." She added abruptly, "Where's Pilo?"

"He's here in Brownsville," answered Alex.

"Is he okay?"

"Yes, he's safe. Why do you ask?"

Alex put the question out there to see if Aurora would tell him anything else regarding the circumstances of the highway accident.

"Well, I would hate for something to happen to him . . . you know, with Border Patrol and everything," explained Aurora. "Have you told him anything about Rosario and his son?"

"No, I wanted to wait until I spoke with you," conceded Alex, not completely satisfied with Aurora's answer.

"Good, I'm glad you haven't told him anything yet. I feel terrible for him, too, but we are also somewhat in the dark. When we started asking questions, doors were slammed shut in our faces. Up until this date, we are still not exactly sure what really happened, *no sabemos nada.*"

Alex glanced at his watch; it was now six in the evening. Hunger was getting the better of him. He felt famished.

"Before you tell me the details, Mrs. López," he said, "let me brew some coffee . . . it will take a second."

"*Sí, está bien,*" responded Aurora as she nodded in agreement.

Alex got up and went to the back room and got a pot of coffee going. He reached down and splashed his face with cold water from the sink. Now the adrenaline was beginning to wear off, and he was starting to crash. His whole body ached as if he'd been in a boxing match, but he had to keep going and get the details from Aurora. He needed to keep her in the office and get as much information as he could.

Alex loaded his cup with two sugars and plenty of cream. He couldn't wait to taste it, feel the caffeine kick in and have the hunger pains subside.

He came back to the desk and sat down. He offered a cup to Aurora, but she declined since she needed to wrap things up and wanted to avoid keeping her husband waiting outside.

"About a year, year and a half ago, maybe more," said Aurora, "I got a phone call from Rosario. I rarely spoke with her because the employers kept her on a short leash. Almost mean, I would say. She confided in me and told me that the *patrón* had made advances toward her and that she no longer felt she could continue to work there. You see, Rosario was very attractive.

"Anyway, she calls me and says that she is at the end of her rope and that she met this guy named Ramón, who apparently works there as the gardener, and that he can smuggle her and the boy up to Houston. This guy Ramón . . . he worked on the side, with people in the smuggling business, and he knew some *coyotes*."

"Do you know Ramón's last name?" asked Alex. "Or do you know where he lives?"

"No, but as I understand it, Ramón was going to set her up with one of those janitorial companies working in downtown Houston. The job paid eight dollars an hour to start and plenty of overtime. She was to take Juan José with her and was supposed to stay with Ramón's relatives until she could get her own place. Unfortunately, they never made it."

"Why, what happened?" asked Alex.

"From what I hear, there was a highway accident, and everyone was ejected from the vehicle. There may have been one survivor. I think it may have been the driver of the van. I'm not really sure. I don't know all the details."

"Was Ramón with the group?"

"I don't think so," answered Aurora, "but of course all we have are sketchy details. The story was reported in the *Valley Shining Star*, although the accident happened on the outskirts of Raymondville right where the Yturria ranch starts. The story never made the *Rio Grand Post*."

"So the accident happened around April or May of 2003?" inquired Alex.

"Somewhere around there. I remember the first showers passing through the area, so it could have been May. But it may have been April, I don't recall exactly. It has been a while."

"What a tragedy," said Alex, trying to comfort Aurora. "Was there a funeral service for Rosario or the boy?"

"That's what I was getting to," said Aurora. "You see, we didn't find out about the accident until sometime after it had happened. Since the story came out only in the Harlingen paper, we never saw it. We only get the local paper. And because it was very diffi-cult for my husband and me to get around, we sent our son, Arturo, to Raymondville to get the details. In Raymondville, the police couldn't find the accident report. That's what they said. I don't know. Anyway, Art was told that the report could not be released to him, only to attorneys or the parties to the accident. Then, when he asked where they had taken the bodies to, he was told they could have gone to Dolly Vincent, Valley Methodist, or Harlingen Medical."

Alex thought about the missing report. Could it be that the Willacy sheriff's office had no record because DPS investigated the accident? Would the county morgue have information? And why hadn't anyone contacted the relatives?

"So, you never heard from Rosario and the boy again?" the young attorney asked.

"No, that's all I know," Aurora replied.

"Did the Mexican Consulate call you to see if you knew any-thing about the victims?"

"No."

"And no one from Willacy or DPS contacted you either?"

"No, *nadie*," Aurora said, "and when we tried to ask questions, we couldn't get anywhere. The doors were slammed in our faces, pretty much. Even the Mexican Consulate said they couldn't release information to us, not until the next of kin were notified."

"Did you tell the officials at the Mexican Consulate of Pilo's existence?"

"That's just it. We weren't even sure if it was really Rosario and the boy. No one would give us any answers. I really have to leave now."

"*¿Algo más?*" asked Alex handing her a homemade business card. "Did we miss anything else?"

"I don't think so. But if I remember any other details I will call you," said Aurora. "I got your number. I'm sorry I can't help you with more information, but we are also in the dark."

"Mrs. López, why was it that you didn't want to tell me any of this over the phone?" asked Alex, hoping she would explain her earlier concerns.

Aurora looked down at the floor and started playing her fingers in a nervous manner. She looked as if she wanted to get something off her chest but for some reason was holding back. Whatever it was, she was struggling with it. Finally, she said, "I don't want to say anything because I don't really know the truth, but I think the people she used to work for may know more about what really happened. We didn't want to make any waves, because I hear they are powerful and dangerous people and we don't need any trouble, so we just left it at that. Besides, *agua que no has de beber . . . déjala correr.*"

Alex nodded his head in agreement. Aurora was right. Sometimes it was much better to just look the other way and pretend nothing ever happened.

"I see what you mean," said Alex as he started to walk Aurora outside. "Very well. Keep me posted, and I'll do the same. I've got your number, but I'm missing your address. Could I have it before you go?"

"Yes," said Aurora, "it's 3414 Magnolia Court, here in Brownsville."

And with that, Aurora left Alex's office. Alex looked at his watch. It was now close to eight o'clock. He'd had one heck of a day. He could hear the wind outside, and the rain was coming down hard, too.

Chapter 9

ALEJANDRO DEL FUERTE HAD DECIDED that Tuesday morning would be a good day to get acquainted with the Cameron County Law Library, located on the first floor of the courthouse. He had decided to spend the early morning there, before his mid-morning appointment with Pilo.

Although the library was a hole in the wall when compared to other law libraries across Texas, it was a good starting point to find information, articles, or anything of value that made reference to rollover accidents involving passenger vans. Alex was also determined to finish drafting the Lawrence divorce petition and get it filed that Tuesday morning.

He found a computer and got on a search engine. In an instant, the computer had pulled several stories from the Internet dealing with rollovers. One caught Alex's eyes. It was a small piece in the Sunday edition of the *Valley Shining Star* about an accident involving a passenger van registered to Rio Transport Company. The accident was still being investigated by the Texas Department of Public Safety. However, preliminary reports concluded that speed and fatigue may have played a role. At least eight passengers had lost their lives. It was believed most of the passengers were illegal aliens. No other details were available at press time.

Alex headed upstairs to the county clerk's office.

"Good morning, can you tell me if I can obtain a copy of a death certificate at this office?" Alex asked the lady in charge, whose name was Nellie.

"Yes, we keep such records here," Nellie answered politely. "I'd need to know if the death occurred in Cameron County because those are the only records we keep. I would also need to know the name of the decedent and an approximate date."

"Oh, I see," Alex said in a worried tone, since the accident appeared to have happened in Raymondville, Willacy County. At least, that was what Aurora had said. And that meant that the death certificate might be located somewhere else.

"Do you think," continued Alex, "that if the fatality occurred near Raymondville, EMS would have transported the victims to a hospital in this county?"

"Yes, Harlingen is only twenty-five minutes from Raymondville, and it has major medical facilities. Raymondville is a town of only five thousand people. They don't have adequate medical facilities. Most major medical emergencies are handled at Valley Methodist in Harlingen."

"So then it's possible that if the victims died at the facility in Harlingen, the death certificate might end up here because it's inside the county?" inquired Alex.

"It's quite likely," said Nellie.

"Then can you see if you have a death certificate for Rosario Medina or a boy named Juan José Medina?"

"Sure, give me a minute. I've got to go look in the vault in the back." With that, Nellie disappeared behind a heavy metal door located at the end of a hallway.

Alex was looking out into the corridor in front of the clerk's office when suddenly, out in the distance, he saw Ms. Montemayor leaving County Court One and heading to her office inside the district attorney's office.

God, how he wished he had another case against her—even if she whipped him! Hell, getting whipped wouldn't be so bad, not coming from someone as beautiful as Ms. Montemayor. He would have to get the goods on her. He was deep in thought when Nellie interrupted him.

"Sir, we have them. Will you be needing copies?" she wanted to know.

"Yes, please. Can you certify them while you're at it?" Alex asked.

"That'll be two dollars a copy and three to certify it, for a total of five dollars. Who do I make out the receipt to?"

"Law office of Alejandro del Fuerte, P.C.," indicated Alex.

"So you're Mr. del Fuerte," said Nellie in amazement. "Joe, the bailiff from County Court One, came in here yesterday raving about a young lawyer. He said you did a terrific job for your client and that Judge Sanchez was thoroughly impressed with you."

"Thanks for the compliment. I was just doing my job," said Alex modestly.

"Oh, by the way," continued Nellie, "this name, Rosario Medina, rings a bell. I know I've heard it before. Were you the attorney for the family?"

"I don't understand," said Alex in shock. "What do you mean?"

"Well, I thought you might have worked for the firm that handled the wrongful death case. I know we have a probate file here in the office with her name. Usually there's an estate administration opened in conjunction with certain wrongful death civil lawsuits. I don't know for sure where the civil case might have landed. I don't even know if there was one. But the county clerk's office handles all of the probate matters. I would think that the civil case, if there was one, would have been filed in district court upstairs. The probate files sometimes have a companion wrongful death suit."

This information blew Alex away. He thanked Nellie and said goodbye. Picking up his certified copy of the death certificate and putting it in his coat pocket, he took the stairs down to the first floor and made his way toward the law library.

He now had more questions than answers. His head was spinning. It had to be a mistake. It had to be! There had to be more than one Rosario Medina in all of Brownsville. Besides, who could have filed a claim on her behalf? Pilo, her husband, had been in Mexico. Something was not right.

Could Rosario's parents have brought the lawsuit? But that was impossible. Surely Pilo would have found out. Rosario and Pilo were from the same village. Had there been a case filed on behalf of Juan José, the boy, also? Who was the firm? He would have to ask Pilo about that.

The whole thing didn't make sense. How could Aurora not have known of the lawsuit? Apparently even Nellie thought that there had been a lawsuit. But if there had been a lawsuit, what had happened to it? Did the case go to trial? Was there a verdict? Did it settle? If so, for how much? Who opened the administration of Rosario's estate?

He began to worry about what else he might find. But now he was in the middle of it, and the questions were snowballing by the minute. The only way to find out would be to try to obtain copies of both files. Hopefully he could get that done without making waves, particularly around the courthouse, where everybody knew everything about everybody.

The district clerk's office was known to be the best run clerk's office along the Texas-Mexico border. The district clerk in charge had been at the helm for well over twenty years and was known to run a tight ship. However, certain local attorneys had found ways to make sure their lawsuits always landed in favorable courts. No one had proof of this, but it just so happened that their cases always landed in the courts that generated the biggest jury verdicts. Some called it coincidence, others sheer luck.

The Honorable Alejandro del Fuerte was about to file his first divorce lawsuit. Yes, it was just the Lawrence divorce, not a multimillion dollar lawsuit or anything like that, but it was all his. He'd drafted it. He'd researched it. He'd spell-checked it and had signed it in the requisite signature block. It was notice to the world and the Brownsville legal community that he was open for business. The cover letter to the district clerk requested that Clint Lawrence be served by having a Cameron County sheriff's deputy hand-deliver the lawsuit to him.

"That's $238, and that includes the citation," said Rick, the young man behind the glass at the window of the district clerk's office.

"Does the fee for the citation include the fee for the service?" asked Alex.

"No, that's two different things," replied the clerk. "There are various methods of service. We can have the sheriff serve, or you can have your own process server handle the service, or we can have our office serve the defendant via mail. It's up to you."

"I want you to issue the citation and have the sheriff's department serve the husband."

"Then it's $288. Fifty for the sheriff's department."

"Okay, let's do it. Here's three hundred, and please mark my copies with your 'received' stamp."

"No problem. Are you new around here?" asked the clerk.

"Yeah, just got back to town a few days ago. Just getting started. Excuse my ignorance."

"*No te preocupes*," Rick said. "We all have to start somewhere, right? I'm new too; I started about three weeks ago."

"Oh, good. It's nice meeting you."

"Here you go, you're all set," said Rick as he handed Alex his copies. "We'll forward the originals to the sheriff's department so that they can serve them ASAP. Is there anything else I can help you with?"

Alex hesitated for a minute. "Yes, do you know how to look up stuff in your computer?"

"What kind of stuff?"

"Like the names of a plaintiff or a defendant involved in a lawsuit."

"Yes, I can do that," Rick replied, "as long as it's a recent case. Cases prior to 1980 wouldn't be in the computer system. We would have to do a manual search."

"You mean an index search?"

"Yes. You got a name?" Rick asked.

"Rosario Medina."

"Plaintiff or defendant?" said Rick, following up.

"Plaintiff."

A few seconds passed that seemed like an eternity. Alex looked over his shoulder. There was no one else roaming the hallways. It was just him and Rick at the window.

"Well, I have a *Rigoberto Medina, individually, and as representative of the estate of Rosario Medina, deceased, and Juan José Medina, a child v. Ford Motor Company, Elizondo's Ford, Firelazer Tire International, Baby Pro Inc., Toro Negro Inc., and Roberto Mendez d/b/a Rio Transport Company*. However, the file is not available to the public. It's sealed by court order."

"I see," replied Alex, rubbing his chin. "Well, can you tell me when it was filed, and who filed it, and where it landed?"

"Yes, that I can tell you. The firm was Harrow & Amaro, P.C., out of Corpus Christi, and it was filed in the 148th Judicial District Court in June 2003. If you want to know more, you would have to ask the court to let you look in the file."

"That's Judge Macallan's court, isn't it?" asked Alex, his heart racing.

"Yes, it is," replied Rick.

"How do I ask the court to let me see the file, do you know?"

"I have no clue. I guess you file a motion to unseal the file," guessed Rick.

"Is that a common procedure?"

"I've never seen it done. But remember, I just started working here, so I wouldn't know," Rick explained.

"All right . . . I see. Well, you've been a great help. Thanks a lot, Rick. I'll catch you later."

Alex headed to the second floor to go look at the probate file. He was pretty sure the case upstairs was Rosario and the boy's. After all, how probable would it be that the plaintiffs in that case had the same name as Pilo's spouse and child? And who the hell was Rigoberto Medina? He'd never heard that name before. Didn't Pilo say that Rosario had no other family but his? He would have to ask Pilo about that.

He reentered the county clerk's office.

"Hi, Nellie. Remember me?" said Alex.

"Oh, yes, Mr. del Fuerte. What can I do for you?"

"I was wondering if you could let me see the probate file on Rosario Medina, the one you told me about, remember?"

"Let me see where it is."

Nellie went to her computer and punched in the name. She waited to see what had been the disposition on the case.

"Mr. del Fuerte," said the clerk, "the computer shows that the file might still be here in the office. The last docket entry indicates that the administration of this estate was closed sometime back in early 2004. Let me see if the file is still here. Sometimes they get shipped to the warehouse."

Alex waited while Nellie went to look for the file. He crossed his fingers and hoped that the file would be available. He wanted to know why it had been necessary to open an administration. He also needed to know if the same Rigoberto Medina had played a role in the probate proceeding. He would not be surprised if the same firm from Corpus Christi, Harrow & Amaro, P.C., had had some involvement with the probate matter.

"Here it is," said Nellie. "It was in a box ready to be shipped to the warehouse."

"Nellie," said Alex, "I'd like copies of the entire file. Would that be possible?"

"Yes, sir," she said. "Can you give me thirty minutes?"

"Sure, let me run to the library to do some research, and I'll be back in a couple of hours. Would that be sufficient time?" Alex said.

"Yes, I'll have your total and your copies ready at three o'clock," Nellie indicated in a polite manner.

"All right, I'll be back later. Thanks."

"See you this afternoon."

After researching the library's resources the rest of the morning, including the Martindale-Hubble directory, Alex discovered that Harrow & Amaro had an AV+++ rating. As best as he could tell, the firm was considered to have the highest caliber attorneys. Several of the fifty associate attorneys were board certified in appellate law. The two partners were board certified in personal injury law, civil trial law, and consumer law. There were several links to court opinions, the firm's website, and other cases the firm had been involved in.

Alex left the law library and hurried across the street to his office to wait for Pilo. It was close to lunchtime, and he needed to give the old man some money. As luck would have it, the client was already waiting for him by the door to his office.

"Hey, Mr. Medina," Alex greeted the old man, "come on in."

The attorney and the old man took their places around the desk. Alex dropped his notebook on the desk, loosened his tie and removed his coat. He reached into his pant pocket and pulled out a wad of one-hundred-dollar bills.

"Here's two hundred dollars," Alex said. "Take it. That should be enough to get you through until Monday."

"Thank you, thank you," said Pilo, smiling. "Are you sure it's okay?"

"Yes, I'll just keep a running total."

Pilo folded the two one-hundred-dollar bills and put them in the pocket of his jeans. "I'll never be able to repay you, Mr. del Fuerte. I don't know what to say . . . Thank you. You've done so much for me."

"Ah, it's nothing," Alex said and quickly changed the subject. "Now I need to send you on your way. I'm starving and haven't had lunch. Besides, I need to get back to the courthouse to pick up some documents." Alex could hardly wait to get his hands on the probate file.

"So on Monday we expect to have some news?" Pilo asked meekly.

"Yes, Monday," said the attorney as he got up and motioned to his client to follow him out the door.

After the old man made his exit, Alex returned to his desk and sat there for a while, thinking. He wondered why no one had moved to seal the probate file, like the case in the 148th. Maybe the judge handling the probate file didn't consider the case to be so sensitive? Or was that Macallan's standard procedure? Was he known for sealing his files? If so, why? Hadn't both files been handled by the same lawyers, Harrow & Amaro?

After a quick lunch at El Torito, a Mexican food diner located within walking distance of the courthouse, Alex went shopping for office supplies. When he was done, the attorney placed the Office Mart bags in the trunk of the convertible. He was dying to get back to the courthouse to pick up his copies of the probate file. The anticipation was killing him.

"Hey, Nellie," Alex said as he walked into the clerk's office and leaned over the counter. "You got my copies ready?"

Reaching back and grabbing a large manila envelope from a tray with the words "pick up" on it, the middle-aged woman said, "Here you go, Mr. del Fuerte. I just finished your request. It's ten dollars."

"Thanks," Alex said as he pulled out two five-dollar bills. He bolted to the attorney's lounge located inside the law library to review the file. There, he would be able to study the documents in peace without being interrupted.

The cell phone came alive as the ringer set to Gypsy King's "Samba de La Luna" went off. The man stopped practicing his putting in the office's portable green, put down his cigar, and answered the call.

"Who is this?" asked Chordelli.

"It's me," whispered Nellie into the phone, "down here in the Cameron County clerk's office."

"Oh, yeah," said the attorney, "what is it?"

"He came back again and picked up the copies of the entire probate."

"Who?"

"The guy."

"What guy? Who is that?"

"The young attorney," Nellie explained. "The same guy who came this morning looking for the death certificate. I think his name is Alejandro del Fuerte."

"Is he a lawyer?"

"Yes, new in town," the deputy clerk said. "At first I thought he may have been one of the attorneys that handled the case . . . one of Harrow's young associates."

"Did he say what he wanted the file for?"

"Didn't say, no."

"Did he take copies?"

"Yes, he ordered copies of the entire file."

"Does the judge know? Have you told him?"

"No," explained Nellie, "should I?"

"No. All right. Thanks, Nellie. We'll take care of it."

"All right . . . I just thought you might want to know."

"We do. Thanks."

Chordelli hung up the phone and went to his computer. He accessed the Texas state bar's website and punched in the name Alejandro del Fuerte. The lawyer profiles section of the site indicated that the kid had graduated from South Texas College of Law in Houston in December 2003 and had received his law license on June 15, 2004. There were no professional complaints registered against the attorney. No current mailing address. No phone number. There were no firms listed for which the attorney worked. And the bar's records didn't indicate if the attorney worked for the government or was in private practice. By the looks of it, the guy was right out of law school and wet behind the ears. Chordelli couldn't imagine why the young attorney would want a copy of the Medina probate file. But he was going to find out.

Chapter 10

IT WAS TEN O'CLOCK AT NIGHT by the time Alex finished researching rollover stories on the Internet and reviewing the contents of the Medina probate file. The evening was hot but the air felt heavy with moisture, as if a cool front was about to blow through town. As he walked across the street to his office, he thought for a moment about his living arrangements. For the next few days, he would continue to crash in his office and shower down at the Y. He'd stay in his office until he could make time to go apartment hunting and find something decent to rent. Maybe he could find out where Ms. Montemayor lived and move into the same apartment complex. For sure, he needed to rent a place overlooking the pool. In his head there were already visions of girls in bikinis, swimming pool parties, volleyball, barbecue, and beer.

When he opened the front door to his office, he noticed that something wasn't right. He flipped on the lights and to his horror saw that the office had been ransacked. On the walls, the words *MUERE PINCHE PERRO!* had been spray-painted in red. His jaw dropped, and his whole body felt anchored to the floor. He was paralyzed by fear and had no idea what to do.

He slowly regained his composure and moved about little by little, trying not to disturb the place. Maybe it was better to have the cops process the scene for evidence. Let them find the responsible party. He picked up the receiver. The line was dead. It was time to get the hell out of there. He pulled his car keys out of his pants pocket and ran to the parking lot, across the courthouse, where he'd parked his car earlier in the day. His was the lone car in the otherwise empty lot.

"¡*Hijos de puta!*" Alex shouted as he approached his M.G. Midget and saw that all four tires had been slashed. The expandable file with copies of the probate file fell to the ground. "¡*Cabrones!*" he exclaimed. The terrified attorney ended up having to flag a cab by the corner and spent the night holed up in a hotel, wondering who wanted him dead.

Chapter 11

THE BUSINESS CARD from the Brownsville Cab Company listed the cabbie's name as Romeo Saldivar, taxi number eighteen. Alex didn't remember picking the card up, but he was now glad it had surfaced in his shirt pocket. He dialed the number.

"Brownsville Cab Company," answered the voice on the other end.

"Can you send Romeo from cab eighteen?" he said.

"Where are you at?"

"Fort Brown Motel," Alex indicated.

"Going to?"

"Downtown, across from the Cameron County courthouse. I'll be in the lobby."

"It's on its way."

"Thanks," said Alex as he headed downstairs to wait for cab eighteen.

Alex spent Wednesday morning assessing the damage to the office. The intruder had not taken anything, although he had gone through all of Alex's drawers, boxes, and class notebooks. Whoever had ransacked his place had even taken the time to flip through his law books, presumably checking to see that there was nothing hidden between the pages. He was looking for something. Something important, but Alex could not put his finger on what that might be.

The envelope with Rosario's return address and the death certificate were in his coat pocket. Pilo's documents and the probate file were in a secure place outside the office. In his pant pocket he had the cash from the Lawrence divorce.

Sergeant Detective Ybarra, the BPD officer who had responded to the call after Alex had reported the break-in and destruction to his car from a pay phone across the street, suggested that it was the work of some gang members belonging to the Tex-Mex Syndicate. The break-in was similar to others carried out by this gang. The *modus operandi*, at least as described by the sergeant, had been the same. The gang members would always steal valuables and ransack and spray-paint to intimidate the victims into not calling the police. Unlike the sites of other break-ins, however, there was nothing of value in Alex's office. His PC was a relic. A pawn shop would have offered ten bucks, max. The lack of valuables had been the reason, the sergeant explained, why the thieves had not taken anything.

Alex listened to Ybarra, but didn't buy his theory. He feared this might be the work of someone wanting to send him a message. And he knew they were intent on finding something they thought he must have. Could it have been Mr. Lawrence? Did he have that much to lose in a divorce? Had someone inside the clerk's office tipped him that the wife had filed first? What if it had been Poncho the bondsman, giving him a warning to get on board and play the game?

Alex was thinking of all these things but said nothing to Ybarra about his suspicions. It was obvious that whoever the intruder was, he was sending him a message, and Alex didn't like the message. He was worried. He cursed his luck. Of all the clients in the world, somehow he had gotten mixed up with one who could very possibly get him killed. This was certainly something he had not bargained for.

As Alex continued to clean and organize the office, he realized that he still hadn't made arrangements to go see his grandfather. He had not even called him to tell him he was already home from Houston. Now that he'd been paid a little money, he would get a cell phone and call him. He owed him that much—at least a call, to tell him how much he missed him and ask him when it would be a good time to drop by.

Alex felt good about having filed the Lawrence divorce right away and not having procrastinated about it. At least it was done, and Clint Lawrence was about to get served. He continued to clean up and made a note to call the painter. He would just have to paint over the graffiti. Maybe the landlord would pick up half the tab. He would call him later.

He took a break, grabbed his keys, and decided he'd had enough for one day. Besides, the last time he spoke with Paloma, his girlfriend, right before leaving Houston, they had agreed to meet on Wednesday at the Brown Pelican, down in Brownsville. "We need to talk," Paloma had demanded, "you better not keep me waiting." He'd given her his standard response, "Is that a threat?"

Maybe later, after the meeting with Paloma, he would go look for Pilo at his hotel and try to come clean. He needed to ask Pilo about Rigoberto Medina.

The Brown Pelican was an ice house off Highway 511 where shrimpers, longshoremen, welders, tugboat captains, port directors, the locals, and even tourists would stop by for the famous blue crab boil and *ceviche*. Due to its proximity to the port of Brownsville, the Brown Pelican catered mostly to the people who worked there. The place was a dive, but the beer was always ice cold, and the food and atmosphere were out of this world. There was always a *pachanga* going on.

"So how's it coming along, your office?" Paloma asked with a fake smile as she sipped on a top-shelf margarita, all the while dying to tell him about the lieutenant governor's latest job prospect for him. She was wearing a sleeveless white Helmut Lang T-shirt, a light blue Giada jacket, linen Capri pants, and BeBe sandals, and she smelled of expensive Gucci perfume. Her hair was up in a bun, her makeup flawless.

"I've gained more practical experience in two days on my own than three years in law school," Alex said, grinning. "And there's no sign of letting up."

"So things are going well, I suppose?"

"Yes, I got retained for big bucks yesterday on a divorce," Alex said, beaming with pride as he reached for a shot glass filled with *caldito de camarón*, which was one of the many free *botanas* served to the Pelican's patrons.

"I don't believe you—really? Who's the client?" she asked in an incredulous tone as she sipped on her shot glass filled with spicy shrimp broth.

"A lady by the last name of Lawrence. Her husband is some hotshot here in Brownsville."

"I hope it's not Clint Lawrence's wife . . ."

"What if she is?" Alex asked in disbelief as he took a long swig from his cold Bohemia beer. His eyes were wide open.

"Clint Lawrence is a millionaire," Paloma said for good measure, "and he owns the largest import-export operation here in Brownsville. He also owns El Valle Trucking. He's one of Daddy's biggest supporters and contributors. I hope it's not him, Alejandro!" Her nostrils were flaring.

"I'm afraid it is. Sorry, I didn't know."

"Well," said Paloma, rolling her eyes and snapping her fingers, "I guess you'll have to call your client and tell her you can't take the case. Refund her the money."

"I will do no such thing," Alex replied indignantly. He finished his first Bohemia and reached into the ice bucket for another.

"If you really care about me, you'll do it. You know Daddy can't let anything or anyone affect his supporters. He could lose heavy campaign contributions. C'mon, Alejandro, please?" Paloma ran her toe up and down Alex's calf.

Alex was an expert at the head games his girlfriend liked to play. The skin contact signaled that Paloma was attempting to change strategy and would try anything to get him to change his mind. But he would not budge, no matter how much she huffed and puffed.

"Look, we've had this conversation before," Alex replied as he played with his beer bottle and tried to peel the label off. "You know how I feel about you wanting me to live my life in a way that won't hurt the lieutenant governor. And I just can't. I've got to make money and pay bills. And that means signing up cases and getting retained by clients. I'm not going to send business away because some Joe Blow—who happens to be friends with your dad—might not like it!"

"But you could work for Dad's friends in Austin," she said, pouting.

"And be their whipping boy? No thanks! I don't want . . . better yet, I don't need any handouts."

"Why don't you just try it? The job at Spain & Wienberg, the lobby firm, is still open. Dad could get you an interview."

"Why don't you drop it?"

"No, I won't drop it. You've been telling me to wait to get married. When we first started dating, you wanted me to wait for you to finish college. And I complied. Then, you wanted me to wait until you finished law school and passed the Bar. And I went along. And now you want me to just wait and sit on the sidelines and watch you struggle as you try to build your practice? You want me to grow old waiting? All my friends are already married. With children. *¡Eres un cabezudo insoportable!*"

"So, I'm strong-headed, so what? You know I'd marry you today. Just like that. In an instant. But you know what, or better yet . . . you know who's holding us back."

"My dad only wants to help, Alex."

"No, your dad wants to control. Control me. Control you and everything and everybody around him. He wants to marry you off, but only if the guy fits a certain profile: he has to be smart, make good money, and work for someone your dad approves of. And if such a person doesn't exist, then he'll create him for his daughter. But that person is not me."

"That's mean!" Paloma cried. Finishing the last of her drink, she called the waiter over and ordered another. "All my parents want is for us not to have to struggle," she continued. "Daddy already busted his chops, so we don't have to. He's paid his dues, so we don't have to. He's paved the way for us, for his family, for his grandkids. Ten years in the house and ten years in the senate, isn't that enough? Do you know what it's like to be married to a public servant? To be the daughter of a public official?"

"No. Why don't you tell me?"

"I mean, for the last twenty years, while the legislature convenes, my mother has been alone. We have been alone. Do you know what it's like to have to endure public scrutiny? To have people talk behind your back and point at you?" Paloma finished her second drink with a gulp.

"No, I don't," replied Alex as he sucked the juice out of a Mexican lime.

"You know what it's like to wake up in the morning and read stuff about your dad in the paper?"

"I'm afraid not."

"Or to have your car, your home, your personal property vandalized because someone, somewhere, doesn't like a bill being considered in Austin? Or to receive threats because somebody doesn't like your father?"

"Look," Alex interjected after a drink from his beer, "you're preaching to the choir. I've heard all this before. Besides, there are a lot of perks that come with being the wife and daughter of Lieutenant Governor Yarrington. Don't tell me that's not so."

Paloma reached over to Alex, took his hand in hers, and looked into his eyes. "All my folks want is for us to be happy . . . raise a family, live a good life."

"Do you hear what you're saying?" Alex demanded. "You just said it. What *they* want. It's always 'what *they* want.' They want this, that, or the other. What do *you* want, Paloma? You, not them. You!"

"I want you, Alejandro. You know that. You've always known that."

"Then why don't you marry me? Let's do it! Right now. Let's go get our marriage license and have the justice of the peace marry us tomorrow."

"I can't . . . Daddy would hit the roof!"

"You see, that's what I'm talking about!" Alex responded. He was on his fourth or fifth Bohemia; he'd lost count. He reached for a Camel cigarette out of his shirt pocket. "Whoever marries you has to have your daddy's approval, have a fine-paying job, and work for the right firm. Daddy has to approve in order to be included with the right crowd."

"So what? You want me to pass up the wedding of my dreams? All my life I've been waiting for this. I want to do it right, in a big church with all of our friends and family . . ."

"And don't forget supporters," Alex interjected.

"See how you are? I can't talk to you!" Paloma shouted. "This is a waste of time. I'm out of here, *estúpido!*"

"Catch you later, then," he answered, ignoring the insult as he reached for the last beer in the ice bucket. His head was spinning.

"*¡No me busques más!*" she yelled as she reached into her purse for her car keys and headed for the door.

"Don't worry. I'm also through with you and your daddy!" said Alex smirking as he gulped down the last of his beer, looking at the TV mounted on the wall, pretending to ignore her.

Oh, well, Alex thought. *I guess this is goodbye.*

Chapter 12

PART OF A PREDOMINATELY HISPANIC COUNTY, the city of Brownsville had the county's largest population cluster at 130,000. The other fifteen municipalities split among them the remaining 200,000 inhabitants. And even though the county was sparsely populated when compared to other urban areas in Texas, its courts were famous for their pro-plaintiff juries and big verdicts.

Insurance companies, big and small, tried to avoid Cameron County. They preferred settling cases rather than facing a Valley jury. A wrongful death lawsuit filed in this part of the country was said to be worth twice as much as any similar lawsuit filed anywhere else. Plaintiffs' attorneys knew this and exploited it to their clients' advantage, and their own.

A few boutique firms were firmly committed to representing their injured clients, and for them the job meant adhering to the highest ethical standards. Regardless of the size of the case or the degree of injury, they thrived because of the quality representation they provided to Valley victims.

On the other hand, a few solo practitioners ran their practices as if they were herding cattle. They signed on large numbers of cases, sent the clients to a chiropractor for two weeks of pre-arranged healthcare, and quickly turned around and settled their claims for pennies on the dollar. Their share of the fees was small, but by doing high volume, they were able to earn a decent living.

The large firms scattered throughout the area consisted of insurance defense firms providing representation to the big insurance companies and their insured. These firms typically employed the brightest associates who were put on the partnership track.

Their starting salaries were in the six figures, perked with all kinds of generous bonuses and incentives.

Alex's rented office was located inside a one-story building that was a true eyesore. Certainly no boutique firms or defense firms rented space there. Although conveniently located, the building was occupied by two other solo practitioners whom he'd never met and a guy running a bail bond office. The office was a block away from the county courthouse and two blocks away from a sprawling, brand-new multimillion-dollar federal courthouse.

Alex was back at the office after a busy morning at the courthouse, trying to figure out how he was going to face Pilo on Monday. Should he just come out and tell him what he'd discovered, that both Rosario and his baby boy were dead? Would Pilo have suspected it?

The young attorney was deep in thought, sipping on a cup of strong black coffee, when a headline in the newspaper sitting on his desk caught his eye. He'd picked out a leftover newspaper from a table at the courthouse cafe. The front page carried a gruesome story about ten undocumented aliens who had burned to death as they slept in a sugar cane field. The cane had been set ablaze to get it ready for harvest.

God rest their souls, Alex thought. He hoped the families had been notified, but then wondered whether the victims would even have been recognizable.

There were no other interesting articles, so Alex threw the newspaper into a box off to the side on the floor. He had just sat down at his desk and was finishing his coffee when the recently repaired phone rang. Thinking it might be Pilo, he became concerned. The old man had probably managed to get arrested and was calling from the INS detention center in Bay View. Who else could it be? No one would call so early. He didn't even have an ad in the yellow pages. And no one knew he was back in town—not any of his old buddies from high school, at least. Unless it was Paloma calling to break up with him. But she never woke up before 10:00 a.m.

He picked up the phone.

"Mr. del Fuerte," said Poncho the bondsman.

Alex sighed. "What are you doing calling me so early?"

"Just wanted to remind you of our lunch date," said the bondsman.

"I haven't forgotten," the young attorney said.

"Good. I'll see you at the Blue Marlin on Billy Mitchell Avenue at twelve noon, then," said Poncho anxiously and hung up.

"Bye," said Alex, as the dial tone returned.

The *chicharrones de catán* arrived by the moundful on a large party platter. The platter was piled high with piping hot chunks of fried gar fish, onion rings, french fries, fresh tortillas, a side of serrano-pineapple relish, grilled jalapeno peppers, and limes. Fresh cilantro was sparingly sprinkled on top of the food for color. It was enough to feed five people.

The Blue Marlin was, in essence, the Mexican version of an American diner. The place was small and packed. It did a great lunch business, and the clientele were mostly work crews of one kind or another. The *catán* was sold by the pound, and the plates came with stacks of homemade corn tortillas. Tartar sauce and ketchup was available, but it seemed everybody ate their fish tacos with just a tad of fresh lime juice and a serving of relish. While in law school, Alex had tried fish tacos with purple cabbage and Thousand Island dressing at Yucatan Sam's on Gessner. But these were ten times better! His mouth was watering. He was putting the finishing touches on his first fish taco when the bondsman spoke.

"Did you hear about the poor bastard they found dead this morning at a hotel downtown?"

"No, what happened?" asked Alex, worried that it might be Pilo. He felt pieces of fish getting stuck in his throat and had to drink from his beer to keep from choking.

"They don't know exactly what the motive was, but sources tell me that it might be connected to an alien-smuggling operation. At least, that's what one of the lead investigators is suggesting," said Poncho as he shoved a huge fish taco in his mouth.

Alex took another swig from his beer, put down his taco, and reached for a french fry.

"The cops seem to think," said the bondsman, "that the man was tortured to get the relatives in Mexico to finish paying the *co-yotes'* fees."

"That violent, eh?"

"Oh, yeah. They cut out his tongue, too. These new guys that are moving in and taking over the organizations are ruthless. They're the same guys that used to move dope."

"When do they think it happened?" asked the young attorney.

"They say he'd been dead well over twenty-four hours. The old man that runs the hotel told the cops that the guy was keeping to himself. Nothing really suspicious." He paused for a moment before adding, as he looked at Alex straight in the eyes, "They're looking for witnesses for questioning. You know . . . see if anybody comes forward and identifies the body. Apparently there was no identification on him, and the room had been ransacked. But they do have a name the guy registered with when he checked in."

"You got the name?" asked the attorney.

"No, they're not saying until the relatives are notified."

"How did the man die?" Alex asked.

"Bullet to the head," said Poncho, pointing to his own large head. "They found some business cards on him, but they're not revealing his name or any other details until they notify the guy's family in Mexico. They think that might take a while. In the meantime, they're processing the scene, looking for evidence and clues."

"So they don't know who the guy is?"

"No, they're not saying," the bondsman answered.

"Well, I'm surprised you don't know. Sounds to me you got BPD wired," Alex said in a sarcastic tone. "Was the guy young? Old?"

"They're not saying. But as I told you, they think it might be related to a smuggling operation. They ran his fingerprints, and the guy had no criminal record or any other type of record. Apparently, he didn't even have a crossing card, or a 'laser visa,' and certainly he didn't have a passport," said the bondsman. "The guy at the front desk said he checked in on Saturday. So they don't have much to go on."

"And who told you all this, exactly?" Alex wanted to know.

"I'm a bondsman, remember?" Poncho said with pride. "I spend all my mornings down at BPD bailing people out. I got my sources down there. The minute someone lands in jail, whether it's at one in the morning or five in the morning, I know what the charge is, and I know if it looks as if the individual might be able to afford a bond. I go and talk to them and help them make arrangements to get them out. So by the time they go in front of the magistrate judge at 7 a.m., I already have something lined up with the guy's family to get them out. And other times, by the time the paperwork is finished and the guy is getting out of jail, I've already lined them up with a defense attorney from my referral pool. Speaking of which . . . Are you in?"

Alex cleared his throat, took a drink from his beer, and looked around to make sure no one was listening. He leaned forward and said, "Thanks, but no thanks. But tell me, how come no one has ever blown the lid on guys like you—guys running cases?"

"It's simple," said Poncho, rolling another fish taco. "Attorneys don't rat on other attorneys. Just like doctors don't rat on other doctors. Attorneys know the folks who are running the cases, just like the judges know, and even the state Bar knows, for that matter. The problem is proving it. Remember one thing: everything is handled in *puro efectivo,* cash. There's no paper trail.

"Then, if the clients are happy and the attorney got them good results, well, they're not going to say anything. There needs to be proof that the firm employed the case runner to go and sign up the case. So there needs to be some type of documentation that the firm paid the runner X amount of money for bringing in the case. And that will never happen. Thirty years in this business, and I have yet to see a firm or an attorney who writes a check to a runner and labels it compensation for soliciting clients. If anything, the one thing you'll see is checks to the runners disguised as salary or bonuses. And how do you prove that it wasn't for salary or for a bonus? So it's pretty hard to make the case, and D.A.'s don't have time for that. The state Bar doesn't have time for that, either. Prosecutors are busy trying murders, rapes, worthwhile crimes, sensational crimes. Not client solicitation cases. They're just plain boring.

"Besides, who's going to be the victim pressing charges? Some whiney-ass attorney crying because someone took a case from him or her? Juries don't want to hear that. The public doesn't want to hear that, either. So you have an attorney who's crying because someone stole a case from him, and now instead of making two million for the year, he'll only make one million? Give me a break! You see how lame the whole thing sounds? It's like the doctors complaining that their insurance rates are going up twenty percent a year due to frivolous lawsuits, and now they stand to gross five-and-a-half million dollars versus the six million they made the year before. Cry me a fucking river! ¡*Son chingaderas!*"

"I guess I see what you're saying," said Alex.

"That's right! Unless someone has a strong case, and the proof is there—and, more importantly, the case oozes guts and blood—don't even bother," said Poncho, shoving a third taco into his mouth.

"So you're saying that no one will pay attention unless it grabs the public's attention or makes headlines?" asked Alex.

"I guess you could say that. They're just not very interesting cases. So, we go about our work. No one bothers us, and we serve an important function. We find adequate legal representation for the people that need it the most, when they need it the most, and we charge a small finder's fee. We hook up clients with attorneys and vice versa. We're providing a service. And what's wrong with making a little money while we're at it? Let me know if you change your mind. Remember, you busted your chops in law school, and now you deserve to make a little money."

Alex replied, "I appreciate it, but I think I'll pass. Anyway, I've got other things on my plate right now. I just don't know how long I'm going to stick around in Brownsville. I might be moving away."

Alex looked down at his plate. He hadn't even finished the one fish taco he'd started on. He was worried the homicide could involve his client. Did Poncho know Pilo had visited his office? Did he have a clue that the old man was his client? Was that the reason he was bringing it up? Or was he throwing him a baited line, to see if he'd bite?

"I heard they ransacked your office," Alfonso piped in as he shoved his fourth fish taco in his mouth. "Who did you piss off?"

"Ybarra talked to you?" Alex snapped.

"Hey, remember, I spend a lot of time down at BPD."

"The detective seems to think it was gang-related," he said.

"That's not what I hear," Poncho said. "None of the other offices in your building were burglarized, were they?"

Alex knew this was a good point. He wondered what Poncho was after.

"True," said Alex, "but then again, the other offices have alarms. I haven't employed an alarm company yet. Just today, I called Monitronics to see if they could come out and give me an estimate."

Had he known that the bondsman was going to bring up all kinds of uncomfortable subjects, he would have politely declined the invitation. Well, now it was too late. He grabbed his beer and finished it.

"Well, I gotta run," Alex said.

"But you hardly even touched the food."

"I know. I just wasn't very hungry. We'll come back and give it another try another day. What do you say? Does that sound good?" Alex tried to make his tone of voice inviting.

"It wasn't something I said, was it?"

"No . . . I just remembered I have to be somewhere else right now," he lied. "Plus, my cab is outside and the meter is running." *I gotta figure out what to do with my M.G. Midget*, he thought.

"All right, we'll be in touch."

Alex pulled out a twenty-dollar bill and threw it on the table to cover his share of the meal. Poncho stayed behind, picking at the crumbs on the platter.

Alex walked out of the small diner and flagged Romeo, the cabbie. After the news of the murder in a downtown hotel, he felt it was impossible to wait until Monday to see his client. It was time to go check on Pilo.

Chapter 13

As ALEX LEFT THE BLUE MARLIN, he was buffeted by curtains of rain and gusting winds. The yellow cab had been waiting parked under a large mesquite tree over on the side of the restaurant. It was one o'clock, and Alex had instructed Romeo to wait for him until he finished having lunch with Poncho. Alex had decided to stick with Romeo Saldivar because for the most part the cabbie kept to himself. The only time Alex remembered the driver having volunteered some semblance of conversation was when Alex asked him if the red fish were biting. The cabbie's eyes grew wide, and he'd begun volunteering all kinds of fishing stories.

"How was lunch?" asked Romeo with a smile, glad to have been hired for the entire day.

"Interesting," Alex replied as he combed off the excess water dripping from his hair. "Let's go to any bank downtown." He needed to find a safer place for the documents entrusted to him by his client.

"Texas Valley Bank all right with you?"

"Sure. It shouldn't take long. Keep the car running," said Alex.

He went inside and began arrangements to secure a safe deposit box. When he emerged about an hour later, he no longer had the folded documents he'd been keeping in his coat pockets. He hurried back to the car and got in.

"To the Hotel San Carlos, on Tenth," ordered Alex.

It was now almost 2:30 in the afternoon. He would pay a visit to his client. Their next meeting wasn't supposed to take place until Monday afternoon, but he was in the neighborhood and it couldn't hurt to check on the old man. Besides, Pilo was probably dying just to get any detail. Anything. Something.

"Hotel San Carlos, here it is."

"Drop me off and drive around the block," instructed Alex. "This shouldn't take but a few minutes."

The rain was coming down hard as Alex got out in front of the hotel. He disappeared through the front door while the cabbie went to circle the block. Alex stopped at the front desk. "Can you give me Porfirio Medina's room number?" he asked.

"Did you know him?" the sweaty old man asked without looking up. He sounded disgusted but continued puffing on a cigar. Smoke rings slowly rose above the newspaper. He was wearing a robe and a worn soldier's beret.

"What do you mean, did I know him?"

"What I meant . . ." said the old man, looking a bit exasperated and still gazing at his paper in front of him, "he's dead, a bullet to the back of the head. Deader than Elvis. Kaput. *Chiras pelas . . . ¿comprende? Capiche?*"

"*¡No chingues!*" exclaimed Alex as his jaw dropped. "You're kidding, right?"

"Do I look like I'm kidding?" the old man snapped, looking up from his newspaper and locking eyes with Alex.

"When did this happen?"

"Sometime Tuesday," replied the man. "Did you know him?"

"Eh . . . oh, yes . . . no!" said Alex as he bolted for the door.

"Hey, come back here!" yelled the old man. "What's your name? The police might want to talk to you."

Alex flagged down Romeo and jumped in the cab.

"You all right?" asked Romeo. "Looks like you just saw a ghost!"

"Just drive!" shouted Alex.

"Where to?"

"Anywhere, I don't care!" Alex barked. "Wait . . . go to 1433 Magnolia Court."

His mind was racing, and his heart was pounding. He felt numb. There was a giant pit in the middle of his stomach.

No doubt the old man at the hotel had gotten a good look at him. It was just a matter of time before the police came around asking questions. Someone would recognize him. And the business cards? Didn't Poncho say the cops had found some business cards on the victim? Were they his?

"What happened back there? You want to talk about it?" asked the cabbie, somewhat concerned.

"No, keep driving."

He was in trouble. *Am I next?* he thought. What if he just went to the authorities and told them what he knew? Would they believe him? Probably not. Who would believe a story coming from someone who could be the main suspect? He remembered what Poncho had told them about cops being on the take, to the point of even working with others to run the big cases. He could already see his interrogators rolling their eyes in disgust at the first mention that Rigoberto Medina was a fake posing as Rosario's husband and that whoever was behind it must have killed Pilo.

The cops will die laughing! Maybe my court-appointed lawyer will believe me, but the cops and the public won't. Yeah, that's right! Court-appointed because neither I nor Grandpa will be able to afford competent counsel. I'm truly screwed!

He felt short of breath and sick to his stomach. He could see the headlines, just like the ones he'd read over the years: "Assistant D.A. Busted in Drug Raid," and "Attorney Convicted for Stealing from Clients," except his would read, "Baby Lawyer to Be Prosecuted by His Own Love Interest." That would be Gigi.

Even if his suspicions were confirmed, and he was right and the fake was nothing more than a figment of someone's imagination and had been created for the sole purpose of filing a lawsuit and stepping up to claim the winning lottery ticket, how could Alex prove it?

Plus, it sounded unbelievable. Who would risk going to jail for committing conspiracy, perjury, insurance fraud, even theft? There was no way the cops, or anyone else for that matter, would believe the court system could not catch a fake plaintiff. No one would go through such great lengths to line his pockets. It was simply impossible.

The more Alex thought about explaining everything, the more he realized the whole thing sounded unbelievable.

"Here we are," interrupted Romeo, "1433 Magnolia Court."

"Keep it running," said Alex as he jumped out of the cab.

He went to the door and knocked, loud and fast. He didn't have time to waste.

"Who is it?" came the voice from inside.

"It's me, Aurora. Alejandro del Fuerte, the attorney."

"*Pásele*, come on in," said Aurora as she opened the door and showed him the way. "Are you okay, Mr. del Fuerte? You don't look so good."

"I don't have much time," said Alex in a very agitated manner. "What is it?"

"Pilo's dead," said the young attorney.

"*¡Ay!* No!" cried Aurora and started sobbing.

"Aurora, I need you to be strong. Listen, stop crying, please!" begged Alex. "I think it's all connected . . . Rosario, Juan José, Pilo. Please, please listen to me!"

"*Ay*, I don't want to know," said Aurora, almost fainting.

Alex had to put his arms around her and hold her. He guided her to the small sofa in the tiny living room and helped her sit down.

"Aurora," said Alex, "I need to go out of town for a couple of days. I need time to think and figure things out. Whoever killed Pilo could be after me. They destroyed my office and left messages saying they wanted to kill me, and now Pilo. They mean business, and I need to go!"

"But . . ." said Aurora, sobbing and trying to ask questions all at once.

"Look," interrupted Alex, "here is a key to a safety deposit box at the Texas Valley Bank on Elizabeth. I want you to have the key. If something happens to me, you go to the bank and open that box. In that box there are important documents. I'll call you later with instructions. Right now, all I can tell you is that this has to do with Pilo appearing and stirring things up. Promise me that you'll be strong and wait to hear from me."

"I don't know, Mr. del Fuerte," replied Aurora. "What if my life is also in danger?"

Alex hesitated and didn't know how to answer. Who was to say that they hadn't followed him to Aurora's house? They had certainly followed Pilo to his hotel room. The organization had ears and eyes everywhere.

"Nothing is going to happen to you," said Alex, brushing aside Aurora's concerns. "You're not the one snooping around. Besides, I made sure no one followed me. I'll call you soon . . . wait for my instructions, okay? If you don't hear from me in a month, then take the documents to this address in Matamoros." He took a business card and quickly scribbled an address in Mexico and shoved the card in her hand.

"Okay, I guess. But tell me, what happened to Pilo?" insisted Aurora between sobs.

"He died of a gunshot wound. The police seem to think it was a case of mistaken identity. I can't tell you more than that because I don't know much more. But as soon as I find out, I will tell you all the details. Look, there's a cab waiting for me outside. You'll hear from me shortly. I promise. Just do as I say."

Alex handed her the safety deposit box key. He knelt down next to her and made sure she held the key and the business card in her hands. He then held her hands and looked straight into her eyes.

"Mrs. López ," Alex started, "I need you to be strong. I just need a few days, and I'll figure out what's going on. All right? We need answers, and we're gonna get them. All right?"

She blew her nose into a pink tissue and murmured a soft "*Ta bueno*, okay."

Alex looked at his watch as he got up from the floor and headed for the door. It was now three o'clock in the afternoon. He wondered how much time he had before the clerk would call the authorities to report someone had come around looking for the dead guy.

"To my office," commanded Alex, "through the alley in the back."

"Yes, sir," replied Romeo.

Chapter 14

THE BACK ALLEY to Alejandro del Fuerte's law office was littered with discarded sofas, rusty water heaters, broken TVs, and other such appliances. Over time, the courthouse complex, along with the surrounding office buildings, had grown and overtaken the center of Brownsville's oldest barrio. Because of this, it was not unusual to see chickens running in some front yards or the obligatory junk car resting on cinderblocks.

"Wait here for me and keep the engine running," growled Alex as he ran away from the cab and into the office building. It was time to move the operation somewhere else. No use becoming an easy target. Working out of that location made him just that. The best thing to do would be to retrieve the Lawrence file and the one box with his old law books and stay clear until Pilo's murder got solved.

He opened the door to the back office and let himself in. He turned on the lights and scouted the place for anything unusual. Everything seemed to be just the way he had left it. Traces of the threatening messages were just visible under the new coat of paint, but the landlord had not wanted to spend more money on a second coat. Alex wasn't going to need an office anymore, anyway. At the rate things were going, his future office was going to be a five-by-eight inside the Texas Department of Corrections Institutional Division.

He walked to the front office and noticed a large manila envelope that had been slipped under the front door. It was addressed to *Hon. Alejandro del Fuerte*, and the words *Personal & Confidential* were stamped on the front. The return address read:

Holiday, Chordelli, Domecq & Flanegan, L.L.P., Attorneys at Law
The Arboretum
1152 Paseo del Rio
San Antonio, Texas 78654

He bent down to pick it up and cursed his luck. Now what?
He wondered who Holiday, Chordelli, Domecq & Flanegan were.
*Perhaps this is the firm that represents Clint Lawrence. Man, they're
quick to answer!*

He sat at his desk and pulled out an old pack of Camels that had
been left in a box with his Bar review materials. He'd tried, off and
on, to quit smoking after sitting for the Bar, but now was a good time
to pick up where he'd left off. Coming home to set up shop had been
full of surprises. Never did he imagine he'd end up in hot water with
his father-in-law, especially over some stupid divorce. It's not like it
was a bet-the-company type of case. It was just a divorce. People got
divorced every day. Could they be countersuing his client?

He took out a cigarette, struck a match, and placed the envelope in front of him. He thought about its contents for a few seconds and took a long, slow drag. As the smoke filled his lungs, he
closed his eyes and waited for the nicotine to kick in and soothe
his frayed nerves. He finally exhaled.

The letter from the attorneys read:

Dear Mr. del Fuerte:

I will be visiting South Padre Island over the coming weekend.
I, on behalf of my partners and the firm, would like to meet with
you and explore the possibility of bringing you on board as local
counsel in the Valley. I will arrive on Saturday to participate in the
GCCA Fishing Tournament and will stay until Monday morning.

From talking to Lt. Governor Yarrington, I understand you too
are an avid fisherman. Would you like to come out and fish for
marlin and tarpon aboard the firm's yacht, *Magillu?* Departure time
will be at 5:30 a.m. on Saturday, from the dock at the Sea Ranch
Marina. I promise you a fun time and a great opportunity to discuss future employment opportunities with our firm.

Jeff Chordelli
Managing partner

P.S. We've included some documents that we think you may find interesting.

Alex pulled out the rest of the documents. One caught his attention. It was titled "Plaintiffs' Original Petition." It was the Medina lawsuit.

Rigoberto Medina, Individually, and as Representative of the Estate of Rosario Medina, deceased, and Juan José Medina, a deceased child, Plaintiffs v. Ford Motor Company, Elizondo's Ford, Firelazer Tire International, Baby Pro Inc., Toro Negro Inc., and Roberto Mendez d/b/a Rio Carriers, defendants.

On or about April 17, 2003, Rosario Medina and her son, Juan José Medina, decedents, were passengers in a 1995 Ford EcoStar Passenger Van (VIN # 1FAFP36P3YW258098) driven by an employee of Rio Carriers and traveling northbound on Highway 77, near Raymondville, Willacy County, Texas, when the front left tire lost its tread, causing the driver to lose control and the unstable and defectively designed passenger van to roll over several times.

The Plaintiffs had been restrained by defectively manufactured three-point seat belts. Despite being restrained, both mother and child were ejected from the van, landing forty feet away from the van's final resting place. The 1995 EcoStar had been serviced at Elizondo's Ford on several different occasions for different types of problems. The problems ranged from faulty belt latches and defective brakes to steering column defects.

Ford and Firelazer manufactured products that were unreasonably dangerous. The Defendants designed, manufactured, marketed, assembled, and tested said products in question to be unreasonably dangerous and defective within the meaning of Section 402(A) Restatement (Second) Torts in that the van and tire were unreasonably dangerous as designed, manufactured, assembled, marketed, and tested, because the Defendants knew that the vehicle was dangerous, inferior, and unsafe, knew that the vehicle was not crashworthy, knew that the seat belts were unreasonably dangerous, and knew that the tire was defectively manufactured.

Furthermore, Defendants were negligent in the design, assembly, marketing, and testing of the van and tire. These foregoing acts and/or omissions of defendants were the producing and/or proximate cause of the Plaintiffs' damages.

Rio Carriers was also negligent because it failed to supervise, drug-test and adequately train its drivers. Moreover, Rio Carriers was vicariously liable for the acts or omissions of Juan Gomez, its employee, agent, and servant. At the time of the incident, Juan Gomez was acting within the scope of his employment. Therefore, Rio Carriers were also negligent and responsible for the Plaintiffs' damages.

United Sports Drinks d/b/a Toro Negro manufactured sports drinks that were unreasonably dangerous. The Defendants designed, manufactured, marketed, and tested said drink to be unreasonably dangerous and defective within the meaning of Section 402(A)Restatement (Second) Torts in that their sports drink Toro Negro was unreasonably dangerous as manufactured, marketed, and tested because Defendants knew that the drink was dangerous, addictive, and unsafe, knew that the drink contained large doses of Ephedra, knew that Ephedra could keep a person up for days and was defectively marketed because it lacked appropriate labels and warnings. These foregoing acts and/or omissions of Defendants were the producing and/or proximate cause of the Plaintiffs' damages.

BabyPro, the manufacturer of child car seats, manufactured products that were unreasonably dangerous. The Defendants designed, manufactured, marketed, assembled, and tested said products in question to be unreasonably dangerous and defective within the meaning of Section 402(A)Restatement (Second) Torts in that the car seat was unreasonably dangerous as designed, manufactured, assembled, marketed, and tested because Defendants knew that the car seat's buckle was dangerous, inferior, and unsafe because it would come undone in a rollover situation. These foregoing acts and/or omissions of Defendants were the producing and/or proximate cause of the Plaintiffs' damages.

As a result of these acts and/or omissions of all Defendants, Rosario and her boy experienced physical pain and suffering prior to their death, and these damages survive their death through their estates. Rigoberto Medina has lost the earning capacity of Decedents in the past and will into the future and has become obligated to pay necessary and reasonable medical liens and funeral expenses.

Plaintiff herein sues for fifty million dollars and requests that a jury be convened to try the factual issues in this cause.

Respectfully Submitted,
Tod Harrow

The other documents included the application for the administration of Rosario and Juan José's estate, which Alex already had.

The applicant had been Rigoberto Medina, and he alleged that the estates required the immediate appointment of a personal representative with powers to hire qualified counsel to investigate a potential claim that his wife and son may have, including a wrongful death lawsuit. Rigoberto Medina represented that he was the only heir and that he was thirty-five years of age, living in Brownsville. He claimed to have been Rosario's lawful husband and Juan José's father. The couple had never divorced, and there were no other surviving heirs.

Alex was surprised by the invitation and the contents of the file. He got up from the desk and decided to head on out. He grabbed the divorce file, the letter, and related documents and proceeded to lock up the office. He wondered what exactly the San Antonio boys wanted. How did they know about him? And how did Harrow end up with the case? Did Rigoberto Medina walk away a millionaire?

He turned off the lights and was walking out the back door when suddenly someone spoke his name.

"Mr. del Fuerte," said the voice.

"Yes?" said Alex, stopping dead in his tracks and not wanting to turn back. In his mind, he could see the shiny blue steel of a gun barrel pointing squarely between his eyes. The hair on the back of his neck rose.

"Have you had time to think about my offer?" asked the voice.

"*¡Pinche, güey!*" cried Alex, somewhat relieved. "You scared the daylights out of me. What do you want? What are you doing here . . . *baboso!*"

"I'm sorry," replied Poncho, smiling, "I didn't want the big one to get away."

"What do you mean, the big one?"

"I can see you got talent, and you'll make a bunch of money," said the bondsman as he huffed and puffed, trying to catch his breath. "So I want to go along for the ride. I can help you make money. You can help me make money. We can both be very happy. It's that simple."

"¿*No entiendes?* Look, I already told you! I'm not interested," the young attorney said. "If I change my mind, I'll call you, all right?"

"So I hear you're going to represent Linda Lawrence," the bondsman remarked, changing the subject.

"Yes. I got retained on Monday. So?"

"Well, let me know if you need anything. I can do surveillance work, if you need me to."

"What for? Everyone knows he had a *movida*, a side dish," the young attorney said, throwing in that last detail. "Maybe even more than one." He was annoyed by the bondsman. *Man, what's wrong with this guy? Why is he so persistent?*

"Well, I'm here to help. Whatever you need," said Poncho.

"I want you to stop following me! That's what I need!" barked the young attorney. "If it wasn't for the fact that you want to do business, I could swear you were stalking me! Now, take a hike!"

"What do you want with the Medina file?" asked the bondsman point-blank.

"What is it to you?" Alex replied, getting in his pudgy face. He was a little shocked that the bondsman would bring that up.

"Look," said the bondsman, taking a step back while at the same time lighting a cigarette. "I don't want you to think that I had anything to do with that lawsuit. Remember, my work is running the small stuff. I don't do the big cases. But that doesn't mean I'm deaf, dumb, and blind. I know what's going on. Remember, this is a small town, and people talk. All I'm going to say is for you to be careful. These are big interests, you know . . . dangerous folks."

Alex interrupted him. He could feel his temperature rising and the adrenaline pumping. "You think I wanted this case? You think I asked for it? You think I want to die? How was I supposed to know that something fishy was going on?"

"It's not too late, Alex," the bondsman said. "Just turn the other way. Let things lie."

"Why? Are you working for them? Are you connected to the case?"

"No, no, no!" said Poncho, lighting up another cigarette. "But the word on the street is that no one was supposed to ever stumble upon the case. It was supposed to be sealed. Both files, even the probate. Now you have a copy of it. There are thousands of cases filed each year in Cameron County, but you stumbled upon the one. It wasn't supposed to happen. They'll stop at nothing to avoid being exposed. Nothing, you understand?"

"It was them, wasn't it? They killed my client."

"I don't know. My sources tell me they think this is a case of mistaken identity. Somebody ordered a hit, but the executioner went to the wrong room. Your client just happened to be there. No one is connecting it to the Medina file. Not that the PD would know anything about that, anyway. But just between you and me, watch your back. The whole thing could blow up in your face."

Alex shook his head in disbelief. "I gotta go."

"*Mira* . . . Alex, wait! I'm in danger, too. If they find out I've been talking to you, I'm dead meat! Watch your back . . . that's all I am saying. *Con cuidado,¿eh*? You know what I mean? You're the lawyer . . . I shouldn't have to remind you."

"Whatever," Alex shot back as he stormed out the back door. The wind and rain pummeled him briefly as he struggled to make his way into the cab.

"Where to?" asked Romeo.

"South Padre Island," said Alex. "The Tuscany Suites."

He needed to be careful . . . and that meant he would keep moving from hotel to hotel until he could find out if Pilo's murder was related to the Medina file or whether it was simply a case of the old man being in the wrong place at the wrong time.

Chapter 15

THE LAW FIRM OF ALEJANDRO DEL FUERTE had been temporarily relocated to an executive suite inside the South Padre Island Tuscany Hotel. With the money from the Lawrence divorce and a pending fishing invitation, Alex and his sidekick, Romeo the cabbie, headed out to Tate's Clothiers on Padre Boulevard to update their wardrobes. Alex paid cash for four pairs of fishing shorts, six open-weave cay caster shirts, and two pairs of Sperry Top-Siders. He also picked up a couple of polarized Ray-Bans for the fishing trip. He doubted they were going to do much fishing, but at least they would look the part.

"Where to?" asked the cabbie.

"Blackbeard's," ordered Alex, "down SPI Boulevard." It was important to spend as much time as they could in crowded restaurants and bars, where it would be difficult to be singled out and pumped full of lead. If these people were after him, they wouldn't dare to pull a hit in a crowded public place or as long as he was with the cabbie. At least, that was the way he was thinking.

Alex walked in ahead of Romeo and told the hostess they were there for drinks only. She waved them through and pointed them in the bar's direction. They stood at the bar and squeezed into a large crowd of professional anglers in town for the tournament. It was loud, and the boisterous fishermen were throwing back drinks like there was no tomorrow. As they compared fishing stories, each new story fast became more unbelievable than the last.

Alex and Romeo were completely out of their element. Blackbeard's was the locals' favorite restaurant and watering hole. It had sprung up in the seventies when two surfing buddies wanted vegetarian fare on the island. In the early days, it had been nothing more than a shack with sand for a floor and a palapa roof. However, due to its strategic location dead smack in the middle of the island, it had grown into a must-stop for tourists, fishermen, the locals, politicos, and spring-breakers. The place was famous for its Primo Burgers and Barrier Island Teas.

Alex and Romeo were sipping ice-cold Barrier Island Teas when a booth in the corner opened up. They made their way to the booth and sat down.

Romeo spoke loudly over the noisy fishermen. "What are we doing tomorrow, boss?"

Alex shot back, "I don't know, I don't have any plans, but perhaps a fishing trip over the weekend."

"You mean, we're just going to hang out? Do some fishing?"

"Yep, if you don't mind. I want you to stick around. I'll pay you three hundred a week," said the boss. "Hang out at the beach, drink . . . relax, have a good time."

Romeo felt excited about the whole thing. He'd never gotten the chance to just "hang out." And certainly he'd never spent time like this on the beach, rubbing elbows with high rollers, staying at fancy hotels, and sipping on Barrier Island Teas. Making three hundred a week! He was having a ball. "I had never experienced South Padre like this. No wonder it's such a hot spot."

"It can be lots of fun, that's for sure," said Alex.

"And trouble too, I suppose."

"You're right," replied Alex, "I'm glad you've noticed. This tropical paradise can pull you in and suck you dry, if you don't watch it. The easy-going lifestyle can cut both ways. You wanna be real careful before throwing caution to the wind."

"I hear you, boss."

Friday morning found Alex and Romeo out by the hotel's pool drinking Clamato Bloody Marys and *micheladas*. They sat at the swim-up bar and were happy to be taking in the beautiful scenery in and around the large swimming pool. The sky was sunny and clear, with no trace of the storm that had passed through days earlier. Behind the bartender, on the wall behind the beer cooler, a small TV was tuned to Channel Five. At noon, the daily news update sponsored by Channel Five came on. Irma Benavidez, a pretty anchorwoman with great hair, reported that BPD had identified a possible suspect in connection with the recent murder of an illegal alien at a downtown hotel in Brownsville. Alex pulled his cap low over his eyes.

The news broadcast showed a five-second clip from an interview with BPD's chief, Abraham Zayas, regarding the investigation. The chief said that they had narrowed their search to a suspect, but didn't yet know his identity. However, a witness had come forward, and sketch artists with the department were putting together a rendition of the suspect's face.

After the interview with the chief, the TV news showed the preliminary sketch of the suspect. It was that of an Anglo male, medium build, about five-feet-eleven-inches tall, probably between the ages of twenty-five and thirty, with brown eyes, light brown hair, and sideburns.

Alex sighed, somewhat relieved that the witness had not gotten every detail right. He knew that even though there was a resemblance between himself and the guy shown in the sketch, the witness had gotten the Anglo part and the sideburns wrong. These errors would save him, for now. At least, that's what he tried to tell himself. He wanted to believe, and he was trying hard to convince himself, that Alejandro del Fuerte was not the guy in the sketch.

The idea of having become a suspect in a murder investigation didn't sit too well. Paranoia began to set in. What if the sideburns didn't matter and people recognized him? He made a conscious decision to keep the Ray-Bans on at whatever cost. He would have to lay low and figure out a way out of this mess. He was also preoccupied with the speed of the investigation. It sounded like BPD was making progress. Maybe they had nothing, and this was just a way to beat the bushes and see if anyone came forward.

"So, what are the plans for today?"

"Don't know yet. I'm trying to figure it out," answered Alex, "maybe we'll go on the dolphin watch tour. Or go horseback riding along the beach. We'll think of something."

"Okay."

Truth be told, Alex was not thinking about which sights to see on the island. He was thinking about Pilo and he was feeling a tremendous amount of guilt. He regretted not having been completely truthful and honest with him from the beginning. He should have told the old man what he had discovered. *Wasn't that his job as an attorney? To keep the client informed?*

He knew he'd never wanted to cause the old man any pain. But who was he to decide what information to keep a secret and what to reveal? He wondered if Pilo had known all along. And why was it that Pilo had not demanded to know, at their last meeting, right there and then, everything Alex knew about Rosario and the boy's disappearance? Did he suspect the worst and didn't want to find out?

It was the vodka that was fueling all these questions, which were not getting any easier. Nor did he have the answers. Maybe God had wanted it that way. Maybe this was exactly what was supposed to have happened. Maybe, all along, he had been supposed to keep quiet and spare the old man the pain. Hadn't he suffered enough? Was Pilo's death intended to serve a higher purpose?

"Boss, can we order some lunch?" Romeo interrupted, forcing Alex to snap out of it and come down to earth.

"Yes, but let's go to the Sea Ranch Marina first."

The bartender totaled their tab and handed it to Alex. Alex took the bar tab, signed it, and charged it to his room. And with that, the pair left the pool.

Chapter 16

THE *MAGILLU* WAS A PLUSH, luxurious, Celestial Craft V, two-hundred-foot yacht that reeked of money and power. It was docked at the Sea Ranch Marina and stood out among the other boats. It looked like the deck hands had been getting it ready for its owners. Up and down the pier, there were other boat owners working on their boats, getting them ready for the upcoming fishing tournament.

Alex thought about taking a stroll along the wooden pier in an effort to get close to her royal majesty. The pier jutted out into the peaceful Laguna Madre. In the early morning hours, the air smelled of diesel being pumped into the surrounding boats and of decomposing fish entrails discarded in the pier's trash cans.

Off to the side of the pier was the Sea Ranch restaurant and convenience store. The restaurant was nothing more than a lunch shack with tables out front, and the mom-and-pop convenience store had a large blue banner reading: ICE, BREAKFAST TACOS, FUEL, BAIT, COLD BEER.

Alex decided to take a peek inside the *Magillu*. He didn't think anybody would mind. Besides, Mr. Chordelli wasn't due in until later that night. At least, that was what his letter had said. Right now it was Friday morning. His home office at the Tuscany sat across SPI Boulevard, on the Gulf side, on opposite sides of the Sea Ranch Marina. The marina had been built right on the Laguna Madre, or South Bay, as the locals called that portion of the bay.

"Do you think anyone would mind if I checked out that boat?" Alex asked Romeo while pointing toward *Magillu*.

"I don't see why anybody would. Anyway, it looks like the deck hands are getting ready to go out to lunch," observed Romeo.

"Pull as close as you can to the pier. Let me go check it out."

"I know it's not my place, but why are you so interested in checking out that boat?" the cabbie asked.

"Because we're going fishing on that boat, you and I," the young attorney informed the driver.

"What do you mean, you and I?" he asked.

"You and I," said Alex. "Don't tell me you don't want to go?"

Alex already knew what the answer would be. An invitation like that only came once in a lifetime.

"When you said we were going fishing, I thought we would go fishing off the jetties. Nothing like this. I've been fishing on tin cans, but never in a yacht like that," Romeo shot back, half delirious from the excitement.

"We're scheduled to go at 5:30 a.m. I thought I'd told you."

Alex got out of the car, and Romeo, who was already dreaming of the fishing trip, waited in the car.

Alex walked down to the yacht and looked around. When he was sure no one was watching, he got on board. The yacht was huge, with three levels. He walked in through the lobby, which was flanked by two marble pillars, and into a beautiful lounge with panoramic views of the water. The Italian fabric sofas, upholstered in soft earth tones, and the artwork on the walls made the spacious lounge feel comfortable and cozy. The lounge opened and flowed into the main dining room.

There were three luxury staterooms with accommodations for six. Two of the staterooms were below the main deck, while the master stateroom was on the main deck. The furnishings were custom-made, and each stateroom had "his" and "her" bathrooms. Each room was finely appointed, with Jacuzzi, entertainment center, computer station, and plasma TV.

Whoever Holiday, Chordelli, Domecq & Flanegan, L.L.P. were, they were doing all right. He figured a boat like this would cost about twenty million. And that didn't include the maintenance, repairs, the salaries for the crew and captain, and the operational expenses. This was a big boy's toy.

Alex had seen enough and decided to leave and rejoin his loyal companion, who had been waiting in the yellow 1995 Crown Victoria cab.

"So, how was it?" asked Romeo as he sped away from the marina.

"Amazing! It'll blow you away!" replied Alex. "And if I tell you, I'll ruin it for you. Just wait 'til Saturday, you'll see."

Alex wondered if Romeo had ever gone fishing in a luxury yacht.

"Have you ever gone deep-sea fishing?"

"No," Romeo said, "Dad and I would go fishing in the ship channel, off Highway 48. Our gear was an empty glass Coke bottle wrapped with nylon string."

"Really?"

"Yeah," Romeo explained, smiling. "We couldn't afford fishing rods and reels. But even with just a Coke bottle, we'd catch reds, trout, and snook."

"Wow . . ." Alex mumbled. He was amazed. "You'll have to teach me some day how to fish like that."

"Mr. del Fuerte," Romeo said as he looked at the attorney through his rearview mirror, "thanks for the new outfit and the hotel stay last night. It was a nice change. Thanks a lot."

"It was fun, wasn't it?"

"You don't know what this job can do to you. My memories consist of sitting in the cab, waiting. Waiting for clients. Waiting out in the rain. Waiting out in the cold. Waiting in hundred-degree weather. Waiting, waiting, waiting. Always with the engine running, it seems. The waiting blurs the days into weeks and the weeks into months."

"How long have you been in the business?"

"Fifteen years. I started part-time after high school as a way to help my folks, and in the blink of an eye . . ." Romeo snapped his fingers, "fifteen years have gone by."

"How old are you?" Alex asked.

"I'll be thirty-four in March."

"Hey," Alex suddenly said, "let's head back to Brownsville."

"Where to?" asked Romeo.

"Ho's Garden on Highway 48."

"All right."

The cell phone showed seventeen voice mail messages, some as old as Monday. Nine were from Paloma, and three were from her father, Lieutenant Governor Yarrington. One was from Grandpa, who wanted to know if he was all right and if he could come visit soon. The other messages were from his client, Mrs. Lawrence, wondering if the lawsuit had been served on Clint. She hadn't heard anything because she'd been staying at the island, but Alejandro could ring her up at the Frankie. She was in 1080, in case he wanted to come out and soak some rays. The forecast called for sunny skies throughout the weekend.

After going through his messages, Alex punched in a number.

"D.A.'s office," announced the pleasant voice at the other end, "how may I direct your call?"

"Gisela Montemayor," requested Alex.

"I'm transferring you, please hold," said the operator.

He waited for Ms. Montemayor to pick up the phone. He wondered what went on inside the D.A.'s office. It was a complete mystery. He had never set foot in that office. Everything he'd heard about it had come via the local newspaper. There was an election coming up for the D.A.'s position, and things were heating up. One candidate had accused the incumbent of being nothing more than a warm body collecting a big paycheck. Apparently, in her eight years in office, the incumbent had never tried a single case.

The incumbent had come out swinging and had called her opponent nothing more than a disgruntled former employee. She claimed that the young candidate was retaliating because her office, at one point, had had to go after him for passing hot checks. The hot checks had been issued after her opponent had left her employment and had gone into private practice. If he couldn't balance his checkbook, how could the voters and taxpayers of Cameron County trust him? She claimed that her opponent could not properly administer the D.A.'s office and its ten-million-a-year budget.

"Gisela Montemayor, can I help you?" said the voice at the end of the line.

"Yes," replied a startled Alex. "Ms. Montemayor, this is Alejandro del Fuerte. I was wondering if you had any lunch plans today?"

"Oh, I don't usually go out for lunch, I just brown bag it. As you may or may not know, starting salaries here at the D.A.'s office are rather slim," said Ms. Montemayor.

"Well, this would be a wonderful opportunity for you to take a break and have a nice lunch. C'mon, what do you say? My treat. Besides, it's Friday . . . time to wind down," insisted Alex.

"All right, but I only have an hour. We have drop docket at one o'clock with Judge Sanchez. And you know how he is, all business and no nonsense. He expects us to be on time."

An hour with Gigi would not be enough, but Alex decided to take whatever he could get.

"So, meet you at Ho's Garden, then?" he asked.

"Okay, see you there."

Alex hung up the phone, got comfortable in the back seat of Romeo's cab, and enjoyed the ride to Ho's. Out in the distance, he could see the oil tankers and shrimp boats on the ship channel that ran parallel to Highway 48. A fifteen-minute ride from Padre Island, Ho's Garden was known to have the best Chinese food. It was a small operation located inside the Port of Brownsville. Ms. Ho ran the front of the house, and old man Ho cooked all the meals in the tiny rear kitchen. To everyone's amazement, even the Ho children, ages five, seven, and nine, jumped in and lent a hand when not in school. They would take the to-go orders and help clean tables.

Ho's packed them in at lunchtime and was the ideal meeting place. Since Alex's ex and her father both detested Chinese food, a chance encounter was highly unlikely.

"You're going to do lunch on your own, all right?" explained Alex to Romeo.

"*Seguro,*" the cabbie said, "that's not a problem."

"See ya back here in an hour, then."

"An hour," shot back the cabbie.

Alex managed to find a table in the back by the large salt aquarium kept by Papa Ho. He sat down and waited for Ms. Montemayor. Five minutes later, she made her entrance. She saw him, and he waved her to the table. She looked stunning. He didn't remember her being this beautiful.

"Hola, Alex. May I join you?" she said smiling.

"Please," said Alex nervously as he got up to help her to her chair.

She reached and shook his hand before sitting down. Alex caught a whiff of her perfume. It was sweet and intoxicating. All kinds of crazy thoughts ran through his head, but he knew he needed to stay cool, calm, and collected.

"¿Qué tal? How's it going?" Alex asked.

"Good. I've been working on a very interesting case that's going to trial in two weeks," said the young assistant D.A.

"What kind of case is it?

"It's an injury to a child, where the mother left a six-month baby girl unattended in her trailer home. The mother went to the corner store, and when she came back the baby wasn't breathing. That's what she's claiming. She ran out with the baby in her arms yelling for help. By the time they got the baby to the hospital, she was unresponsive. She'll now be on life support for the rest of her life."

"Isn't that a felony charge?" asked Alex, wondering why she was handling it.

"They're pulling me from the misdemeanor courts. I'm being promoted to second chair felony prosecutor. My supervisor has asked me to get this case ready for trial—trial by fire."

"Who's your first chair?" he asked.

"Armando Saenz," she replied.

"That's great! Congratulations," Alex said. "So, they think the mother had something to do with it?"

"Yes, but the defense attorney has raised some interesting issues," added Ms. Montemayor. "He's claiming that the defendant didn't have the mental capacity to waive her rights and make a declaration."

"So there's a confession?"

"That's just it. There are two confessions, made four hours apart from each other. One is exculpatory and the other is inculpatory. Apparently the cops took her downtown and kept her there for well over twelve hours. She was also seven months pregnant at the time with a second child."

"Well, that doesn't look good," added Alex.

"Exactly, plus her attorney is claiming that she's mentally retarded. Apparently she's been in and out of several mental institutions."

"Ouch!" concluded Alex. "So if the judge throws out the confessions, what do you have?"

"Nothing. The whole case is circumstantial. We might be able to prove the reckless portion of the indictment. Leaving the child alone, unattended. But that's only a misdemeanor. A probation case. We don't want her on probation. She's pregnant again, remember?"

"I see," said Alex, and with that the waitress interrupted the small talk.

"Are you ready to order?" she said.

"Yes," said Gisela, "I'll have the Kung Pao with steamed rice and iced tea to drink."

"I'll have the same, but switch the soup du jour for a cup of won ton," Alex indicated.

"Make my soup also the won ton soup," interjected Gisela, "and would you tell Mr. Ho to kick my Kung Pao up a notch with the chilies?"

Wow, we have similar tastes! Alex thought. *And she loves spicy food! What are the odds? She sure is different from my ex—Paloma couldn't stand Chinese or Vietnamese or any crazy food like that. Sushi? No way! "¡Ay, no, qué asco!" she would say. "Yuck! ¡Guácatelas!"*

"So, how come I haven't seen you around the courthouse lately?" asked Gisela.

"Well, I've relocated my office to the island, but only temporarily."

"Really?"

"Yes."

"Any reason?"

"The landlord is repairing the building, and I've always wanted to live on the water. So in the meantime I'm working out of a suite apartment at the Tuscany."

"I see, must be nice."

"It's great!" he answered, covering up.

"And what kind of law are you going to practice?" she asked.

"Looks like it's going to be criminal and family law. That's what God's hand has dealt me in the last few days. I can't complain. Although I am working on another matter that has nothing to do with either."

The soup and iced tea arrived, and both of them instinctively reached for the Sweet & Low. They both laughed, feeling a bit clumsy in front of each other. There was no more pretending. Neither of them put up the façade of tough lawyer. Alex didn't have to pretend to be the pit bull, fresh out of law school, trying to make his mark on the world. Everything between them seemed uncomplicated and simple. Obviously she was interested. She could have politely declined to meet him for lunch, and that would have been it. He felt all kinds of emotions and was glad he'd decided to come into town for lunch.

"Tell me about the other case," said Gisela.

"I got hired to help this guy find his family," he said. "It looks like the wife and son might have vanished without a trace. The last thing my client heard was that they were here in Brownsville, but after that the trail went cold."

Alex didn't want to tell Gigi anything else. Why speculate? He really didn't know everything there was to know about the case. Besides, if he told her, would he put her at risk?

"So, I'm just getting started. I'll see what I can find out for the guy," he concluded.

"Well, let me know if I can help. You know we have four investigators working at the office. Sometimes they moonlight. Although no one is supposed to know that," whispered Gisela.

"Who would you recommend?"

"Jaime," said the assistant D.A. "He's the most trustworthy. He's retired FBI, all kinds of credentials. He got bored after retirement and decided he wanted to keep on working. And, let me tell you, he doesn't mind getting dirty . . . so just let me know."

Lunch arrived at the table, and both attorneys in unison asked the waitress for chopsticks. Again, they both chuckled. This was too much. Not bad for a lunch date. It didn't get any better than this. Good company, good food, good conversation, and very few worries. Alex was so happy that he'd invited her. He wondered if she felt the same way. He wished lunch would never end.

Chapter 17

THE ALARM CLOCK WENT OFF AT 4:30 A.M. on Saturday. It took Alex and Romeo an additional half hour to get up, and it was 5:00 by the time they walked out of the Tuscany. After lunch at Ho's the day before, the pair had gone to a hole in the wall called The Cove. They had spent the evening hours eating raw oysters on the half shell and the best blackened red drum fish north of the Rio Grande, although there were a few locals who claimed the stuffed flounder was as good, if not better, than the drum.

The food and the ice-cold Bohemias had been the perfect way to end a day of leisure while anticipating the fishing trip. From the bar, they had watched the fishing boats coming in and out of the bay. The GCCA was a two-day tournament starting on Saturday, but already the anglers in town had been going out to sea to scope out the hot spots for the best fishing. Alex had caught sight of the *Magillu* as its crew took it out to sea to get it ready. It was impossible to miss the show, since the mom-and-pop eatery sat on the jetties.

Romeo was now driving the pair to their rendezvous at the Sea Ranch. It took less than a minute to arrive. They found a parking space near the marina's restaurant and walked to the pier. It was 5:25 in the morning, but already on board the *Magillu* the deck hands and skipper were hard at work readying her majesty for a day of fishing.

"Excuse me!" yelled Alex from the pier to one of the deck hands on board. "Is Mr. Chordelli around?"

The deck hand disappeared for a second and resurfaced a minute later. He motioned the pair to come on board and signaled them to wait in the lounge on the middle deck. Alex knew the way. Romeo followed closely and couldn't believe the display of opulence.

"Look at this place," Romeo whispered, eyes wide open. "This lounge alone is bigger than the two-bedroom frame house I grew up in."

"It's pretty amazing, isn't it?"

They were taking it all in, when out of nowhere a deep voice with a southern accent startled them both.

"Mr. del Fuerte," said the man, "how the hell are you? It sure is good to meet ya! I'm Jefferson Chordelli, but call me Jeff."

Mr. Chordelli reached out for Alex's hand and gave him a Texas-size hug as if he had just run into a long-lost friend. He apologized to both of them for keeping them waiting and demanded to know if Sophia had come by to offer them coffee or juice. He was dressed in pressed cargo khaki shorts and khaki shirt and was sporting leather loafers. He was lean, with a full mane of wavy silver hair, and wore wire-rimmed glasses. He looked not a day past fifty and radiated energy and confidence.

"Nice to meet you. Please call me Alex," said the attorney, somewhat taken aback by the warm reception. "This is Romeo, my investigator."

Mr. Chordelli turned around and shook Romeo's hand forcefully. "So, tell me guys, can we get you an espresso, cappuccino, or a bagel, anything?" said the host.

"We're good," said Alex.

"Well, make yourselves at home. Help yourselves to whatever you want, or if you see Sophia, the only girl on board, have her get you whatever you need. She's an excellent hostess and will make you feel right at home. Have either one of you ever gone deep-sea fishing?"

The pair looked at each other, not knowing what to say, almost embarrassed. Neither had.

Chordelli could sense their discomfort and decided not to push for an answer. "We're going to travel about three hours away from shore into deep waters," he informed them. "As a matter of fact, you won't see South Padre once we get out there. On the way out, we'll be trolling for marlin and tarpon. As it sometimes happens, it's quite probable that we'll catch other fish, too. But we're only interested in those two. We won't be back until six or seven this evening. All the weighing in ends by seven, so we'll be gone most of the day. We'll have plenty of time to talk. If you don't mind, I need to go and make a couple of phone calls to my partner at the office in San Antonio. She and I are usually at work by 5:00 a.m., every day. But I'll be back. Make yourselves at home. I've been hard at work since four o'clock."

Mr. Chordelli disappeared, and Alex and Romeo walked out on deck to catch the crew prepping the yacht and gear for the tournament. The skipper, who was up on the third level at the helm, had turned on the two turbo diesel engines and was carrying on a conversation over the radio with other captains. They were discussing weather conditions in the area. The forecast called for sunny and warm weather, with winds blowing out of the south at fifteen miles per hour.

At six o'clock, tournament officials blew an air horn and fired flares into the sky to signal the start of the tournament. The yacht's captain carefully maneuvered the yacht out of the marina and pointed her in the direction of the intercoastal channel. The *Magillu* navigated the waters effortlessly and in style. The skipper then guided her from the intercoastal through the jetties and out to sea. The first rays of sunlight were beginning to light up the sky, and Alex and Romeo watched in silence. It was the most beautiful sunrise they had ever seen, and the yacht's plush accommodations only heightened their senses. Both were thinking they could get used to this.

An hour into the trip, the deck hands started baiting the hooks with artificial lures resembling squid. There were four massive fishing reels prepped with their lines in the water. The lures were trolling on the water surface about one hundred feet behind the boat. The two deck hands were constantly going back and forth from fishing pole to fishing pole, checking the drag on the reels, looking for tangled lines, and making other adjustments.

Although he was having a wonderful time, Alex couldn't help but think the whole thing was a dream. Who were these attorneys from San Antonio? Why had they wanted to talk to him about employment opportunities? Were they for real?

He took out the pack of Camel cigarettes from his shorts pocket and lit a cigarette. He was now alone on deck. Romeo had gone up to the tower to speak to the captain and learn about the yacht. Alex looked at his watch; it was 7:30. The sun was out and the skies were clear. He wondered if Pilo had ever seen a sunrise as beautiful as this one. Had he ever seen an ocean?

Alex was deep in thought when Sophia approached.

"Mr. Chordelli would like to see you, Mr. del Fuerte, alone in his office," she said. "Would you please follow me?"

"Sure," he replied and followed Sophia to Mr. Chordelli's office.

They made their way down to the deck below and knocked on the office door.

"Come on in," came the voice from inside.

Sophia opened the door for Alex and let him in. With that, she was gone.

"Come in, and please sit down," said Mr. Chordelli in a warm and welcoming tone.

"Thanks."

"I was doing a little work before the real fun begins. I might be in trial in Hidalgo County on Monday in Judge Noah Gonzalez's court. So, I hope you will excuse me," he said. "Anyway, are you guys enjoying yourselves?"

"Yes, the whole experience is very nice. We're having a good time," answered Alex, but he had decided it was time to cut the pleasantries and get to the point. He added in a serious tone, "But Jeff, what do you want? Did your firm have anything to do with my client, Porfirio Medina, disappearing? What do you know about the Medina file?"

Jeff got up from behind the desk and went to look at an antique Texas map on the cabin's wall. He was facing the map on the wall when he spoke. "Alex, have you ever heard the story of Gilgamesh?" Chordelli asked, sidestepping the attorney's questions.

"No. Why?"

"It's a story about a king. Believed to be the oldest written record that still survives to date, it was written in Sumerian. Shin-equi-unninni was the author, the oldest human author civilization has known. His story was written on twelve stone tables found in ancient ruins. Are you with me so far?"

"Yes, get to the point."

"Well, I won't bore you with all the details, but let me say this. King Gilgamesh undertakes a journey. The reasons are not important. What's important is this. There is a passage in the story where Gilgamesh has to cross a river. It is the river of death, and anyone who touches its waters dies. So he has to rely on his faith and trust the ferryman to deliver him safely to the other side. The boat is called *Magillu*. I've invited you here today because I would like to extend an invitation for you to cross the river with me. To come along, if you will."

"What are you asking?" asked Alex.

"We need a lead attorney with *cojones* to file a lawsuit in Brownsville. We think that is you. Of course, we are prepared to compensate you for your efforts. And you have to trust us on this. We'll be behind you all the way and lead you through the exercise."

"You're not telling me everything. What do you know about Rosario Medina and her son?" Alex demanded.

"I'm getting to it. Hear me out."

"Do you have anything to drink?" interrupted Alex. His mouth was getting dry, and he could feel his pulse quicken. He was starting to feel the adrenalin going. He was in for a ride.

"I'm with you—let's order a drink." Chordelli paused. "What would you like?"

"I'll have a Pinch on the rocks, if you have it."

"Hm, I see you have good taste. I'm sure we have it."

He pushed the intercom button and barked into it, "Sophia, get Mr. del Fuerte a Pinch on the rocks and get me a Glenlivet neat. And make sure Mr. del Fuerte's friend is taken care of. Make him feel right at home, okay? Don't interrupt, and hold all my calls."

"Yes, sir," replied Sophia over the intercom.

Within a matter of minutes, the drinks arrived. Chordelli sat down across from Alex on a plush leather sofa and took a big swig. Alex was playing with his drink, twirling it around and making sure the scotch was ice cold.

"Alex," said Chordelli, "Holiday, Chordelli, Domecq & Flanegan didn't get to be a leader in the area of product liability litigation by standing on the sidelines. We didn't get to be the top litigation firm in Texas by settling cases. That's why we're *número uno*. We try the hell out of every case. We have been in this business almost twenty years. We pride ourselves on our ability to change with the times. When car wrecks were paying one hundred thousand a pop, even soft tissue cases, we were churning them out like sausage. Then the insurance companies got real chicken-shit with their payouts, and eventually soft tissue cases dried up. We saw the writing on the wall and moved on to bad faith insurance cases, consumer law, and commercial litigation. Eventually we moved on and focused on medical malpractice cases. We did very well for a number of years on those, too.

"Unfortunately, the HMOs and the doctors got smart and convinced Joe Public that frivolous lawsuits were causing their insurance rates to skyrocket. The bad doctors, the ones that got sued all the time, were eventually denied coverage. Without coverage, these doctors couldn't operate and either closed down or left Texas. They went crying to the legislature. They claimed that frivolous lawsuits were the reason they had to stop practicing. What the public wasn't told was that everyone's rates were going up, not only the doctors'. The truth was that when the stock market crashed due to terrorist acts throughout the world, the insurance companies' reserves dwindled to nothing. So, they needed to raise premiums to be able to pay out on claims. Tort reform was a bag of goods! It had a good poster child, the doctors, and the HMOs used their mighty muscle to convince allied Republican legislatures across the United States to pass tort reform."

"Is that what happened?"

"Yep," answered Chordelli, taking a sip out of his single malt scotch. "You see, good doctors don't get sued. So they don't need tort reform. It's the bad doctors who get sued, and now they have tort reform to protect them, because with tort reform all they pay out is $250,000. They can kill your child, your wife, and your elderly parents, and they would only be on the hook for a quarter of a million."

"Is that it?" asked an incredulous Alex.

"Sad, but true . . . that's what those cases are worth," said Chordelli. "You wait until them 'sumbitch' Republicans have a son or daughter killed by a doctor, and then they're going to be crying that their son's life is worth more than that."

"I hear you," said Alex.

"The worst part is that they don't realize that no attorney will even file their case, because it no longer makes economic sense to file that kind of lawsuit. So, in essence, tort reform denies the true victims access to the court system. I dare you to find a good attorney who will file a med mal case where the recovery is $250,000. Shit! It takes, at a minimum, $100,000 to develop a med mal case. Conventional wisdom tells us that in such cases the client, after paying expenses and forty percent in attorneys' fees, will have nothing left. How can you justify to clients that they end up with nothing but the attorney gets his expenses back and his fee?"

Alex replied, "I guess you can't."

"Sophia," yelled Chordelli through the intercom, "get us two more drinks and bring some Cohibas." He turned back to Alex. "Am I boring you yet? Wait till I explain the 'offer of settlement' concept. That one will leave you crying."

"I can't wait. Keep going."

"Anyway, my firm saw the storm coming, and about eight years ago we started concentrating on product liability cases. We eventually got completely out of the med mal racket. Since then, we've done nothing but product cases. But, remember one thing, Alex. We are attorneys, but we are also businessmen. We don't like competition if we can avoid it or eliminate it. We're the leaders in the legal arena when it comes to spotting new trends in product liability, with the exception of that Mikal Branson. He ate our lunch on the defective tire litigation. That was the only time when all of us, including my firm, were following his lead."

"Oh yeah, I heard about him," interjected Alex, "the twenty-something kid out of Nueces County."

"He's good. I hear he's now after the folks that make SSRI prescriptions—that's selective serotonin reuptake inhibitors." Chordelli paused for a second before continuing. "Those drugs are known to trigger suicide attempts in certain people."

Alex took a drink from his scotch, and Chordelli proceeded to light up his Cohiba. He puffed on it a couple of times and slowly let the thick clouds of smoke cascade out of his mouth. Alex followed his lead, but lit up a Camel instead. He thought about Romeo and wondered if he was having a good time. Maybe he needed to go check on him. He hoped Chordelli would get to the point soon enough. It was obvious that the powerful lawyer liked to hear himself talk.

"Anyway, where was I?" asked Chordelli.

"You were talking about how your firm got into product cases," said the young attorney.

"Yes . . . in the product arena, we've always taken pride in putting forth innovative legal theories to win big verdicts for our clients. Have you heard of 'aggressivity and incompatibility?'" asked Chordelli.

"No, what is it?"

"It's a novel theory we're pleading in car crash cases. With SUVs now dominating the market, chances are there will be tons of wrecks involving compact cars and SUVs. Obviously the smaller cars will come out losers. The problem is that manufacturers know that the bumpers on the SUVs don't match up with the lower bumpers on the compact cars. So, there is this danger with 'override' where the larger vehicle ends up on top of the smaller car, usually with tragic results. Manufacturers know this, but their profit margin is so big on the SUVs that they'll keep on making them. The smaller cars in the market have no way to protect themselves from the override. All car makers, in an effort to get to market first, have failed to conduct testing to find a way to cancel out or prevent the override. We know for sure that no manufacturer has ever conducted any rear collision override testing. And ever since the forties, they've known that this could be a problem."

"So, when do we talk about Rosario and the boy?" asked Alex impatiently.

Chordelli replied, "Alex, it's only nine in the morning. We're going to be out here all day. You might as well kick back and relax. I promise you that my proposal will interest you. We are attorneys, but we're also businessmen, remember?"

"Well, hey! Time is money!" said Alex, cracking a smile as if telling Chordelli to give the "businessmen" song-and-dance routine a rest.

"Look, there's a ton of money to be made on product liability cases," Chordelli continued. "Holiday, Chordelli, Domecq & Flanegan is always looking at ways to expand its share of the market. We've been marketing our firm's services in the lower Rio Grande Valley, Mexico, and South America. We've seen tremendous potential for new cases because the so-called *transmigrantes* from Honduras and El Salvador are purchasing American-made cars and transporting them down to their homeland for resale. Likewise, we've marketed our firm to the Mexican nationals living on the Texas-Mexico border, from Matamoros all the way to Ciudad Juárez, including Monterrey."

"You mean," interrupted Alex, "you've started running cases down there?"

"We would never stoop so low," the partner replied.

"Yes, but you just said that you were also businessmen," Alex reminded him.

"Anyway . . ." continued Chordelli, brushing aside the comment. He was clearly not going to give Alex a straight answer. "We recognized early on that twenty percent of the Mexican nationals living along the border would buy and drive American-made cars. Matamoros alone has a population of one million. So, in Matamoros alone there will be, circulating on the streets at any given time, about two hundred thousand American-made cars. The research shows that about one percent of those vehicles will fail because of some engineering or manufacturing defect. That's about two thousand cars, just in Matamoros alone. Weed out the bad cases that have zero or negligible injuries, some contributory negligence, alcohol or drug issues, and you have fifty to a hundred viable cases worth between $50 million to $200 million every year. That's just the Matamoros market."

Chordelli took a swig out of his drink and paused for a moment. Alex followed and took a drink from his Pinch. Alex was crunching numbers in his head. If the firm was able to get and sign up twenty-five cases per year, that meant they were probably earning from twenty to forty million in fees per year. And that was just from Matamoros! Then there was the rest of the border and all the cases in the Rio Grande Valley. The numbers were huge!

"Go on," said Alex. It was finally beginning to get interesting. For a moment he thought he would rather run Chordelli's operations in Mexico and South America. The proposal to file some lawsuit on behalf of the firm no longer sounded interesting, anyway. After all, he was fluent in Spanish and knew his way around all of Mexico.

"Remember how I said that we like to eliminate the competition?" asked Chordelli, checking to see if Alex had been paying attention.

"I remember."

"Well, we want you to file a lawsuit that we believe will sink Harrow & Amaro out of Corpus Christi," Chordelli said, looking intently into Alex's eyes. Alex didn't flinch.

"Why?" replied Alex in a firm tone.

"Because, my friend . . . they're a thorn in our side."

"Come again?"

"They run all the cases from South Texas. And now, they're even stealing our cases along the northern Mexican border," Chordelli explained.

"And?"

"If we had healthy competition," the partner said, "that would be one thing. For example, if they were better marketers or had better advertising and the clients signed up with them . . . well, more power to them!"

"They're not doing that?" Alex asked.

"No! They have bought and paid every Mexican cop, tow truck driver, judge, coroner, investigator, and federal agent. Even the postman. They pay them to keep their eyes open and ears to the ground and find cases. Anybody who comes in contact with a fatality, they've got on their payroll. So the cases are being snatched from under our noses."

"So, they're better at playing the game?"

"They're thieves."

"And you want them out."

"Look, Judge Walter Macallan and I were roommates in college. I'm sure by now you've heard of him, haven't you?"

"Yes, I've heard a thing or two."

"He and I went to law school together and practiced together right after law school. We did insurance defense work for the first few years. Then I went to the plaintiff's side, and he got appointed to the bench. Through every election year, my firm has supported him, and we've donated large amounts of money to all his reelection efforts. Lucky for us, we've been successful. Over the years, I'd say we've pumped well over thirty million to his campaigns. Not every amount has been reported, if you know what I mean. But we needed to make sure he'd get elected. This is no small feat in Cameron County, because as you know the Democrats control all the politics. Anyway, when Rosario Medina and her son died, obviously he didn't want anyone to know that she had been working illegally in his house. Rosario had in her purse a small address book, and the judge's name, address, and telephone number were in it. When the accident happened, he called me and asked me to handle the mess discreetly. Within minutes, we had our people at the scene. They made sure the address book never surfaced."

"So you guys are running cases too, eh?" Alex asked. He was not amused.

"Sometimes, not always," Chordelli said. "We have to in order to stay competitive. It's survival of the fittest. Eat or be eaten." Chordelli took another puff from his cigar and said, "But we will never steal a case from underneath another colleague, and we will never conspire to commit insurance fraud or commit murder in order to cover our tracks. It's one thing to get to the case first and sign it up. It's another to pay off the client to switch lawyers."

"Oh, so you tamper with evidence, solicit cases, and pay bribes, but would never commit insurance fraud or murder. Is that what you're saying? Is that what I'm hearing?" said Alex, laughing under his breath and nodding his head.

"Look, Alex," said Chordelli, in an impatient tone, "If you insist on believing in Santa, maybe I'm wasting my time. Maybe I'm talking to the wrong guy. I'm offering you a way to sock it to the really bad guys, make a million or more, and walk away a hero. In the process, we'll eliminate one of our biggest competitors. And I can guarantee that Mr. Medina's murder won't be pinned on you. That's pretty good. You should think about it. And I wouldn't be so cocky if I were you. You don't think witnesses can be created? You don't think false identifications can be coerced out of people? It's a miracle that you're still walking out and about. So, don't lecture me on morality. Think about it in business terms. You've got something I want, and you want something I've got."

Alex knew Chordelli had a point. Spending life in prison was not a pleasant thought. Especially for a crime he didn't commit.

"So, why Harrow & Amaro?"

"Because they deserve it."

"How so?"

"They stole the Medina case from us. They invented Rigoberto Medina to defraud the insurance company out of millions of dollars. They committed mail fraud, theft, and other crimes and ended up costing me and my firm millions of dollars in fees. And we suspect they're behind your client's murder, too. When your own colleagues turn into crooks and murderers, it's time to take them out."

"Wait," said Alex, "this doesn't make sense."

"What doesn't make sense?"

"If Harrow filed the lawsuit and you had no involvement, why have you been following me? What is it to you?"

"Look," Chordelli said with a toothy grin, "it's simple. Our people found the case, and we filed lawsuits on almost everyone. However, we never found the Medina relatives. . . . We didn't have anyone to sue with."

"And?"

"We filed the lawsuits we could make. In other words, we sued on behalf of everyone but the Medinas. We finally tracked down all the relatives and spouses and filed the lawsuit in Raymondville. We made a ton of money."

"Then?"

"Then we just gave up on Rosario Medina and her son. We never found anyone who could file their lawsuits."

"So, let me guess," Alex volunteered. "Then you come to find out that Harrow had filed the lawsuit in Brownsville, and you wondered how the hell they did that?"

"You want to guess what happens next?" Chordelli asked, as if challenging Alex to piece the puzzle together.

"I can just imagine. Your cronies kept tabs on the files, and lo and behold, months later some young attorney, new to town, comes knocking around. What's more incredible is that apparently he's been talking to some old man. And since the attorney is new and the old Mexican Indian looks to be his only client, you figured they have to be connected."

"Go on," Chordelli instructed, smiling.

"You then figured that the decrepit old man can't possibly be Rigoberto Medina, because Rigoberto made a ton of money."

"And don't forget," Chordelli reminded Alex, "Judge Macallan is my friend, and since the case landed in his court, he knew that the defendants paid Harrow millions."

"So then," Alex concluded, "you had to wonder how an old man, obviously broke, was connected to the file?"

"Well, we had never found the relatives, so we figured if the old man was related, then who was Rigoberto Medina? I mean, after all, Medina disappeared without a trace. Which led us to believe that Harrow must have manufactured the guy."

"Okay, but why do you need me?"

"Because we believe you've got the proof that the fake was not Rosario's husband. And the old man that was murdered was your client, wasn't he?"

"The name was Porfirio . . . and yes, he was my client. Except, I never had him sign a contract."

"My friend . . . there's always nine ways to skin a cat. You remember that Texas recognizes oral contracts, don't you? That won't be an obstacle. Besides, if my firm came forward and blew the whistle on them, don't you think they'll also expose us? We can't get involved because we've been running cases, too. There aren't many attorneys in Texas that haven't run cases. That's where you come in. You're new to town, no one has heard of you, and there's no dirt on you. We've checked you out. You're squeaky clean. We'll provide all the litigation support. We don't think there will be a trial, so you won't need to worry about trying the case. And you won't have to draft a single document. Everything will be provided for you. Plus, we'll teach you and help you use the media to your advantage and provide you with a defense team in case your client's death blows up in your face. I doubt that will happen, but we've got to be prepared. We estimate taking out Harrow & Amaro will cost the firm about a million, but it's an investment we're willing to make. Once Harrow & Amaro is gone, their market share will be worth an additional $150 million to $200 million a year to us. We would like to have the suit filed by the middle of next week. Interested?"

"I don't know. You make it sound so easy. There's got to be more to it than that."

"Yes, there is," said Chordelli. "You'll have to sign a confidentiality agreement. No one can know that we're behind you. And certainly, no one can know that we've assisted Judge Macallan. Do you know what I mean?"

"I see," said Alex, "but the person who could have filed the suit is dead. Did you forget about that?"

"No, I've thought about that," the partner added. "The Texas Probate Code allows categories of people to represent the estate of the deceased. Even creditors are entitled to file claims to recover fees owed to the estate. Anybody can do it."

"Anybody?"

"Yes," said Jeff. "Do you know if there are relatives out there? They would have priority in representing your client's estate."

"Yes, there are."

"There you go. That's how we do it," Chordelli said, making it sound simple.

"But what if they don't want to get involved?" Alex asked.

"The code allows the representative to keep a percentage of whatever they recover on behalf of the estate. It can be very good compensation. I don't see a problem finding someone to take charge."

"Let's talk about compensation first," Alex said as a clearer picture began to emerge in his head. "Then we can figure out who should represent my client's estate."

"All right, we're offering you five hundred thousand for your services. That's a lot of money to take one for the team, to be deposited into an offshore bank account in the country of your choice."

"It's not enough," barked Alex. "Besides, you just said I could make a million or more. Now you want to nickel-and-dime me?"

"I like your attitude . . ." the partner answered.

The young attorney cut him off. "You know that attorneys aren't supposed to sue other attorneys. I'll burn my bridges and probably never be able to practice law in Cameron County ever again. That means I'll have to leave and go practice law somewhere else. I want two million," said Alex with conviction.

"You are good! Nah, I'll tell you what. One million now. The other million after you survive motions for summary judgment. I hate to give you two million and have Harrow pour you out way before trial starts."

"Okay. But wait, there's more," said Alex. "You want confidentiality. I'll give you confidentiality, but you need to add another million."

"You're busting my balls, Alex," protested Chordelli, "but if we have your total commitment that none of this will surface and our name will be kept out of the headlines, then it's worth it to us. You got it. What else?"

"I'm going to need an office with staff and a paralegal to be able to handle the litigation. The way I'm set up right now, I couldn't even sue a fly. You'll need to pay for that."

"We can arrange that. Is that it?"

"I need some cash now to buy a car and survive until I can touch the money in the offshore accounts. So, before I file the lawsuit, I need to have confirmation that the money has been safely deposited into the offshore accounts under my name and that my operations account has been funded."

"That sounds doable. So, we will deposit one million right now in your offshore account. When the court denies their summary judgment motions, then we'll deposit the remainder. As for the operating funds, give me your operations account number for your bank in Brownsville so we can fund it. Will two hundred thousand be okay?"

"Yes, I think that can get me through the first few months or so."

"Where are you going to have your offshore account?"

"Cyprus."

"We can help you set that up, too. No problem."

"How long do you anticipate the litigation will last?" asked Alex.

"We don't know, but I can guarantee you this. If the Cameron County D.A. opens a parallel criminal investigation, then the Corpus Christi boys are going to want to settle real quick. And if a grand jury returns an indictment, then that will be the firm's death sentence. Either way, they'll be gone. And that's okay with us."

"I have one last request," said Alex.

"Let me hear it."

"I'll need a place to live until I'm convinced no one suspects I had anything to do with my client's murder. Otherwise, I'll have a problem moving about freely in Brownsville. And I'm going to need backup on a nasty divorce where I'm representing the innocent spouse. The guy is well connected."

"What court did you land in?" asked Chordelli.

"Judge Trey Ramos's court."

"He's a personal friend of mine. We were on opposite sides during the Value Jet litigation years ago, then we became friends. My firm represented ten Texas families who lost relatives on that flight. I'll put a phone call in to him, and if the guy's attorney gives you any trouble, then Trey will help you equalize the playing field. Don't worry, he'll take care of your client. He always does. You can anticipate that the just and right division will be, at a minimum, fifty-fifty. With the right set of facts, then he'll side with the innocent spouse eighty-twenty."

"Well, we do have pictures of the guy with his lover," Alex volunteered.

"Then you have nothing to worry about. Trey will take care of you. I'll see to that. In the meantime, you should continue to live at the Tuscany. You'll have enough money to be able to afford it. As soon as the lawsuit is filed, then the first thing we'll do is to arrange a meeting with criminal defense attorney Rusty Chapa, you, and BPD to answer any questions they may have. Tell them the truth, that he was your client. This will eliminate you from their suspect list and will allow you to go about your business. If you want to move back to Brownsville, then you can. Hey! More power to you if you point BPD Harrow's way."

"Okay, then," said Alex, "we have a deal."

"I'll have San Antonio email the confidentiality agreement to my office here on the yacht, and we can have it signed before the weekend is over. Also, I think it would be wise to keep our contacts to a minimum once we drop the bomb. Other law firms in Texas wouldn't like it if they knew it was us trying to sink Harrow. As far as office space goes, we'll set you up inside the Artemis Plaza off Central Boulevard. I can make some calls and have a crew start getting it ready. By the time you walk in on Monday, you'll see in the conference room five boxes of documents waiting for you. These boxes will contain sample lawsuits, some press releases, sample letters to the clerk, discovery forms, and standard motions typically filed in disgorgement lawsuits. There will be sample questions for any depositions you will need to take, plus a library of CDs with more litigation forms. There will be some instructions as well. Just follow those. If you have any questions, and it's absolutely necessary to communicate, let's do it via email. I don't think anyone will try to get into your computer. It's your work product, and it's privileged information. Finally, your office keys will be waiting at the manager's. I'll need your personal info to set up the offshore account and your Bar number so we can input it into the documents we're assembling for you to file."

"I see you've thought of everything," Alex said in astonishment.

"Well, I don't anticipate any major problems. But if something does come up, we'll just have to work through it together. Right now, I doubt Harrow & Amaro suspects anything. My sources tell me that Poncho sent word that you were still in Brownsville, hiding somewhere. But you can be certain that when news of the lawsuit hits, they'll try to discredit you and bury you with paper. After the lawsuit is filed, I anticipate they'll be watching your every move."

"Poncho is in on it?" asked Alex with raised eyebrows.

"Yes, he was ready to do the bait-and-switch on you. I'm glad you didn't get involved with him."

"What do you mean, bait-and-switch?"

Chordelli got up and went to the cabin's porthole. He was enjoying the view of the sun coming up over the horizon. "Poncho always convinces all the new lawyers to take his referrals. Once he sets the hook, and he's got you paying him kickbacks, then he'll tell you it's time for you to repay the favor."

"How so?"

"If you land a big case, he'll want you to refer it to his boss, Harrow. By then, it's too late. He'll have you bent over a barrel, and you won't be able to say no."

"And if you don't play ball?"

"He'll threaten you with all kinds of stuff . . . of course, to a young attorney, the thought of coming up before the Bar's ethics committee and losing his license will prove too much."

"So the young attorneys are extorted and have to play along," Alex said, catching on.

"Exactly. So we have to be careful . . . . I'm sure they'll be watching your every move."

"I think they're already doing that," Alex indicated as he sipped his scotch.

"Here is my secured email address," said Chordelli, handing him a business card. "After this weekend, I don't think we should be seen together. A lot of heads are going to roll."

"So, do you know how Harrow pulled it off?" asked Alex.

"Well, we scorched the earth looking for a relative and found no one. The black book had nothing on your client. After Harrow filed suit, we learned Harrow had negotiated with a Mexican marketing firm for the purchase of registered voter and driver's license rolls to do target advertising. They were fishing for wrongful death cases involving tire and rollover cases. We suspect the impostor came from the rolls. He sure as hell doesn't live on Honey Dale Street here in Brownsville. We checked that out already. That address doesn't even exist. I don't know how they're going to explain that one."

"Well, if I was Harrow, I'd say that that was the address the guy gave, and I believed him. How are you going to disprove me?" countered Alex, showing Chordelli more thinking-ahead moves. The case looked to be full of holes. Alex could already anticipate that "lack of knowledge" was going to be the cornerstone of the defendants' defense.

"We've got that covered," replied Chordelli nervously. "The evidence weighs heavily to them hiring to play the part. It won't matter; I doubt they'll want to take the case to trial."

"And to think that had been on my list of things to do," sighed Alex. "After reading the probate file, I was going to go and look for Rigoberto at that address," he mumbled, shaking his head.

"Well, don't bother. 175 Honey Dale is the location of a Water Mill Express," said Chordelli in disgust.

"Talk about no shame."

"I know, I know," said Chordelli while rubbing his hands and looking as if he was getting ready to inflict some pain on whomever got close.

With that, the meeting was over. Chordelli and Alex shook hands, finished their drinks, and headed out to the main deck, where they found Romeo screaming and yelling with sheer excitement. The cabbie was busy fighting a giant yellow fin tuna. And at the moment, it looked as if the enormous fish was getting the better of him.

"Go help your buddy," said Chordelli, "I need to call San Antonio and have them email me the documents. As soon as I finish taking care of a couple of other things, I'll join you on deck. We'll do some fishing."

Alex was delirious with excitement. At the end of the day, he stood to make millions of dollars. He was going to have his own fully staffed office and, in the process, take out a few bad guys. Not a bad gig, if you could get it. Maybe he could buy Gigi an engagement ring. It was premature, he knew this, but at the rate things were going, why not? Everything was possible. It was time to show the Yarringtons a thing or two. Who needed them?

He thought of his classmates from law school, probably struggling and still having to beg for court appointments. They would barely be able to pay the bills and would even be fending off the Sallie Mae hit man. And yet he, in a twist of fate, was about to become a multimillionaire. *What a life!* he thought. *I could get used to it. No doubt! Good scotch, a nice boat, life on the beach, Gisela by my side, and a couple of babies. I would make her proud and happy. If only Mom and Pop were around to see all of this.*

Everyone at Holiday, Chordelli, Domecq & Flanegan was expected to work Saturdays, and no one dared complain. That was the price they paid for the privilege of working at the Alamo City's premier plaintiffs' firm. Recent law grads killed and trampled over one another for the opportunity to work at such a firm. Likewise, the support staff knew that the firm offered the best-paying legal jobs in town. No other firm had such a lucrative caseload.

"Holiday, Chordelli, Domecq & Flanegan, how can I help you?" said the receptionist.

"Pass me through to Laura," said Chordelli.

"Yes, Mr. Chordelli, right away."

There was a brief silence as the call was being transferred. Chordelli played with his pencil-thin moustache. He was anxious to talk to his partner in San Antonio.

"Hello," said the voice at the end of the line.

"Laura?" asked Chordelli.

"Yes, Jeff, what is it?" said Ms. Holiday.

"I closed the deal," Chordelli said in a proud tone.

"Did he take the bait?" asked the female attorney as she played with her hair and looked out her office window overlooking the beautiful riverwalk down below. It was teeming with tourists who were out and about, enjoying the fine weather that Saturday morning.

"Yes."

"Does he suspect anything?"

"Not a thing. I fed him the story of Gilgamesh. I had him eating out of my hand," Chordelli said, smiling.

"Boy, you're good," the female partner purred. "Maybe when you get back to town, we can celebrate . . . just you and I."

"We'll see," Chordelli replied. "I've got that three-week trial against Nissan over in Hidalgo County starting on Monday. I don't know when I'll be back."

"But I miss you, Jeff. We haven't spent any quality time together lately."

Chordelli was now sitting down. He looked down at the cabin's floor and rubbed his temples. "Look, when I get back, I need to spend a few days with the wife and kids. I promised her I would take the family to Orlando for Thanksgiving. You and I, we'll spend some quality time during the firm's winter retreat in Aspen."

"That never works!" cried Laura. "We have to do all these activities with the partners and the associates. You and I can never have just some one-on-one."

"I promise we'll spend some time together," Chordelli said. "Who knows? If the Hidalgo case settles right at the start, I'll tell my wife I'm still in trial down here, and you can fly down here and join me on the *Magillu*. What do you say?"

"You think she'll buy it?"

"Sure. She doesn't suspect a thing," Chordelli said. Switching topics, he added, "I had asked my paralegal to send me a confidentiality agreement."

"Do you have it yet?" asked Laura.

"I checked with her, and she's supposed to be emailing it to me in the next hour."

"Should I look it over before she sends it to you?"

"Yeah. Can't hurt," he said. "Ask Clara to provide you with a copy of it. Make corrections if needed."

"Will do," interjected Laura and added, "Do you think the boy can pull it off?"

"He's pretty sharp and can think on his feet. But what I liked the most is that he's got balls."

"Good."

"And he can negotiate pretty good, too," added Chordelli as he puffed away on his second Cohiba. "He's no dummy, if that's what you're asking."

"How much did it set us back?"

"Three million."

"All right, then," said Laura, "let's go to work."

"Looks like we might get out of this deal for under three million or thereabouts," advised Chordelli. "Anything is better than taking a direct hit."

"Sounds reasonable. Let's set the hook and reel him in."

"Right," said Chordelli, "let's get it in black and white, before he changes his mind. He can still walk away."

"Is Sophia there with you?"

"Yes."

"Good, he won't resist," said Laura. "Have her seal the deal."

"All right, gotta go," Chordelli said.

"Bye," Laura Holiday replied.

"Sophia," barked Chordelli into the intercom.

"Yes, sir?" she asked.

"How's Mr. del Fuerte doing out there?"

"He's having a great time," said the hostess.

"Make sure he reels in the next big one. Tell the captain and the deck hands that the next one is his. And make sure you keep his scotch filled to the rim. Cater to his every wish, okay?"

"Yes, sir."

"And I mean his every wish, understand? We wouldn't want this new associate to get away, all right?" Chordelli mumbled under his breath.

"He won't get away, sir, I promise."

"Good," answered Chordelli, "that's exactly why I hired you. You're my closer. Make sure the boy enjoys himself."

Chordelli hung up the phone. He felt a bit of remorse, but the wheels had been set in motion. There was no turning back.

Chapter 18

MONDAY AFTERNOON FOUND ALEX AND ROMEO still wearing shorts and Hawaiian shirts as they drove to Brownsville from Padre. While on their way, they made small talk and touched on some of the highlights they experienced aboard the *Magillu*. They had been wined and dined, and Romeo could barely wait to get invited to the next fishing tournament. The cabbie still couldn't believe that people lived and played like that.

During the commute, Alex had been thinking about the confidentiality agreement he'd signed and the task at hand. Had he gotten in over his head? How could he possibly bring down one of the biggest firms in Texas—by himself? Maybe it had all been a dream. He also swore off scotch. For as long as he lived, he was not going to touch that stuff again.

"Romeo, before going by the office, I'd like to stop at Artemis Square first." It was time to start thinking about assembling a legal team.

"*Sí, jefe*. No problem, boss," responded Romeo as he turned west on FM 802 and headed for Central Boulevard.

Twenty minutes later, the cabbie pulled into the parking lot at Artemis Square and parked in front of the manager's office. Alex got out and asked Romeo to wait in the car. He went inside and came out a few minutes later with a set of keys in his hand. He motioned Romeo to turn off the car, get out, and follow him. The cabbie obliged.

They walked from the manager's office across the parking lot to Suite 100. On the door, shiny brass letters spelled out "Alejandro del Fuerte. Attorney." Romeo was impressed.

Alex opened the door and was pleasantly surprised. The space smelled of new paint, new furniture, and success. The walls were painted hunter green and the floors were hardwood. There was a reception area with the mandatory twelve-inch brass letters announcing *Law Office of Alejandro del Fuerte* mounted on the mahogany wood paneling. On the reception desk were his business cards with the new address, telephone and fax numbers, and even the Internet address to his own website.

Past the privacy door behind the reception area, there were two workstations for a secretary and paralegal. The stations were ready to go, equipped with computers, printers, and a fax machine. The copy room and file room were located off to one side of the hallway. Further down the hallway, on the right-hand side, there was a large library that also accommodated a large Italian marble conference table for twelve. On it sat the five promised boxes with documents. Alex peeked in the conference room but decided to wait before opening the boxes. He couldn't believe his luck.

At the end of the hallway was his office. The desk was in Louis XV style with gold appliqués. Beveled glass tops protected the Parisian mahogany veneer of the desk and a matching credenza. He took his place at the desk and pulled a Cohiba from the stocked humidor strategically placed behind on the credenza. Chordelli had thought of everything. No doubt about it, they were pros. The big leagues. It was obvious they wanted to take care of their investment.

Alex lit the Cohiba and puffed on it for a while. With his legs up on the desk, he started to go over the events of the last few days. Things were happening too fast, at a roller-coaster pace, and now all he could do was hang on, go along for the ride. But he wasn't complaining. All in all, things were looking up.

He reached for the remote control on top of the desk and pointed it to the TV that was inside the armoire at the opposite wall from his desk, past the mini seating area with the coffee table. Turning on the TV, he started surfing the local channels for any updates on the murder at Hotel San Carlos. There was nothing.

The office seemed fully stocked. All he needed to do was to hire the help and get to work. He called out to Romeo, who was going from room to room checking things out.

"Hey, Romeo, come in here. I need to talk to you."

"Yes, boss. What is it?" asked Romeo, still marveling at the whole setup.

"Where do we find a secretary or receptionist?"

"You could run an ad in the local paper. Or call the placement office at the college," suggested Romeo.

"Do you know anybody you can trust? Someone you would recommend with good secretarial skills?"

"I have an aunt who just last month was forced to take early retirement when Wells Fargo took over Mercantile Bank. I could ask."

"What's her name?"

"Beatriz. But we call her Betty," answered the cabbie. He was standing up, leaning against the door to Alex's office.

"Why don't you call her and see if she would be interested. Offer her thirty-six thousand a year to start. See what she says," instructed Alex.

"You don't want to place an ad?"

"I don't want to waste time going to the *Rio Grand Post*. They'll get it wrong, and we'll have to correct the ad. And then I'll spend a week interviewing applicants. I trust your instincts. If she wants it, then let's hire her."

"Okay, I'll call her today."

Alex puffed some more on his cigar and let the smoke slowly escape his mouth. "Come in and sit down," he said, pointing at one of the empty leather chairs across from his desk.

Romeo sat across from his desk.

Alex asked, "How much do you make a year driving a cab?"

"Fourteen to eighteen thousand," replied Romeo. "It depends."

"How would you like to be my office manager and personal assistant?"

"Get out of here!" said Romeo in disbelief. "*¿En serio?*"

"You want it, yes or no?"

Romeo sat there thinking for a few moments and then spoke. "I barely finished high school, Mr. del Fuerte. You think I have what it takes to be an office manager?"

"You want the job or not? *Sin miedo,*" Alex said.

"I'm not afraid, Mr. del Fuerte. I just don't want to mess up."

"Messing up . . . that's how people learn," explained Alex. "But I can't force you. You're right, maybe you'd rather be a cabbie for the rest of your life."

Romeo's eyes grew wide, and he scratched his head. He thought about the child support cases, filed by two old girlfriends months earlier, now pending against him in Judge Nelson's court. "Yes, I want it," he said, and then murmured under his breath, "whatever the position is."

"You'll make forty thousand a year, plus bonuses. But the job will be demanding, and at times we'll have to work 24/7. Can you deal with that?"

"Forty thousand? Wow! Yes, I'm in for the ride," said Romeo with confidence.

"Good," said Alex, "it'll be a ride, brother. I promise. All right, let's lock up and go to my old office. I need to pick up a few things and figure out what to do with my old M.G. Midget. Last time I checked, it was still parked at the county courthouse parking lot."

"Let's go," said Romeo with a smile from ear to ear. "And Mr. del Fuerte, before I forget, one more thing?"

"What is it?"

"Thanks for trusting me," Romeo said as he extended his hand to shake the attorney's. "This means a lot."

"It's nothing. Don't mention it. *No es nada.*"

Romeo drove down Central Boulevard to the Jefferson Street intersection. At the light, he made a left and drove two miles past the original López supermarket and Villa Maria High School. Jefferson Street dead-ended at Washington Park, and he took the mandatory left, past the Brownsville Police Department to Harrison. He pulled up in front of the office building. Alex could see his old car still parked in the middle of the parking lot down the street from his office.

"Go around the block and park in the alley," instructed Alex. "I want to go in through the back."

"Sure, boss" said the newly promoted office manager, still smiling.

Romeo parked in the back. Alex asked him to come into the office and give him a hand. Once inside the office, Romeo could still make out the remnants of the writing on the wall.

"You must have pissed somebody off," observed Romeo.

"Can you believe it?" said Alex in a playful tone. "And I've only been back in town a few days, eh?"

Alex chose not to explain. Besides, there was a confidentiality agreement already signed. He boxed up a few leftover notebooks, outlines, and knickknacks and checked his messages on his voice mail. There had been calls from Mr. Nino, the telephone repair guy, and from Grandpa, who was calling to check on Alex. He wanted to know if everything was all right since he hadn't heard from him. There were two other calls, but they were hang-ups. Mr. Nino's message indicated that he'd come by on Friday, but had missed him. He left his number in case Alex still wanted to talk to him about a new telephone system.

The two of them cleaned out the office in less than twenty minutes. Alex left his desk, chairs, and small filing cabinet behind. He would need to call the landlord and give him notice that he was moving out. He didn't think it would be a problem, especially since he'd signed a month-to-month lease. Besides, it was time to close that chapter and start a new one.

On the way back to the new office, Alex took inventory of the situation. He had an office manager and a secretary lined up. But he still needed a receptionist.

"Keep going. Let's first go to Dillard's at Sunrise Mall, and then we'll come back to the office," ordered Alex. "We need to get out of these clothes."

Romeo answered, "I agree."

Romeo parked the car by Luby's Cafeteria, and both entered the recently remodeled shopping mall. They walked to Dillard's and stopped at the men's department. A pretty young lady named Astrid approached them and offered to help them find whatever it was they were looking for.

"We need suits, shirts, ties, socks, belts, and shoes," said Alex.

"Very well," said Astrid, "I've got everything you're looking for. Right over here."

They walked to where all the two-piece suits were.

"What size coat are you?" she asked Alex.

"I'm a forty-two regular, with a thirty-four waist," said Alex.

"Are you sure? Your broad shoulders make you look like you're at least a forty-four regular," she said, pumping him up. She was good.

"I need a solid navy blue, one blue with pinstripes, one black with pinstripes, and a charcoal gray," ordered Alex. "Maybe one or two sports coats with interchangeable pants and button-downs. Get him a couple of suits as well. Whatever he wants."

They spent about two hours at Dillard's buying suits, getting them tailored, and trying on different shoes. During the whole episode, Astrid had been smiling and helpful, catering to the pair as if they were the only customers in the store. And even though under normal circumstances suits couldn't be tailored in less than a week, she had managed to convince Francisco, the tailor, to have them ready by six that same day.

Alex liked her resourcefulness and work ethic. "How long have you been working at Dillard's?" he asked.

"Just over three months," she answered.

"Do you like retail?" he asked.

"It's tough. You've got to be on your feet all day and work on commission. But I do all right."

"How much are you making a month?"

"Fourteen hundred, take-home."

"Come work for me instead. I'm looking for a receptionist for my law firm. I'll give you two thousand take-home, plus year-end bonuses. The hours are eight to five, Monday through Friday. You would start tomorrow."

"Are you serious?"

"Yes, here's my card," answered Alex as he handed her one of his new business cards with the Artemis Square address.

"You're not pulling my leg, are you?"

Romeo interjected, "He's for real and Mr. del Fuerte is fair and will treat you like a human being. If that's important to you, then this is the job for you."

"I'll take it. I'll see you in the morning, then. Thank you so much." She was obviously overcome with excitement.

Chapter 19

H<small>IS</small> <small>DESKTOP COMPUTER FLASHED</small> *Y<small>OU'VE</small> <small>GOT</small> <small>MAIL.</small>* With a push of a button, Alex opened his Hotmail account and checked his emails. One caught his eye. It was from Barclays World Bank on the island of Cyprus. The email had been sent to pescador@sbc.com, and Pescador had forwarded it to Alex. There it was. Confirmation that the first million had been deposited into his account. He wrote the account number and password on a yellow sticky, folded it, and looked for a place to hide the information. No place looked safe enough. He decided to memorize the information instead and proceeded to destroy the yellow sticky and the email.

All right, he thought. Now it was time for him to deliver. His office was almost fully staffed. It was Tuesday, and there was only one day left before he had to file the lawsuit. Chordelli had wanted it filed on Wednesday, and he was going to fulfill Chordelli's wishes.

Betty had come on board and was getting familiar with the computer system and its word processing software. Astrid was at the front office getting used to the telephone system and practicing her greetings.

"Law office of Alejandro del Fuerte," she could be heard saying. A few minutes later she would try a different approach. "Law office. How may I direct your call? *Oficina del licenciado del Fuerte. Buenos días, bufete jurídico del licenciado del Fuerte.*"

Everyone was in good spirits. Romeo was looking spiffy in his new business suit, and he was already making himself useful, trying to learn how to make coffee and copies.

Alex had started reviewing the documents contained in the boxes. His hands had started trembling as he'd read the plaintiff's original petition. It contained some serious allegations. Harrow & Amaro were being accused of having committed some unspeakable acts. The allegations ranged from conspiracy to commit fraud, aiding and abetting the fraud, intentional fraud, misrepresentation, conversion, and racketeering. The allegations stopped short of calling them criminals. His stomach started churning. He sure hoped the evidence existed to prove all the allegations. Everything was on the line—his life, license, and reputation. If the evidence didn't support the allegations made in the petition, he would never recover. He sure hoped Chordelli and his people had gotten it right.

"Romeo," he called.

"Yes, boss?" he shouted back from the copy room.

"Make yourself a note to call Ms. Aurora López in the next few days. We need to give her our new address, tell her we've moved."

"What else, boss?" asked Romeo.

"I need to return a stack of old photos to Paloma Yarrington. I have them at home. Remind me to look for the box so that I can get that done in the next few days," said Alex.

"Who's Paloma Yarrington? Sounds high-class."

"Just an old girlfriend."

"Okay, I'm on it. Anything else?" asked Romeo.

"Yes, one last thing. Remind me to call Grandpa in Matamoros, and let's have an employee meeting in the conference room. Call everybody back here," ordered the young attorney.

Betty, Astrid, and Romeo came in and sat at the conference table. Alex was holding a yellow pad with notes scribbled on it and was sitting at the head of the table. At the other end of the table were some of the boxes containing the lawsuit against Harrow & Amaro.

"Okay," said Alex, clearing his throat. "You see those boxes at the end of the table? They contain a lawsuit that will be filed tomorrow in state district court. As you can see, you're all now working in a law firm. As such, there are certain rules that we need to follow. First of all, everything that happens here in the office is confidential. All of you are prohibited from discussing any aspect of any case with outsiders, not even your families. Loose lips sink ships.

"After the lawsuit is filed, I expect the phones to start ringing off the hook. It's a very sensitive lawsuit, so I don't want anyone talking to the press about anything. Whatever happens here in the office stays here. If the press comes around looking for an interview, have them leave a fax number where we can fax them a press release. Understood?"

"Yes," the three replied.

"Secondly, after the lawsuit is filed, I expect bad things will be said in the press about the firm and even some of us. The enemy will try to discredit us and take their case and try it in the court of public opinion. We'll stick with the game plan, and we'll win our battles in the courtroom. Because that's where it counts.

"I also expect the firm we're suing to try to bury us in paper," Alex continued. "There are only four of us. The enemy firm has at least fifteen seasoned trial attorneys and a staff of at least seventy-five employees. At a minimum, I would expect that five attorneys and fifteen staffers will work on this case, alone. And they will work on this case twenty-four hours a day, seven days a week. Because if we prevail, Harrow & Amaro, the biggest plaintiff's firm in Corpus Christi, will cease to exist. Their livelihood is at stake. And they will fight us with everything they've got. Tooth and nail."

The three employees of the firm had stopped smiling. They were giving each other looks, not yet grasping the magnitude of the task at hand.

"The good news is that, for all intents and purposes, this will be the only case that we'll be working on, as well. So all of our attention will be devoted to this one case. Harrow & Amaro can't say the same. They're a big firm and will have other cases that will take their time. So we have a slight advantage because we won't have other distractions.

"Now having said that, we won't be taking on new clients. I expect we'll get a bunch of new calls because we're the new kids on the block, and obviously we have guts to take on a Goliath such as the firm from Corpus. So, I expect people will want to retain our services. Astrid, I want you to let the potential clients talk to Romeo. And I want you, Romeo, to run interference and handle their calls. You will tell them that our firm believes in commitment and excellence. And because of our high standards, we are only able to provide quality representation to one client at a time. So right now, one case has our firm's undivided attention. But you will be more than glad to give them the number of the Cameron County Bar's referral section. They will be able to help them. Any questions?"

"But what if we get walk-in traffic?" asked Astrid.

"You'll let Romeo handle it," said Alex, looking at Romeo. "He's the office manager, and that's part of his responsibilities."

"So, boss," interjected Romeo, "can we ask what the lawsuit is about?"

"Sure," said Alex, "let me explain it to you all over lunch. Wait, there is one more thing. There's actually one other case we'll be working on. Our client is Linda Lawrence, and she's a divorce client. I'll tell you all more about it later. But now, let's go grab a bite. I hear Romeo is going to take us to a special place where they serve the best seafood soup in Texas."

"And we need to hurry," added Romeo. "If we get there late, we'll have to fight for a table. Let's beat the noon lunch crowd."

La Fonda Chiquita was located on Southmost Street, between Canal and 14th Street. The place was so small, with six tables, that it was not unusual for people to have to wait outside in the parking lot for a table. It had the best seafood soup in the Valley, but the locals didn't like to divulge such secrets. The owners didn't promote the place and never advertised the day of the week when the *caldo de mariscos* would be served.

Only those with an ear to the ground, "in the know" as they said, knew when *la Doña* would be making the seafood soup. Rumor had it that the folks at Snodgrass Seafoods—where *la Doña* shopped in the early morning hours for the freshest shrimp, red drum, and blue crab claws—would normally tip the locals.

They were sitting at a table for four, enjoying their spicy *caldos grandes*, when Alex leaned forward and spoke softly.

"The guys we're suing took some money that didn't belong to them. I don't know the exact amount, but it's somewhere in the ten to twenty million dollar range. These lawyers found this case, with a dead mother and child, but couldn't find any surviving relatives to bring a lawsuit on their behalf. So they hired somebody off the street to play the role of the widower and mourning father, and in this manner, they collected big. Once they got millions, they made sure the actor disappeared into the night. That, my friends, is called 'making the case' and is also insurance fraud."

"How do you know all this?" asked Romeo.

"Because I was hired by the legitimate husband and have the evidence to prove it," explained Alex.

"I would have never believed attorneys would stoop so low," said Betty, almost embarrassed, trying not to offend Alex, who happened to be the only attorney present.

"I wouldn't have believed it myself," said Alex, "but you know what they say. Life is stranger than fiction."

"Amen," said Astrid.

"Speaking of life being stranger than fiction, what if the guy played the firm, and they didn't know he wasn't the real husband?" proposed Romeo.

"No, the firm set it all up," said Alex with conviction. He knew this because Chordelli had told him so, although Romeo had made an interesting point. The fake could have conned the firm into believing he was the husband, which would not have been too difficult, given all the identity thefts going on all over the place. All it would take to pull it off would be for someone to surf the Net looking for those kinds of accidents with fatalities, then follow up on the dead victims. If no one came forward to claim the bodies, the imposter could step in and play the part. How would the firms know? If the fake said that he was the only surviving relative and he produced fake Mexican birth certificates or marriage licenses, how would American-trained lawyers detect the fraud? They wouldn't!

"So our firm then represents the real husband?" asked Astrid.

"Well, not exactly," said Alex with sad eyes. "The real husband died a few weeks ago. But a representative of his estate is suing on his behalf. Basically, we represent the estate's representative, and we are suing to undo everything that Harrow & Amaro and the imposter did and to have them return the money. Then those monies will be distributed to any legitimate heirs of the family. However, the money isn't the real issue. The real issue is that firms like that need to be exposed because they're manipulating the system, and if that goes on, then the system cannot be trusted. People go to court because they want fairness, truth, and justice, and it turns out that we have lawyers making witnesses up and manufacturing plaintiffs in order to scam the system and the insurance companies."

"I see your point," said Betty, "but you mean a judge can't tell what is going on?"

"I don't think so," explained Alex. He had now become an expert on the court system. "You see, a judge doesn't have time to worry about those things. It's the job of the attorneys to make sure that they're representing the proper parties with legitimate claims. A judge has to run the court, handle hundreds of files assigned to his court, and keep things running smoothly. If I'm the defense attorney and the plaintiff's attorney tells me that his client is the father of the victims, I'll believe him. I, as the defense attorney, expect that you would have done your homework and that you would have established that the client is the real father. Defense attorneys usually ask for a copy of a driver's license, and that's it. In some instances, they might even ask for a social security number, but that's rare. Everyone takes the plaintiff at its word. You say you're the father, then the attorneys and the system will believe you are the father. There are no security mechanisms. The attorneys must know if their clients are for real or not."

"And what makes you think that your client was the real husband?" asked Astrid.

"Well, he provided me with some documents that backed up his story," replied Alex matter-of-factly.

"What happens if we don't win?" asked Betty in an innocent manner.

The way Chordelli had made the whole thing sound, losing had not been an option. Had Alex not been so high on scotch, he might have considered a negative outcome. He knew that anything was possible in a jury trial. Seasoned trial lawyers were always complaining that they sometimes lost cases they should have won and sometimes won cases they should have lost.

"If we don't win, we pack our bags and go home," said Alex, somewhat humbled. It was a possibility, but he tried to convince himself that he didn't care. He was set for life, all because of Pilo. And to think he almost sent him away. Alex added, "But not without first having given the guys from Corpus a bloody nose and a black eye!"

Romeo, Betty, and Astrid broke into laughter, and the BPD cops having lunch at the adjoining table looked in Alex's direction. Alex became alarmed, although his staff didn't notice anything unusual. He leaned forward, as if trying to conceal his face, even though it was impossible for him to do so. He wasn't able to relax again until the officers finished their lunch, paid their tab, and left the restaurant. The thought of being recognized as the guy in the photo in the Pilo murder case had him a bit concerned. He still had to make arrangements with Rusty Chapa and meet with the BPD detectives.

However, what really worried him now was losing the lawsuit. Romeo and Astrid had raised good questions. What if the fake had played the firm and the boys at Harrow had no idea of what was going on? Could he prove otherwise? What if Jeff was wrong? And if he lost the case, would Harrow turn around and sue him and his firm for libel, slander, and other horrible scenarios too painful to mention? Then maybe he would cave and point the finger at Chordelli. But he would surely be finished as a lawyer. His career would be over before it even started.

Alex was deep in thought when Romeo interrupted. "Boss, are you ready to go?"

"Yes," said Alex, "I'm finished."

"*Ándale*, let's go then," indicated Romeo. "There are people still waiting for a table."

"Right," replied Alex, "let's get back to the office. We have work to do."

Chapter 20

THE LAWSUIT WAS FILED RIGHT BEFORE LUNCHTIME on Wednesday as per Chordelli's instructions. Alex sent Romeo down to the Cameron County courthouse to file it, along with instructions to the district clerk to have a Nueces County sheriff deputy serve Todd Harrow, managing partner of the firm.

Romeo returned to the office after lunch with his copy marked "filed" and handed it back to the boss.

"It's done," said the office manager.

"Good," said Alex. "Anything unusual?"

"Nah. Except the clerk said it would take about a week to receive the officer's return detailing exactly when the defendants got served."

"Okay. I guess we'll just sit and wait before the storm hits. In the meantime, I need you to help me buy a car for the firm. Who has the best prices and selection on Ford pickup trucks?"

"Oh, that's easy, Tipton Ford. As a matter of fact, I know a salesman over there. I can call him right now and tell him we're coming in. What are you looking for?"

"An F-350, extended cab with four-wheel drive."

"What are you going to do with one of those monsters?" asked Romeo.

"Do I live at the beach?"

"Well, yes," acknowledged Romeo.

"Okay then. That's what I need it for. Besides, there will be days when I'll have to go out of town on my own. I'll need you to stay behind and watch the office. I need something that's strong and reliable. That way, we'll be more effective."

"*Ta bueno*. Let me call my buddy, Harrison, and tell him we're coming in."

"Here," said Alex, handing Romeo the receiver, "call him from my office."

Romeo dialed the number for the local Ford dealership and asked the operator to transfer him to his friend. After a few minutes of silence, the salesman got on the phone, and Romeo greeted him and explained the object of the impromptu visit. After about thirty seconds of conversation, Romeo hung up the phone and addressed his boss.

"They have twenty in stock. And right now the dealer has all kinds of incentives and rebates."

"Well, let's go," said Alex.

"*Vámonos.*"

"Tell Betty and Astrid we'll be right back," added Alex. "And if they get any phone calls about the lawsuit, have them tell the caller that someone from the firm will get back to them. Ask them to take a name and number where the caller can be reached. Have them call Ms. Lawrence and advise her of our new office location."

"Will do," said Romeo as Alex grabbed his coat and a blank check and headed for the parking lot to wait for his right-hand man.

Chapter 21

IN THE LOWER RIO GRANDE VALLEY, news of the allegation that some law firms were faking plaintiffs and that the scam had been uncovered had brought the legal community to a halt. The feds and Texas Rangers had descended to investigate the fraud, and this had the effect of sending everyone scurrying off into hiding.

In fifty years, the legal community in the Rio Grande Valley had managed to stay out of the limelight, and things were better that way. Local players could make large campaign contributions and influence the judges. The judges helped level the playing field any time it was necessary, particularly when local practitioners went up against well-heeled defense firms from Dallas, Houston, or Austin. Now the rumors were that the scam had far-reaching implications and that many a head would roll, including judges, politicos, and other high-ranking officials.

Events that no one could have predicted had led to the opening of Pandora's box. The buzz around the courthouse was that had Porfirio Medina not decided to come looking for his family, the racket would never have been discovered. The crushing blow was that it had taken a member of the legal profession to expose corruption within the ranks. And a baby lawyer at that! The amazing thing was that this was the baby lawyer's first case and first trial, and there was much speculation about whether he would succeed in proving his case to a jury.

The profession's image was at stake. Harrow & Amaro's survival and the livelihood of its one hundred employees were at stake. Attorneys, and judges' reputations were at stake. The state bar's ethics committee's credibility was at stake. Everyone had something at stake. There would be no winners.

To the million or so Valley residents, the spectacle proved intoxicating. Just a few years back, proponents and opponents of tort reform had dominated the airwaves. It hadn't been enough that doctors, HMOs and lawyers had been at one another's throats, campaigning vigorously to either pass or defeat measures to cap monetary awards in medical malpractice cases, but now lawyers, insurance companies, and even judges were making news, again. This time it was about conspiracy, insurance fraud, and murder.

In the coffee and beauty shops, in the hallways down at the courthouse and governmental office buildings, in the bleachers at the White Wings games, the arena boxes during Killer Bees hockey games and Little Miss Kickball, on the sidewalks down at market square, in the *cantinas* lining 14th Street, the Valley talked of nothing else.

Everyone knew someone who either knew the people involved or knew someone who knew someone who knew the people allegedly involved. A lawyer suing another lawyer was almost a crime in itself. Brownsville had been such a friendly venue and had had such a friendly local Bar for so long that the mere fact that someone could now slander and libel another attorney was a disaster for South Texas.

All the Valley newspapers had run articles about the lawsuit. The reporters had begun digging around to find out about Rosario Medina and her son. Judge Macallan had changed his home phone number and was not returning phone calls. The newspapers wanted to know if he had a comment about hiring illegal aliens, even though he was a judge sworn to uphold the laws of the State of Texas and the United States. They wanted to know if he was somehow involved in the scam to defraud insurance companies. Macallan's silence and refusal to make a statement only added fuel to the fire. The locals felt he knew something and wasn't talking.

The front page story in the *Rio Grand Post* was the most objective. The newspaper called for the public to keep in mind that this was a civil case and nothing more. It reminded its readers that there were no criminal charges pending against anyone mentioned in the lawsuit. Even if the parties or other third parties were found to have engaged in fraud, that finding still did not amount to a criminal conviction. That was the beauty of the American judicial system. Anyone could accuse anyone of anything but the accuser had the burden of proving the case. The accused would get his day in court as well and present evidence exonerating himself. There were always two sides to every story.

Since Alex usually skimmed the local newspapers, and because he didn't want to read falsehoods in the paper about his case, he almost missed another story in the back pages. The newspaper article laid it on thick and explained how Harrow & Amaro was already preparing a separate lawsuit against Alejandro del Fuerte and his firm for libel, slander, and defamation. There was a picture of Shelby Tinning, the name partner of the firm Tinning Williamson, hired by Harrow & Amaro to sue the pants off Alex. The digitally enhanced photo had Tinning standing in front of the witness box ready to cross-examine anyone or anything into oblivion.

Alex was troubled by the article, which stated that Tinning had never lost a case in Corpus Christi and that the lawsuit had been filed in Corpus Christi in Judge Rose Gorman's court. As an aside, the article mentioned that when Judge Gorman had run for district judge the first time, Mr. Tinning had been her campaign treasurer.

Alex stared at the photograph and wished he had never bought into Chordelli's story. How could he have been so stupid? He had just filed his first major lawsuit, and now he himself was a target. Less than ten days had passed since the filing. To say that he was concerned was an understatement; he was freaking worried. Tinning was a name partner and founding member of the firm that specialized in libel, defamation, and slander lawsuits. It was a niche that had been very profitable for the boutique firm that represented the rich and the powerful, including the Hollywood elite, and had made its reputation suing the *National Enquirer, The Sun,* and other British tabloids. It appeared that he was going after Mr. del Fuerte and was not going to stop until the attorney surrendered his law license and left the state, or better yet, until he left the country. "What better poster child for frivolous and meritless lawsuits than this case," the paper quoted him as saying. "It's time the folks in Austin wake up and introduce legislation to stop lawyers like Alejandro del Fuerte who are trying to hit the lotto." Alex wanted to run and hide under a bed.

The paper added that Tinning was doing the lawsuit *pro bono* to help his friends at Harrow. That showed how much he believed in the firm's innocence and in the justice of its case. The story also gave the down-and-dirty on the creation of Alex's firm. Of course, it was all speculation. The news article threw in, just for good measure, the rumors that Alex's firm was laundering drug money for some powerful drug cartel in Mexico.

The paper also ran a photo of Alex. It was obvious that it had been downloaded from the driver's license rolls, since it was an old picture from Alex's college days. His eyes were half closed, and he looked drunk. It was a bad picture, but Tinning had managed to find it. The hostile spin now was that Alex was a drunk, possibly even a doper, trying to hit the lotto. The plaintiff's attorney was nothing more than a beach bum, a South Padre Island druggie and low-lifer.

Alex was also horrified to see that the newspaper had procured a copy of his law school transcript, which reflected poorly on him. He'd been a C student. He'd received no As, only three Bs and two Ds. To make matters worse, they had dug up and published his Bar exam results, which he had barely managed to pass. A passing grade was 675 points out of a possible 1000, and Alex had scored a 679.

Reading slowly each bit of the story, Alex felt more and more depressed. He read how Tinning explained that the Corpus Christi jury would hear from the name partners at Harrow, and how they could attribute losses in the hundreds of millions of dollars to Mr. del Fuerte's false statements. Tinning went further and added that the jury would hear from other firms that used to refer cases regularly to his clients and how after the allegations surfaced these referring firms had ceased to do business, altogether, with his clients. For good measure, the article reported that fifteen percent of Harrow's workforce had already been let go, and more cutbacks were coming.

"When I am done with him, Mr. del Fuerte will have to go back to Mexico, where he came from," Shelby Tinning was quoted as saying, and Alex could also feel the twenty-inch blade of a razor-sharp *machete* piercing his heart. He crumpled the article and tossed it in the trash. He wished he'd never agreed to file the lawsuit, never agreed to help Pilo, never discovered the probate file, and never thought about going to law school.

He called Romeo to his office and told him to get the pickup truck and his fishing gear ready.

"Where on the bay are we going?"

"We're not going bay fishing."

"I'm sorry?"

"We're going surf fishing. I need to clear my head. We'll camp out for a couple of days. Maybe we'll drive down to Mexico and go fishing at Nicho's lodge. I don't know yet."

"I don't think the reds are running now, are they?" Romeo said. "And, by the way, shouldn't we be worrying about the lawsuit we just filed?" Romeo was taking his new job title extremely seriously.

"Yes, but Harrow has about three weeks to file an answer. That gives us plenty of time to squeeze in a little fishing. Right before we get busy . . . the big battle." Alex didn't want to let his office manager know that he was now a legal target. He wanted to go underground so that he could avoid getting served with Tinning's lawsuit.

"I'll have everything ready in an hour, then," said Romeo.

"Very well, then."

He needed time away from the city, the courthouse, and everything that reminded him of this miserable lawsuit.

Chapter 22

THE THREE-DAY WEEKEND at Nicho's fishing lodge down by Puerto Mezquital helped a little in calming his worries. Alex would have liked to spew his fears and guts to Romeo, but he thought that Romeo probably wouldn't understand. Tinning was trying to take his license, skin him alive, bankrupt him, and even send him back to Mexico! The result was Alex overmedicating on liquor, cigarettes, and entirely too much food.

Alex kept checking the web through his cell phone for stories on the lawsuit. There was nothing else, for the moment, on Tinning. And he had not even been served with the lawsuit. He wondered if Chordelli was going to step in and help him defend the other lawsuit? How much time, effort, and resources would it take to defend a lawsuit against Tinning Williamson?

While the staff at Nicho's lodge prepared lunch, Alex went swimming in the green waters of the Laguna Madre and tried to forget about the lawsuit. Late Saturday afternoon, after a day of fishing, drinking, and eating, Alex placed a phone call as he lounged on the deck overlooking the Gulf of Mexico.

"¿*Bueno?*" said the voice on the other end.

"Grandpa, it's me, Alex. Can you hear me?"

"Yes, *m'ijo*," said Grandpa, "where are you?"

"I had to go out of town, but I promise, as soon as I come back we'll get together, okay?"

"Sure, *m'ijo*, don't worry about it. I know you must be very busy."

"I miss you, Grandpa. I can't wait to see you," cried Alex. "Anyway, I just wanted to call and say hi. I hope to see you soon."

"I miss you too, *m'ijo*," Grandpa replied, "just let me know when you want to get together. Take care."

"Bye, Grandpa," said Alex as he hung up and immediately dialed another number. The call went through. "Professor Fetzer?" asked Alex.

"Yes, who is this?"

"It's me, Alejandro del Fuerte, one of your ex-students. I emailed you a while back asking for advice regarding a situation I'd come across while trying to help an illegal alien. Do you recall?"

Professor Mike Fetzer had been a Marine drill instructor in his younger days, and the training had carried over to his teaching style. He had been the toughest, most demanding professor, and a fifteen-year stint as an assistant U.S. attorney battling the New York Mafia had only added to his toughness, resourcefulness, and reputation. As a special prosecutor on several high-profile cases, he won praise for his legal ability and tough-as-nails approach. Law students, on the other hand, had other opinions. Having students for breakfast, lunch, and dinner only cemented the professor's reputation as the hardest nose in the annals of the law school's history.

"Oh, yes, I saw the email. Something about a Mexican national . . . ," said Fetzer. "Did I answer your email? I can't remember now."

"No, but it doesn't matter now. I'm in trouble, serious trouble. I need your help, that's why I'm calling now." Alex blurted out.

"What do you mean?"

"Well, do you have a few minutes?"

"Sure, I've got more than a few minutes. I took early retirement, Alex. My days are spent here at the house. I'll be honest. I still miss the classroom and the courtroom. I'm afraid I have too much idle time on my hands."

"All right, then. If you recall the email, I opened my office a while ago. You'll be amazed to hear what's happened to me since I passed the Bar and went into solo practice—stuff law school does not prepare you for. Anyway, I'm involved in a case against a Corpus Christi law firm, and it's blown up in my face. The firm has hired Tinning Williamson to sue me for defamation, libel, and slander. Have you ever heard of those guys?"

"Sure, Tinning was my student. I hear he's done pretty well for himself," Fetzer said.

"Well, now he's after me, and I don't know what to do. I can't fight two lawsuits on two fronts, not against mega-firms."

"Tell me about the lawsuit against the Corpus Christi firm. Who are they?"

"Harrow & Amaro. You know them?"

"The product liability guys?"

"Yep, those."

"What are you doing suing them?"

"I know, I know. Please don't rub it in. I already feel like a complete nincompoop," admitted Alex. He couldn't disclose the real reason for his actions.

"So what happened in that case?" asked Fetzer.

"Do you remember that I emailed to consult you about helping an illegal alien?"

"Yes, I now remember, go on."

"My client, Pilo, that was his nickname, was here looking for his family. Remember?"

"Yes."

"I investigated their whereabouts and discovered that the wife and child had died in a horrific rollover accident."

"Okay, and . . .?"

"Well, I also discovered that someone stepped in and pretended to be the husband, and there was a lawsuit filed against the van manufacturer and Firelazer Tires. There was a sealed, confidential settlement. The guy who pretended to be my client, in other words the father and husband, does not exist. At least, not here in the United States. So someone had to create him to act the part, bring a wrongful death lawsuit, and recover millions of dollars in insurance money."

"So, you've got a case where somebody saw an incredible opportunity to make lots of money, except they didn't have an integral part of the puzzle, so they just created the missing piece."

"Exactly!" Alex said. "And the Harrow boys handled the lawsuit."

"Sounds to me like someone ran the case," the professor explained. "Did I ever tell you about case running down in your neck of the woods?"

"No, but since I've been down here, I've found out a thing or two about it," the young attorney replied as he opened another beer.

"Well, you might as well get used to it. It's a way of life down there," said Professor Fetzer. "It's something you were going to deal with sooner or later. Of course, they don't teach you that in law school. It's kept hush-hush . . . swept under the rug. Otherwise, first-year law students might change their minds about becoming lawyers. Here we have young students, full of ideals, anxious to become lawyers, wanting to help people such as the one you just described, and lo and behold there are other attorneys who will snatch cases even after someone else has signed them up! South Texas is full of them."

"Does it go on in other places?"

"Not like in the Valley. You have a *compadre* system in place that helps perpetuate the ambulance-chasing and the running of cases. You see, that kind of stuff isn't as prevalent in Houston, Dallas, or Austin. In those places, if a lawyer knows of somebody running cases, he'll report it to the state Bar, even sue the bastard. That sort of thing never happens down in your area. It's such a small Bar, and everybody knows one another, that it would be embarrassing to have to report a colleague, much less sue them."

"So everyone just kind of tolerates it?"

"Sure. Why do you think the big boys from Corpus, San Antonio, and Houston run cases down there?"

"Why?"

"Because the Valley attorneys aren't going to do anything about it. They don't want to turn in their own colleagues. Call it professional courtesy or lack of balls," the professor explained. He added, "But then it gets more complicated."

"What do you mean?"

"Since there are no checks and balances," the professor explained, "and because neither the Bar nor the attorneys down there do anything about it, the runners end up taking first an inch, then a yard."

"I don't get it."

"They get careless, greedy. To the point where they might even manufacture a plaintiff or two to hit the jackpot. Which is what you might have with the Harrow boys."

"So this sort of thing then has been going on for a while, eh?" Alex asked.

"Yep. But you see, had you known that this went on, you might have ended up going to dental school instead. So it would have been pretty dumb for your Ethics professor to have discussed the subject with the students. I mean, even here in Houston we've heard of people like Israel Cantu. Answer me this. How do you explain that an attorney from Starr County ended up representing all the Baytown refinery explosion families? It's obvious, don't you think?"

"Who is that?"

Professor Fetzer cleared his throat and whispered in a low voice, "Your neighbor. The scumbag controls the highway from Rio Grande City to Harlingen. He's the one with the big bankroll. He's part of the problem. With his money he's able to finance the parasites that lurk on the edge of the legal profession. It's rumored that he runs a sophisticated network. He and another big one, Francois Margoux, have been investigated, even prosecuted. They ended up with a slap on the wrist."

"Well, it sounds to me like that might be the situation I'm dealing with here," confirmed Alex.

"Do you know or have evidence that would indicate that Harrow set this whole thing up?"

"No, not really," Alex said, not willing to reveal the information he'd received from Chordelli. "All I know is that my guy is legit."

"Did Harrow have knowledge, or do you have any evidence that proves they had knowledge that the actor was just that . . . an actor?"

"No, but he's vanished without a trace, and I know that my client was the real deal. I have the proof."

"Aha," Fetzer responded.

"It gets more complicated. As I dug deeper, I got death threats, my office was ransacked, and Pilo was murdered. I guess you could say they were trying to get rid of the smoking gun. And they did just that."

"So they mean business. Well, that's pretty brave of you to hang in there. Why are you still in it?"

"To get to the truth and expose the bastards," Alex said. "I suspect they were also behind my client's murder. No one should get away with that." Alex knew this was not the entire truth, but he didn't think Fetzer needed to know anything else at this time.

"Where is the criminal investigation in connection with your client's murder?"

"It went nowhere. These guys are pros. Not a trace, not a fingerprint, not a piece of fabric, not a suspect, no DNA, nothing. Vanished into thin air!"

"So, why are you still around, then?"

"They must think that I have the evidence that will do them in, and since they don't know where it is, they need to keep me alive until they find it."

"So do you think Harrow also had something to do with the murder?"

"I don't know what to think anymore. At one point, I thought they may have set the whole thing up. Maybe even ordered the hit on my client. But then I have my doubts. Would a bunch of lawyers do that? I mean . . . order a hit? That's extreme. But then I think of the hundreds of millions of dollars at stake. Then I think that maybe Harrow didn't know a thing. They trusted this stranger and believed his story and signed him up. Who wouldn't sign him up? If someone had walked into my office and told me he was the husband, and I saw the dollar signs, and he showed me a fake Mexican driver's license or a fake Mexican marriage certificate, I wouldn't know the difference."

"So how are you going to prove that Harrow had something to do with it?"

"I don't know. I'm in trouble here," said Alex. "I mean, I have evidence that Pilo is the genuine husband. I have evidence that Rosario never remarried. I have evidence that the guy pretending to be my guy is not and cannot be the real Pilo Medina."

"That doesn't mean anything. You need more—to prove fraud, anyway."

"I know, and then I sometimes think that somebody from the outside set the whole thing up. Somebody could have thought of this. They came on the scene or found out about the accident. Then, they followed up and realized that no one came forward to claim Rosario and the boy. They saw the perfect opportunity. Millions waiting to be claimed. So, they hired someone to come in and play the role. When the whole thing was done, they gave him his cut. They sent him on his merry way and they kept the bulk of the money."

"I see what you're saying. It could be a case runner, the coroner, a state trooper, anyone really."

"Yep, and maybe Harrow knew nothing. So, I'm screwed."

"Well, they must have suspected something and maybe decided to overlook it, don't you think?"

"I would like to think so," Alex said.

"I would think so, too, and let me tell you why," said the sage professor. "It's because attorneys like Harrow always investigate their cases before filing anything. They don't take a case unless they're going to win it. So they do their homework because they're going to sink two to three hundred thousand dollars to develop the case, hire experts, and take it to trial, with the guarantee that they can prove liability and damages. Part of preparing their case involves going over everything with a magnifying glass."

"I see where you're going with this, Professor," interjected Alex. He was getting excited. The lightbulb had gone on in his head.

"You follow?"

"Yes! They're not going to lose a case over some small, over-looked detail. Which means if the guy was an impostor, they probably caught it. They must have known about it, but maybe decided to press forward, thinking no one would know. No one would find out. Now, if they didn't catch it, then they should have caught it and thus were negligent. Especially a firm of that caliber. At a minimum, they should have caught it."

"Now you're thinking," Fetzer chimed in. "You need to focus on the intake part of the case. I think that's where the secret lies."

"I would have to agree with you, Professor," Alex concurred. He was beginning to feel a little better.

After a long silence, Fetzer asked, "What happens if Harrow walks?"

"That will only bolster their defamation suit against me, I would think."

"Actually, the defamation suit should probably be thrown out of court. Especially if the alleged defamatory statements against Harrow came from within the four corners of your lawsuit. Have you made other communications to anyone, besides what is contained in the lawsuit?"

"No."

"So, there's immunity. So you should be okay," Fetzer said.

"Yes, but the judge in Corpus Christi is not going to throw it out. She's buddies with Tinning. In the meantime, they'll run me to the ground."

"And it will cost you a bunch of money."

"That's not what I want to hear."

"There might be other ways to handle the defamation suit," said the professor. "File a motion for summary judgment, asking the judge to dismiss the lawsuit. When she denies your request, which she will, immediately file an interlocutory appeal. The underlying suit will be stayed until the appellate court rules on your appeal. That could stall things for a while," Fetzer concluded.

Alex took a big swig from a cold Bohemia beer. "I might just do that, see what Tinning does. I doubt the court of appeals, which also happens to sit in Corpus Christi, Tinning's playground, will help me much. Besides, wasn't the chief justice of the court of appeals Tinning's roommate in college?"

"Yes, that's what I've heard."

"Do you want to come out of retirement, Professor, come soak your toes in the warm waters of the Gulf of Mexico?"

"Is that an invitation or a job offer?"

"Both."

"I can't get involved right now. My health wouldn't allow it. But thanks for the offer," Fetzer said.

"Well, I figured it can't hurt to ask."

"Let me ask you, who's defending Harrow in your lawsuit?"

"Slick Stevens," Alex said.

"Well, it's going to be an uphill battle. But you should come out okay. Sometimes if you get pounded in front of a jury, that can turn things around. I've seen it happen hundreds of times. You'll have the jury rooting for you because you're the little guy fighting Goliath. Of course you don't have the experience Stevens and the boys at Harrow have. To get there, it takes years in the courtroom. But this will be a fantastic introduction to the big leagues. After a trial like this, you'll be able to take on anybody. If you're still standing, of course."

"Well, I'll let you go, Professor. Thanks for listening."

"Call anytime if you need anything else, Alex."

"Yes, Professor . . . thanks."

"Alex, one last thing before we hang up. Remember this. Whether you prove or not that Harrow had knowledge of the fake, that won't matter."

"Come again?" said Alex.

"They still have to disgorge the fee. Whatever their fee was, it goes to your client's estate."

"You're right! They don't get to profit from their mistakes or incompetence," concurred Alex. Things were looking up.

"All you need is a relative to prove Pilo was the real spouse and the boy's dad. If you filed the lawsuit, that means you must have someone representing the estate. I would hope it's a relative, right?"

"Yes, it is."

"So even if you can't prove fraud because they lacked knowledge or intent, it won't matter. If their guy is a fake, they have to return the fee. What do you think the fee was?"

"I'm guesstimating about five to seven million. We're still doing discovery."

"Great! There's enough for the heirs and to pay your fee. You should come out all right, then."

"I'm glad I got to talk to you. I feel somewhat better. Thanks, Professor." They exchanged goodbyes and hung up.

The truth was, Alex didn't feel much better at all. As much as he wanted to get justice for Pilo, it was obvious that he was alone on this one. The initial excitement he'd felt on board the *Magillu* in thinking, if for a minute, he could sock it to the bad guys was now mostly gone. He must have been seriously high on scotch and highly impaired, thinking of all those millions in the bank when he signed on with Chordelli. He was about to get the spanking of a lifetime.

Chapter 23

ON MONDAY MORNING, after a brief visit with his grandfather, Alex and Romeo drove south on the two-lane highway away from Matamoros. They were on Highway 101 to Ciudad Victoria, the state capital of Tamaulipas. As Romeo drove, Alex called the office and left a message for the staff. He and Romeo would be driving down to Tepantitlán, Pilo's hometown, and would return in about a week.

He read his emails and news reports on his laptop as Romeo negotiated the steep and deadly curves of the Sierra Madre. One of the emails was from Betty, wanting to know if she should sign for some documents a deputy sheriff had brought over. The documents were from a firm in Corpus Christi and were addressed to Alejandro del Fuerte.

MSN also ran a story about Harrow's press conference in which it had announced that Tony "Slick" Stevens would be defending the meritless lawsuit filed by Alejandro del Fuerte. Stevens had not lost a lawsuit in five years. "Damn, now what?" Alex mumbled to himself.

At 10:00 p.m. they stopped to rest at a motel on the outskirts of San Luis Potosí. They were now getting into the highlands of Mexico, and they would continue their journey in the morning. Finding Tepantitlán would not be easy. The Mexican map given to them by Nicho, back at the fishing lodge, didn't even show the place. The city of Teotihuacán was shown, but not Tepantitlán. Alex remembered Pilo saying his hometown was near the pyramids, and he hoped that would help them find it.

Early Tuesday, they headed to Mexico City. It was necessary to loop around the Mexican capital, avoid its bottleneck traffic, then drive southeast to Teotihuacán. By three o'clock in the afternoon, as Romeo crested a hill and the pyramids outlining the horizon came into view, Alex saw a sign in both English and Spanish:

BIENVENIDOS A TEOTIHUACÁN Y A LAS PIRAMIDES DEL SOL Y LA LUNA.

WELCOME TO TEOTIHUACÁN AND TO THE PYRAMIDS OF THE SUN AND MOON.

They were both relieved when Romeo spotted a barely visible sign to Tepantitlán, and they left the main highway in the direction it indicated. They took a rough drive in the mountains, during which there was no reception on the radio. After about an hour, they arrived in Tepantitlán, which looked like a ghost town. Romeo parked the truck next to the town's main square. Wearing fishing khaki shorts and sweatshirts, roped sunglasses around their necks, and four days' worth of beard stubble, they both stuck out like sore thumbs.

They walked into a tiny general store across from the square and grabbed two carbonated apple drinks from the icebox. The store owner asked them if they were hungry and both said yes. He brought out pork *carnitas* with a stack of handmade tortillas, and the pair devoured the succulent feast. The keeper couldn't make the tacos fast enough. As he worked on the food, he kept giving the pair the look-over. The strangers sure had come to the wrong place to go fishing.

A few feet from where Romeo and Alex were standing, two Tlahuica Indians were speaking in their native dialect. *So this was Pilo's birthplace*, Alex thought. The place was even worse than Pilo described it. It was a hellhole in the middle of nowhere. Alex wondered if anyone there would remember his client.

"Excuse me, do you know Porfirio Medina?" Alex asked the storekeeper in Spanish. The two Tlahuica Indians nearby looked up at the mention of Pilo's name.

"Yes," answered the man, "he left to El Norte to go in search of his wife and son. That must have been a while back, two, three months maybe. We haven't had any news of him since. Where are you from?"

"Brownsville, Texas. On the other side of Matamoros," Alex answered.

"Pilo was supposed to cross into the United States near Matamoros."

"Pilo did cross there," Alex said. "He was my client. I was trying to help him find his wife and son."

"What do you mean, you were trying? What happened?"

The two Tlahuica Indians had stopped talking and were now paying special attention to the exchange. It was obvious that they also spoke or at least understood Spanish.

"He disappeared," Alex lied. "He never returned to my office. And I was wondering if he had come back to his hometown. I was worried for his safety, him being old and all."

"No, like I said, we've had no news of Pilo or his family. We all knew that he had been worrying about them a lot. The month prior to his departure, he came in here and told me that he was going to go search for them. Then he was gone."

"Where did they live, Rosario, the boy, and Pilo?" Alex asked.

"Down west by the quarry," said the storekeeper, pointing in the direction.

"Is it easy to get to?"

"Macario and Chemo here can show you the way," said the man, pointing to the Tlahuica Indians standing nearby. "Just throw them a bone . . . twenty or thirty pesos, and they'll be happy."

The keeper motioned to the two Indians and gave them instructions in Tlahuica. They quickly headed for the truck across the street. They climbed into the bed of the pickup truck and waited for Alex and Romeo to come out of the store.

"What do we owe you?"

"Twenty pesos."

Alex pulled out a one-hundred-peso bill and laid it flat on the counter.

"*Así está bien*," he said, winking at the storekeeper, "keep the change."

Alex pushed the makeshift door to Pilo's hut aside. Nearby, Alex had noticed the one-room brick *casita* was half-finished. It was the one his client had mentioned he was building with the money Rosario sent every month.

The shack was nothing more than a small, empty room with dirt floors and patched-up sheets of tin metal for a roof. Off to one side were rolled-up straw mats. On a small wooden table, there was a Bible and pictures of Pilo, Rosario, and the boy. Alex noticed other pictures, too, of his daughter María Luisa, her husband, and their children.

Off to one corner, he saw a blackened metal *comal* sitting on three large rocks, and that served as support for the stove. There were a few metal cups and three or four chipped plates strewn about the floor. The hut had no running water, no indoor plumbing, nothing. It was bare. Hanging from a nail on a wall was a cross showing Jesus Christ crucified.

Romeo stepped outside and went back to the truck to wait for Alex. Alex could hear him talking to the Indians and asking them questions about their Tlahuica dialect. Alex stood alone in the middle of the empty shack as the last rays of daylight barely filtered through the tree branches that made up the hut's walls. It was there, in the middle of the dead silence, that new questions came to him.

Why had his destiny crossed paths with Pilo's? What if he'd decided not to go to the office that Saturday morning? Would somebody else have helped the old man? Would that other person have uncovered the scam? Was that it? Was it all about the scam? If it was, how would uncovering it help Pilo, Rosario, and the boy? They were dead. Gone forever. If he hadn't gotten involved, would his client still be alive today?

He pushed aside some wool blankets on the floor and noticed an old shoe box sticking out of the ground. He dug it out and dusted it off. In it, he discovered bundles of love letters from Rosario to his client, all postmarked "Brownsville." They were neatly wrapped with red ribbons. The case against the boys from Corpus had just gotten better.

Chapter 24

ALEX AND ROMEO STAYED IN TEPANTITLÁN for a week. The village was nestled in a high valley surrounded by green, lush mountains. It was a beautiful area, but it was so remote and isolated that it was barely noticeable on anyone's radar screen.

As far as getting any meaningful work done, or preparing the Medina case for trial, Alex got very little accomplished. However, the time spent down in Tepantitlán allowed Alex to do some serious soul searching. Of all the people in the world, why had he crossed paths with a piss-poor, illegal alien that Saturday morning? Had it been an accident or was it destiny? They rented a room from the storekeeper and spent most of their time either digging up stuff about Pilo, Rosario, and the boy, or hiking up the surrounding mountains and swimming in the icy cold Caracol River.

The Lawrence divorce was put on the back burner after Clint's attorney called the office to say that the couple wanted to go to counseling and give the marriage another chance. Alex was not opposed to the idea, despite the fact that he had done very little work on the file and felt guilty hanging on to Mrs. Lawrence's five-thousand dollar retainer. Yet he knew that even if his client went to counseling, there was a ninety percent chance the couple would still end up divorcing. If that happened, the retainer would not be enough for the fight that awaited him when it came time to divvy up the assets. The exercise would certainly consume a lot of time. The days spent exploring the mountains in and around Pilo's birth place helped clear Alex's head.

Finally, Alex decided it was time to face the music. If he was to go down in flames, he would go down fighting. Pilo had lost his

life searching for the ones he loved the most. He had paid the ulti-
mate price for them, but at no time had his resolve wavered or
diminished. At no time had he thought of giving up. He'd done
everything that he was capable of doing.

What kind of lawyer was Alex, shaking at the knees because
someone had filed a lawsuit against him? What was he made of?
Pilo, his heirs, and his estate deserved their day in court. They had
a valid claim, and if Harrow had engaged in wrongdoing, then a
jury would see that. That was his job. Put on a case, present the
evidence, and let the jury decide. There would always be certain
things that no one could control or predict. A jury trial was just
that—a big, open-ended question or a roll of the dice. Even the
biggest plaintiffs' lawyers lost occasionally. As the big names in the
business said, "If you're not losing some cases, that means you're
not trying them." Besides, what if the jury returned a verdict in his
favor? Certainly the defamation case would go away, because a jury
would have validated Pilo's allegations. Ha! He would present his
case to the jury and let the jury decide. He owed that much to his
client. Now there was a trial date set. It was time to fish or cut bait.

Mexico City was a two-hour drive from Teotihuacán and almost
four hours from Tepantitlán. It was Alex and Romeo's first trip to
Mexico City, and Alex had decided to catch any available flight out
of the Aztec capital to Houston. Romeo would drive the truck back
to Texas, and they would meet up in Brownsville in two or three
days.

There was no time to waste. Alex needed to visit his old mentor in Houston. He wanted to discuss some aspects of the upcoming Medina litigation and discuss trial strategy. He needed to
bounce and share ideas with someone. He had to do it in person,
a phone call would not do.

Alex had never flown Aeromexico. The uneventful nonstop
flight to George Bush Intercontinental Airport in Houston took
two hours. The Mexican capital had been cold and covered in
smog when the jet took off, and when Alex stepped off the plane

in Houston and cleared customs, the heat and the humidity were so intense it felt like a sauna.

He flagged down a cab for the forty-five-minute ride downtown. The Four Seasons Hotel would be his home during his stay in Houston. The suite was luxurious, with marble floors, dark wood paneling, and lots of brass. It overlooked the George R. Brown Convention Center and the Minute Maid Baseball Stadium, home to the Houston Astros. He ordered room service from the Deville menu: Texas Mixed Grill—charbroiled boneless quail, beef tenderloin, and venison medallions—apple wood smoked bacon with grilled jalapenos, wonton potatoes on pepper corn cabernet sauce and a bottle of Duke de Lalande.

After eating, Alex stumbled onto the bed for a power nap. Later in the evening or the next day he would try to reestablish contact with Professor Fetzer. It was time to bring on a gunner.

The next morning, Alex called the office to check in. He and Romeo had been gone for almost two weeks, and now it was time to fire up the troops and go on the warpath. Alex let the phone ring about nine times and was about to hang up when Astrid picked up.

"Del Fuerte Law Firm," Astrid answered.

"*Hola*," said Alex, "it's me, Alex."

"Hi, Mr. del Fuerte. Sorry I didn't pick up right away, but you can just imagine the phone has been ringing off the hook. I was on the other line with the producers of Court TV. They want to negotiate a deal with you in order to televise the trial. Apparently, Judge Robles is okay with it, if the lawyers in the case agree."

"What did you tell them?"

"I said only you could decide and that you were out of town, to please leave a call-back number, and that somebody would get in touch with them as soon as we gave you the message."

"Good. How are you and Betty doing?"

Astrid explained that without Alex around, not much had gotten done. For the most part, she and Betty had spent their time returning phone calls from several newspapers across the nation that had picked up the story from the wire. In addition to the inquiry from Court TV, Greta Von Windershcraft with Univision had been calling every day to try to get an exclusive with Alex and invite him on her show, *Final Judgment*.

"Okay, good," replied Alex. "Did you get my last emails from Nicho's lodge?"

"Yes, we did. How was Tepantitlán?" Astrid asked. "I know it's Pilo's hometown."

"Sad," Alex said, "but at the same time it was an eye-opener. I'll tell you all about it when I get back."

"When will that be?"

"Tomorrow night. Tell Romeo to pick me up at the airport. He should be back in the office in the morning. My flight comes in at 10:00 p.m. And call Ms. Lawrence. See if she will come in Friday afternoon around four. I need to have a status conference with her on her case."

"Will do," the receptionist said. "Anything else?"

"Nah. I'll see you and Betty when I get back. Take care and keep up the good work."

"Thanks. Bye-bye now."

Alex took a twenty-minute cab ride from the Four Seasons downtown to 2222 Woodway, an address just outside loop 610. It was in the Tanglewood area where former president George H. Bush lived, just five minutes from the Galleria and Post Oak Boulevard. Post Oak Boulevard was to Houston what Rodeo Drive was to Beverly Hills.

The cab pulled into the long driveway, and Alex got out and rang the doorbell to the New England-style home. He had the taxi driver wait in the cab with the engine running.

"Who is it?" said a female voice through the intercom.

"Alex del Fuerte," said Alex into the intercom. "Is Professor Fetzer home?"

"I'll go and check. Please wait."

The intercom came back on. "Alex," said Professor Fetzer, "let me buzz you in. Please come in. I'm in the library. It'll be to the left off the stairwell."

When the buzzer came on, Alex pushed the door open and went inside the house. He found his way to the library and discovered his old professor reading the *New York Times* by a large bay window.

"Ah, it's good to see ya," the professor said, squeezing Alex's hand. Fetzer was wearing a robe and slippers and had not shaved for two or three days.

"Likewise," replied Alex.

"Can I offer you coffee, juice, anything?"

"No, Professor, I won't be staying long. Thanks."

"Well then, what brings you here?"

"I need your help, and I need it bad. I came to ask you if you would be interested in second chairing me."

"Alex," Fetzer said slowly. "I'm retired now. It's been a while since I've been in a courtroom. I'm afraid I wouldn't be much help, son, not to mention my health."

It was obvious the professor's health had declined recently. His white hair was thinning, and he looked pale. His booming voice was gone, and his left hand trembled a bit as he held the newspaper on his lap.

"Professor, hear me out before you say no. If, after I'm finished, you still decline, then I'll go quietly. That's it."

"Okay," Fetzer said, appearing somewhat exasperated with his former student.

"Remember when we first met, when I started law school about four years ago? Well, when I first took your class, I, along with the other students, had no idea what was in store for us. You were so tough and demanding that some students would even faint when called on to recite. There was one incident that I recall involving Ms. Stoval, do you remember? She fainted as you started drilling her on the facts of *United States v. Vega*. Do you remember the episode?"

"How could I forget? The opinion discussed police manufacturing exigent circumstances. One of my ex-students argued that case in the Fifth Circuit Court of Appeals and won."

"And remember Marcus Soleil?"

"The time I stormed out of the classroom because Soleil wasn't prepared?"

"Yes! Do you remember that time?"

"Yes, looking back I should never have jumped on poor Marcus the way I did that day," the professor said. "I lost my composure, and for that I apologize."

"Ah, let bygones be bygones, Professor. In time, everyone caught on and realized that all you were trying to do was to make us true lawyers, lawyers that could make a difference. Lawyers that would leave no stone unturned to help a client and fight for justice. You made me realize that being a lawyer was not about making a hundred grand a year, dressing in Brooks Brothers suits, or driving around in a Mercedes. No, to you, being a lawyer meant going the extra mile for the client. Putting in the extra effort, whatever it took. If it meant burning the candle at both ends, then so be it. To give it your all. You took us to 'a higher level.' Do you remember that? Do you remember those words?"

"It was just a show, Alex. That was it."

"Well, this case I'm trying against Harrow is the kind of case that can make a difference. It's the kind of case that the state Bar will be watching, as well as the legislature and others across the country. It's the kind of case that will have serious consequences for all those who engage in case running or ambulance chasing. It could be a landmark case. It could also restore honor to the profession or at least be a catalyst for change. But I can't do it alone. I wish I could, but the reality is that I'm being outgunned, outnumbered, and outlawyered."

"But I have poor health. I don't think I can handle the stress, Alex."

"Look, I'm proposing that you come down and stay at Padre with me for just two weeks. The trial is still a few months away. If, at the end of your stay, your health has not improved, then you can come back to Houston. I promise you the fresh Gulf air will do wonders for you. Plus, you'll get to experience the culture, the food, and meet the friendly locals."

The professor looked outside the window as he thought over Alex's proposition. "Well, the sea air couldn't hurt my condition. And I hear Padre is paradise, right here in our own backyard. Plus it's a stone's throw away from Mexico."

"Come on," Alex pressed on, "what do you say?"

"Well," the old professor said, mulling it over, "it has been twenty years since I've been to the beach . . . and the kids don't call anymore, after the divorce and all."

"Let me call my office," Alex said, bursting with excitement. "I'll have them make your flight reservation as well. You can fly back with me tonight. I promise you won't regret it. There's a cab waiting for us outside."

"Martha!" the professor called out to his home health provider, who was hovering somewhere in the background, "pack my swim trunks, I'm going native!"

Alex and his old professor started laughing.

Chapter 25

ROMEO WAS WAITING IN THE LOBBY at the airport. The Continental jet was due to arrive at any minute now. Although it had been a couple of days since he had last seen his boss, he had no idea what Alex had been doing in Houston.

As Alex emerged at the gate, he looked refreshed and reinvigorated. He was walking alongside a distinguished-looking elderly gentleman with white hair and horn-rimmed glasses. They looked to be together.

"Can I help you with your bags?" Romeo asked Alex.

"Help Professor Fetzer," Alex answered, pointing to the professor and his bags. "He'll be staying with us for a couple of weeks."

"Welcome to Brownsville, Professor," said Romeo as he reached to shake hands with Professor Fetzer. "My name is Romeo."

"Nice to meet you," Fetzer said.

"Follow me. I parked right outside. I gave security a tip so that I could just pull in and pull out," Romeo said, proud of himself for being able to secure special privileges. "And of course it helped that he remembered me from my cab-driving days."

Alex and Romeo both helped the professor climb into the truck and then headed out to Padre. It was time to get Fetzer settled into his own suite at the Tuscany and allow him some rest. Alex needed to get the professor healthy again, even though it was obvious that his mind was as sharp as ever.

It was Monday morning, and Astrid and Betty had been hard at work since seven as they anticipated the arrival of Alex and his special guest. They had made fresh coffee and ordered a gallon of fresh-squeezed orange juice, along with a basketful of giant flour tortillas filled with eggs prepared all kinds of ways. There was *jamón con huevo, chorizo, papas, tocino,* and *barbaco*a. Las Brasas down the street sure came in handy when it came time to enter-tain or impress the guests. The flour tortillas were fluffy and twelve inches across, at least. Alex had said that a serious crisis couldn't be handled on an empty stomach, so Astrid and Betty did their best to make sure the office was stocked with snacks. The boss had acquired his appreciation of fine food while waiting tables in college and law school.

Alex and Fetzer greeted everyone and then quickly went to the conference room. Betty asked Alex to buzz if they needed any-thing else.

"Professor, let me give you an update as to what's been going on with the Harrow litigation," Alex said.

"Alex, wait," the professor said, "let me ask you something. You just passed the Bar exam. How can you afford to run a place like this?"

"I have friends at the bank," Alex replied with an answer that he had prepared just in case the topic came up. "Friends I grew up with, both here in Brownsville and Matamoros. They were very helpful in advancing me a $200,000 credit line. I spent about $75,000 getting the place going and have in reserve about anoth-er $125,000."

"Ah," Fetzer said, apparently satisfied with Alex's answer.

Alex felt remorseful for not being honest with his old profes-sor. But he had decided that he would reveal the truth only on a need-to-know basis. For now, that was all the professor needed to know.

"The Harrow litigation has been worked up," started Alex again. "Discovery has been done, depositions have been taken, and experts have been hired. The only thing my office needs to do, since we're getting close to trial, is one last discovery supplemen-tation. I plan to drop a bomb on Harrow."

"What's the bomb?"

"Stacks of letters from Rosario to my client . . . which, I might add, prove they were still married and very much in love. Also, some family photos."

"Don't you think," Fetzer asked as he took a bite out of a steamy potato and egg taco, "that they'll run to the judge and ask him for more time, since you've dropped new evidence on them and their experts haven't had a chance to review it?"

"Maybe," Alex responded. "Judge Robles has given us a preferential trial setting, and he's also known to run a rocket docket."

"That's what I would argue," added the professor. "The first thing I'd say is that the letters could be fake and I need my experts to analyze them."

"Let them try. It's just a delay tactic. But in the end, the letters will be admissible as evidence. The envelopes with the U.S. postmark are public records and an exception to the hearsay rule. The letters come in as recorded recollections," Alex explained as he displayed a mastery of the Texas rules of evidence.

"What's in the photos?"

"The wedding. The boy when he was a little baby. I'll also produce their birth records from the *registro civil* in Puebla and their marriage license and other documents."

"Are they authenticated?" Fetzer asked as he delved into a *machacado* and egg taco dripping with salsa. He was quickly getting some skin color, Alex had noticed.

"Yes, and I've also hired and listed an expert who will testify that this is the real McCoy and that all these documents can now be obtained through due diligence. Long gone are the days in Mexico when it would take you two to three months to obtain certified copies of government records."

"So, it would have been easy for Harrow to ascertain that the individual they were dealing with was a fake."

"Exactly," Alex said, excited. "Red flags should have gone up all over the place. Unless, of course, they purposefully stuck their heads in the sand."

"No jury is going to buy that," said Fetzer convincingly, drinking from his cup of coffee. "Not with this firm."

"I would think," Alex continued, "that the jury will think they were either too stupid not to notice, which we know they're not . . . I mean, Harrow recruits the brightest and sharpest talent from Harvard, Yale, and UT Austin to work for the firm . . . or the jury will say they were in it from the get-go."

"Plus," Fetzer added, now beginning to show traces of excitement, "it's a lawsuit against lawyers and their mega-firm, with hundreds of millions of assets. It reeks of greed, and lawyers already have a bad name. It makes for a sexy case. And if you pick a jury made up of people who live at, or under, the poverty line, then you could certainly hit a home run. On the one hand, you have poor Pilo, demanding justice from the grave. And on the other, you have greedy attorneys. I would think the jury will hate these guys. All in all, I think that the trial should not take longer than two weeks. If we get to the punitive damages phase, then I think that'll take an additional three days. So, two to three weeks total."

"So, we've got our work cut out ahead of us."

"As far as the trial presentation, yes. . . . "

"Other than that, Professor, the case is ready to go," Alex said with pride.

"Have you listed all your witnesses?"

"Yes."

"Are your trial exhibits ready?"

"Yes."

"Are your motions *in limine* ready?"

"Yes."

"Have you missed any deadlines?"

"No."

"Have motions for summary judgment been filed and argued? How about your responses?"

"They're still pending. The judge will hear us on announcement day, at the pretrial conference."

"Deadline for joinder of additional parties?"

"Fifteen days from today."

"What's the deadline to wrap up discovery and depositions?"

"Twenty days from the day of trial," said Alex.

Alex relished the exchange. It was just like in law school, and Fetzer had not lost any of his sharpness.

"I see you know the case inside and out," Fetzer said.

"My caseload has been quite small, so all the cases get a lot of attention," Alex replied, again with a prepared response.

"Well, your credit line has to be much larger than two hundred thousand dollars," Fetzer mumbled. "I just don't see how you've been making money in order to support this nice office and staff. Particularly if what you say is true, and you're being selective in the cases you pick and choose."

Alex began to feel uncomfortable with the direction the conversation was taking. He quickly changed the subject.

"I have my opening and closing arguments ready," he said. "Would you like to hear them?"

"I'll tell you what. Why don't you give me a tour of the courthouse, show me the battleground?"

"That sounds great," Alex said, somewhat relieved. He jumped to his feet and quickly dialed Romeo's extension.

"Romeo, please bring the truck to the curb. Professor Fetzer would like a tour of the courthouse."

"Right away," replied Romeo.

Chapter 26

THE CALLER SAID HE WAS LOOKING for Mr. del Fuerte on behalf of Paloma Yarrington. It was a personal phone call. Alex took it in the conference room, which he now thought of as the war room.

"Alejandro del Fuerte speaking. Who's calling?" said the attorney. *I guess Paloma couldn't handle the box of photos. I knew she'd come crawling back,* Alex was thinking.

"Alex," said Lieutenant Governor Yarrington, "what are you doing for lunch? Can you get away?"

"Lieutenant Governor! What a pleasant surprise," Alex said, biting his tongue. "It's good to talk to you."

"Likewise," the lieutenant governor said, cutting the pleasantries out. "I'd like to take you to lunch, bounce some ideas off you."

"I can't get away right now, Lieutenant Governor. I'm working on the Harrow litigation."

"Oh, I see. It's keeping you busy, eh?"

"Yeah, that's all I'm doing nowadays . . . you know, with the trial coming up in less than a month. The judge got us on the fast track. It's just around the corner."

"Well then, sounds like you're working too hard. Why don't you take a break?" insisted Yarrington. "C'mon, let me take you to lunch. Like the old days. Just you and me. We'll go to the Longhorn in San Benito, eat ribs, get messy, what do you say?"

Alex was in no mood to deal with his pressure tactics. But he had to admit, in the last six months he'd had no news of Paloma, and he was still a little curious. He wondered whether she was dating anyone new. Yes, things had gone downhill between them, but they'd shared some good times. After all, he'd known her since the seventh grade. They'd met at St. Ignatius Catholic School. Grandpa had sacrificed to send him there. That had been his parents' last wish.

"What time?" Alex asked, bowing his head after losing that round.

"Twelve-thirty. I'll be in the back room."

"I'll see you there, then," Alex replied as he hung up the phone. Boy, was he going to have a talk with Astrid, who had put the call through!

The Longhorn was the Valley's hot spot for barbecue. It sat right outside the San Benito city limits, in the middle of old man Williamson's land. The old barn had been converted into a restaurant, and people drove in from all over the Valley for the atmosphere, the ribs, and the banana pudding. Several years back, the restaurant, along with its pudding recipe, had even been featured in *Bon Appetit* magazine, the Best Bar-B-Que edition.

"Counselor," the lieutenant governor greeted him, smiling as he extended his hand to shake Alex's.

"Lieutenant Governor," the attorney replied, shaking hands.

"It's good to see you again, son. It's been what . . . six, eight months? Since law school graduation, right?"

"Yes, sir, you and your family were gracious enough to take me and my law school buddies to dinner. Remember, you took us out to Churrascos on Shepherd Drive?"

"How could I forget? The *puchero de camarón* was excellent!"

"Have you ordered anything?" Alex asked, trying to change the subject. Graduation dinner at Churrascos had started on a great note but had deteriorated when Yarrington, who had had one too many glasses of Chilean wine, started up with the lobby job offer. It was not a good topic. But for now, at least, he was safe. The Longhorn didn't serve alcohol.

"Just tea. I was waiting for you."

"Thanks," Alex said, "you didn't have to wait. I know you're a busy man."

"Never too busy for my future son-in-law," Yarrington said, "and never too late to try and mend fences, right? Like the Mexican saying goes, *mejor un mal arreglo que un buen pleito, ¿no?*"

"I hear you," Alex said, again wanting to change the subject. *Man! Where is he going with this?* Twice in the span of a minute, Yarrington had tried pushing his buttons.

"Are you ready to order?" interrupted the waitress.

"Yes," said Alex, jumping in ahead of the lieutenant governor, "I'll have a tea and the three-meat platter, extra barbecue sauce."

"I'll have the eighteen-ounce bone-in cowboy rib eye, medium rare, and a baked potato, dry."

"Sir," said the waitress, a little embarrassed, "we only have steaks at nighttime. Right now we're serving barbecue."

"Tell Bob, your manager, that it's for Lieutenant Governor Yarrington. He'll make it for me," Yarrington replied as he dismissed the waitress with a hand gesture. What the lieutenant governor wanted, the lieutenant governor got.

"So where were we?" he asked.

Alex sighed. "Mending fences? You were saying?"

"Ah, yes. Never too late to mend fences. Speaking of, did you know that I've been asked to support and help pass the Anti-Meritless Exposure and Gain Opportunity Bill, known as the AMEGO legislation?"

"What is it?"

"It's legislation designed to prevent attorneys from suing each other. It would cap the amount of damages one attorney could recover from the other and would apply retroactively to all pending litigation in the State of Texas. The committee studying the proposal is also recommending to shorten the statute of limitations to six months, instead of two years."

"Who's pushing for this?" Alex said angrily. The lieutenant governor had pushed yet another hot button. This bill could very well kill his lawsuit.

"Both houses. Everyone thinks it's a great idea. For the first time, both the Republican and Democratic leadership see eye to eye. You see, the legislature is made up of mostly lawyers, so this helps everybody. Not too mention the profession, which, I might add, has gotten a couple of black eyes lately."

"What kind of caps are we talking about?" Alex wanted to know.

"Ten thousand per incident, with a maximum of twenty thousand in the aggregate," Yarrington acknowledged.

"That's ridiculous! What happens to real victims? For example, the client who's left holding the bag because his attorney screwed up?" asked Alex.

"The same thing that happens to the victims of medical errors or medical negligence, as the plaintiff's Bar likes to call it. Nothing. They go away. Never to be heard from again," said Yarrington with a smile.

Alex felt that the lieutenant governor had him on the ropes. Maybe the legislator was exacting his revenge on him because he'd strung Paloma along for so long—six years, to be exact. Alex had heard Yarrington had ways of getting back at anyone who crossed him. It was just a matter of time. Sooner or later, he could find a way to ram a legislative bill down your throat and make you pay for it.

"Who's pushing for this, the insurance lobby?" Alex demanded to know.

"Who else? They have their hands in everything. You know how the game is played. Big money, big interests, big legislation, that's Austin for you."

"Since when do you care about what attorneys do to each other?" Alex said point-blank. "I would think you'd be happy letting them kill each other."

"You're right. My position was always to keep them at arm's length. Just monitor them and rein them in when needed to offer protection to small business. I also felt doctors and hospitals needed protection from frivolous lawsuits. That was especially true here in the Valley. And I coauthored legislation to achieve that." The lieutenant governor smiled as he relished his accomplishments.

"So, since when do you care if lawyers sue each other?" Alex said as he furiously pierced the jalapeno sausage on his plate. "What is it to you?"

"What is it to me, you ask? I'll tell you what it is to me! It becomes my problem when my future son-in-law is suing the second biggest firm in Texas . . . which also happens to be one of my biggest supporters and contributors."

"But they're plaintiffs' lawyers. They make their living suing big business," Alex said. He didn't understand.

"There's a subtle difference."

"What difference? How come you guys at the legislature can take money from them and turn around and protect doctors and hospitals? I don't get it," said Alex, wanting to finish the sentence with the words *you hypocrite*, but he just couldn't do it.

"See," Yarrington explained, "the product liability Bar and the asbestos-mesothelomia Bar contribute big, big money to both houses. So there is an unwritten rule or gentlemen's agreement, if you will, that we just don't tinker with their livelihoods. Besides, Ford, GM, Chevrolet, the big three, they're Delaware corporations. Those lawsuits don't affect the people of Texas. You just don't see the big guys packing it in and going home. That's the difference. When you guys sue doctors and hospitals, insurance gets so expensive that hospitals shut down and doctors leave the state. Now, that affects my constituents. And it's the same story with small business. As far as the auto manufacturers or asbestos producers are concerned . . . well, they can take a hit."

"I knew there was a catch to this impromptu lunch invitation," Alex snapped. "I should have known better. You don't give a damn about me, or your daughter, for that matter . . . all you care about is not upsetting your contributors." He was about to reach his melting point—and maybe even reach over and deck the lieutenant governor.

"That's bullshit!" Yarrington shot back. His cheeks were changing color and almost matched the tomato slices on his plate. "I don't want to see you be left holding the bag. Taking the fall for somebody else. I care about you. Paloma has nothing to do with this. I know you're your own man. I respect that. Sure, I don't like it, and I disagree with the fact that you don't let me help you. But I do respect the hell out of you."

"What would you know about taking the fall for somebody else, anyway?" Alex demanded.

"Look, Alex, I'm not an idiot. I suspect somebody is behind all of this. You couldn't possibly afford to develop a case like this on your own. C'mon! Just nine months ago Paloma was lending you money so you could eat while you studied for the bar," Yarrington reminded him. "And now you have a three-thousand-square-foot office, fully furnished and fully staffed in one of the most expensive rental districts in town. Where were we when you hit the lottery?"

"I don't have to explain shit to you!" Alex barked. At this rate they would surely end up in a fistfight.

"I've known you since you and Paloma were friends in the seventh grade," said Yarrington quietly as he looked down and played with his napkin. "I was always impressed by your independence and your determination. With all due respect, when both your parents died—in that rear-end collision between their Pinto and the eighteen-wheeler outside of Mexico City—we were all worried that you wouldn't bounce back. But you surprised the hell out of us all, and you pulled yourself together and finished high school in the top twenty-five percent. Then, when we all worried that you might not be able to afford college, again you showed us wrong. You waited tables, even tended bar, and paid your own way. And what I remember the most was when you and Paloma were seniors in high school working on the science project. Do you recall?"

"Yes."

"That day," Yarrington continued, "you happened to catch an article in some old newspaper that discussed how Ford Motor Company knew of design defects and other problems with its Pinto. Yet the car maker had decided to go ahead and sell the car anyway, putting profits before people. That day was the day you decided to become a lawyer. You even told my daughter. And I know this because she told me. In time, you went off to law school. And again, we worried that you wouldn't finish. We worried that you wouldn't have what it takes. After all, you were the first in your family to attend American schools. Hell, never in a million years did I dream you could even get into law school, much less graduate. I mean, you didn't have the luxury of a mom who was a judge or a dad who was partner in some fancy law firm somewhere. But again, you proved us wrong. Now, I must admit—when I heard you were graduating from law school—I always felt that you'd practice immigration law or international law. Never in a million years did I, or anybody else for that matter, imagine you would want to sue other lawyers—and some of my friends, at that."

"I didn't go out and deliberately choose this case, Lieutenant Governor! That's just the way things happened, and I will not walk away. *¿Me entiendes?* Do I make myself clear?" barked the young attorney.

"Am I interrupting?" said a man's voice behind Alex. "I just wanted to come over and say hi."

Alex was caught totally by surprise. He could feel the hair on the back of his neck rising.

"Judge Macallan!" the lieutenant governor said, getting up. "How the hell are you? It's good to see you! Do you care to join us?"

"Oh no, I couldn't . . . I'm expecting company over there," he said, pointing at his table at the other end of the barn.

"Sit down for a minute. I want you to meet a family friend. This is Alejandro del Fuerte, a young attorney who recently moved back into town," the lieutenant governor explained as he introduced the two men to each other.

"I've heard about you," said the judge as he firmly shook the young attorney's hand so hard it nearly hurt.

Is he trying to inflict pain on me? thought Alex. *Maybe send a message?*

"You need to come see me in chambers," the judge continued. "I'll give you some appointments."

"Will do, Judge," Alex said. "Thanks."

Alex thought the lunch was becoming like a scene out of a Fellini movie. The only thing that could top it would be for Chordelli and Harrow to show up together and come over to say hi. Or for Rigoberto Medina to show up, for that matter. The whole thing had to be a setup.

"All right, I'll leave you two alone," the judge said. "Lieutenant Governor, please call me to discuss the new proposed legislation. And if you need me to testify in committee in favor of

AMEGO, I'll gladly do it for you. You know where to reach me. Anything for you, Lieutenant Governor."

"Thanks, Walter," Yarrington said, "I'll call you on Monday."

"Nice meeting you, Alex," the judge said as he walked away.

"Alex," started Yarrington again, "I don't have to put that bill on the calendar. As a matter of fact, I don't give a rat's ass about that bill. If I want to, the bill will never be introduced or even make it out of committee. It will be dead, just like that."

"Why are you telling me this?"

"Look, I think I can get the boys from Harrow to settle with you. They don't want their names splashed all over the newspapers. They don't want the publicity. Whether it's true or not, that's irrelevant. Let's put an end to it. You could walk away with six figures, plus. I don't have to carry that stupid bill. Look, I might even be able to squeeze more money out of them. Two, three hundred K. That's not pocket change, Alex. Especially since you just passed the bar. And then, I promise, I'll get my friends up in Austin to send you work down here. You could be hired as local counsel for all kinds of different cases. Hell! My colleagues even get hired to obtain legislative continuances. You could make a decent living just getting hired to delay cases."

"I'm not a legislator, remember?"

"What I'm trying to say," Yarrington said as he cut into his steak, "is that I can help you make a ton of money. Good money. You won't starve. Who knows? Maybe you'll even renew your relationship with Paloma. Buy her a ring, get married."

"Good day, Lieutenant Governor," Alex said as he suddenly got up, ready to bolt out of the restaurant. "And don't call again!"

Chapter 27

THE MESSAGE ON ALEX'S DESK was written in Romeo's handwriting:

> *Jim Schlaeter, with Fiesta Pages Phone Book. Please Call 555.561.2800. Wants to know if you'd be interested in running an ad.*

The message had come in at 4:45 p.m.

After the lunch fiasco, Alex had driven out to the country to clear his head. The lieutenant governor's words were still resonating in his head: *Settle the case . . . Walk away . . . Why are you doing this?*

Alex sat down at his desk to review the day's messages. Astrid, Professor Fetzer, Betty, and Romeo were gone. He decided to return Schlaeter's call. He dialed the number, but there was no answer. Instead, the voice mail came on.

"Hello," the voice said, "this is Special Agent Jim Schlaeter with the FBI. I'm either away from my desk or on another call. Please leave your name and number where I can reach you. I'll return your call. Thanks."

Alex's heart started racing, and he felt like it was about to jump out of his chest. First the nasty encounter with Yarrington and now an FBI agent calling. What the heck? What exactly was going on? Whatever it was, it didn't sound good. Why would the FBI want to talk to him? Could it be that they wanted to keep an eye on the Harrow trial and maybe even bring racketeering charges against them? Lately, it seemed the feds were charging everyone with racketeering. Alex convinced himself that racketeering was what the agent's call was about, and he felt a little better. *This reminds me*, Alex made a mental note, *I have to set up a meeting with Chapa and BPD. I need to get on it.* Either way, he wouldn't call that number again. If the agent really wanted to talk to him, he would call again. Besides, it was better to wait for the agent to call. And then again, maybe it was nothing. There was no need to stir things up.

An email message from Mark with Sea Garden Marine indicated that Alex's fishing boat had been delivered to the dealer in Port Isabel and that it would be ready for pickup anytime after Wednesday. In an instant, the encounter with the lieutenant governor and the FBI agent's message were nothing but a distant memory. Alex was transported to the warm, shallow waters surrounding King's Island in the Laguna Madre and could see himself in his brand-new boat sneaking up on the schools of red fish. Stalking them. Casting for them. Fighting them as he reeled them in! It was all about presentation and placement. One by one they'd fall prey to his skill and his Flats Cat. After all, only serious anglers owned a Flats Cat. It was one of the few boats on the market made specifically to fish the flats, as the locals called the shallow water. It worked well in as little as six inches of water. The reds stood no chance. Turn off the engine, push off the pole, and sneak up to the big ones. There was nothing the reds could do when spotted from the casting deck. Alex couldn't wait to show off his Flats Cat to Professor Fetzer and Romeo. They were going to love it. *If Dad could only be here!* he thought.

He was dreaming of the bull reds when the newspaper on his desk caught his eye. The headline read, "More Questionable Cases Surface as Probe Intensifies." It was a list of cases handled by three of the biggest plaintiffs' firms in Texas in which all victims had been illegal aliens involved in rollover accidents along the border counties in Texas. Jesse Saunders, a tenacious reporter with the *Rio Grand Post*, had uncovered a number of other cases involving illegal aliens in which no relatives either in Mexico or the United States could be found. Yet the cases had settled for millions under confidential terms. Most of the files had been sealed by court order. The paper had had to sue to get the courts to unseal the files and make their contents available to the public.

The paper also ran some figures and estimated that in one year Harrow had collected, in jury verdicts alone, over $150 million. The settlements, on the other hand, topped the half-billion-dollar mark. Harrow had to be one of the most profitable firms in Texas. The only other law firm that was more profitable than the Corpus firm was San Antonio's own Holiday, Chordelli, Domecq & Flanegan. The story also suggested that there may have been other Texas firms filing and settling cases where no plaintiffs could be found. Was it a coincidence that the litigants appeared to have gone underground?

The story got Alex pumped up again. Newspaper headlines, whether good or bad, were always good publicity. And now the story was out there, in the court of public opinion, and the public was learning that Harrow may have been involved in many other similar cases along the border. All questionable cases. At least, that was what the paper suggested. People would be asking why the files had been sealed. Weren't the courts supposed to be public forums?

The investigation had revealed another interesting point. It appeared that in all of Harrow's cases dealing with child victims, the same guardian *ad litem* had been appointed to protect their legal interests. This raised another interesting issue. How come it was Lieutenant Governor Yarrington who'd received all those appointments, since he was not a lawyer? The article explained that the legislature had left a loophole in the law that allowed anyone to be appointed *ad litem* as long as the court determined the appointee was qualified. The article mentioned that at press time, the numerous calls that had been made to the lieutenant governor's office had gone unanswered. Were the judges in on it? the paper asked. Other politicos? How much money had the lieutenant governor made off of *ad litem* appointments? The whole thing didn't pass the smell test, and maybe Alex del Fuerte's lawsuit had some merit to it, after all. Maybe the Medina case was only the tip of the iceberg, the paper said.

Who was the *pendejo* now? That had been the way Yarrington always expressed disdain for his enemies. He loved the word and used it frequently when insulting others less fortunate than himself. The word meant "pubic hair" but was akin to "stupid jerk" or "dumbass." Even though Alex had never been called that by the lieutenant governor, at least not to his face, he was sure Yarrington had called him that behind his back. And now the newspaper article was suggesting the lieutenant governor's involvement in the matter was questionable and perhaps even in violation of the legislature's rules of ethics.

The Texas Ethics Commission had issued a statement that no public official was above the law and that it would look into the matter closely. How much compensation had Yarrington received for his work? Had he earned his fee? The few files that so far had been ordered unsealed showed that, in a period of a year, Yarrington had pocketed more than half a million dollars in *ad litem* fees.

The article spewed venom. Someone at the *Rio Grand Post* did not like Rene Yarrington. Alex thought of the Yarrington household. Right about now they were probably circling the wagons, talking strategy, and finding a way to put a lid on the latest attack. Paloma had always been the one who took it the worst any time her father had gotten bad press. The smallest criticism or innuendo was enough to send her into hysterics. Alex's relationship with her had suffered because of it, and he now wondered why he hadn't walked away from her sooner. Why had he stuck around for all those years? Did he think she was going to change?

Then he started thinking back over some of the better times they had had together. The few occasions when Paloma had come up to visit while he was in law school had been magical. What a difference it made to her, being away from her dad and the family, away from the voters and supporters, and away from the press and the public eye.

García's in Mexico had been the place. It was a place where the tough DWI laws of Texas had no meaning and where thirsty American teens could stretch their drinking dollars. It was famous for its dollar margaritas made with Everclear liquor and free *panchos*. The place had been witness to their budding romance. Paloma had come home one year for spring break and had gone drinking with friends at García's when Alex had run into her.

She had been so happy to see him that they soon ditched their respective friends and spent all night dancing together. By the end of the evening, their bodies pressed close together as they slow-danced to Luis Miguel. Love letters followed and weekend visits to her college campus at Texas A&M, without her parents suspecting a thing. The relationship had been kept secret from the family for almost two years.

Funny how, six years later, their relationship was a mess, and he was the legal profession's *persona non grata*. How things had changed in just a few years! There was only one thing left to do. He dialed the number.

"Hello?" Paloma answered.

"It's me, Alex. Can you talk?"

"Oh, I wasn't expecting you," said a startled Paloma. "Your number didn't show on my cell."

"I didn't want to leave any loose ends," he began, then cleared his throat. "And I know it's been a while since we've talked."

"There's nothing to talk about, Alex," she said, knowing where he was going. "Wouldn't it be better to leave things unsaid? Leave things as they are, and both of us just . . . move on? Go on with our lives and close this chapter?"

"I never thought it was going to get this complicated. I never saw it coming. I'm sorry."

"Don't feel bad, Alex. Things happen for a reason."

"Well, I won't pretend to understand what the reason is. But I will say this. I want you and your father to be happy."

"There we go again! Leave Dad out of this."

"Can we? Can we leave your dad out of this?"

"Look, Alex, I don't know why you called. But now that I've got you on the line, you must know this. I'm getting married. I'm getting married to Calvin Macallan, Judge Macallan's oldest son. The wedding is in two months."

"But . . . but he's at least fifteen years older than you," Alex said, surprised.

"I've already dated people my age," Paloma hissed back. "I don't need to waste any more time with immature fools. I need a man who knows what he wants. I need a man who wants me the way I am . . . family and all."

"So that was the family friend you traveled Europe with while I clerked down in Laredo that summer?"

"Yes! I'm sorry. I never told you."

That had been the summer from hell. She had wanted him to come home and clerk at Royston Chaney. He had picked the Laredo firm because they were a litigation boutique. In the end, the friction had been unbearable, just like Laredo in the summer, and the romance was put on hold. She had gone to Europe to clear her head.

After the breather, to her family's dismay, they'd managed to patch things up. And for the first time in several years, Alex had finally dropped hints of marriage. Yes, the lieutenant governor was still a thorn in their side, but maybe a grandkid or two would create enough of a distraction to keep him at bay. But no one could have predicted the effect the Harrow lawsuit was going to have on their relationship. It was the final nail in the coffin. They both knew it, and there was no way around it.

"I'm sorry I never told you about Calvin."

"It doesn't matter, Paloma. You and I know it's not Calvin. Calvin is a pretext. We both know the truth."

"Alex, there's no getting around it. You're smart and resourceful. But your downfall is that you are a *cabezudo*, too independent. Some would say maybe even too proud or headstrong. It's always your way or the highway! And you can't see a good thing, even when it's right there in front of you. Even if it begged you all night!"

"I don't want handouts. Why can't you and your father understand that?"

"What is wrong with getting a little help or having Dad open a few doors for you? I don't understand. That's his job as a public servant, helping his constituents."

"Look, I never told you this, but I guess now is as good a time as any. Growing up in Mexico, I saw what the *hueso* system did to my dad. He grew up having his friends throwing him a bone here and a bone there. Him and his buddies, that's all they could talk about: what they needed to do to position themselves to get the next bone. When his *compadre* got appointed to head the water utility district, Dad got a cushy job as treasurer. Then, when his childhood friend got elected mayor, Dad got appointed to head the city's tax collection department. It was always like that. Every few years, the opposition would get elected . . . and Dad would be out of a job. It was a struggle, and we went through some hard times. He would sell insurance, try his hand at farming, or even sell used cars, until the next *compadre* would take office. Then a close friend got elected to Congress."

"I know how the story ends, Alex," interrupted Paloma.

"No, you don't. You have no clue!"

"Do you think I'm an idiot or what? You're going to tell me that your dad got a juicy job again, and then things were all right for a while, and then things dried up. Like it always happens in Mexico. So what's new? That happens here in the States, too. It's not what you know, but who you know, Alex. Haven't you heard?"

"Let me finish! Then you can go back to your same old song and dance!"

"Ha! Song and dance! I do know this. Dad could have hooked you up, and we would have been all right. We could have had a nice life. But you chose to throw it all away."

"Whatever. Did you know that on their trip to visit Mr. Botti in Congress to hit him for a handout, that's when my parents were killed in the car wreck outside of Mexico City? I bet you never knew that was the reason my parents had gone to the capital."

"I never knew. This is the first time I've heard this."

"I will not take a handout. That's just the way it is."

"I hear you. But I still think you're making a big mistake," Paloma said.

"My loss, I guess."

"You guessed right. Goodbye, Alejandro. And listen, you won't get any sympathy from me. Oh! And one last thing . . . don't call again, and don't even think about showing up at my wedding!"

Chapter 28

THE MEETING SCHEDULED BY CHORDELLI was to take place at his firm's main conference room overlooking the river walk down below. It was the firm's calling card. Whenever big, million-dollar cases needed to be brought to fruition, they were mediated in the cash room, as the associates called it. It was intoxicating, and even the big boys from Titan Wheels, Smith-Johnson Pharmaceuticals, or the big three car manufacturers had been known to start throwing cash around once they loosened their ties and rolled up their sleeves as they worked through settlement conferences.

The wood paneling was gorgeous African rosewood, covered with expensive works of art. There were paintings by Botero, Serrot, Rivera, and even Tintoreto. The conference table for twenty-four had been cut out of a single large tree from the rain forest —a Brazilian *palo blanco*. The supple, exquisite Argentinean leather chairs still smelled new. The whole place reeked of success, power, and money—some would even say a little greed. Others would label it opulent. It was hard not to feel the effect.

"I called you in because I needed to update you on a little business opportunity that came up . . . something the firm is involved in. It's an incredible opportunity," said Jeff Chordelli as he stood near the window looking out over the river walk.

"You call it a business opportunity, I call it trouble," said Willy Hankins. "I've heard the rumors going around the Cameron County courthouse." He was sitting at the conference table drinking a Maker's Mark on the rocks and puffing away on an Arturo Puente Gran Reserva.

"Look, Willy," retorted Chordelli, "I don't know what you've heard, but I can guarantee you this. The kid doesn't suspect a thing. He bought my story hook, line, and sinker. All this time, I've had him believing Harrow was the devil and that Harrow set the whole thing up."

"I still don't like it," said Hankins. "Look, Jeff, you and I have been doing this long enough and have made a ton of money together. But when you allow a snot-nosed kid to first-chair a law-suit . . . it could very well blow up in our faces. It's risky. Besides, why couldn't you just let him sue Harrow on his own? I mean, hell . . . the old man found him, and he in turn found the file on his own. Who knows? Had we stayed away, maybe he would have done it on his own. Or just given up and quit."

"That's just it. We got involved, and then the kid continued to dig stuff up," Chordelli replied. "This way is better; at least we have some control over him. I don't think he would have just quit. You know . . . keep your friends close and your enemies closer."

"How do you know? Don't you think he would have gotten discouraged? I mean, his client died. With no client, why pursue the case?"

"Maybe," Chordelli replied, "but this kid is tenacious . . . he would have kept digging stuff up."

"You barely know the guy!" snapped Hankins. He got up and went to fetch another Maker's Mark. This time, he poured himself a double.

"Easy, Willy. It's not even twelve o'clock yet," the partner admonished him.

"Don't lecture me!" scowled Hankins.

"Look, I worked this thing out in my head. I know it will work. All we need is a little help with the dirty work, and Mr. del Fuerte is doing that for us. And in the process, we put out of business our biggest rivals. It's perfect."

"Perfect, my ass! One thing is to let him do it on his own and we watch from the sidelines, and another is to give him a hand. Even if he didn't win, it would still be okay. By then it's too late for Harrow, anyway; they've been dealt a public relations nightmare. No one will want to refer cases to them, and the Bar will watch them like a hawk. They're dead in the water, either way. But now you've got the firm involved, and that doesn't sit right with me."

"Look," Chordelli replied, "how long have you been running cases, Willy? Fifteen? Twenty? Thirty years?"

"Twenty-five."

"Well, you know what this business is like. You've seen it change. Competition is fierce. And then public opinion changes, and the clowns in Austin change the laws and screw with us! Even at the federal level, they're threatening national tort reform. Then it becomes tougher to make a buck! I don't have to tell you. How many of the big plaintiffs' firms are still around?"

"Five or so. Not many," snorted Hankins.

"Exactly! So, this way we take out the competition. It guarantees our survival for at least another ten years. We'll be the only game in town. The rest of the firms in Texas will have to refer their big, complex cases to us. We're the ones with the large bankroll, great trial lawyers, and impeccable record."

Willy was looking at his drink, digesting the partner's words. "I don't have a problem taking out the competition," he said slowly, not looking up. "I just don't think throwing money at a young attorney to do it for us is sensible. Since when do we pit young attorneys against one of the most successful firms in Texas . . . hell, in the nation? This is not the case to do it on. There are no safety valves."

"What do you mean, no safety valves? All the kid knows is what he already discovered on his own. The old man found him. Neither you nor I could have predicted that. So . . . he does some research and finds that somebody else filed a lawsuit and not his client, the real husband. Big deal! He knew that then! Then he stumbles upon the file and discovers that it was Harrow who filed the lawsuit. Nothing has changed."

"How can I be sure?" Hankins cried in a worried tone. He was already working on his third drink. "How can we be so sure this thing won't blow up in our faces?"

"You just have to trust me."

"I worked real hard to stay one step ahead of the state Bar," explained the case runner, sounding disappointed. "I've fought off other law firms trying to steal our clients. I even wrote my house representative asking him to vote against tort reform. And all for what? To have you and some punk screw everything up?"

"No one is going to screw anything up . . . not if we keep tabs on him."

"All those years honing our skills . . ." Hankins began as he slammed his drink down. "And for what?"

"Come again?"

"You know what I mean! All those years developing our network. Millions of dollars spent greasing the skids, setting up our networks in South Texas, Mexico, and South America. Training doctors and coroners to produce the most favorable reports. Showing them what to look for, what to put in their reports, how to submit their findings, how to testify, putting money in everyone's pockets . . . and now we're this close to giving it all away."

"Hey!" Chordelli screeched. "Give me a break! I taught you everything you know. When I first met you, you were chasing assholes with traffic citations. I taught you how to pick the good cases from the bad cases. And how to get the coroners to give us the right findings in the autopsy reports. I taught you how to get cops to change their police reports and fault the party with the most insurance. I taught you the concept of setting up the case from the beginning. If it wasn't for me, you would still be chasing traffic tickets!"

"The hell with you!" Hankins yelled as he got up and starting pacing back and forth. "I made you your first million. Did you forget that? Sure, you taught me that 'God is in the details,' but until the day we met, you were only handling fender benders! You could barely pay your bills, or have you forgotten? It was me who brought you the first wrongful death case worth millions. Have you forgotten the Hardwood case?"

"Which one was that?"

"Come on!" Hankins was standing by the window, looking out over San Antonio. "How quickly we forget. Remember the drunk girl who rear-ended the eighteen-wheeler properly parked on the road's shoulder? The one on FM 510."

"What about it?"

"What about it? What about it?" jeered Hankins. "I put you on the map with that case. It was your first multimillion dollar settlement. . . . I signed up the family of the drunk girl, even though the chick was completely at fault. And I bribed the driver to get him to say that he'd been parked on the shoulder without lights or hazards . . . and to add that his employer had not provided him even with emergency flares. I got him to stick with his testimony."

"Yes," Chordelli reminded him, "but I had to mortgage my house to come up with the hundred thousand for the driver's testimony. I came close to losing everything . . . even filing for bankruptcy."

"But," Hankins said, "you made out like a bandit."

"*We* made out like bandits," Chordelli reminded him. "We."

"I gave you the bankroll with that case," Hankins yelled, "for you to play in the big leagues. For you to have the ability to make whatever detail was needed, no matter how small, miraculously appear. That's how you made the Gayman Fisheries case. With the money from Hardwood, we were able to bribe the coroner to say that he had managed to find traces of the deadly chemicals in the lungs of the dead workers. With that case, you doubled your fortune. Thanks to my tweaking!"

"Don't worry," Chordelli interjected, switching topics, "nothing is going to happen. Besides, the state Bar has no teeth! Remember the one lawyer the Bar prosecuted and convicted?"

"Margoux?"

"Yes, that guy! The scum bucket hired lawyer friends of the judge, and the judge granted them a new trial. It was such a slap in the face to the D.A. that they got disgusted at the whole thing and just dropped the case. The guy still has the biggest yellow-page ad in the directory . . . and he's still in business, and everybody knows he runs cases."

"Well, I don't want to end up in front of the Bar . . . or the Texas Rangers, for that matter."

"I don't have to tell you," Chordelli replied, "but violating the rules of ethics is a joke when you think about it. We've tampered with evidence, bribed foreign officials . . . and you're worrying about the state Bar. Give me a break! Besides, the rules allow for us attorneys to advance money to the clients. It's perfectly legal."

"Are you sure the kid doesn't suspect a thing?" Hankins asked, wanting to be reassured.

"I told you," Chordelli reiterated, "all I told him was that we believed Harrow was manufacturing plaintiffs." He reached for a cigar from the humidor in the middle of the conference table. "He knows nothing else. And I told him nothing else! All we did was point him in the right direction . . . and away from us."

"What if he suspects us? Think about it! It doesn't make sense. A firm, out of the blue, gives me a ton of money to go sue a rival firm. Why would anybody want to do that? Why? Why me . . . why now? What's the motive? There's got to be a catch."

"Because it's competition! It's time to take them out. And he has the client who can prove that Harrow's case is a farce, remember? Of course, it helps that the kid is hungry, too, and wants to make a buck."

"*Had* the client, remember?" Willy corrected him. "Or did you forget that we put a number on him?"

"No one could have predicted that was going to happen. They were supposed to just rough him up a bit and order him to get the hell out of Brownsville and go back to Mexico," the partner said as he blew smoke rings. "A slight turn of events . . . some would call it the cost of doing business."

"What if he figures it out? Have you thought of that?"

"It won't happen. You and I are the only ones that know how Harrow came to file the Medina lawsuit. And neither you nor I are going to say a word. So how would he ever find out?"

"You and I? You and I? Listen to you!" growled Hankins as he pounded his fist on the desk and got close to Chordelli's face. "And what about Macallan? Did you forget about him?"

"Okay. So three of us know," the partner whispered, taking a swig out of a snifter half full of Louie XVIII cognac. "If the judge opened his mouth, that would signal his demise. And he won't do that."

"But my point is," Hankins explained in a hushed tone, "that you and I and the judge and Laura, your lover, know. So the circle keeps getting bigger. All it takes is for somebody to slip up, and by you getting behind that punk . . . it has the word 'disaster' written all over it."

"He isn't going to say anything . . . he signed a confidentiality agreement," the partner said matter-of-factly.

"You think your confidentiality agreement will mean anything when the feds get him in a room alone? I can't believe you still believe in fairy tales!"

"Why would the feds care?" asked Chordelli. "This has nothing to do with them!"

"Because people talk!" Hankins said. "For the past several months, people around the courthouse have been asking how is it that a baby lawyer is funding a mammoth lawsuit and supporting a large office. The feds are watching everything that goes on down there in the courthouse. Have you forgotten the string of scandals? What about the district clerk in Hidalgo County next door? The one that was taking bribes to backdate documents? And Sheriff Conrado Zapata? And JP Judge Ed Harris? Judges under federal investigation . . . even the D.A. was accused of employment discrimination! It's been one corruption scandal after another! Or have you forgotten how hot things have gotten down there?"

"So the kid has a sizable credit line at the bank," Chordelli said as he lit a second cigar, trying to downplay Hankins' concerns. He knew the risks. It was the nature of the business.

"No one will believe that!" continued Hankins. "What's he going to say when the feds ask him how he got a two-hundred-thousand-dollar credit line? Have you thought of that? Right out of law school? What is he going to say?" He was now working on his fourth glass of Kentucky whiskey. "The problem, the way I see it, is that you're up here in your glass castle and you no longer have your ear to the ground. While you're up here in your hundred-thousand-a-month penthouse, counting your millions, you've lost touch with reality. I, on the other hand, am down there in the trenches. I know what's going on, and I can read the writing on the wall. This protégé of yours will be our demise. I say we eliminate him."

"What are you talking about?" the partner barked. "That's all we need!"

"Why not? It won't be the first time. Besides, once he's gone, the lawsuit will be gone, and that will be the end of that. Close that chapter. The exposure is over."

"Don't be ridiculous!" Chordelli said as he poured himself a second glass of cognac. "Then you're opening a can of worms. First the client, then the attorney? Now we'll really end up the target of a criminal investigation. That's a no! We are not having this conversation. Got it? Besides, if he's gone, then Harrow walks. Right now is the perfect opportunity to finish them—crush them!"

"Since when do you care who we put a number on?"

"Every time you get high on whiskey, you get sloppy and start talking crap," the partner ordered. "We're not going there. End of story!"

"What about the retired law professor he's got working for him? Have you thought about that?" Hankins demanded.

"Think about what?" said Chordelli with a confused look. "I didn't know he had hired another lawyer. No one told me. We'll see about that!"

"That's exactly my point. You don't know him from Adam!" Hankins said as he ran his fingers through his oily white hair. "Did you know that this Fetzer guy used to be a federal prosecutor? Doesn't that concern you?"

"Should it?"

"Of course it should concern us!" Hankins yelled. "He used to prosecute white-collar crime—in particular, those involved in insurance fraud. I've checked him out. By the way, that was his specialty. Does that ring a bell? Rosario Medina? Insurance? Fraud? What if your boy and the professor get chummy, and the boy tells him of the arrangement . . . our involvement?"

"I don't think he'll do that," Chordelli answered, by now quite tired of Hankins' gloomy outlook.

"I don't know . . . but look! We never in a million years thought there was a husband out there. We searched and searched and searched, and nothing. But there he was! And then he shows up and starts asking questions. Then we never thought Macallan would leave the probate file unsealed, but he did. He dropped the ball. Now all we need is for Fetzer to smell a rat and figure it out!"

"Well, the judge did drop the ball on that one," Chordelli said, agreeing. "I had instructed him to order all companion cases to the civil case sealed. And either he forgot or he ordered it, but the attorneys at Harrow dropped the ball."

"No! If he ordered it sealed, the attorneys would have complied with the court order. That's not what happened, and you know it. He dropped the ball. Stop covering for the old bastard! And you . . . you should have made sure that never happened. For the kind of money we throw at him to keep him on the payroll, he should have known better. Remember, this isn't the first case we've done when the judge was involved in it. He's getting sloppy, and I bet you never called him on it."

"I think I may have mentioned it," Chordelli said.

"Mention it, my ass!" Hankins shouted, by now very high on alcohol and almost slurring his words. "Next time we put a case together like the Medina case, I'll handle everything. I didn't bust my chops to put your firm on the map with big cases so that some smooth idiot can come ruin the whole thing. And by the way, you can bet your ass I'll have a word with the judge!"

"You will do no such thing."

"Watch me!" snapped Hankins. "We spent hundreds of thousands of dollars keeping the district clerk happy to make sure the cases land in Macallan's court, and then the judge himself screws them up!"

"Keep it down, Willy!" demanded Chordelli. "That's enough!"

"Well, your boy . . . he better not screw up, or we'll all go down," said Willy Hankins, the most famous case runner in South Texas.

"I'm keeping tabs on him. This way I can make sure the job is done right and he has enough support to sink Harrow once and for all."

"What if he figures it out?" Hankins asked, truly worried. "What if he suspects something?"

"That," Chordelli replied, "will never happen. And if it does, I'll be the first to know, remember? That's why I decided to get involved. This way I keep him on a leash. A preemptive strike, if you wish. There won't be any other surprises."

"I hope you're right, Jeff. In my twenty-five years, I've never found myself in front of a grand jury and I've never been investigated by law enforcement because I've always covered my tracks. In the hundreds of cases that I've run, there was never a direct link back to me or the attorneys. I'd hate to start now."

"Don't worry about it," Chordelli said as he finished his snifter of Louis XVIII. "You have nothing to fear."

"I gotta go!" announced Hankins. "I've had enough of your bull." He stormed out of the room.

Chapter 29

LAS BRASAS GRILL AND CANTINA was owned by the Martinez family. Originally from Mexico City, the whole family had migrated north thirty years ago. The restaurant was a staple in Brownsville and the locals' favorite spot for authentic Mexican food. Las Brasas' breakfast was the best in the Valley. Alex had visited the restaurant even as a child with his parents and Grandpa. It had been the family's favorite place to get together on Saturday mornings, share the week's ups and downs, and eat the restaurant's famous *machacado · con huevo*. The locals joked that the flour tortillas were so big and wonderful that one could use them as a poncho for cover on a cold winter's day.

After saying his goodbyes to Paloma Yarrington the night before, Alex had stopped on his way home at the Brown Pelican for a few beers. Unfortunately, he had drunk one too many, and he was now paying the price. Luckily, he'd never met a hangover that couldn't succumb to a spicy bowl of Las Brasas *menudo*. It was a hangover antidote.

He pulled into the packed parking lot. It was Saturday, a day when the folks from across the border also came to sample the restaurant's specialties. It took him a few minutes to find a parking space, and then he went inside and found a small table in a corner. He sat down and waited for the waitress. In the meantime, he wanted to clear his head, forget about the previous night's conversation with Paloma and then go to the office to get some work done.

"May I take your order?" said the waitress. She wore a name tag that read, *My name is Cruz.*

"Yes, please, let me have the *huevos rancheros*, with a double slab of ham on the side and a small *menudo*."

"Corn or flour?" she asked.

"Flour."

"To drink?"

"Black coffee and a glass of ice water."

"Would you like the beans *refritos* or *charros*?"

"*Refritos*, please."

"Be right out."

After the waitress left, Alex went back to his thoughts. He wondered when Paloma had decided to marry that putz. Why had he been the last to know? The wedding had her father's signature all over it. He was sure it was Daddy who had arranged the whole thing. Yeah, marry a Macallan, run around in the power circles, and create profitable alliances. How else could anybody explain the marriage? He now remembered Yarrington talking about some guy named Calvin who wanted to make Paloma's acquaintance. He vaguely remembered the details. The exchange between Paloma and her father had happened during brunch with the Yarringtons at Rancho del Cielo Country Club years ago. He now made the connection.

The coffee and water arrived, along with a basketful of warm tortilla chips and a small *molcajete* filled with spicy salsa.

The food arrived soon after, and Alex dove right in. It was magical. In an instant, his problems had become manageable. He had very few cares in the world. Paloma and her father could go to hell. Her groom, little boy Macallan, was in for a big surprise. And the Harrow boys were about to have a "come to Jesus" reckoning. Alex was thinking of all this when he was suddenly interrupted.

"May I join you?" asked a young man as he discreetly flashed a badge from under the jacket of his red Adidas running suit.

"What do you want?" Alex responded, somewhat surprised. He didn't want his food to get cold.

"Jim Schlaeter, FBI," said the clean-cut agent.

"I'm eating. Can't this wait?"

"I won't take much of your time. May I sit down?" asked the special agent.

"Suit yourself. You have five minutes."

"Listen," started the agent as he leaned closer to the young attorney, "for the last five years I've been working on some insurance fraud cases. I have reason to believe you might be on to something . . . I mean, with your lawsuit against Harrow and all."

"I plan to expose them, if that's what you're talking about," Alex countered, trying a spoonful of steamy *menudo*.

"Would you mind sharing information with us?"

"No need to do that. You know very well that court files are public record. Go to the courthouse, read the file, make copies, I don't care!"

"That's not what I meant," explained the agent.

"Well then, get to the point."

"It seems that you think that Harrow manufactured the plaintiff to bring forth the lawsuit."

"Isn't that what happened?" Alex asked, somewhat surprised by the agent's explanation. Did this mean his whole theory of the case was wrong?

"We used to think the same. At first, the guys in my antifraud task force thought that Harrow had simply found the case, but then we realized that maybe the fake worked alone. Maybe he's done this before. Maybe he finds cases like the Medina case on the Internet. Looks for relatives, and if there's no one there, he creates an identity and plays the role. He walks away rich."

"And?" Alex asked, wanting to know more but trying not to appear too eager.

"Well, then we investigated, put some wiretaps here and there, and talked to some people, and . . . nothing. We came away thinking that Harrow had no reason to suspect anything unusual and believed, in good faith, that they had a good client."

"What about the client? Did you ever find him?" asked Alex.

"Rigoberto Medina?" asked the agent.

"Yes, him."

"We didn't get much cooperation from the Mexican authorities. However, the little information that we were able to obtain was sketchy. We believe the guy has done lawsuits up and down the border posing as the father, or spouse, even a son. He's a chameleon."

"Sure," said Alex, "but I believe it had to be Harrow. Who else?" He had to admit, the agent had gotten him thinking. Could it be that he had it all wrong?

"We're not so sure," the agent said. "There might be others out there."

"So?" Alex asked. "How does any of this concern me?"

"Well, you're suing them, and we thought maybe you knew something we didn't know. Maybe we missed something."

"The bottom line," said Alex, thinking on his feet and at the same time trying to get rid of the agent, "is that my guy is the real guy. I can prove it. So we sue and make Harrow give the money back. Who cares about good faith? If your guy was a fake, then that's your problem. In the meantime, disgorge and give the money back to my client's estate. You had the wrong client. That's your problem. Too bad!" He was not about to give the agent any other explanation. Certainly, he couldn't tell him what he knew from Chordelli.

"We want to get this guy. I've been after him for years now."

"Well?" replied Alex, trying to send the agent away. "You and I are after two completely different things. You're chasing a fake who spends his time defrauding insurance companies, and I'm suing Harrow to get them to give back the money because, in my opinion, they knew they were dealing with a fake. In the end it won't matter, because Harrow still has to disgorge the fee."

"Let me tell you a little story," the agent said as he reached for a chip and scooped up some salsa. "Nine or ten years ago I was hot on the trail of a hotshot attorney who was rumored to have the largest organization of case runners all along the Texas border. At that time, I was working for the Texas Rangers."

"Why are you telling me this? I don't care," Alex said, somewhat exasperated.

"Hear me out. I'm almost done," said Schlaeter as he dipped another chip in the salsa bowl. Salsa was dripping from the side of his mouth. "So, as I present my findings to my supervisor and ask to send the file to the D.A. in Starr County, I get assigned to another division."

"Well, there you go, stuff happens," Alex said without facing the agent. He was busy working on his food. Maybe the agent would get the message and just leave. At least, that was the idea. Besides, he didn't need to talk to him. He knew his rights.

"Later on, I come to find out the guy is very well connected in Austin," the agent continued as he waved at the waitress to bring him more chips and salsa. "And his friends in Austin are covering for him. Apparently, the guy is a big campaign contributor and has given millions away to Republican state senators and representatives."

"Isn't that always the case?" Alex said, rolling his eyes. "Why didn't you just call it a day and move on? *Vámonos*, case closed. Life is too short, no?" Alex was waving at the waitress to get her to bring him his tab. He'd had enough of the agent. The meeting was over.

"You don't want to know the guy's name?" the agent said as he reached for Alex's arm to stop him from getting up.

"No. It's none of my business," Alex replied.

"If you say so," said the agent, "but I'll tell you anyway. His name was Jeff Chordelli. Does it ring a bell?"

They stared at each other in silence for a few seconds, the agent still hanging on to Alex's arm. Alex could hear the name going round in slow motion in his head, J-E-F-F C-H-O-R-D-E-L-L-I, but yet needed to pretend he'd never heard of the guy.

"It sure doesn't," he said as he pulled his arm away and threw a ten on the table.

"Anyway, I figured you'd heard of him. I'd almost given up on the case until I heard that the Harrow case down here might be connected to the fake or Chordelli. So, since I'm with the FBI now, I asked for permission to dig into the old case. Unfortunately, people in Washington are now running interference for this guy. It had to happen, I mean his firm in San Antonio has donated over ten million dollars to the president's reelection campaign. As always, a lot of doors have slammed shut."

"Well, I wish I could help you. But you know as much about the case as I do. Sorry you wasted your time," Alex said as he tried to make his way to the door.

"Wait, Mr. del Fuerte," the agent said as he pushed something into Alex's hand. "Here's my card, call me if you hear anything. Or take me fishing with you, next time you get to go."

"Right!" Alex said, quite disgusted. "That'll be the day."

On Saturdays the office was usually quiet. That was the day when Alex could go in and get some work done. No phone calls, no questions, no distractions. Unfortunately, although he would never admit it, the meeting with Agent Schlaeter had rattled him. It was extremely difficult to concentrate, much less get anything done. He reached for a beer from the office cooler and went and sat down at his desk in the semi-dark room. He needed it. First Paloma, and now the FBI. What next?

He was worried. Did Schlaeter know about his meeting with Chordelli aboard the *Magillu*? Their plan? The money? What if the agent was right, and Harrow had nothing to do with fabricating the lawsuit? What if they too had been set up? Was Chordelli setting him up as well, to take the hit? But why? For what reason? And what if they tagged him with Pilo's murder? Having the FBI snooping around was not good.

It sure sounded like Schlaeter had his number. Why else would he have mentioned the fishing trip invitation? That had to be it! Or was he just saying that because Alex had recently bought himself a Flats Cat? Did he know about his fishing boat? What else did he know?

Alex picked up his cell phone and stepped outside his office to the private courtyard. He dialed a number in Matamoros. It was no use making the call on a hard line. Maybe the telephone lines were tapped. At this point, anything was possible. The cell phone rang about ten times until somebody picked up.

"*¿Bueno?*" said the voice at the end of the line.

"Grandpa, it's me, Alex," said Alex as he took his last swig of the Negra Modelo Especial.

"*Dime,*" said Grandpa, sounding excited, "to what do I owe the pleasure?"

"Are you going to be at the house?" Alex asked.

"Yes, *m'ijo*, I'll be here all day. Are you coming?"

"Yes. I'd like to take you to Portales, if that's all right with you. Have some *cabrito.*"

"How wonderful I get to see you again, so soon. Maybe you can spend more time now. Like the old days?" asked Grandpa. Those had been some happy times. Every Sunday, after mass, the whole family, including young Alex, had paid a visit to Portales in Matamoros. It was famous for its *cabrito al pastor*. But since Alex's parents had died, the old man hadn't gone back to the place.

"*Así mero*, Grandpa," Alex answered, "just like in the old days. I think it will do us both good."

"I can't wait until you get here," the old man said in a delighted tone. "Is everything okay?"

"We'll talk when I see you."

"I've been reading about you in the paper. You make me so proud, Alex. I'm sure your mom and dad are watching from heaven."

There was a long silence.

"Okay, Grandpa," Alex said, breaking the uncomfortable silence, "so I'll pick you up at two. . . . Is that all right?"

"I'll be ready, then."

"*Bueno*, I'll see you at two o'clock."

"*Muy bien*," Grandpa said and hung up the phone.

Grandpa's home in Matamoros had been built in the 1930s with the hacienda look and feel in mind. It had the requisite water fountain in the middle of the courtyard. There were avocado trees, pomegranates, guavas, and overflowing bougainvilleas. Grandpa had built the house himself after his honeymoon stay at Hernan Cortez's Hacienda Encantada in Cuernavaca. It was a trip that he relished reliving and retelling, as long as he had an audience.

Alex had lived off and on at his grandfather's house since Dad had stood in the unemployment line more than once. Alex was looking forward to lunch with Grandpa.

The young attorney pulled the cord to the bell at the front door, announcing his arrival. After a few minutes, Grandpa finally managed to get the door open.

"¡*M'ijo!*" exclaimed the old man, "how are you?"

"I'm doing all right, Grandpa," replied Alex. "How about you?"

"Please, please come on in. I just have to get my coat and my hat, and we'll leave in a minute."

"Lots of stuff going on, Grandpa. Paloma and I are no longer a number."

"I never told you this," Grandpa shouted from his room as he continued to search for his coat and hat, "but that girl came with a lot of baggage. And I don't mean her own. I mean her father's. He was going to be a thorn in your side. *Mejor así.* You know what they say: *Más vale solo que mal acompañado.* Better to be on your own than surrounded by terrible company."

"I hear you. We could never get past the dad factor. I was always going to have to compete with him," Alex answered as he looked around the house. It was as if time had stood still. Everything was in the same place, as always.

"It still hurts, doesn't it?" asked Grandpa.

"*Un poco,*" admitted Alex. "It's disappointing. I mean, we've known each other since the seventh grade. You kind of get used to that other person."

"*Dímelo a mí,*" Grandpa agreed. He was now digging for the house keys inside the desk in the living room. "I was married to your grandmother for fifty years. And to this day, I still miss her."

"I guess that's the way it is."

"I can still remember our honeymoon in Cuernavaca as if it was yesterday," Grandpa started.

Alex interrupted him, not wanting to hear the story about the honeymoon again. "So what have you been reading about me in the paper?"

"Oh, yeah, yeah," Grandpa now remembered, "I saw the article about you and your old law professor taking on a giant law firm. How's that going?"

"Good, I guess. We're going to trial in a month or so. That's why I've been so busy, getting the practice up and running, training people, getting everybody up to speed and stuff." Alex shrugged his shoulders. "You know, just busy."

"Are you worried about losing the trial?" Grandpa asked. He was now trying to find his reading glasses in the kitchen. "I don't know how you can get up and argue in front of a jury, without getting nervous. When I practiced law, many, many years ago, I'd always get nervous the night before I had to go to *tribunales* and argue in front of a judge. And that was just one judge. That's why I ended up giving up litigation work and became a Notario Público. You lawyers in the United States have to face a jury. Now that has to be nerve-wracking."

"Honestly . . . yes, I am worried. There's a lot at stake here," Alex mumbled, "things you couldn't even imagine."

"Try me," Grandpa said lovingly as he stood there in front of his only grandson. He'd finally found the things he was looking for. It had taken him thirty minutes. But he'd finally gathered his coat, hat, keys, reading glasses, and a pair of indispensable white handkerchiefs with the words *C. del Fuerte* embroidered on them.

"I'll tell you over lunch. Are you ready to go?"

"I'm ready," Grandpa replied.

"*Bueno, vámonos,*" Alex said as he led Grandpa by the arm and out the door.

Chapter 30

Los Portales was the place in Matamoros for *cabrito al pastor* and *carnes asadas* cooked over the open flame on mesquite charcoal. The restaurant's trademark was to serve the cuts of meat piled high on sizzling hibachi grills brought out to the diners' own tables. *Cabrito, fajitas, chuletón, agujas, costillas*, grilled onions, peppers, and *nopalitos*, grilled just right. The guests sang loudly along with the restaurant's Mariachi band while waiters went from table to table offering free tequila shots. The gringos and the Mexicans were united by food, drink, and music. It was a sight to see.

"When would you like to come and see my office, Grandpa?" said Alex as he took a sip out of an ice-cold Bohemia beer.

"Anytime. Just give me an hour's notice before you come pick me up."

"Maybe next week would be a good time. Tuesday or Wednesday."

"Sounds good," said the old man as he struggled with his enormous *chuletón*.

"Good. I would also like you to meet Professor Fetzer. He decided to come out of retirement and come down and help try this case."

"That's what I read," Grandpa said.

"Yes, he went through a divorce and then became ill. The loneliness, coupled with retirement, was doing nothing for his health. So I invited him to jump back in, come down here and get some fresh Gulf air."

"And he likes it down here?"

"*¡Claro!*" replied Alex. "And he's taken up fishing, too. He loves it!"

"Once you get hooked on fishing, it's hard to give it up," Grandpa said. "I should know. The only time your grandma and I ever fought was over my spending entirely too much time fishing."

"I never saw you and Grandma fight."

"Oh yeah, once your father got older and he became my fishing buddy, we were never home on weekends. From November through April, until the bull reds stopped running, César and I were gone every weekend. God, how I miss those days!"

Grandpa motioned to the waiter to come over. He was now in the mood to do one tequila shot. He also wanted a beer chaser.

"Grandpa," Alex asked, "are you sure it's okay to mix liquor with the medications you're taking?"

"I'll be all right. A drink once in a blue moon never killed anyone. Besides, today we're celebrating your big case. *M'ijo*, you remind me so much of your father. I'm glad you decided to work close by."

"I'm glad to be close, too, Grandpa," said Alex as he raised his tequila shot and drank it.

"To your dad and your mom's memory. May they glow with pride for their son and his accomplishments. *¡Salud!*" said Grandpa as he raised his shot glass. "To the biggest jury verdict Cameron County has ever seen!"

"*¡Salud!*" echoed Alex, and with that, grandfather and grandson downed their shots. A bottle of Cofradía Centenario tequila frozen in a block of ice was now sitting at the table. It was another distinct way of serving tequila and was first introduced to the rest of the world courtesy of Portales.

"*¡Ajúúúúa!*" shouted Grandpa. "That went down smooth. Let's do another one!"

"Easy, old man," said Alex, "slow down. Maybe we'll do another one after dinner." He'd never seen him this happy and so eager to throw back more tequila.

"So what's on your mind?" asked Grandpa as he put another small piece of meat in his mouth.

"Lots of things," Alex said, not really knowing where to start. The mariachis in the background were now playing "*Sabor a mí*," grandpa's favorite love ballad. He claimed it reminded him of the love of his life, grandma. Curiously enough, it was also Alex's favorite love song.

"*¿Entonces?*" Grandpa said over the loud mariachi music. "So, what's going on with you, *m'ijo*? Is it money problems? Work? A girl?"

"It's work."

"Work? What can be so bad about work?" asked Grandpa.

"I don't understand why everybody is trying to dissuade me from taking the Medina case to trial."

"Who is everybody?" Grandpa asked as he cleared his throat and put a grilled serrano pepper down. All the food and drink was getting the better of him. Beads of sweat were forming on his forehead.

"Yarrington, his friends, judges, people around the courthouse."

"Well, maybe you stumbled onto something. It obviously has generated some interest. Answer me this," said the grandfather. "Are you financing it?"

"That's just it. Have I told you how I came upon the case?" Alex said as he took a swig of beer.

"No. But we've got all day. I'm with you, so I'm not going anywhere. *Dime, ándale.*"

"It was the day when I was moving into the office building where I had my first office."

"You're already on your second office?" Grandpa interrupted. He sounded amazed.

"My first one got ransacked. That's what I'm telling you . . . this whole thing is very strange. I don't know what to make of it."

"*Bien*, go on."

"So, I'm driving up to my office, and there's this old man sitting on the curb down the street. He is disheveled and frantic. I invite him to come in," explained Alex as he squeezed more lime in his beer, "and he tells me that he's here illegally, that he had to come to search for his wife and kid. Apparently the wife had been working for somebody in Brownsville, but then she stopped writing. Not knowing anything got the better of him, and he came searching for them."

"Then what happened? Did you do the Christian thing? Did you agree to help him?"

Alex motioned the waiter to bring another beer. "I hate to admit it," he continued, "but at first I didn't want to. I didn't think I could help him, and he had no money to hire me. So my intentions were to send him away, and I did. Then, just like that, something inside of me told me to help him. I practically had to chase him down the street and ask him to come back to the office."

"I was the same way when I practiced law," Grandpa said. "There were times when I just couldn't say no. And sometimes you just can't help everybody. Well, I am glad you chose to help this poor soul. And then?"

"So the old man—I come to find out his name is Pilo and he happens to have another daughter named María Luisa who lives in Mexico City—hands me an envelope with an address where he thinks his wife might be working. I find the number and call. The lady who answers the phone seems surprised and hangs up on me. Then I call another number he gave me. I dialed the aunt, a lady named Aurora López , who apparently placed the wife or got her the job with the family." He paused. "Are you ready for this? Can you guess what happens next?"

"No. What happened?" the old man asked with eyes wide open. "But first, can I have another tequila?"

"What the heck," Alex said, giving in, "but only half a shot."

"Okay, go on," Grandpa motioned as he salted his fist and squeezed a lime wedge in his mouth. Down went the shot.

"Both the wife and the child are dead."

"No!"

"Yes."

"How did it happen?"

"*Carreterazo*," gestured Alex with his hands, "tire blowout, and then the van they were in rolled over several times."

"That's sad. How did the old man take it?"

Alex paused. He turned away, embarrassed and ashamed. Pilo had deserved to know. Wasn't that his job? To find out and tell the old man what had happened to his wife and kid? And yet he could never bring himself to tell him. "I didn't have a chance to tell him. I wanted to. I thought that he should know, but I didn't have a chance to tell him."

"What do you mean, you didn't have a chance to tell him?"

"The old man was murdered," Alex whispered. "Somebody killed my client."

"You're making this up, right?" the old man asked. "*Puro cuento, ¿verdad*? You're pulling my leg, right?"

"*Ojalá*, I wish I was. But it's the truth," the young lawyer said.

"*Pero*, how can that be . . .?"

"A week or so after our initial meeting, Pilo was found dead in his hotel room, murdered execution-style. He died of a gunshot wound to the back of his head."

"I'm confused."

"I know it sounds unbelievable. But bear with me . . . I need you to listen," Alex requested.

"The wife's dead! The child's dead! And now the client's dead, too! How can that be? Who's next, you?"

"I hope not. But listen. After I started asking questions to see if there was a death certificate, I found a probate file, which in turn led me to another file. It turns out somebody had filed a wrongful death lawsuit. This somebody collected millions in a suit against Ford and Firelazer Tires. The impostor stepped in and filed a lawsuit pretending to be my client." Alex paused and took another swig of beer. "Then I ran into this bail bondsman who tells me that everybody is running cases, and he wants me to work with him. He tells me that the Corpus Christi firm that filed the lawsuit involving my client's wife and child are known to run cases all over South Texas."

"So he opened your eyes, eh? Welcome aboard," Grandpa said, disgusted. "That's what I hated about the profession. That even went on in Mexico."

"Really?"

"Oh yeah, and not just the legal profession. Did you know that even funeral homes in Mexico run the corpses?"

"Come again?"

"Sure. The funeral homes have people on the payroll to lay claim to the bodies first. Once the body is being prepped, the family is stuck and has to pay that particular funeral home . . . or else."

"Or else? What do you mean?" asked Alex.

"Or else the body isn't sent to the cemetery for burial. That corpse won't leave until everything has been paid. Trust me, someone usually pays. Corpses translate to money."

"What a racket. I had no idea," Alex said as he took a bite of *cabrito*. "Well, let me tell you, I started putting the pieces together." Alex paused to see if Grandpa was paying attention. "And next thing, I'm being proposed to run cases. Putting pressure on me to join, or asked to purchase cases brought in by case runners. Putting pressure on me to join, but then never be able to leave, you know. Like the Mafia. You start working with scumbags running cases and then what? Next thing you know you're caught on tape bribing a judge. Or worse yet, you stage a little accident where someone gets killed in order to sue and collect."

"Someone is trying to bait you," Grandpa added, "that's what I think. Once you join, you're one of them. So, if you had the goods on them, now they also have the goods on you. Then you'll keep quiet. *¡Fácil!* They got you by the short hairs!"

"But how did they know I had the client or where to find him, for that matter?"

"*Fácil,*" the old man said, "it's easy. Once you started snooping around the courthouse, somebody alerted the guys who filed the lawsuit. These guys have eyes and ears everywhere. They got clerks on their payroll."

"Well, now that you mention it, I did ask the clerk about the companion wrongful death case in Macallan's court. But it was off-limits . . . under seal."

"There you go. That's your answer," Grandpa said, grinning as if he had solved the mystery. "Someone told the judge that you were snooping around, and they started watching you. Whoever 'they' might be. I would bet it's the firm that filed the suit. One and the same."

"That's what I would have thought," said Alex as he poured himself another shot of Centenario. "But wait. Now the story gets really weird. You're not going to believe this. Remember you asked about financing the lawsuit I filed?"

"Sí, and . . . ?" said the old man as he reached for the *agujitas* on the hibachi grill. "Oh! before I forget, I read about Paloma and Macallan's kid's engagement in the paper. I would have never guessed."

"I know. The whole thing makes me sick," Alex replied as he downed his tequila shot followed by more beer. "Talk about kicking a man when he's down."

"*Y luego.*" Grandfather cut him short; it was better not to go there. Especially now that the tequila was having its effect on his grandson and the mariachis were playing "*El reloj*" in the background. "So then what happened?"

"I got this mysterious envelope with copies of the pleadings from the sealed file. Someone slipped it under my office door."

"Like they wanted you to have it?" Grandpa asked. "Sort of helping you so that you keep on with your digging for answers. Maybe uncover the whole thing."

"Yep, and then I get invited to meet the person that sent it. A guy named Chordelli, he wants to talk business."

"*Pero, ¿cómo?* What kind of business?"

Alex went on, explaining excitedly, "You see, the firm from Corpus that filed the case and this guy Chordelli's law firm—a mega outfit from San Antonio—have been having a turf war for the last few years. They're both trying to control the Valley and the Texas-Mexico border. There's billions and billions of dollars in fees to be made from product liability cases. So, the guy tells me that they want to help me bring down the Corpus Christi firm."

"And?"

"Well," the young attorney continued, "he then explained that this Corpus Christi firm is known for running tons of cases down in the Valley, but that recently he began to suspect that the boys from Corpus had the Medina lawsuit manufactured. The Corpus firm brought in somebody to play the part of the husband and father. Then they sued in Cameron County, and the county's jury pool, being what it is, forced the defendants to settle for an undisclosed amount. Probably tens of millions."

"And what does any of this have to do with you?" Grandpa asked.

"Chordelli somehow knew that my client was the real deal," Alex said, clearing his throat as he motioned the waiter to bring him a pack of cigarettes. He had no idea how the old man was going to react. He needed a cigarette.

"How did he know you had the client?" asked Grandpa.

"He knew! He just knew. . . . So . . . are you ready for this?"

"He offers to finance the lawsuit?" Grandpa answered, as if he'd lived this same scene before. Déjà vu. Seventy-eight years had not been wasted on the old man.

"Yep."

"You told him no, right?" Grandpa sighed and nodded his head as if he already knew the answer.

"No," an embarrassed Alex replied. "I wasn't able to say no." He lit a cigarette and took a long draw, blowing the smoke away from Grandpa.

"You couldn't say no? Why would you want to sue other lawyers? In my day, that was a clear no-no. Why would you want to be a pawn in his chess game?"

"I was going to have to sue them anyway to find out how they came upon the lawsuit," the young lawyer tried to explain.

"No! You were supposed to find out what happened to the wife and kid and simply tell your client," Grandpa scolded him. "That was your job! Or did you forget?" The old man motioned to the waiter to come clear his plate and bring him some coffee.

"Well, I guess you're right, if you put it that way," Alex acquiesced and fell silent, a bit embarrassed. Although it was hard to come clean, he needed to tell his grandfather. He hadn't been able to tell anyone else. Not Romeo. Not Fetzer. No one. And the whole thing was eating him up inside. Was he really doing this on principle, to get the answers that Pilo should have received? Or had it been Chordelli's money? He wondered whether he was any different from the guys running cases and why he was still in the case.

"Of course, I'm right!" the old man snapped as he poured milk in his coffee. "Your job was to find his family's whereabouts. That was it!"

"In my defense," countered Alex, "let me say this. How could I have told him anything if he was dead?"

"Then, the guy is dead. And your job ends. Simple," admonished Grandpa. "You move on to the next case."

"But I couldn't just sit there and do nothing. Besides, if I didn't file a lawsuit, I would have never gotten to the bottom of things. All Pilo and I would have known was that the family had died in an accident and somebody filed a lawsuit. He deserved more than that."

"Have you asked yourself why Chordelli is throwing money at you? Have you?"

"Yes. I've gone over it in my head, not one but hundreds of times. Why? Why? The only plausible explanation is that they don't want to get their hands dirty, and it's a business decision. Take the competition out and rake in billions."

"How much money did they pay you?" asked the old man.

"Two million plus."

"That much!" Grandpa said, amazed. "No wonder you're going through with it. That explains a lot." Grandpa was shaking his head.

"I didn't want to do it. But I have a feeling that Harrow and his boys are also responsible for Pilo's murder. So, if I can expose them, maybe even take them out, put them out of business, can you blame me?"

"You're playing with fire, Alejandro, and I don't want to see you get burned."

"Why do you say that?"

"The whole thing doesn't pass the smell test," the old man said. "And I think you're dealing with dangerous people. They'll stop at nothing to get what they want. Think about it. If what you're saying is true, and Harrow is capable of murder, don't you think they could take you out . . . just like that? Don't you think that's a sure-fire mechanism to make the case go away? Who's to say they won't do it?"

"Grandpa, I can't live my life wondering what if? Thinking every day, I wonder how it feels to have a couple of million in the bank. Or not knowing how I'm going to pay my bills, support a family, or pay the mortgage, like my father. I don't want to go through life wondering what would have happened if I had taken the case to trial. Or having regrets. That's what I'm talking about."

"Money isn't everything, son. Your father was an honest man."

"I'm not talking about money. I'm talking about taking a chance . . . going for it, putting everything on the line. Remember when dad was young and was invited to join Mexico's PRI? Remember?"

"Yes, I remember."

"And he hesitated and hemmed and hawed and came up with a million excuses," explained the young attorney, "and eventually all his friends who took the chance and jumped in the fray in time made a name for themselves. Some were elected mayors, others were senators, congressman and even the neighbor's kid, Cavazos-Lerma, became governor. Remember that?"

"How could I forget? We went to Manuelito's inauguration ball in Ciudad Victoria."

"Well, that's what I'm talking about!" exclaimed Alex. "I don't want to wait on the sidelines and see everybody go by. I guess that's also part of the reason I decided to take the case."

"Well . . . I can accept that," Grandpa said reluctantly. "Your father loved you and your mother very much, but you're right . . . he was not a go-getter. Happy-go-lucky, yes, but not a go-getter. And I can't blame anyone but myself for that. Your grandmother and I spoiled him rotten. He was our only son. We babied him too much. We tried having more children, but your grandmother always lost the babies. And then, we thought we'd been blessed again with a child, but the little girl died."

"What was her name?"

"Carlota," said Grandpa as he got teary-eyed.

"How come this is the first time I hear this?"

"She died at six months," Grandpa explained as he wiped away the tears with his handkerchief. "Your grandmother was devastated. You could say she also died the day her baby girl died. She never really recovered. She was never the same after that."

"I am so sorry, Grandpa," said Alex as he reached over and grabbed the old man's arm, trying to comfort him.

"Please be careful. You're all I've got. I don't think I could go on if something happened to you."

"I will, Grandpa. I will. But I did not want to worry you, make you sick," Alex added and called out to the waiter to bring the tab. It was getting late.

Chapter 31

THE *RIO GRAND POST* PUBLISHED a short feature on the upcoming trial with a picture of Alex and Professor Fetzer at counsel's table, looking ready for battle. The feature had all the makings of an epic drama: baby lawyer fighting a mighty mega-firm from Corpus Christi. It was two attorneys against twenty, not to mention Slick. It was substance versus image, David versus Goliath. The paper quoted sources saying that no matter what happened in the end, the real tragedy was going to be the blemish on the legal profession.

Some were already predicting that legislatures all across the United States would overhaul their canons of ethics and rules of professional conduct. Others were quoted saying that the case could potentially criminalize conduct that everybody engaged in and was, at worse, unethical, and at best, a true example of a capitalism. The story didn't directly attack any of the lawyers involved in the case, but the implication was that all of them were bloody piranhas, circling, hungry, willing to even devour each other.

In the back pages there was another interesting story with Yarrington's picture splashed alongside it. It was a new dawn in Texas. The legislature was overcome with joy because the AMEGO legislation had made it out of the Senate and was now heading to the House for debate. The new bill was designed to cap the damages any lawyer suing other lawyers could recover. According to the story, a clear example of this type of frivolous lawsuit was the Medina case now coming up for trial in Cameron County. The story quoted lawyers who had been sued before by other lawyers and how those cases had been settled for pennies on the dollar because they posed claims with no merit. It was just another blatant attempt by young, inexperienced lawyers to make a quick buck. AMEGO would dissuade lawyers from suing each other, especially in light of a new trend in litigation surfacing from case running or lawyers stealing cases from other lawyers.

Since legislators were lawyers and everybody at one point in time or another had run a case, they were making it harder to sue. If the bill passed, it promised to have a retroactive effect, and Alex's suit against Harrow could end up being worth peanuts. The word on the street was that the big firms, known for running cases, were behind this new legislation, and Harrow had Clint Jones and Joe Smith, two of the highest paid and most influential lobbyists in Austin, on its payroll. They had been hired specifically to get this new legislation passed.

The story mentioned that the lieutenant governor supported, wholeheartedly, the AMEGO bill. He was quoted saying that he and the governor's office were prepared to call a special session if they couldn't get it done during the regular session and that the State of Texas needed this bill to restore honor and reasonableness to the legal profession. There were graphs and charts and numbers that purported to show how all these lawsuits were bankrupting the system, because baby lawyers like Alejandro del Fuerte knew nothing about screening a good case from a "dog with fleas." Amateurish lawyers were mostly at fault here. They were trigger-happy and loved filing frivolous lawsuits just to see their signatures on the page. They were clueless when it came time to carefully choose and file cases where the liability was clear-cut and the economic damages were big and absolute. Instead, these novices filed cases that were weak on liability or, worse yet, where the losses were minimal. The lawsuits clogged the court system. They were a waste of time and money.

"Don't let it get you down," Fetzer said as he walked into the war room with a cup of black coffee in each hand. "They were already complaining about lawyers when I first became a lawyer thirty years ago. It's part of the game in the court of public opinion. This is when the tough get cranking."

Maybe Fetzer had seen his share of legal battles and was hard as nails. After all, he had been a marine in his younger days, but Alex didn't feel that formidable at all. And as the trial date grew closer, the young attorney had begun experiencing all kinds of self-doubt. Could he really go up against the big boys and give Slick Stevens a bloody nose? Could he and the professor take on so many? Did he really have what it took? Could he go the distance? And what about Fetzer? He hadn't been in a courtroom in over twenty years! Could he still try a case?

"It's just butterflies," replied Alex.

"This is nothing," the old professor said. "Wait until the night before trial. See how you feel."

"It gets worse?"

"Oh yeah," said Fetzer, "it always gets worse before it gets better. But once you get past jury selection, your butterflies will subside. It used to happen to me every time I tried a case."

"I hope you're right," the young attorney said. "Trial is less than two weeks away. And I feel like I could try this case today. I mean, I'm ready to go. I just hate having to wait around with all this adrenaline building up inside, and all."

"Well, let's go over the order of witnesses, the substance of their testimony, and then you can practice your opening argument on me," suggested the professor. "And by the way, we don't have to do it in that particular order."

"I don't have anything prepared for my opening," Alex said. "I've vaguely glossed over some themes and stuff."

"That's even better," Fetzer said, getting all excited. "Show me you can think on your feet."

"All right," Alex said, getting up from the conference table and clearing his throat, "here goes nothing."

Chapter 32

SEMANA SANTA, as the folks from south of the border called holy week, was not necessarily the best time to be at the beach. The locals resented the vacationers who descended in droves from neighboring Monterrey and Mexico City. And Alejandro del Fuerte was no exception. Although his standard of living had improved—he'd moved out of the Tuscany and purchased a villa at La Contesse di Mare—he hated all the distractions. With the trial looming less than two weeks away, both Alejandro del Fuerte and Professor Fetzer were spending more and more time at the office and less time at the villa. The tourists were such a nuisance that Alex decided that sleeping at the office was better than dealing with late-night parties, loud music, and bottleneck traffic.

Of course, to Jeff Chordelli, *Semana Santa* presented just the right opportunity to come out and check on his investment and play at the same time. Besides, he'd never met a pretty girl who could resist an invitation to board the *Magillu*. The crowds and the excitement made it easy to blend in. All he had to do was send his wife shopping in New York for a few days, lie to Laura by concocting a story about some fishing trip, and he would have the island to himself. Besides, his two kids were away at college. He loved staying at the Boardwalk, where the million-dollar villas each had their own berth. The *Magillu* dwarfed them all. Holy week was the perfect opportunity to mingle, meet single women, and get to know the *crème de la crème* of Mexican society. Rumor had it that two of the wealthiest families in Mexico, the Torres-Parra and Alemán families, also happened to own villas there at the Boardwalk. The other, smaller villas, which were just as luxu-

rious, were owned by famous writers, TV personalities, intellectu-
als, industry magnates, and politicians.

Chordelli's adult life had been spent, for the most part, inside
the courtrooms across Texas. And just like the legal world, his
marriage had been dull, frigid, and boring. Therefore he liked to
mix things up a bit any chance he got. He was always trying to see
how much he could get away with, always living for the thrill,
pushing the envelope.

"*Hola,*" said the distinguished-looking woman waiting by the
elevator, "*¿vas a la fiesta de los Torres-Parra en el penthouse?*"

"*Hablo poquito español,*" Jeff Chordelli answered, pretending
to be terribly embarrassed, his cheeks turning red. "I apologize,
but I don't speak Spanish."

"Are you going to Don Fernando's party at the penthouse?"
asked the woman, with a slight accent.

"I didn't know there was a party," responded Chordelli. "I was
heading for a drink aboard my yacht. Watch the fireworks from
the upper deck."

"What's your name, stranger? Do you live here?" she asked,
apparently interested and wanting to know more about the lawyer.

"I'm Jeffrey Chordelli," he answered while looking her over.
"My friends call me Jeff. This is my first time down here during
Semana Santa. I didn't know the island got like this."

"Well, what do you think so far?" the attractive Mexican
woman asked. She appeared to be in her early fifties and was sporting a beautiful tan. Her green eyes sparkled like bright emeralds.

"I like it. I could get used to it."

"I'm looking for a date for Don Fernando's party. Are you
interested?" she asked.

"Sure, I would need to change, though. I'm not dressed for any
party." The attraction was immediate, and Chordelli was not about
to let this one go.

"All right, come by my place in thirty minutes. I'm in 1221," she
instructed the suitor as the elevator opened up. She jumped in.

"What's your name?" yelled Chordelli through the elevator
doors as they were closing.

"Isabel," shouted the woman as the doors slammed together.

"Isabel," mumbled Chordelli under his breath. It was a beautiful name. And when she said it with a slight accent, it sounded even better. "Isabel, Isabel," he kept repeating as he waited for the next elevator. Nicer sounding than Jane, for sure, his wife's name.

Jeff knocked three times on the door and waited out in the hallway. He was thinking of his wife and children, his lover Laura, and his new acquaintance Isabel. If Jane and Laura only knew. Man, what a lucky man he was. He'd been married for twenty years and had never been caught once. He'd probably cheated on his wife and Laura at least three hundred times. Neither suspected a thing.

"Hey, stranger!" Isabel greeted Jeff as she opened the door. She looked radiant and smelled delicious, her perfume wafting out into the long hallway.

"Ready?" he asked.

"Almost," she answered, "come on in, make yourself a drink while I finish up."

"Thanks."

"The Grey Goose vodka is in the freezer," she yelled as she disappeared down the hallway leading away from the living room, "or if you prefer, there's wine in the cellar, next to the help's quarters."

"I'll find my way," he shouted back and went in search of a nice bottle of red. "Who are all these people in the pictures?" he shouted across the living room as he rummaged through the kitchen drawers for a wine bottle opener.

"My daughters and my husband, *descanse en paz*," Isabel replied.

"What does *descanse en paz* mean?" he asked.

"May God rest his soul."

"He passed away?"

"Yes, five years ago. He was a wonderful man."

"I'm sorry to hear that," he said. Trying quickly to change the subject, he added, "Would you drink a glass of Bordeaux with me?" It was time to get the party started.

"Certainly," she answered and, without missing a beat, further explained, "Rafael died in a boating accident. He raced cigar boats as a hobby. I never approved, but what are you going to do? He died doing what he loved best. So he went happy."

"What did he do for a living?" Chordelli asked.

"He was a businessman. Have you heard of Grupo Omega?"

"I'm afraid I haven't."

"He started a TV network. We're Televisa's biggest competitors. Anyway, suffice it to say that my daughters and I do all right. *Semana Santa* we spend here at the island, summers at our ranch down in Durango. And Christmas we spend in Lake Tahoe. Talk about a white Christmas. The rest of the year, we stay in Monterrey. All my girls are on the board of Grupo Omega. Running the company and spending time with their families take most of their time. However, we try to get away every chance we get. I don't know what I'd do without them."

"It gets lonely, eh?" said Jeff taking a sip out of his glass of wine. He was in for a ride. A lonely widow, rich, good-looking, and searching for excitement, just like him.

"You can say that," Isabel answered, sipping from her glass and staring into his eyes. "Come, let's go outside to the balcony and enjoy the view of the Gulf."

The pair leaned against the rail and stared out into the distance. They were twelve stories up in the air, and the view was magnificent. Far away and deep into the ocean, they could see the small, flickering lights from a local shrimp boat flotilla. They were both quiet, taking it all in. The Gulf breeze was blowing gently, and they could hear the surf softly in the distance.

"So," Chordelli asked, "who's Don Fernando?"

"Have you heard of Dorado beer? Carta Suprema? And Águila Real?" Isabel asked.

"Of course. The drink of choice of college students, right?"

"Well, Don Fernando Torres-Parra is the son of the founder of that beer company," she said as she sipped her wine. "Of course, the family nowadays also owns industrial parks throughout Mexico, hotels, a steel mill, and other ventures. They're nice people. Fernando and my husband were roommates at Yale. Our families have been friends ever since I can remember. You'll like meeting them."

"If they're as nice as you, I think I will like them," he said, smiling, as he took another drink of wine and poured her some more. He was laying it on thick.

"Oh, that's sweet," replied Isabel, "but tell me about yourself. What do you do?"

"I'm a businessman," Jeff explained, "from San Antonio. I own several car dealerships."

"How long are you in town for?"

He leaned on the balcony and glanced at the moon. "I don't know, depends. My friend has a trial starting in Brownsville in two weeks, and he might need me to testify on his behalf."

"Oh yeah? What kind of trial?"

"A custody battle. The wife is fighting my buddy for custody of the children. I've been subpoenaed to testify as a character witness for him." Chordelli was impressed by his own lies. Boy, he was good.

"You think your friend will get custody?"

"Yes, the wife has mental issues. Can barely take care of herself," he said, making it up as he went along. "She also suffers from multiple personalities, so I don't see why not."

"How about you? Are you married?"

"No, never been married," lied Chordelli.

"Have you always lived in San Antonio?"

"Oh no. In my younger days, I was in the military. The Navy Seals, to be exact. I lived in San Diego and then was stationed in Germany." The lies just kept coming.

"So what happened, how come you never married?" She caught herself, hesitated, and then said, "Maybe we shouldn't go there. I'm sorry." She started to blush.

"No, it's okay," Jeff, the used car dealer, said. "I don't mind talking about it. After the military, I came back to San Antonio. There I met Sandy and was engaged to be married. I mean, we dated for almost eight years. And then, two months before the wedding, she just walked out on me. She said that she was moving to New York to pursue other interests. She said that she was bored. Bored with her dead-end job. Bored with me. She had been a librarian at Trinity University. We'd met at the Oyster Bake Street Festival."

"Just like that, eh?"

"Yep. There you have it. Just when you think you know the other person." He poured them more wine from the last of the bottle. "But I guess things happen for a reason."

"I agree," she replied, *"por algo suceden las cosas."*

"So, I devoted myself to work and never looked back. Next thing I knew, twenty years had gone by. After that incident, I never gave marriage much thought. I guess you could say the incident left a bad taste in my mouth."

"I'm sorry I asked," Isabel said reassuringly, looking into his eyes. And before he could realize what was happening, she closed in and gave him a kiss on his cheek. "What was it like to be a Navy Seal?"

"Exciting, scary, all at once," pretended Chordelli.

"Did you ever see any action?"

"Yes, Vietnam. Let me show you," said Jeff as he rolled the short sleeve of his stylish Cubera all the way up his shoulder. "You see this scar?" There was a two-inch scar from when Chordelli had had surgery to repair his right shoulder after a snow skiing accident. "That's where the bullet went in and exited past the shoulder blade."

"Wow, what nice big biceps," she marveled. "You're in great shape. If my friends had told me that on this trip I was going to meet a single, gorgeous man and a Navy Seal at that, I would have never believed it. This is amazing."

"Stop. You're embarrassing me," he said, chuckling.

"Are there others?"

"What? Scars?"

"Yes," she said. "I had never seen a bullet wound."

"Yes, I have a few others," he said as he rolled down his sleeve. "Why don't we go inside and sit down? It's hot and humid out here. We'll be drenched in sweat by the time we make the party."

"If we make the party," she corrected him, winking. "Do we need more wine? Let me get another bottle. I insist. You make yourself comfortable. I'll be right back."

Jeff Chordelli followed her inside to the sunken living room and sat down on the floor, on the silk pillows that were scattered on the large hand-painted Oaxacan wool rug.

"So, where were we?" started Isabel as she held another bottle of wine, handing it to Jeff so he could open it.

"We were checking out each other's scars," Chordelli said.

"Oh, yeah," Isabel said, raising her wine glass, "speaking of . . . I can't wait to introduce you to my friends and show them your battle scars."

"Aren't we going to be late to the party?" Jeff said while pouring Isabel wine from the newly opened bottle.

"No, Don Fernando's party goes on all night. We've got plenty of time. *Salud.*" She raised her glass and toasted to their good fortune.

"Cheers," replied Jeff, smiling. "To true love, romance, and adventure."

Chapter 33

THE UNEXPECTED JUDICIAL ORDER came in through the fax line. It was the court's order sending the parties to mediation *sua sponte*. The court on its own had decided to give the parties one last chance at resolving their dispute through the Valley's foremost mediator, Reagan Denham. If Denham couldn't settle the case, then no one else could.

The mediation had been prearranged by the court and was to take place all day Saturday in McAllen, before trial on Monday. The directive sent everyone at both firms scrambling, since they had been expecting to spend the weekend getting ready for trial and not for a last-minute mediation. The usual fee for a full-day mediation, middle of the week, was one thousand dollars per party. However, for a "must settle" weekend mediation with Reagan Denham, the fee was ten thousand dollars per party.

The firm's navy-blue Ford F-350, Heavy Duty, rolled to a stop under the shade of a large oak outside Denham's parking lot. Alejandro del Fuerte, Professor Fetzer, and Romeo got out and reached for their files and exhibits. Everyone was pitching in and in good spirits. Alex adjusted his tie and collar, put on his coat, and for a few seconds thought about the opponents. Were Tod Harrow and Slick Stevens ready to play hardball? Had they brought enough money to get the case settled?

It was hard to believe that just a few months earlier he had been sleeping on his office floor, and now he was about to go into his first mediation and start throwing around figures with seven zeroes next to them. *Enjoy it*, he kept repeating to himself. He knew that million-dollar cases didn't happen every day. *Let's get this case settled!* he kept repeating silently, over and over, as he walked alongside Fetzer and Romeo.

He was about to make his grand entrance into the office of the Valley's premier mediator. The office building was located within the historic district of McAllen; its small lawn was perfectly manicured, and the narrow one-way street was lined by tall, skinny palm trees. The district was dotted with boutiques, coffee bars, and restaurants. He'd visited the area once with Paloma, and they had tried out the bistros and teahouses along Pecan Boulevard. Now he was about to play hardball with some of the most seasoned lawyers in all of Texas.

They walked into the building and entered the well-appointed offices of Reagan Denham, certified mediator, arbitrator, and neutral party. In his younger days, Denham had been a top trial lawyer in Hidalgo County. He'd made so much money suing doctors and hospitals that he retired from the practice of law and opened up a mediation practice, just for fun.

His mediation center had three large "caucus" or conference rooms, all beautifully appointed. Each caucus room had its own large conference table made out of black Italian marble, plush leather couches, wet bar, flat-screen TV, and a video library. The object was to make the parties feel comfortable and get them to the negotiating table in good spirits and feeling good about themselves.

Vanessa, Denham's assistant, greeted the plaintiffs and guided them to the main conference room. She advised the party of three that Mr. Denham would stop by and talk with them in a few minutes. At the present time, the mediator was on his way from home. The defendants had called and were running a tad late but were due to arrive any minute, she said with a pretty smile. In a minute, Manny the office clerk would come by with different menus from various restaurants in the area to take their lunch and dinner orders. Mr. Denham wanted to get the case resolved even if it meant working until midnight. That was why the staff was anticipating working through dinner. Manny would also get them coffee or drinks. All they had to do was call.

After he had exchanged pleasantries with Denham's staff, Alex heard Slick and his party arriving at the front office. Stevens was barking orders. "Tell Reagan we're all here. Let's get the show on the road. I've mediated enough cases in my lifetime to know this is a dog and pony show."

Vanessa greeted the defendants and made the terrible mistake of taking the defendants into the large conference room where Alex, Fetzer, and Romeo were still setting up for their presentation.

Slick dropped his briefcase on the large marble table with a loud thud and boasted in his southern drawl, "Weeell, looky heeere, if it's not the golden boy and his mentor, Mr. Washed-up Marine." Salzman, the attorney for the carrier insuring Harrow & Amaro, didn't appear amused and had a frown on his face, but Tod Harrow was smiling and enjoying the spectacle. "Don't worry, del Fuerte, having an old federal prosecutor by your side isn't going to help you on Monday when we go toe to toe in the courtroom."

Alex and the others continued to set up and ignored Slick's comments. Slick, Harrow, and Salzman took their respective places on one side of the large conference table, and Slick started up again.

"I don't know why we're wasting our time with this exercise," he cried. "I want to try this case. I'm gonna open a can of whoopass on you and the old man. You won't know what hit ya." He had now propped up his cowboy boots on the table and loosened his tie. He was waiting for an answer and was obviously ready to pick a fight.

Salzman tried to diffuse the tense and uncomfortable situation. "Counsel," he started addressing Alex and Fetzer, "I don't know if we've met before, but I'm the attorney for the carrier insuring the defendants. Let me assure you we've come in good faith and with the best intention to get this thing resolved, once and for all." He turned to Slick and gave him the look from hell.

Out of the blue, Fetzer reached over to shake Salzman's hand, grabbed it, and staring straight into his eyes he said with a grin, "Well, I've guess you've come prepared to pay top dollar, then?"

The move surprised the hell out of everybody in the room, including Stevens, who sprang to his feet and got into the professor's face. "As far as I'm concerned, your case isn't worth six figures, and if you want more than that, you'll have to get it from the jury."

Alex, who'd never once in his life attended a mediation, was certain they were close to throwing punches. He motioned over to Romeo to get Vanessa, the assistant, and find out where the hell Reagan Denham was. The mediator needed to get in there, pronto, and calm things down.

Finally, after a brief, tense moment, Denham entered the conference room. Like a guided missile he went straight to Salzman, the guy with the money, and introduced himself. Alex knew the mediator needed to work on Salzman. Salzman had to be convinced that it was better to settle than to try the case. After all, it was his company's money. There was a policy with twenty-five million in coverage, and his company was on the hook for the whole amount if the defendants took a hit. Even if Tod Harrow wanted to settle, the case couldn't be settled unless Salzman agreed.

As he noted the way Denham worked, Alex liked what he saw. Quite possibly, Denham had instructed Vanessa to put everyone together in the room, get everyone's juices flowing, mess with their minds. Tweak them a bit. Obviously the guy knew how to play the game. Alex had been told by Fetzer that the best mediators were part actors, part bullshit artists, part masters of ceremonies, and part magicians. "The trick," Fetzer had said, "is to keep everyone talking, on their toes."

"Gentlemen," Denham started in his deep voice, "is there anything I should know before we get started? Are all the representatives that have the authority to settle available?" Denham was standing up at the head of the conference table, straight and tall. He was wearing a dark suit, and his broad shoulders, gray sideburns, and moustache added greatly to the impressive effect. "Mr. del Fuerte, where's your client? Can you get him on the phone to authorize the settlement if need be?"

"It's a she," Alex said, clearing his throat, "and yes, she is available via phone."

"Mr. Stevens?" Denham asked pointedly. He was now determined and serious, all business.

"Can't you see? Do you need glasses?" Slick answered, getting in Denham's face. "We're all here . . . Tod, Salzman, we're ready to go. Enough of the pleasantries."

"We'd rather settle for something reasonable," Harrow chimed in, meekly, "and avoid the publicity and a costly trial, if at all possible. Although we'll never admit any wrongdoing, we don't think the public needs to know the profession's dirty secrets."

Alex and Fetzer turned to each other, somewhat surprised. The exercise had not even started, but Tod Harrow sounded like he was ready to wave a white flag.

"I gotcha," Denham said, poker-faced. "Anything else?"

"Yes," Slick said, "considering the rookie trying the case, I don't think they'll get past a directed verdict. And in the event they survive a directed verdict and get the case to the jury, I don't think a jury will give them more than one hundred thousand dollars, max. So, I value the case at that. However, if it was my call, I'd rather try the case than give them a miserable penny."

"Let me say something," Salzman added, gesturing at Stevens. It was obvious that they couldn't stand each other. "I've read the mediation memorandum, and, irrespective of what Mr. Stevens thinks, I have valued the case differently. Now, that does not mean I'm simply going to roll over and heed the plaintiffs' demands. Yet, let's not underestimate our opponent. Maybe they don't want to settle this case. Maybe they're here because the court ordered them to be here, and nothing else. There's nothing else that they would rather do than try the case. Now, with that said, I hold the money bags here. Yes, granted, my client Harrow & Amaro may have wanted to settle. But it's I who authorize the settlement. I call the shots. All right?"

Slick Stevens was playing with his tie as he addressed Denham. "Reagan, you've known me for a number of years. As a matter of fact, I think I've mediated probably about fifty cases with you in my lifetime. Now, I don't care much for bluffing or posturing. The fact remains that the golden boy here has never tried a case in his life. And I doubt old geezer Fetzer can find his way to the courthouse. Plus, I don't have patience for fancy-schmancy mediators like you and your feel-good mumbo-jumbo. As far as I'm concerned, there's nothing more enjoyable than a good ol' knockout, drag-down fight all the way to verdict. A nasty, mean, bloody courtroom ass-kicking. That's what I get hired to do. Mediations are for sissies."

"Very well," interrupted Denham as he sized up everyone's egos, "the plaintiffs are ready and have a presentation waiting for us. Why don't we take our places . . . Do the parties want to make an opening statement?"

"Yes," said Tod Harrow, standing up and buttoning his double-breasted blazer. "I'll speak on behalf of my firm."

"Very well," Denham said, "we'll let you go first, if the plaintiffs don't mind?"

"No," Alex said smiling, "save the best for last."

Harrow rolled his eyes at the young attorney's comment and began speaking. "There's no question that the plaintiff's case is full of holes. For sure, it's not a 'laid down,' as I'm sure Mr. del Fuerte and his paralegal, Mr. Fetzer, believe."

Alex and Fetzer did a double take. Who was Tod Harrow calling a paralegal?

"Professor Mike Fetzer to you, jerk," Alex said, correcting Harrow.

"Whatever," the name partner said and pressed on. "We all know there's no evidence that my firm knew that Rigoberto Medina was an impostor. Sure, a jury could choose to believe otherwise, but it's unlikely. Think about it this way. Why would a mega-firm risk everything for ten million in fees? Why would Harrow & Amaro, P.C. set up some scam for a small case when my firm grosses over three hundred million in fees a year? It just doesn't make any sense. Lose everything over such small change? The whole idea is ridiculous! A jury is not going to pin any fault on us."

Tod Harrow paused briefly, took a swig of coffee out of a mug, and continued, "Sure, I'll be the first to admit that it appears as if we dropped the ball and didn't check the plaintiff out, but this is the first time something like this has ever happened. Besides, Ford, Firelazer, and Rio Carriers should have also caught it, and they didn't. Which, in my opinion, only goes to show just how skilled and well-rehearsed the impostor was. We were all conned. Now, having said that, we've come to negotiate in good faith, ready to work it out and get this thing behind us. Let's get this thing settled."

Professor Fetzer got up slowly, struggled with his wire-rimmed glasses, fixed his bow tie, and quietly began to address Harrow and his cronies. "This is a simple case. And it has nothing to do with whether your firm knew or not that the plaintiff was an impostor. We now know that the guy was a fake. You and I both know that Porfirio Medina was Rosario's real husband and the boy's dad. That's undisputed. Those are the cold hard facts. So, knowing that, Harrow & Amaro does not get to keep any of the fee generated from a case it had no right to file. A jury will not let you profit from somebody else's misfortune. Certainly a jury will not let you profit from your own mistakes, i.e., 'dropping the ball and not checking your client's background.' So you need to return the fee. According to our calculations, that's ten million dollars. Those ten million dollars need to be paid back into the estate of Rosario and Juan José Medina and then distributed to the rightful heirs, whoever, wherever they may be. Now, I haven't even addressed the issues dealing with case running or illegal solicitation. And I don't have to remind you that such an act is a felony in the State of Texas. You know better."

Slick jumped up, got in Fetzer's face, and shouted, "Are you threatening criminal sanctions? Is that what you're doing? Because if you are, I'll also file a grievance with the state Bar against you . . . and against your flunky recruit, too!"

"Hold the insults," Fetzer replied. "First of all, no one has threatened criminal sanctions. Obviously you haven't been listening to a thing I've said. But if you think it's a threat, then I'll see you at the grievance hearing. You think the state Bar is going to do anything? They couldn't catch a crook if he bit them in the ass! Just to give you an example, they have never busted your client's firm for case running, have they? And everyone knows they're the biggest case runners out of Corpus."

"Listen!" Alex said, jumping up, his chair flying as he kicked it out from underneath him. "Have you forgotten we're the good guys here? Have you forgotten that it was us who caught your clients with their pants down? Save your screaming for the jury. It won't work here, and it won't work on us. Sure, you might want a trial, but I can tell your client doesn't. And I wouldn't either if I had to explain to a jury the reasons why I should get to keep a fee that I'm not entitled to. Let me see, I gross over three hundred million in fees a year, but now I also want to keep these other ten million . . . um, even though the law says I can't. Even though the right thing to do would be to disgorge and pay them back. Let me see, what do I think the jury is going to do? Hm?"

Alex knew he was making a valid point. To a jury, the whole thing was going to reek of greed, greed, and more greed. A mega-firm that grossed hundreds of millions in fees per year was fighting and trying to keep a chunk of change. Ten mil here, five mil there. Who knew, maybe less or maybe more. But at the end of the day, the jury was going to be disgusted. And whatever the result was, it was not going to be pretty.

In an attempt to regain control of the situation, Reagan Denham interjected, "Gentlemen, let's break and separate into groups."

"I'm not finished," Fetzer reminded the mediator. "Let me finish my presentation, and then we can start mediation." He was firm but calm.

"Go ahead," the mediator said, embarrassed. He quickly sat down.

Alex noticed that Denham was quickly losing control of the situation. At the rate things were going, the mediation might not even make it to lunch, much less dinner. The animosity was such that any party, at any moment, could choose to walk or start throwing punches. Then the exercise would be over even before it started. It wouldn't be the first time a party had walked out. Hell, walking out wouldn't be so bad. It was better than coming to blows. Alex remembered reading in the *Texas Lawyer* a story about the mediator who had to break up a fistfight between an attorney from Brownsville and some knucklehead defense attorney from Houston.

"Where was I?" Fetzer asked. "Oh yes. Your opening settlement offer should be at least ten million. If you didn't come to the table prepared to pay that amount, then we're just wasting our time and we should all go home."

Salzman and Harrow were scribbling furiously. Stevens was now yawning and staring out the window, apparently uninterested. Alex wondered what was going through Slick's head. Did Stevens just plain not care, or was it all an act? Didn't trial lawyers know that going to trial was a roll of the dice? Wasn't it always better to settle, to take the money and run? Certainly Stevens had to know that the jury might possibly hate his client.

"Gentlemen," interrupted Denham, facing everyone in the room, "if we're going to settle this case here today, we all have to be reasonable. We are going to have to compromise and give up some of the marbles."

Salzman and Harrow were both nodding their heads as if agreeing with the mediator, especially the "reasonable" part.

"We might not like it," continued Reagan, "but we do need to keep an open mind and not hang on to any ill-conceived notions. So let's roll up our sleeves and get to work. At the suggestion of Judge Robles, I've set aside the whole day for you. Let's break, and why don't the defendants follow me into another conference room?"

Alex wondered about Denham's last comment. Certainly, being reasonable was a two-way street. Sure, Fetzer had made an opening demand of ten million, but he'd done that for a reason. There was a lot of room for movement. One thing for sure, the case was not going to settle for six figures. The plaintiffs needed to convince the defendants to start talking in terms of seven figures. Then a trial could very well be averted.

After Denham and the defendants left the room, Alex, Fetzer, and Romeo sat there staring at each other in silence.

Fetzer finally broke the silence. "You know, if we get them up to one or two million dollars, that would be a reasonable settlement and would put anywhere from half a million to a million dollars into Pilo's estate for the heirs."

"Not bad for a day's work," Alex said, smiling. "More money than María Luisa would see in a lifetime working minimum wage jobs in Mexico."

"And if she structures the settlement, she could double or triple her money and make it grow tax-deferred," said Fetzer. "She could be set for the rest of her life. Some structured settlements even pay a monthly living stipend and large lump sums every five years. It could be retirement money."

"What sort of figure do you think they'll come back with?" Alex asked the professor.

Fetzer removed his glasses and set them on the conference table. "You watch. They'll try to lowball us. Hopefully Denham can get them to stop playing games and have them start throwing around some serious numbers."

"We'll see what they come back with. Now it's just a waiting game."

"Well," Fetzer added, "we'll let Denham do his job . . . let him tell us how much money they brought to the dance."

"What do you mean?" Alex asked.

"Remember, if we don't settle today and their last offer was one hundred thousand . . . you can betch'a on Monday they'll have two hundred thousand, and so on and so forth. Today we need to find out what their limit is. On Monday, it will double."

"I hope you're right . . . Slick sounds like all he wants to do is to try the case."

"That's just posturing. He doesn't want to try this case. He's worried, I can tell."

Alex loosened his tie, removed his coat, and set it on the table. "I hope you're right. I don't like him."

"Well, let's wait and see what kind of counter offer they come back with," Fetzer replied. "Let's give the three stooges some time."

While waiting for the mediator to come back with a figure, Alex thought of numbers, structured settlements, percentages, and disbursement statements. He was wondering how much money Salzman was truly prepared to pay. Would he give in and agree to the ten million? Alex crunched the numbers in his head and was already dreaming of the things he could do with four million dollars, his firm's forty percent. For sure, he would let his old professor have at least one million. After taxes, the professor would get to keep five hundred thousand. Fetzer could also put his Houston house up for sale, buy a duplex on the island, and put the rest of the money to work for him. It could be a nice life. And if Fetzer wanted, he could still try cases side by side with his pupil. Alex had nothing but the utmost respect and admiration for his old professor.

At the end of the day, the key would be how much money Salzman had at his disposal. Each side could lowball and highball the other to death, all day long if they wanted, but in order to settle the case each side would have to get close to the number in Salzman's head. That was the trick, figuring out the number in Salzman's brain.

Alex was practicing settlement gymnastics when Denham walked into the conference room.

"Whew!" Alex said. "Where have you been? You've been gone almost an hour."

"I always have to spend more time with the defendants," Denham explained. "They're holding the bags with the money, remember? That means my job is to convince them to part with their money . . . and that can be tough and time-consuming."

"Alex," the professor said, "Mr. Denham's real work is in the other room, convincing the defendants that it's better to pay than to try the case."

The mediator was nodding his head in agreement. "Professor Fetzer is absolutely right, Alex. Today, I expect to spend eighty percent of my time with the defendants, giving them reason after reason after reason why it's better to pay than to try the case."

"Remember," Fetzer said, "Harrow might want to settle, but it's Salzman's company's money. Harrow might value the case at half a million, but Salzman only brought two hundred thousand to play. And then you have Slick, telling Harrow he shouldn't pay a dime, that they're better off trying the case."

Denham nodded. "It sure can get complicated with so many different personalities in there."

"So what kind of number did they send you back with?" Alex asked, cutting to the chase.

"Gentlemen," he said, "I've got a number for you . . . it's just a starting point."

"What is it?" asked Alex. He was impatient.

"Fifty thousand," said Denham, his head hung low, almost embarrassed.

Fetzer, Alex, and Romeo glanced at each other.

"I know fifty thousand is not the number you had in mind," Denham volunteered, "but remember, it is only ten in the morning . . . and we're just getting started. Honestly, I think your next move should be in the low millions."

"Tell those bastards, especially Salzman," Alex said, "that his insurance company is on the hook for a lot of money, in case Harrow takes a hit. The experts, the mock jury, and the focus group that evaluated the case agreed that it's a twenty-million-plus case. They also agreed that it's a punitive damages case. Especially if the jury believes that the firm set up the whole thing from the beginning." *I hope my bluff about the mock jury and focus group works . . . so we can get this thing settled,* he thought.

"What Alex is trying to say," Fetzer clarified, "is that they can go to hell. Now, let's see how serious they are about settling this thing. Go back with nine million. See what happens. With their next move, we'll know if they came prepared to play ball."

"All right then," Denham said, turning around and heading out the door, "I'll be back in a while."

By five o'clock Saturday afternoon, the plaintiffs had dropped their demand to seven million and the defendants had come up to two hundred thousand. Movement was coming about slowly, but the parties were still going at it, and it seemed they were prepared to work until midnight. Romeo appeared to have enjoyed the exercise and the tremendous spectacle. The entire afternoon, Alex had been quietly observing Romeo's reactions as the demands, offers, and counter-offers in the millions of dollars flew back and forth. To the uninitiated, it must have sounded as if money grew on trees or there was a printing press in Denham's back office.

Denham walked back into the plaintiffs' room. He was now stripped down to his trousers, shirt, and suspenders. The coat and tie were gone, and his shirt sleeves were rolled up. "They're offering $250,000," the mediator said. "They also told me to tell you that they're running out of money. They don't have much more than that. Not much room to negotiate."

"Do you believe them?" Fetzer asked.

"No, but maybe that's all they brought today," Denham clarified.

"Oh, pleeease," Alex said rolling his eyes, "we've moved down three million, and they have only come up to two hundred thousand . . . I'm ready to walk. Let's go try this thing. The hell with them!"

"Between us girls," Denham said, trying to be humorous, "the problem is Slick. He's wielding a lot of influence over Harrow, and he's convinced Harrow that you can't try this case."

"Is that so?"

"Yes, he really believes that you and the professor are going to be fumbling idiots, come Monday. And that the jury will see your inexperience and, ultimately, will side with them."

"All right," Alex said, jumping up and motioning over to Romeo to start packing it up, "tell the defendants we're walking, to stick it where the sun don't shine, and we'll see them down at the courthouse. *¡Qué chinguen a su madre!*"

"I'll give them the message," Denham said with a grin.

And with that, Alejandro, Fetzer, and Romeo walked out.

Chapter 34

THE HEADLINES IN THE *RIO GRAND POST* READ, "Last Ditch Effort at Settling Medina Lawsuit Fails." It was the day of trial, and the Cameron County courthouse in Brownsville was abuzz with the media. It was packed with potential jurors, lawyers, and reporters covering the epic battle about to take place.

Alex, Fetzer, and Romeo had headed for the courthouse armed with boxes, exhibits, and projectors ready to set up for jury selection. *Voir dire* would commence promptly at 1:30 p.m. in the 347th Judicial District Court. The presentation of evidence would start the next day, Tuesday, when the plaintiffs would call their first witness. Judge Robles would require the attorneys to select twelve jurors and two alternates. Romeo and Alex were busy setting up and playing with the overhead projector, when Gigi walked into the courtroom.

"Am I interrupting?" she asked.

"No, not at all," said Alex. "We're just making sure the equipment works before we get started. Last minute stuff." Alex knew his nervousness was showing.

"I've tried enough cases to know what you're going through right now," the prosecutor said. "In your head you're always going over the details. Did I get my subpoenas out? Are my experts in town? Did the client dress appropriately? Do I have my order of witnesses? My exhibits pre-marked? Am I ready to give my opening? It's one thing or another. It's inescapable."

"So what I'm feeling is normal, then?" asked Alex.

"Yes," she said as she got closer to the attorney and grabbed him by both hands. Her eyes fixed on his. "Alex, listen to me.

You're ready to try this case. You know it inside out. And you've done everything you could to get it ready for the jury." She got even closer and whispered in his ear, "You're going to be fine. Those lawyers aren't any better than you. You've got charm, personality, and the jury will like you. People tend to like you. I like you. Everyone is rooting for you. We all hate case runners. And you, well, let's just say we're all glad somebody is doing something about it. Now, go kick some ass!"

"Thanks," Alex said, "that means a lot coming from you."

"All right . . . good luck. I've got to go, they're paging me from the 404th District Court."

"*Hasta luego.*"

"We'll celebrate later," said Gigi as she exited the courtroom.

The Honorable Benjamin Robles had set aside the months of May and June for the showdown. It was only early May, and the temperature was already pushing one hundred. Alex and Fetzer had been working eighteen-hour days preparing for trial. And even though the case had not settled at mediation, both Alex and Fetzer had gained some insight into how Harrow and Slick would be trying the case. By now, Alex knew that the defendants were prepared to offer $250,000. That had been their last offer on Saturday. He hoped there would be more to come.

The morning would be spent going over pretrial motions, and no jury would get to witness the exercise. After all, these were all preliminary matters. It was better that way. Everyone could be saved the spectacle of the attorneys, with tempers flaring, nit-picking each other's motions apart.

The firm of Harrow & Amaro and their counsel took up one side of the arena. Fetzer and Alex had picked the table closest to the jury box. Tod Harrow, the name partner, would second-chair Slick, the smoothest litigator this side of Corpus Christi. Alex and the professor were by now very familiar with Stevens' antics and were expecting the unexpected. After all, "Slick" Stevens had always managed to drop huge bombs on his opponents or pull rabbits out of a hat. In five years, he had not lost a trial. All his corporate clients had dodged big verdicts.

When the large panel of potential jury members was brought into the courtroom, Chordelli and a junior associate took seats with the other spectators, of which there was an impressive number from Lieutenant Governor Yarrington's staff. The state Bar would also watch the trial very closely. It would be a continuing saga in legislatures and Bar ethics committees all across the country. Not to mention a complete and utter embarrassment for lawyers in all of Texas. Now the cat was out of the bag. The entire nation had become aware of the legal profession's dirty little secret. Of course the worst vultures, firms like Harrow from Corpus Christi and others lesser known, had a lot at stake in the outcome of the trial. Even Chordelli had to wonder if their boy had revealed anything to Fetzer or if Fetzer suspected anything. Now they were in too deep, and there was no turning back. They would just have to let things take their natural course. Let the chips fall where they may.

Fetzer moved about the courtroom purposefully in slow motion. Playing the part of a distinguished, brilliant professor, bow tie and all. His voice was clear but soft, and his words were always eloquent. He was the old sage warrior, with a set of reading glasses perched on top of his wavy gray hair. At times he appeared to misplace the glasses, only to find them miraculously on his head, again and again. Occasionally, he pretended to lose his place while arguing an important legal point. It was all a well-rehearsed act.

Slick Stevens, on the other hand, was decked out in border brawler cool: black cowboy boots, suede leather jacket, big silver turquoise pinky ring, slicked back jet-black hair. He had a strong chin, and it was rumored that in his younger years he'd won the golden gloves championship as a boxer, although this had never been confirmed.

The one thing that the Corpus Christi Bar did know for a fact was that Stevens always managed to get the biggest and juiciest *ad litem* appointments from all of the Nueces County district courts. It was rumored that he had every district judge in his pocket, and of course there was good reason to believe this. Not a month went by when Stevens made less than a hundred thousand dollars in *ad litem* appointments. The rest of the Nueces County Bar averaged two to three thousand dollars in *ad litem* appointments a year, if they were lucky.

Coincidentally, every major holiday or three-day weekend, Stevens could be found in Las Vegas in the company of all the male district judges and their wives. His firm was believed to foot the bill for these so-called judicial conferences.

Stevens didn't use fancy words or complex grammar. To add drama, he would pepper his arguments with a little Spanish here and there. He let you know, or at least faked, his Mexican ancestry during arguments. When he began arguing a point, he got down to the common man's level so that everyone could understand the points he was trying to drive home. He was very effective, and he always had the talent to sway the blue-collar Hispanic males in the jury. Women, on the other hand, thought he was cheesy. This, however, didn't concern Slick very much. It had always been almost impossible to assemble an all-woman jury in Cameron County. He had no fear of Fetzer or Alex, no fear of big-city lawyers, or of juries.

When Slick argued even the smallest legal point, Alex, like everyone else, found himself drawn into his act. At first he had not noticed the effect Slick was having on him, but when he did, a lightning bolt of fear struck him. If Slick was having that effect on him and he was the opposition, what effect was he going to have on the mostly Hispanic jury? Slick was good, no doubt about it. Alex and Fetzer had their work cut out for them.

While Alex was fighting to keep his concentration and not fall for Slick's spell, Chordelli realized that Slick was a force to be reckoned with. If Slick successfully defended Harrow & Amaro, then they might just emerge as the biggest, strongest law firm in South Texas. Certainly, as the saying went, what doesn't kill you will make you stronger.

Judge Robles called a fifteen-minute recess so he could visit with the attorneys in chambers. Chordelli's young associate left the courtroom and went to use his cell phone. He wanted to place a call to the partners up in San Antonio who were monitoring the trial. Alex, along with Slick and a horde of Harrow & Amaro lawyers, headed back to chambers to confer with the judge. Fetzer stayed behind in the courtroom, which had emptied out while the judge had called the recess. In the background, Chordelli was reviewing some notes he'd taken earlier in the morning, when a voice interrupted him.

"Hello, Jeff, what brings you here?" called Fetzer as he walked closer to the bar, near where Chordelli was sitting.

"Professor Fetzer? How the hell are you? What are *you* doing here?" said Chordelli, pretending to be pleasantly surprised.

"I'm helping one of my ex-students try his first case."

"I didn't recognize you, Professor."

"Well, it's been, what? Twenty years?"

"At least," replied Chordelli.

"Just wanted to say hello," Fetzer said. "No surprise to see you here."

"We're monitoring this trial. You could say we have a small interest in it," Chordelli said.

"Why, you run cases, too?" the professor asked.

"Hey," snapped Chordelli, "I don't appreciate that. But if you feel that way, why don't you file your grievance with the state Bar? See if you can prove anything. Put your money where your mouth is."

"I don't have to prove anything," Fetzer replied, "but if the shoe fits . . . "

"Whatever," Chordelli said. He tried to ignore the professor and go back to his notes.

"Why would you say that you had a small interest in the case?" Fetzer continued as he picked up a yellow pad from counsel's table and scrambled around trying to find a pen. They were alone in the courtroom.

"We want to see what happens to our competition," Chordelli explained. "Is that so wrong?"

"I doubt it has anything to do with the competition," Fetzer said matter-of-factly. "Maybe your firm put Alex up to this. How did you manage to convince Alex to come on board?"

"What are you talking about?" said Chordelli in a shocked tone. "Are you suggesting he's working for us?"

"I never said he was working for you," replied Fetzer. "Why, is he working for you?"

"Of course, not," Chordelli said, realizing he may have slipped. No doubt about it, Fetzer still had the smarts, just like in the old days. He could turn things around on you in a blink of an eye. And you might not even notice.

"It amazes me . . . Alex just graduated from law school, and there's no way in hell that he could have put together the law firm he's got on his own, and in such a short period of time," said Fetzer. "I also happen to read *Texas Lawyer* and know that your firm and Harrow's don't get along."

"So? Lots of firms don't get along and are always competing against each other," replied Chordelli. "That doesn't mean a thing."

"I just find it highly unusual that Alex, all of a sudden, came into money and has a fully staffed firm. You're here with members of your firm, monitoring the trial. And it's Harrow & Amaro who are on the other side. Too much of a coincidence, don't you think?"

"This is the hottest ticket in town. And it's free! Why would anybody miss it?"

"Maybe," Fetzer answered, "because you have more than a slight interest in the case?"

"Well, then, looks like you've done your homework," said Chordelli, content just to smirk and stare back at Fetzer.

"Something like that," Fetzer shot back.

"I'm surprised you're still around. Wasn't your license to practice law suspended 'cause of the bottle?" Chordelli was making drinking gestures with his hands.

The unsolicited comment caused Fetzer's temperature to shoot up. That had been a period in his life that he'd rather not remember. Fetzer shot back, "I was not born yesterday. I can smell a rat when I see one! And I would bet that you're somehow involved here. I can't put my finger on it just yet."

"Oh, you're reading too much into things, Professor Fetzer. And I've never met the young lawyer trying this case. As a matter of fact, I have no idea who this Alejandro del Fuerte is. I couldn't tell him apart from a baby prosecutor assigned to misdemeanor intake in Podunk, Texas."

"Well, I've got a case to try," Fetzer said. "We'll talk later."

"Whatever."

Right at that moment, all the lawyers came back into the courtroom and walked to their places. The bailiff called the court into session. Judge Robles sat down, and Chordelli went to join his associate in the gallery.

Fetzer leaned over to Alex and whispered, "What happened in chambers?"

"The judge is trying to get us to settle this thing before blood is shed," Alex replied. "He thinks the spectacle is going to hurt the profession's image. There won't be any winners."

"Well, did they put any money on the table?"

"They came back with five hundred thousand on the table, but with no admission of guilt or liability on the part of Harrow & Amaro," Alex replied.

"There will be more. We'll revisit the issue after we put on our case in chief," Fetzer said. "Let's start slaying some dragons."

"Let's," said Alex.

At 1:30 in the afternoon, the courtroom was filled with forty-five potential jury members who sat in their numbered places. The remaining seats were taken by other lawyers, insurance company representatives, reporters, and the staff of Alex and the defendants' firms. Judge Robles took his place on the bench.

"Ladies and gentlemen of the jury panel," said the judge, greeting the panel members, "this is jury selection. How many of you have participated before in an exercise similar to this, whether in a criminal case or a civil case?"

A few members of the jury panel raised their hands.

"Okay, I see that about fifteen of you have had some jury experience," said the judge, counting the hands in the crowd. "Well, for those that have never served, the lawyers representing the parties will talk to you here shortly. They're going to ask you some questions. Please answer the questions. If they ask something embarrassing and you don't want to answer, then wait, and during the break you can approach the bench and tell me what your answer would have been, got it?"

The members of the panel nodded their heads in agreement.

"Very well then, with that said, I will turn it over to the attorneys," said Robles. "Mr. del Fuerte, you have thirty minutes for jury selection."

"Thank you, Your Honor," answered Alex, "may I have a five-minute warning?"

"Sure."

"Well, then," Alex continued, "may it please the court. Professor, Mr. Stevens, Counsel. Ladies and gentlemen of the veniree."

With that, jury selection got underway.

The all-Hispanic jury in the box was made up of five men—a truck driver, a retired migrant worker, a high school coach, a mechanic and a farmer—and seven women. Five of the women worked for the Brownsville Independent School District; three were teachers, one was an assistant principal, and the other was a high school counselor. The other two women were stay-at-home moms. The two alternate jurors were a male and a female, both Anglo, and both in law enforcement. The male worked fo the Border Patrol and the female was an assistant U.S. attorney.

"Ladies and gentlemen of the jury," Judge Robles greeted them. "Good morning. In a few minutes, the plaintiffs will start with their opening arguments. Then defense counsel will also have an opportunity to give an opening argument. After that, the plaintiffs will put on their case in chief, and then the defense will have an opportunity to do the same. 'Case in chief' means that each side would get a turn to call their witnesses, ask questions, present other forms of evidence—photos, recordings, diagrams, records, letters, etc. Once they do this, each side will 'rest' to assess if they have something else to present. If they don't, they will 'close' and deliver closing arguments, and then you will start your deliberations. We don't anticipate the trial to last more than two weeks. Any questions? No? All right. Mr. del Fuerte, you have twenty minutes for your opening statement."

"Thank you, Your Honor," said Alex as he rose from counsel's table and stood up in front of the jury box. "Ladies and gentlemen of the jury, this is a simple, straightforward case. What is this case about, you ask? It's about these defendants keeping some money—money that never belonged to them—in the amount of five million dollars, maybe more. The evidence will show that we represent the estate of the person and the heirs who are entitled to that money. We are going to ask you to order these greedy attorneys to disgorge their fee and return the monies to the rightful owners. In a nutshell, that's it. It's quite simple, *sencillo, fácil* . . ." He paused and waited for the words in Spanish to resonate with the jury. Alex would pull no punches, even if it meant letting the jury know that he was one of them.

"*Bien*," Alex added, "we anticipate, and the evidence will show, that the defendants will try to confuse this simple issue. They'll say that they didn't know that the client they represented was not the real husband of Rosario Medina. That they had no clue that this so-called Rigoberto Medina, the guy they represented, was not the father of baby Juan José Medina. And that they would have never guessed in a million years that somewhere in Mexico there existed Rosario's real husband and Juanito's biological father. They will get up on the witness stand and tell you that they were also conned. Tricked. That they're a mega-firm and would never intentionally dupe anybody. But if you let them," Alex said, getting up close to the face of the migrant worker juror, "*si los dejan*, they will dupe you, too." He walked away from the jury box, walked over to Harrow, and stood there pointing at him.

"The evidence will show, and Mr. Harrow will argue, that his firm, too, was conned. That no one at his firm ever suspected a thing. That Rigoberto Medina was an impostor who duped everybody: their firm, Ford, Firelazer Tire, even Rio Carriers. And we will agree with them. Yes, they were duped. They were conned. But the law says they don't get to profit from their mistakes. The law firm of Harrow & Amaro does not get to keep the millions of dollars in fees it made on the Medina case. The law says they must disgorge the fee. They're going to kick and scream. They're going to put up a fight. Sure, I, too, would want to keep several million dollars. Who wouldn't? As a matter of fact, I, too, might kick and scream and bite. But the law is the law, and we live in a country where we follow the rule of law. So, just because their firm was duped, don't let them dupe you. You need to make them give the money back to the estate of Porfirio Medina. Thank you."

"Mr. Stevens," snapped Judge Robles, "you're up."

"Judge," Slick Stevens replied, as he slowly got up to address the court, "the defense is going to reserve its opening statement until after the plaintiff's case in chief."

"Very well, Mr. del Fuerte, call your first witness," instructed Judge Robles as he gestured over at counsel's table.

Alex stood up and announced, "We call Aurora López to the stand, Your Honor."

Aurora made her way to the witness box and sat down, struggling to keep her composure.

"State your name for the record," said Alex without missing a beat.

"Aurora López ."

"Who were Rosario and Juan José Medina?" Alex asked.

"My cousin's wife and her son," the lady replied, "but because of her young age, I'd call her my niece or *sobrina*."

"Are they still alive?"

"No, they died in a car accident in the outskirts of Raymondville."

"When was this?"

"About two years ago."

"Did you know that there was a lawsuit in connection with their deaths, where these attorneys recovered several millions of dollars?" asked Alex, who was standing next to the witness box, pointing directly at Tod Harrow.

"Objection!" shouted Slick. "Calls for speculation."

"Overruled," Judge Robles said.

Alex pressed on. "You can go ahead and answer, Mrs. López."

"That's what I've learned," Mrs. López said, sounding amazed. "I never understood who could have filed the lawsuit . . . her husband lived in Mexico. She had no other relatives to speak of."

"What was her husband's name?"

"Porfirio Medina, but we knew him as Pilo."

"Was Pilo your cousin?"

"Yes," Aurora replied.

"While Rosario lived and worked here in Brownsville, do you know if she ever remarried?"

"No, she wouldn't do such a thing. She loved her husband. And that was the reason she came to the States and sacrificed so much. She was trying to provide for her family. Just like a normal parent would want to provide for his or her family."

"What do you mean?"

"She would send money to her husband in Mexico, so he could build the family a home. Before, they basically lived in a *choza*, a shack. I'm sure she also wanted . . . "

Slick jumped up. "Again, Your Honor, we object! Calls for speculation!"

"I'll rephrase, Your Honor," said Alex.

"Very well," Judge Robles said. "Rephrase the question."

Alex returned his attention to Aurora and asked, "Did Rosario ever confide in you about her dreams and goals for her son . . . her family?"

Before the witness had a chance to respond, Slick rose again. "Objection, Your Honor! Calls for hearsay."

"Dying declaration," countered Alex, quickly thinking on his feet. Alex knew that the dying declaration exception to hearsay did not necessarily apply to the testimony he was trying to elicit from the witness, but sometimes the judges themselves didn't remember all of the exceptions to the hearsay rule. Besides, the jury didn't know either way. It was worth a try.

"Overruled," cried Judge Robles, taking the bait.

"But Judge," started Slick, "clearly . . . "

"I made my ruling," interrupted the judge. "Mr. del Fuerte, please continue."

Alex directed his attention once again to the witness and added, "You were saying, Mrs. López?"

As if on cue, Aurora finished her thought. "I'm sure Rosario also wanted her baby boy to have a better life, to somehow find a way to give him a piece of the American Dream. Isn't that what we all want . . . for our children to do better than the generations that came before them? You know, raise them in a place where there is still freedom and opportunity to make something of yourself and become productive members of society."

The jurors were all nodding their heads in agreement with the witness. When Slick noticed this, he jumped up to try to cut the witness short. "Judge, this is turning into a narrative. Where's the question?"

"Question and answer, counsel," said the judge, "question and answer."

Alex switched gears. "Do you know if she dated anybody or started another romantic relationship while being married to your cousin Pilo?"

"No, when she worked for the Macallan family, she barely got time off. Plus, she didn't like to go out . . . because of her situation, you know?"

"We'll talk about her situation right now, but first let me ask you. When you say Macallan family, you mean she worked for Judge Walter Macallan. That's the Macallan family you're referring to, right?" Alex peeked at the jury to gauge their reaction. Some were scribbling on their yellow pads, others were looking intently at the witness, and all were paying close attention.

"Yes, sir. I believe that's correct."

"Now, what do you mean by her situation?" Alex asked as he turned and tried to read the jury. "Do you mean she had no papers, that she was here illegally?" Alex knew that it was better to bring out the fact that Rosario and her son were in the States illegally than to give Stevens the opportunity to bring out and exploit this fact himself. The tactic was called "stealing thunder," and it was a way for lawyers to preempt the other side from making a mountain out of a molehill when dealing with touchy issues.

This way, the "wetback" factor was out and in the open. If Slick revisited the issue, it would then no longer be a surprise.

Aurora was firm with her answer. "Yes," she said.

Alex pressed on. "So, it would be fair to say that Rosario's lawful wedded husband, at the time of her death, was Pilo Medina?"

"That's right."

Alex reached for a stack of photos at counsel's table and approached Aurora on the witness stand. "I'm handing you what has been marked as plaintiff's exhibits one through ten. Do you know what they are?"

"They're photos of my cousin Pilo and his wife, Rosario."

"Is that it?"

"Well," the witness said as she flipped through the rest of the photos, "actually some photos are of the whole family, Pilo, Rosario, and Juanito. Then there are two wedding pictures from the day Pilo married Rosario. It looks like the plaza or main square down in Tepantitlán. As a matter of fact, here in this picture you can see María Luisa, Pilo's daughter from a prior marriage."

Aurora was looking over her reading glasses and pointing to María Luisa, who was sitting at counsel's table next to Professor Fetzer.

"May I publish them to the jury?" Alex asked Judge Robles, while walking over to the jury box. "And admit them into evidence?"

"I'm going to object!" shouted Slick. "I've never seen these photos before."

"Your Honor," Alex replied, "that's misleading. Maybe Mr. Stevens hasn't seen them before, but certainly we've produced copies of the photos in discovery months ago."

"When were the copies produced?" Judge Robles asked the attorney.

"Six months prior to trial," Alex said in a matter-of-fact way. "There's no unfair surprise."

"They'll be admitted," the judge ruled.

"Publish to the jury?"

"Go ahead."

While the jury examined the photos, Alex walked back to counsel's table and sat on the other side of Pilo's daughter. "Pass the witness," he said.

The second week of trial was now fast becoming a repeat of the first week. Tony "Slick" Stevens had swaggered around the courtroom like the bully in the school cafeteria, throwing hissy fits, balking at the judge's rulings and not getting anywhere with his courtroom antics.

"Your Honor, we call Mr. David Amaro as a hostile witness," announced Professor Fetzer from counsel's table in his rich and deep voice.

David Amaro walked with a slight limp and used a cane. He sported a straw fedora hat, a white poplar suit with blue pinstripes, and white shoes. He looked thin and frail, probably from his many years of boozing, womanizing, and burning the candle at both ends. He was the complete opposite of Tod Harrow, his partner. Alex thought the old geezer had to be at least seventy.

"Mr. Amaro, where do you work?" Fetzer said, jumping right into his cross-examination of the witness.

"At the firm of Harrow & Amaro, in Corpus," replied the witness.

"Are you the 'Amaro,' as in Amaro, the name partner?"

"Yes, I'm the name partner and founding member of the firm. Two of my sons also work at the firm."

"How long has Harrow & Amaro been in existence?"

"Fifteen years."

"What kind of cases does your firm handle?"

"Product liability cases."

"Tell this good jury what that means—product liability cases," Fetzer instructed.

"Okay," Amaro answered as he played with the microphone in front of him. "To put it simply . . . if a defective product out there in the marketplace injures, maims, or kills somebody, we'll sue the manufacturer of the product."

"Typically," Fetzer continued without missing a beat, "what kinds of product liability cases does your firm handle?"

"Rollover crashes with fatalities or catastrophic injuries, meaning someone is seriously injured, sometimes even paralyzed."

Fetzer got up from counsel's table and approached the witness. He was holding some pictures in his left hand. "Are you familiar with the Medina lawsuit against Ford, Firelazer, Rio Carriers, and others?"

"Yes," Amaro answered, "I was the lead attorney in that case."

"Was that a rollover accident involving a defective product?"

"Sure, the van's high center of gravity made it dangerous, the tires were poorly constructed, and the restraining systems, seat belts, and airbags didn't function properly."

Fetzer approached the partner. "Let me show you a set of pictures from the Medina lawsuit. Do you recognize these?" He handed the old partner the picture set.

"Yes, I recognize these."

"Is this the van in which Rosario Medina and her son, Juan José Medina, lost their lives?"

"Yes."

"Judge!" shouted Slick, jumping up from his chair. "Can counsel get to the point? Where is he going with this?"

"What's your objection?" Fetzer asked Stevens. "Either make an objection or stop interrupting."

"What's your objection?" asked Judge Robles, glancing over at Stevens.

"My objection," Slick said, "is relevancy. Where's the relevance of all this?"

"I was getting there," Fetzer said, "before I got interrupted."

"Move on, counsel," instructed the judge. "The objection is overruled."

"Mr. Amaro," Fetzer continued, "what was the amount of the global settlement for Rosario and Juanito's lawsuit?"

Springing up again from his seat like a rocket, Slick shouted, "Objection, Your Honor! The terms of those settlements were confidential. I'm instructing my client not to answer."

The judge, who was obviously getting tired of the pit bull defense attorney, replied, "I'm instructing the witness to answer. If you have a problem with that, then I suggest you take that issue up on appeal when the case is over, Mr. Stevens."

"Your Honor," cried Slick, "I would re-urge my objection. We are treading on uncharted territory here, Your Honor."

"Your objection is overruled, the record will so reflect," Judge Robles admonished Stevens.

"Mr. Amaro, what was the amount of monies recovered on the Medina lawsuit?" asked Fetzer, pressing on with the same line of questioning.

"Again I object," Slick shouted nervously. "Can we take a five-minute break? Visit in chambers?"

All eyes were on Slick Stevens, including those of the jurors, the audience, and Alex and his legal team. Harrow's support staff, also present in the courtroom, looked nervous, and their demeanor gave the impression that the trial was going badly for them. This was only the beginning of the second week, and the defendants already appeared slightly frazzled.

"Answer the question," demanded Judge Robles of David Amaro, the witness in the hot seat.

Amaro looked at the judge, then looked over at Tod Harrow and finally muttered, "Thirty million." He let out a sigh and looked down.

"How much is your firm's net worth?" Fetzer followed up in rapid-fire fashion.

"Objection!" Stevens interjected again. "Improper."

"I'll allow it," instructed Judge Robles.

"Half a billion," Amaro said, shaking his head. Tod Harrow was also shaking his head over at his counsel's table, as if saying, *You've let the cat out of the bag.*

"And from the thirty million, how much in fees did your firm keep from the Medina lawsuit?"

"Ten million, plus we got back our expenses. All in all, about twelve million."

"So Rigoberto Medina walked away with eighteen million?" Fetzer asked nodding his head, disgusted.

"Yes, sad but true," said Amaro.

"Why do you say that?"

"Because we got duped by an impostor, and he got away with eighteen million," explained Amaro.

Fetzer quickly read a note Alex had passed to him. It contained a question that Alex wanted answered. "Well, let me ask you," Fetzer continued, "in connection with the two million in expenses from the Medina case: What does 1MJWMS mean?"

"What?" asked Amaro with eyes wide open.

"What does 1MJWMS mean? Explain that to the jury, please," Fetzer instructed the witness.

"Objection!" shouted Slick. "I'm instructing the witness not to answer."

"On what grounds?" asked Fetzer.

"State your objection," demanded Judge Robles as he looked over at Stevens.

"I'm advising the witness to take the Fifth, Your Honor," Slick said, "on grounds that any answer may incriminate him or others. He pleads his right to remain silent."

"Judge," Fetzer said, "the jury is entitled to know what 1MJWMS means. Besides, this is a civil trial. Please instruct the witness to answer. Is it a payment to somebody or an illegal referral fee?"

"Objection!" shouted Stevens.

Fetzer pressed on in rapid-fire form, "Or a finder's fee to an investigator? What exactly is it? Would you care to explain? Is it a payoff to a judge? A bribe?"

"Your Honor!" Stevens exclaimed, addressing the court, "again, I'm instructing my client not to answer."

Perfect! thought Alex, sneering, as he enjoyed the spectacle from counsel's table. *Now the skunk is in the jury box . . . and nothing can clear the stench. To the jury, these guys now look like crooks. They're screwed!*

"I can't make him answer, Mr. Fetzer," advised Judge Robles. "He's invoked his Fifth Amendment right against self-incrimination."

"What are they hiding?" asked Fetzer out loud so that the jury could hear, along with the members of the public.

"We're not hiding anything!" Stevens shouted back, not realizing it was looking worse and worse for Harrow's firm.

"Judge," Amaro said from the witness stand, interrupting the heated exchange, "I want to answer. I will answer, and I'm not invoking my right to remain silent."

There was a loud collective gasp in the courtroom. Fetzer, Alex, Slick, Tod Harrow, Salzman, Romeo, and even Judge Robles did a double take. All eyes were focused on David Amaro. A heavy silence came over the courtroom, the only sound coming from the interpreter sitting next to María Luisa and whispering into her ear the latest exchange in Spanish.

"No, you won't!" screamed Slick Stevens loud and clear so everyone would hear. "Mr. Harrow, as partner to Mr. Amaro, and being that this witness' testimony is prejudicial to the firm, the defendant in this case, invokes on behalf of himself and the parties their right to remain silent. We are instructing this witness not to testify."

"I'm instructing the witness not to answer," said Judge Robles. "I can accept Mr. Harrow wanting to invoke his and the firm's right to remain silent. And since Mr. Amaro is still part of the firm, then he is not to answer anything else in connection with this one question."

Alex, Fetzer, and Romeo were enjoying themselves immensely. Alex had had no idea things were going to turn this ugly. When he'd thought of the question, he just wanted clarification. He just wanted to know where the two million dollars in expenses had gone.

"How many wrongful death lawsuits does your firm handle a year, on an average?" asked Fetzer, switching gears.

"Between fifty and one hundred."

"And what is the average recovery per death, per case?" Fetzer demanded to know.

"Five million."

"So, would it be fair to say that your firm averages in gross recoveries between two hundred fifty million and half a billion a year?"

"Yes, give or take a few."

Fetzer turned around and looked at the jury as he asked his final question. "So in a year's time, your firm, on the average, nets between one hundred and two hundred million in attorneys' fees? Would that be a fair statement?"

"Yes, thereabouts," answered Amaro.

"No further questions," Fetzer said. "Pass the witness."

The next day, the *Rio Grand Post* paraphrased Amaro's testimony in its front-page article, "Firm Pockets Millions of Dollars." It ran a photo of the name partner on the witness stand, handkerchief in hand wiping his forehead, with the caption, "Corpus Christi lawyers in hot water." There was also an inset photo of Tod Harrow scratching his head in disbelief at some of the judge's rulings. A brief summary of the trial followed, along with a few quotes from the Court TV analyst, Wanda Myers. The reporter referred to Alejandro del Fuerte as the shining star and future hope of the legal profession.

First thing in the morning, the courtroom was overflowing with litigants, observers, news reporters, and others. At 9:30 the parties took their places at the two large rectangular tables.

"This court is now in session," announced Roy, the bailiff. "Please turn off your phones, pages, and cell phones. The Honorable Judge Benjamin Robles presiding."

"Are we ready to proceed?" Judge Robles asked the parties as he took his place on the bench.

"Present and ready," replied Alex.

"We're ready," said Slick. "Again, I would like to renew my objection from yesterday on the confidentiality issue and ask the court to instruct the jury to disregard Mr. Amaro's testimony concerning his firm's net worth. That was highly prejudicial and irrelevant to the issues of the case."

"Overruled."

"May I have a running objection, Your Honor, on that point?" Slick pressed again.

"You may not, but you may sit down," snapped the judge. "Mr. del Fuerte, call your next witness."

"Your Honor, we call Professor Jeremiah Treeze to the stand."

The law professor made his way to the witness stand but didn't sit down. He stood next to the hot seat and awaited the judge's instructions. His actions showed great respect for the judge and the system and was done on purpose to make an impression on the jurors.

"You may take your place," acknowledged the judge with a smile.

"Thank you, Your Honor," said the tall and distinguished-looking professor, who had a head full of white hair and a perfectly trimmed matching beard. He was meticulously dressed in gray trousers and navy-blue blazer, and he sat down with great dignity. He looked at the jury and smiled, acknowledging their presence and the importance of their service. After years and years of testifying as an expert, he was the consummate courtroom professional.

"Professor, state your full name for the record," Alex asked.

"Jeremiah S. Treeze."

"You are a law professor, correct?

"Yes."

"Where do you teach?"

"Harvard University, in Cambridge, Massachusetts."

"What subjects do you teach?"

"Legal ethics."

"Have you always taught legal ethics?"

"No," the professor said, addressing the jurors, "I've taught morality and the law, remedies, comparative law, and other similar courses."

"Have you written any articles or published any research?"

"My book on ethics is used by law schools all over the country. I'm also on the advisory board for several state Bar ethics committees throughout the country, and I was invited by Chief Justice Valdez, in Texas, to help him rewrite the Texas Professional Rules of Conduct."

"Besides teaching and publishing, do you do anything else?"

"Well, before joining the world of academia, I worked in the real world, if that's what you're asking."

"Let's talk about that, Professor. Tell us a little about your work history," Alex said.

"After graduating at the top of my class from Harvard Law School, I joined Schonberg, Wolens, Napp & Cox in Washington."

"What kind of work did you do for that firm?"

"The firm handled legal matters dealing with banking, governmental affairs, labor, employment, securities, media, real estate, environmental law, and other regulatory matters."

"How long did you work for the firm?"

"Close to ten years."

"And after working at that firm, did you work anywhere else?"

"Objection!" shouted Stevens. "This is all irrelevant, Your Honor. Can counsel move it right along? Get to the point? Who cares where this witness has worked?"

"Judge," replied Alex, "the jury is entitled to learn something about Professor Treeze's background."

"I agree," Judge Robles concurred. "Even I want to learn something about his background. The objection is overruled."

"Where was I?" asked Alex. "Oh yes, after leaving the Washington firm, Professor, where did you go?"

"I and two other associates from the Washington firm formed Treeze, Scofield & Beckman."

Alex turned and looked at the jury and said, "So you left to form your own firm?"

"Yes."

"And then?"

"Harvard came calling," Professor Treeze answered.

"How so?"

"As the founding member of the firm," Professor Treeze explained, "I had the opportunity to defend and prosecute a wide variety of significant cases that made national news. Headline grabbers, if you will. Some of those cases went all the way to the U.S. Supreme Court. I guess you could say that having argued and 'won' at the Supreme Court made people take notice. So Harvard called and offered me a teaching position. It was a dream job, and I couldn't refuse."

"Very well," Alex said, clearing his throat, "besides teaching, do you do anything else?"

"Spend time with my wife and grandchildren. My two oldest sons met and married beautiful *mexicanas* that they met in college, and they live in the great State of Texas with their families. Every chance we get, we come down to San Antonio and Austin to visit. We love the food. You can't get *enchiladas* like that up north."

The answer caught everybody by surprise. Even Alex was taken aback, for that matter. The jurors' ears perked up at the mention of the great State of Texas, and they immediately felt a connection with the expert when he mentioned that his own sons had fallen in love with Hispanic girls from Texas. Even Judge Robles had cracked a slight smile. It was as if Professor Treeze and his family had instantly been welcomed and embraced into the Valley's Hispanic community. But over at counsel's table, Stevens was rolling his eyes in disgust and seemed quite distraught by the fact that Alejandro del Fuerte was exploiting every advantage at his disposal. No doubt about it, Treeze was what they called "an expert's expert." He knew exactly what to say to sway the jury, without overdoing it.

"I'm sorry, Professor," said Alex, smiling, happy with the way things were going, "I meant, do you do any work anywhere else, outside of Harvard?"

"Oh, yes. Sorry, I didn't understand the question." The professor was now smiling, too, and making visual contact with Judge Robles. "I do consulting work for all the major law firms and teach seminars on ethics, professional conduct, and responsibility."

"Do your peers consider you an expert in the area of legal ethics, canons of conduct, and disciplinary matters?"

"Yes."

"Your Honor," Alex said, looking over at the jury box, "we would like to tender Professor Treeze as an expert in matters dealing with legal ethics, professional responsibility, and lawyer conduct."

Judge Robles pushed his reading glasses up his nose and looked over at Stevens. "Any objection?"

"None," said Stevens, his nostrils flaring.

"Please continue, Mr. del Fuerte," the judge said.

"In order to prepare for this case," Alex asked the professor, "what documents did you review prior to testifying here today?"

"I reviewed the entire Medina file, which was produced by the defendants."

"So you're familiar with the facts of that case, is that an accurate statement?"

"Yes."

"In your professional opinion, can a lawyer keep fees that don't belong to him or her?"

"Of course not," said the professor addressing the jury.

"Along those lines, can a law firm keep fees that do not belong to it?"

"No."

"You've heard what happened in the Medina case, have you not?"

The professor was now addressing the jury, explaining to them the facts of the Medina lawsuit. "Yes, the defendants got duped, supposedly, by a con artist who pretended to be the spouse and father of the victims."

"Assuming that it is true," Alex continued, "do the rules of ethics and professional conduct allow the defendants to profit from their mistake?"

"No, they have to give up any monies wrongfully recovered."

"Why is that?"

"Because they filed a lawsuit that should never have been filed in the first place. They're not allowed to profit from their mistakes."

"Who could have filed the lawsuit, then?"

"Only the husband or the father, parents, sons, or daughters. The law allows what we call 'ascendants and descendants' to sue. Also the spouses."

"So Porfirio Medina was the only person who could have sued?"

"Yes."

"Could María Luisa, sitting here in the courtroom, have sued?"

"No."

"Why not?" Alex pressed on.

"Because she's not a descendant or ascendant of Rosario, even though she's Porfirio's daughter. However, the law does allow her and Mrs. Aurora López to sue as representatives of the estate of Porfirio, her father, to recover the monies that should have been paid to him, had he filed a lawsuit on behalf of his spouse and his child."

"In your professional expert opinion, what would you call a defendant who still refuses to return what is not rightfully his?"

"A thief."

"Objection!" shouted Slick. "That's totally improper."

"Sustained."

"Withdraw the question," instructed Alex. "In your professional expert opinion, do you seriously believe that a firm like Harrow & Amaro could have made a mistake and didn't catch something as basic as that?"

"It's highly unlikely."

"Why is that?"

"They are professionals. They don't sink a dime into a case unless they know that they can win it and that all their t's are crossed and i's dotted. So, I just don't see how they could have been duped."

"So what do you think happened?"

"Objection, calls for speculation!" Slick yelled.

"I'll rephrase, Your Honor," replied Alex. "Do you know what happened?"

"Yes . . . to a reasonable degree of legal certainty. After reviewing their file, I noticed that their intake sheet was not even documented. There was nothing on this man Rigoberto Medina. There was only a copy of a Mexican driver's license, a fake. From what I know, anybody can get a Mexican license for forty dollars. You can even buy them at flea markets. And not only licenses—ID's, working papers, even social security cards. Harrow & Amaro were blinded by greed, saw big money signs, threw caution to the wind, and basically made a ton of money for an impostor who played them because they weren't careful."

"What's that called?"

"Well, at best," the professor said, looking intently at the jury, "negligence, at worst, fraud, theft."

"What do you mean?"

"If it was an oversight, they committed negligence. But if they intentionally set the whole thing up, then they've committed fraud, conversion, and theft . . . insurance fraud, too. Look, it's like this. Tod Harrow and David Amaro both graduated summa cum laude from their respective law schools; both were Order of the Coif, Law Review. One was president of the Law Student's Association, the other clerked for the chief justice of the Texas Supreme Court. Both of them are brilliant. Both are great lawyers. But now, they're here telling us they got duped? They want us to believe that somehow they didn't know? That would be absurd. It just doesn't make sense, not if you apply common sense."

Alex leaned on the witness box, turned to the jury, and said, "Bottom line, Professor Treeze. If the impostor walked with five, ten, or even the entire eighteen million and that money is gone, can the defendants, from a legal standpoint, keep the other five, ten, or whatever millions they made in attorneys' fees?"

"Absolutely not. They have to surrender their fee."

"Thank you," Alex said as he made his way to counsel's table. "Oh, Professor . . . one last thing."

"Yes?"

"Has the Texas state Bar ever investigated Harrow & Amaro for running cases?"

"Objection!" Stevens shouted, his face turning red. "Counsel's comments are highly prejudicial and inflammatory. We move for a mistrial, Your Honor!"

"In chambers, all of you, now!" barked Judge Robles. "We'll be in recess."

All the litigants had been severely admonished by Judge Ben Robles. There would be no more courtroom antics, no more low blows, and no more delays. The next morning, the *Rio Grand Post* ran another brief summary of the contentious trial. Unnamed sources who happened to be outside chambers the day before had plenty to say. Judge Robles had read the parties the riot act. And he'd also admonished Slick that he was close to being found in contempt. For all intents and purposes, Stevens had one foot in the holding tank. The trial would resume promptly at 9:30 the next morning.

"Your Honor, we call María Luisa Medina de García," announced the plaintiff. "She'll need an interpreter."

"The witness has been sworn in," advised the judge. "Please continue, Mr. del Fuerte."

Without wasting any time, Alex jumped right into his direct examination of Pilo's daughter. "Who was Porfirio Medina?"

"My father," the witness replied through the interpreter.

"Let me show you," Alex said as he walked over to the witness stand. "Have you ever seen a marriage license from Mexico?"

"Sure, I have one, since I was married in Mexico."

"How about the order confirming marriage signed by a judge?"

"You mean the *constancia de fe*?"

"Yes."

"Sure," she said, "in Mexico you're also given a copy of that document after your civil ceremony. It's usually signed by the witnesses, too."

"All right," Alex said, handing her a stack of documents, "have you ever seen these documents?"

"Yes, I've seen them before as part of this case."

"Tell the jury what they are and who they belong to."

"The documents are the marriage license and the order confirming."

"Signed by whom?"

"Rosario Medina and Porfirio Medina, my father."

"Are you sure those are their signatures?"

"Yes."

"How can you be so sure?"

"That's my signature here. I was also a witness at their wedding."

"How old were you when your dad remarried?"

"Twenty-seven. I was already married, living in Mexico City with my husband and three children."

"Did he have any other children besides you and your half-brother, Juanito?"

"No, just us two."

"Did your dad love Rosario and his son?"

"Oh, yes! They were everything to him. Just remember what he went through when he came searching for them. He hitchhiked thousands of miles from Tepantitlán to the border. He risked life and limb, even to the point where he was beaten senseless by highway robbers. He even risked drowning and getting thrown in jail . . . all in an effort to find his loved ones. In the end, he paid with his life . . . when he was murdered. To this date, no one has been brought to justice in connection with his murder. If that's not love, then I don't know what is."

Alex took a look at the jury. They were hanging on María Luisa's every word. The women were teary-eyed and the men were staring down at the floor, obviously concentrating hard, trying to restrain their emotions. The entire courtroom had fallen silent.

"Did Rosario ever divorce your father?"

"No."

"Do you know if Rosario left your father for another man?"

"No, she did not."

"Do you know a Rigoberto Medina?"

"No."

"Do you even have a relative by that name?"

"No, sir."

"After Rosario and Juanito passed away, do you know if your dad had a chance to even say goodbye?"

The witness looked down at the floor, overcome by tears, and said between sobs, "He never had a chance to say goodbye to his wife or my little brother. I don't think he even knew they had died, much less how they died or what happened to them. As for myself, I never had a chance to say goodbye to my father."

"I'm so sorry," Alex said as he offered his handkerchief to the witness. "I know what a tremendous loss you have suffered. Not only was your father a client of mine, but I have to tell you, Pilo was also a dear friend of mine." Alejandro del Fuerte had also become teary-eyed. He was standing in front of the witness, glaring down at the floor, trying to regain his composure and contain the tears. "Pass the witness," he said, his voice cracking.

After the plaintiffs ended their case on a high note, the defense began to put on its case in chief. A parade of defense witnesses testified that Rigoberto Medina had managed to dupe them all. Paralegals, secretaries, file clerks, associate attorneys—everyone at Harrow that had worked on the file—all testified that they were dealing with a master in identity theft. Harrow's highly paid defense experts, testifying about insurance fraud and identity theft, explained how easy it was nowadays to con the average Joe, and even the insurance companies.

There was no way to predict that anybody, or Rigoberto Medina, for that matter, would have the nerve to pull such a stunt, to the point of walking away with millions in his pocket. That was what made the whole thing more believable. The impostor had seized a momentous opportunity and had caught everyone at Harrow with their pants down.

Alex and Fetzer took turns cross-examining each witness and were able to show that with a little elbow grease and sweat equity, Harrow could have discovered that Rigoberto Medina was not for real. Had they double-checked the impostor's background in Mexico or the United States, they could have easily discovered that the man did not even exist.

The defense called as their last witness a professor of Economics. The expert was called to explain to the jury that grossing half a billion dollars in attorneys' fees per year did not automatically translate into half a billion dollars in profit, by any means. No, the firm paid salaries, bonuses, overhead, CLE's—Continuing Legal Education—litigation costs, and health insurance for its employees and participated in matching retirement programs for all willing employees. The expert broke down for the jury the expenses normally associated with each lawsuit. There were filing fees, investigator fees, fees for medical records, X-rays, MRIs, CAT scans, deposition expenses, retainers for the experts, postage, copies, referral fees, trial exhibits, storage fees, preservation of evidence fees, laboratory testing fees, animation fees, translator fees, jury consultant fees, even mock jury expenses. There were times when the firm even had to advance the client money for reasonable living expenses. Everything but the kitchen sink. On the average, Harrow sank half a million dollars in expenses per case.

So to bankroll about seventy-five to a hundred cases a year took approximately fifty million dollars.

Alex forced the expert to concede that even though the numbers sounded huge, the fact remained that the firm averaged a hundred million dollars in profits per year. And no one other than the name partners were entitled to share in the profits. A spreadsheet prepared by the plaintiffs' experts showed that the value of the firm was five hundred million and that the good will in the community added another three hundred million to the business.

"We rest," announced Slick Stevens after their last witness, "and close."

"Mr. del Fuerte?" the judge asked. "Your announcement?"

"Your Honor," Alex said, "we call Professor Kauffman, a documents expert from Mexico, for impeachment purposes."

"Very well," Judge Robles said, sounding tired, "put him on the witness stand."

Alex put on his impeachment expert that Thursday afternoon and, after a brief cross-examination by Slick, rested and closed. The impeachment expert was brilliant; Alex used him to steal the thunder of the defense team's economics expert. Kauffman had the jurors nodding their heads in agreement with everything he said. The expert had testified that in Mexico, everything was now computerized, and it was quite simple to obtain information about a person.

Moreover, the viewing of all public records was available for free to anyone with a computer and a modem. Had the defendants cared even a little about finding out who they were really dealing with, they could have done it with a few strokes of their keyboard. Likewise, Professor Kauffman, who was instrumental in bringing about Mexico's legislative reforms for a more open and transparent government, told the jury that there were hundreds of web services available, for pennies, to check people's backgrounds.

The rebuttal expert also testified that for Harrow to allege that his firm had no clue, in this day and age, bordered on sheer stupidity—especially with everything the public knew about cyber crime, credit card fraud, and identity theft. Even the U.S. government for decades had required employers to check their employees' papers. The employer must ask if the worker has the required papers to work in the United States, legally. Does the employee have a social security number? A valid ID? A birth certificate? The fact that the defendants were trying to hide behind a copy of a fake Mexican driver's license didn't pass the smell test.

Professor Kauffman also told the jurors that the defendants in the case must have known that Rigoberto Medina was a fake. He himself had run the name in all the search engines available in Mexico and the United States and had found several matches, but none matched the photo in the fake license in Harrow's file. There was a simple explanation to it. The guy in the photo did not exist. Someone manufactured the license and made up the identity of the fake. It would be interesting to know who was behind all of this.

On a final note, Professor Kauffman reminded the jury that his job was not to testify as to whether or not Harrow had actual knowledge that they were dealing with an impostor. He was there to show the jury how simple it was—particularly nowadays with all the recent technological advances—for a law firm, especially one like Harrow, to know who they were dealing with. In his professional expert opinion, Harrow must have suspected something was not quite right. They had a duty to investigate further.

Alex knew that the jurors had probably already made up their minds after the first week of trial. All the available literature on jury psychology indicated that by the end of the first day of trial, most jurors had already made their decision on the case, one way or another. Any additional evidence would probably be swept under the rug, unless such evidence was overwhelming. For the most part, the studies showed, fifty percent of jurors made up their mind by the time jury selection had ended. The other fifty percent would side with one party or another by the close of the evidence on the first day.

"Ladies and gentlemen of the jury," announced Judge Robles, "both sides have rested and closed. That means they have presented all the evidence in the case. We'll have closing arguments Friday, starting at nine. Remember, when you go home tonight, do not discuss this case with anybody, not even your spouses. I'll see you here tomorrow morning promptly at 8:30 a.m."

"All rise for the jury," announced the bailiff as he held the courtroom door open for the jurors, who exited the courtroom one by one.

The headlines in the *Houston Chronicle* that Friday morning read, "Documents Expert from Mexico Bolsters Plaintiff's Case in Medina Trial." It was a brief article by Samantha Liles with the Associated Press. In it, the news correspondent described how Professor Kauffman told the jury that the evidence supported the plaintiff's contention that the Corpus Christi firm must have known or suspected that they were dealing with an impostor. The defendants either had not cared, which would make their conduct reprehensible, or, the most likely explanation, they knew and went along and helped perpetuate the fraud on the real victims and their families. The article concluded by saying that the defendants had decided not to call any impeachment witnesses themselves in order not to risk opening the door to further cross-examination, which would have allowed the plaintiffs to explore some more of the inner workings of the Corpus Christi law firm.

That Friday morning, Alejandro del Fuerte and Tony "Slick" Stevens delivered their closing arguments to a packed courtroom. The exercise took most of the morning as the attorneys went over the evidence and reminded the jury to use their common sense. Judge Robles allowed the jury to break for lunch before starting deliberations at 1:30 that afternoon. Finally, after three weeks of trial, the twelve-member jury had received the case. The jury deliberated the entire afternoon, but they did not reach a verdict and were sent home for the weekend.

Chapter 35

MONDAY AND TUESDAY CAME AND WENT without any news, extraordinary jury notes, unusual developments, or a verdict, for that matter. Outside the Cameron County courthouse, the scene had all the makings of a county fair. The parking lot across from the judicial building had been taken over by all the different news teams from in and around the Valley and all the major U.S. networks, as well as some from Mexico City. The entire area was dotted with Winnebagos, RVs, large buses, makeshift news camps, satellite dishes, cameras, miles of cable, and reflector lights.

By the time Wednesday rolled around, the jury had been in deliberations for almost thirty hours. The legal analysts broadcasting from the footsteps of the courthouse all had different views as to what the delay meant. Some argued that any progress the jury might have made on Friday had been negated by the lengthy weekend. Others speculated that the weekend break was good for the defense because the emotion that Alejandro del Fuerte might have stirred in the jurors' hearts was now gone. Others volunteered that the delay was probably due to the fact that the jury had requested lengthy portions of the trial transcript, along with all of the evidence to be delivered to the jury room. They had to be slowly reviewing all of it, and that would necessarily take some time.

The five-day wait was killing Alex and the others. Alex and his law professor had poured their hearts into the case, but now it was out of their hands. All in all, it had been a pretty good showing. The plaintiffs had socked it to the Harrow boys and given them bloody noses, but not without Slick inflicting some damage and giving the student and his professor a couple of black eyes. It was now up to the jury. The jurors had gone about doing their jobs dutifully and admirably, and they had not sent a note that might indicate the status of the deliberations.

Wednesday morning found Alex, Fetzer, and Romeo waiting impatiently in the law library on the first floor of the courthouse. They had camped out at one of the tables in the back of the library and were waiting to hear any news. If the jury had a question or had reached a verdict, the lawyers would be paged through the PA system. Judge Robles wouldn't take up the question or receive a verdict unless all the litigants were present.

Alex had just opened the early edition of the *Rio Grand Post* when his cell phone rang. It was Chordelli, who couldn't contain himself.

"Can you talk?" Chordelli asked.

"Yes," Alex answered.

"I heard you and your second chair put on a helluva show," Chordelli said in a congratulatory manner. He was calling from his headquarters in San Antonio; he had not had the chance to stay behind and catch all of the action.

"Thank you. We're waiting, like everyone else," Alex answered, trying to play down the unexpected phone call.

He walked out of the library with the phone to his ear and headed out of the courthouse to the sidewalk near the street.

"What do you want?" demanded Alex. "You know you're not supposed to be calling."

"I just wanted to tell you that we are very pleased with our investment. My sources tell me that you were fantastic during your closing argument. You had the jury eating out of your hands. The Harrow boys and Slick were strutting around when the trial started, and now with the jury out for three days straight, I think they've begun circling the wagons. I think they'll want to talk settlement again. Especially after Fetzer had a field day with their legal experts. Man! I hear he really tore their experts apart. The jury paid attention. I tell you what, all those years as a federal prosecutor and expertise in white-collar crime paid off. My sources tell me that the cross-examination may have tipped the jury in your favor. Everyone was thinking that there was no way the firm couldn't have known they were dealing with an impostor. They had to be in it, or so everyone thought."

"I'm glad you're pleased," Alex said, somewhat annoyed because he knew the case was not over, "but you know the jury is still out. Anything can happen." All the compliments and all the accolades didn't mean a thing until the court said those famous six words: *Has the jury reached its verdict?*

"This is what I really wanted to tell you, Alex. I just got off the phone with one of our young associates who has been down there monitoring the trial. He's been eating breakfast at the same restaurant Harrow and his boys have been visiting. He's been keeping vigil, trying to get some scoop, see what they're thinking. He tells me that last night, Salzman, the risk manager for the insurance company defending Harrow, spent all night talking to Slick and Tod Harrow. They were having drinks in the lounge, discussing the possibility of tendering policy limits."

"Excuse me?" Alex exclaimed.

"You heard me. Slick and Tod Harrow, at this very moment, are thinking about settling with you. They must be terrified. When Slick pours out a plaintiff, it's usually within the first three hours of deliberations. Never before has one of his juries stayed out more than that. And now, the jury is getting ready to start its fourth day of deliberations. I'm telling you, they're terrified. They're convinced, like everyone else in the courthouse, that you're about to do the unthinkable to Harrow. That the jury is about to pull the switch on them. That's exactly what I want!"

"Well, that's good, no?"

"Yes and no," Chordelli said, sounding concerned. "If you settle, you must settle for policy limits. They have twenty-five mil in coverage. Now, if they want confidentiality, you must make it so that they can't afford it. Ask for another twenty-five million. So either they pay to keep everything under wraps or take their chances and wait until the jury reaches its verdict and makes the whole thing public. So, you have to make it real hard for them to settle."

"Okay, gotcha. Gotta run. We'll talk later," said Alex as he headed back to the library inside the courthouse. He would hate to miss anything.

The first question from the jury came right before lunchtime on the fourth day of deliberations. It was signed by the jury foreman and was addressed to the judge. All the parties were paged to Judge Robles' chambers.

"Gentlemen," said Judge Robles, "the jury wants to know who gets to assess punitive damages. I would guess they've reached a verdict on liability. Here's the jury's note."

The judge passed the note around. Harrow and his clan went from pink to ghostly white. The note read:

> *Judge,*
>   *When do we get to assess punitive damages? And do we get to decide the amount, or does the court decide the amount of punitive damages? Are there any limits as to how much we can award?*
> *Signed,*
> *Joe Martinez, foreman*

"With all due respect," Slick jumped in, "I disagree, Judge. The question by itself doesn't mean anything. And if I might add, it can't be answered until the second phase of the trial. To do so at this time would be premature and would constitute the court's comment on the evidence and may be reversible error."

"Was there a motion to bifurcate filed in the case?" asked the judge. "So that we only get to the issue of punitive damages if the jury finds gross negligence or fraud first?"

"Yes, of course," said Harrow and Slick in unison. The motion was designed to split the trial into two stages. The jury was to decide liability first. If they also found gross negligence or fraud, then there would be a second phase of the trial in order to determine the amount of exemplary damages.

"What do you recommend we do, Judge?" Fetzer interjected, giving the judge his proper place.

Everyone could see Slick was starting to get a little hot around the collar. The same went for Harrow and his boys.

"I'll answer the note this way," said the judge, who had been busy writing. His reply read:

Members of the jury,
   Answer only the questions before you based on the evidence before you, at this time.
Signed,
Judge Robles

"We don't have an objection to your response, Your Honor," Alex said.

"I don't think it can be answered in any other way," said Harrow in a trembling voice.

"Yes, to do so might send the wrong signal," Slick added, somewhat relieved that the way the judge had handled the question could conceivably keep the jury from reaching the question on punitive damages.

The judge handed the note with the answer back to the bailiff and directed him to deliver it to the jury waiting in the deliberation room. As soon as the bailiff left chambers, the judge asked Harrow, Amaro, Slick, Alex, and Fetzer to stay while ordering all the rest of Harrow's minions to leave.

"Gentlemen," the judge started as he directed his comments to the Harrow boys, "you need to settle this thing. And I'll tell you what. Before the jury reaches its verdict, I'm going to send them to lunch. So, that gives you an hour and a half to talk settlement. I'm doing you all a favor."

"Judge," cried Slick, "there's five hundred thousand on the table. That's more than the case is worth!"

"Give me a break, Stevens," the judge said, growling. "You need to talk to your clients and talk real numbers here. The jury is already considering punitive damages, and you want to settle this thing for pennies. Didn't your client testify that the firm earned ten or twelve million in fees from the lawsuit? I'm giving you one and a half hours to settle this thing. Now go and settle it!"

Once out of chambers, Alex, Fetzer, and the others stopped to talk in the hallway.

"Well, boys," said Alex, grinning, "the judge wants this thing settled."

"Look, you little shit," hissed Slick, "you know my clients haven't done anything wrong! You filed this lawsuit to hit the lotto."

"Whatever," Alex shot back, getting in Slick's face. "Obviously the jury disagrees with you, Mr. Stevens. So, I'll tell you what. Why don't you come back with real numbers, not chicken shit. And you better start at policy limits."

"Ha! In your dreams!" shot back Slick.

"Well, you heard the judge," Alex retorted. "I won't waste my time with *pendejos*! You know where to find me. You've got my cell number."

Fetzer, Romeo, and Alex headed back to the library. Fetzer and Alex took their place at the same table they had left just minutes earlier.

"Can you believe it?" said Alex. His head was spinning.

"The jury is upset, something pissed them off," said the professor.

"Well, whatever it was, it sounds like it's good for us."

"I agree."

"Anybody hungry?" interrupted Romeo. "It's lunchtime, twelve o'clock exactly."

"Yes," replied Alex and the professor.

"I'll go get us some sandwiches from the coffee shop while we wait for them sum'bitches to call," Romeo said, happy to be part of a winning team.

Alejandro del Fuerte's cell phone started ringing. Fetzer jumped out of his chair and got close to Alex to see if he could hear anything. The two were anxious to hear from the defense and start talking some real numbers.

"Mr. del Fuerte," a female voice said.

"Yes," said Alex, waving to Fetzer that it wasn't the call they were waiting for. He didn't recognize the female calling, and his cell showed the call was from a private number. *Was it somebody calling on behalf of Paloma? What did she want?*

"Mr. del Fuerte, I can't tell you who I am, but I can tell you this. I've been reading about you in the newspapers, and I'm glad to see someone doing something about all the sleaze balls out there."

"Thanks," said Alex, somewhat impatient, "but I must hang up. I'm waiting for a really important phone call. I don't mean to be rude, but do you have a number where I can call you?"

"What I have to say will interest you, Mr. del Fuerte. And it will only take one minute. I promise."

"Make it snappy. Go."

"You got the wrong guys," said the female on the other end of the line.

"What?" Alex asked.

"Harrow & Amaro run cases, but they're not murderers or serious white-collar criminals."

"Who is this?" demanded Alex.

"There's a private restroom inside the library that is rarely used. There's a magazine rack in there. In between the magazines, there will be a manila envelope. I think its contents will interest you."

There was a click, and the line went dead.

Alex was completely speechless. He didn't get the caller's name and had no clue how the woman could have obtained his cell number. He had not had the presence of mind to get Fetzer to listen to the caller.

He got up from his chair and went to the restroom the caller described, which was at the end of the stacks off to the south side of the library. There was a lounge area for attorneys furnished with sofas and coffee tables, and adjacent to it sat the restroom the caller described. Alex pushed the door open and found the envelope between an old *Texas Monthly* and a *People* magazine. Inside the envelope, there was a micro tape and a typed transcript. Presumably it was a transcript from the conversation possibly contained on the tape.

Alex was afraid to even begin reading the transcript. His mind was racing. It appeared that he had Harrow and the boys in his hands, and now somebody wanted him to get to this mysterious envelope. Standing there in the bathroom, he decided that nothing was going to derail the settlement negotiations with Harrow. They would be calling soon. It was only 12:30, and there was still an hour to go. Fetzer was waiting back at the table, and Romeo had not yet come back with the sandwiches from the coffee shop.

If he read the transcript or listened to the tape, he might not like its contents, and maybe the whole settlement would be sabotaged. He needed to keep focused and finish with Harrow before doing anything else.

Was this Harrow trying to send him on a rabbit trail? After all, Tod Harrow and Slick Stevens did have his cell number. Were they trying to point him in another direction as part of their settlement strategy? Was the female caller working for them? Why did the call come now, just as he was about to settle this case for millions of dollars?

He was intrigued and afraid. What if the contents revealed something that was too big for him to handle, or a new scandal? What if he needed to come clean with Fetzer and reveal the deal with Chordelli? Would that kill his friendship with Fetzer?

He noticed his hands shaking a little as he held the envelope and its contents. Sweat beads were forming on his forehead. He splashed cold water on his face and patted it dry with paper towels. He threw them down the toilet and flushed.

"That's where I'm headed," Alex mumbled to himself as he glimpsed down into the swirling water being flushed into Brownsville's sewer lines.

His head was still spinning when his phone rang again. Alex thought that this time it must be Harrow and the boys with a juicy offer with real numbers. It was time they came back with big numbers. Even Judge Robles had laughed at their last settlement offer of five hundred thousand, especially after the last jury question. By the sound of it, it seemed the jury was ready to punish Harrow and its cronies. His heart started pounding again. He wondered what their starting number would be.

"Did you get the envelope?" asked the female at the other end.

"Yes . . . I've got it, but I haven't read its contents," Alex said, trying to play the whole thing down. He needed to keep the line open. "Who is this?"

"Let me tell you what's on the tape," the caller said. "The transcript covers only the first five minutes of a conversation that I think you will find very, very interesting. Maybe even shocking. When you're finished listening to the tape, I hope you run with it. It seems you're the only one around here who's willing to stand up and fight for what's right."

"Who are you?" demanded Alex.

"That's not important right now."

"How did you get the tape?" Alex asked. "At least answer that."

"I can't right now," replied the woman, "but you'll know in time, I promise. Let me say this. The tape contains conversations between Judge Macallan and various attorneys. These conversations took place in chambers over different periods of time. They're very telling of the kind of criminal you're dealing with. Of course, I could be in trouble for taping the conversations. For those reasons, I can't reveal my identity right now. However, I believe the end will justify the means, someday. The rest is up to you."

"So, who are the other lawyers on the tape?" Alex asked.

"Powerful lawyers, the kind that always make headlines and hit the big verdicts, large enough to make substantial contributions to Macallan's campaigns. They also happen to be close friends of his. I've got to go. We'll be in touch."

Alex closed the door to the small private restroom and agonized for several minutes about whether he should go over the transcript or not. He glanced at it and noticed the names Macallan and Chordelli scribbled in the margin. It was dated May 2003. He stopped staring at it and forced himself to put it away. Nothing, or better yet, no one was going to derail the negotiations with Harrow. He convinced himself that he must finish the task at hand. He was still in trial mode. It was time to eat what he and Professor Fetzer had killed.

His mind was still racing, and his senses were getting the better of him. He needed to get out of the small bathroom and catch some fresh air. Yet he couldn't help but wonder how the caller had ended up with the tape. Did she know he'd been talking to Chordelli as well?

He was putting the contents back into the envelope when the phone rang again. It was Fetzer, looking for him. The boys from Harrow were outside the law library and wanted to have a one-on-one with the plaintiffs to discuss a proposed structured settlement agreement. He stuffed the envelope into his coat pocket and walked to the table to meet Fetzer and Romeo.

Chapter 36

SLICK, HARROW, AND SALZMAN wanted to talk, and since they were supposed to keep quiet in the law library, Alex suggested they walk across the street and get a cup of coffee at Zydeco's Cajun Kitchen.

All the lawyers were trying to keep it together, especially after that last jury note. Tempers were frayed, and everyone was tired. Alex was thinking of the tape and its transcript. Had it been Chordelli all along? Had he been playing Alex like a record? And what about the lawsuit against Harrow? Could it be that it was really without merit? Could it be that maybe, this once, Harrow had done nothing wrong?

"Here we are," said Alex, as he held the door open for everyone, including Slick. At that very moment, he felt empowered. The jury note had had that effect on him and Fetzer. They were holding the aces.

Everyone took a seat at a round booth far away from the door. The place was empty, and they ordered coffee.

Alex got straight to the point. "How much do you want to pay to get out from under this mess?" he asked Salzman. The risk manager was still holding the money.

"Mr. del Fuerte, before I can settle this case, two things have to happen," Salzman began slowly. "I need you to lower your demand. I cannot possibly pay you policy limits. This case is not worth twenty-five million dollars, and you know that. Secondly, I need to get consent from my clients to settle this thing. And I think you're well aware that my clients have a problem giving you anything above and beyond what was offered at mediation. My clients don't believe they've done anything wrong. Now, with that said, I know the judge wants this thing resolved. I know the jury is considering assessing punitive damages. And I know you and the professor tried a hell of a case. You have us against the ropes. But there won't be any significant movement unless you make a move and come down from twenty-five million."

"Are you finished?" Alex said, yawning.

"You are certainly aware," Salzman continued, "are you not, that the Texas Supreme Court won't let you keep any excessive punitive damages award. Sure, the Corpus Christi court of appeals might let you keep some of it. But at the end of the day, the Texas Supreme Court will, at best, reverse and remand. At worse, reverse and render. And then what are you going to do? How are you going to explain to your client that you could have made her some good money right now, but you chose to gamble it all away because your ego wouldn't let you see straight? I think you need to read to her the Supreme Court's opinion on *South Texas Valley Bank v. Martin*. That should provide some enlightenment."

"I've read the case," Alex said, "and you may be right. The Supremes won't let us keep a huge punitive award. So let's do the math. Harrow settled Rosario and her son's case for thirty million. The firm kept ten million in fees plus two million in expenses. The jury will order your client to disgorge these amounts. The other seventeen or eighteen million are gone, and we'll never see them again—unless we find the impostor. So, ten million in fees times two and a half for reasonable punitives. That's thirty-five million. You come back with a number close to that, and then we will have some movement. So far, all I've heard is five hundred thousand. The ball is in your court."

"You do good work negotiating," Salzman said. "I'm impressed."

"I might be young, but I'm not stupid, Mr. Salzman. Talk to your client and his attorney . . . see where they want to go from here," Alex said, pointing at Harrow and Slick.

"I know the bottom line, Mr. del Fuerte. We've had these discussions before. I have authority to settle for ten million."

"Now you're talking," Alex answered and hit Fetzer under the table with his knee. They were finally talking real numbers.

"We could have the money wired to your trust account before noon tomorrow," Salzman offered, trying to get Alex to just take the offer and get the case settled once and for all. In a few more minutes they would have to report back to court.

"I appreciate the offer, but if you want to settle the case, we've valued it at twenty," Alex replied. He was trying to squeeze the last dime out of the insurance company. After all, he hated insurance companies. They were the scum of the earth. In Texas they had masterminded Proposition 12, caps on jury awards, and every other type of trick to limit victims' rights. It sure was nice to have them against the ropes.

"Can we split the difference?" Salzman asked, exasperated, almost begging. "Will fifteen do?"

"Let us talk to our client." Alex motioned over to Fetzer and María Luisa. "We'll step outside and discuss it."

Fetzer, Romeo, María Luisa, and Alex walked to the parking lot and stood there quietly staring at each other. Alex broke the silence and addressed María Luisa.

"*Han ofrecido quince millones*," he said in Spanish. "There's fifteen million dollars on the table. It's a good amount. Do you want to take it?"

"*Lo que usted diga*," the young woman answered shyly. "Whatever you think, Mr. del Fuerte."

"Professor, what do you think?" asked Alex.

"They have a point," Fetzer replied. "Any large punitive award won't hold up on appeal. Not with this Supreme Court, anyway. Fifteen million is plenty. More than the Texas Supreme Court would let you keep. Sure, it would be nice to let the jury answer the punitive damages question. But with the ultraconservative makeup of today's Supreme Court, I'd say take it."

"Okay, then. Let's go back inside," Alex ordered everyone.

"Well?" asked Slick, Harrow, and Salzman in unison when they saw the plaintiffs come inside.

"Fifteen is fine, but no confidentiality and no structured settlement," Alex indicated. "All in a lump sum."

"Fine," Salzman replied, "but no admission of liability."

"All right, then," Alex said, smiling, "we got ourselves a deal."

Everyone at the table shook hands, except Slick and Alex. Alex knew Slick's pride had to be wounded. The litigator probably would have rather taken the case all the way to verdict. Alex would have liked to hear the jury read the punitive award out loud as well. That would have sent a strong and loud message to all the case runners in Texas. But he would have to wait for that. Maybe the truth about case running would come out another day. Maybe someday, all the law schools would teach a course on it or talk about it. Or maybe the state Bar would decide to really do something about it. Maybe what was needed was to teach all law students not to be afraid and to turn in all those involved in the scheme. They should be encouraged to speak out against the jailer and the bondsman running cases for the solo criminal defense attorney, turn in even the dirty cop who got paid to change police reports and accident investigations, and report the big firms with entire sophisticated networks in place. Even people inside the Mexican consulates along the Texas-Mexico border were notorious for running cases. Maybe what had happened in this courtroom would be the next wave—lawyers suing other lawyers who solicited cases and ordering them to disgorge their fees. Would it come to that?

"I'll call Judge Robles," Slick interjected, "and tell him that the case is settled."

"Sure, make yourself useful," Alex declared. "Let's head on back to the courthouse."

Chapter 37

THE TEXAS LITIGATOR HAD CALLED and said that they were sending a reporter to do a feature on future powerhouse law firms and their founding members. The firm of Del Fuerte & Fetzer LLP was to be included in the next edition, and so a reporter by the name of April Wingate would be dropping by.

When Wingate showed up at the office, she was greeted by Betty and Astrid who were busy returning phone calls and opening mail. The boss was in his office in the back making plans with Romeo to go fishing up at Port Mansfield. The change in seasons, as the latest fishing reports confirmed, was the cause for the migration and return of the fighting tarpon to the South Texas coast. Along with the tarpon fish, there had been sightings of giant bull reds running near past the jetties. Alex and Romeo were arguing over which way was the best way to set the hook on a tarpon when Astrid's voice came over the speaker phone.

"Mr. del Fuerte?" Astrid said.

"What is it, Astrid?"

"The reporter from *The Texas Litigator* is here. Do you want her to wait or do you want me to show her to your office or the conference room?"

"In the conference room. Ask her if she would like something to drink. I'll be right there."

Alex walked into the conference room and greeted Ms. Wingate. He sat at the head of the conference table and loosened his tie. Romeo followed with coffee and a box of crispy crème doughnuts. The *The Texas Litigator* reporter pulled out her micro recorder and hit the record button.

"We're on the record," the attractive twenty-something said, and the interview was on.

Alejandro del Fuerte played with his coffee cup for a few moments and sat there reflecting in silence. He finally peeked at Ms. Wingate, gave her a smile, and began to tell his story. It had all begun the weekend before he'd opened for business. It had been a chance meeting, although other folks might call it something totally different, such as luck, circumstance, destiny, or the hand of faith *o la mano de Dios*. In any event, it had been a meeting that had had an impact on his life. A chance encounter, an envelope, a street address, Rosario, the boy, a rollover, their death, and a mysterious lawsuit. That's how it all had happened. He explained how he had found the probate file and the sealed file and how he had failed to tell his client the truth about his wife and his boy. How not a day went by in which he didn't think of Pilo and his family. And how, deep inside, he thought that maybe it had been better that Pilo had never found out about their deaths. And here he was: famous, rich, the new kid in town. He had even been invited to testify in Austin, at the legislature, but it had all been at the expense of Porfirio Medina. Ultimately, he, Alex, was still here and his client wasn't, and that was the irony of the whole thing.

"Did you ever find out who was the fake plaintiff in the Harrow lawsuit?" Wingate asked, wanting to take the story in another direction.

"Unfortunately," started Alex, "his true identity will never be known."

"Really? You don't believe this individual will surface again?"

"I don't know. It's possible, I guess."

Alejandro del Fuerte reached for his coat pocket and pulled out a white envelope and slid it over to Ms. Wingate. "In the envelope, there is a micro-cassette. There are two male voices discussing a potential case. I think, if you listen closely, you'll be able to recognize the voices on the tape. When you do that, then it's quite possible that you'll find what you're looking for. In any event, if you can pick up the trail, you'll discover all kinds of interesting things."

"You can't tell me who's on the tape?" the reporter asked, batting her pretty blue eyes.

"Oh, I can tell you, but then it won't be any fun."

"When I find out who the voices on the tape are, what happens next?"

"You'll have the biggest story of your life, I promise," said Alex.

"That big, eh?"

"That big. And you'll be famous because you broke the story," Alex said, smiling. He had just fulfilled a reporter's dream. Ten minutes earlier, the interview was just another interview. Now, the reporter was on her way to breaking the biggest story of her life.

"How did you get this tape?" she asked.

"Attorney-client privilege. I can't go there," Alex replied. This wasn't necessarily true, but Alex thought that was all she needed to know at that time. Besides, claiming the attorney-client privilege would stop her cold in her tracks, and she wouldn't press for more details.

"So, how does it feel to be a millionaire at twenty-five?" Wingate asked, switching gears.

"I haven't given it much thought," Alex said, squirming in his chair. "To be honest with you, I just want to try cases. I want to get back into the courtroom and talk to the jury. Try to get in their heads. Lock eyes with them. What are they thinking? Do they view the case the same way I view it? Are they with me or with my opponent? Am I getting through? Do they identify with my client and feel the justice in our case? Now that's exciting! That's a totally different feeling than knowing you have money in the bank. Money is nice, don't get me wrong. But when you connect with the jury . . . there's nothing like it."

"So, what's next on your plate?"

"Take some time off. Maybe take my grandfather fishing," Alex answered. "Spend some time with the old man. He's getting up there in age, and he won't be around much longer. He's the only family I have."

"Well, that's sweet," April said. "One more thing, do you think it's all right for lawyers to sue other lawyers?"

"There's a difference between righting a wrong and suing for the specific purpose of lining your pockets. If it's to right a wrong, I don't have a problem with it. It's not pleasant, but I don't have a problem with it."

"Have you yourself ever been sued?"

"Yes. The case was dismissed, totally frivolous, and I hear our illustrious Texas legislature is revamping AMEGO to further restrict lawsuits filed by lawyers against other lawyers. No surprise there. They've taken the teeth out of everything else."

"Is that because most of the members of the legislature are lawyers?"

"I guess," he replied. "What gets me is that no one is asking how this new legislation is going to protect the public. Sure, it will protect the lawyers, the firms, and the insurance companies that have to pay the claims, but not the real victims."

"Do you want this off the record?" April asked, wondering where Mr. del Fuerte was going with this.

"No," he said, "on the record. I don't mind speaking up. The public needs to have access to the courts. The victims need to have access to the courts. And we need a strong tort system to punish corporate defendants as safety, environmental, and health regulations are done away with by Republican-controlled legislatures. You can't have both. You can't have mild regulatory schemes and a weak tort system."

"Is that what happened in the Harrow case?"

"Absolutely," Alex explained. "Once lawyers realized that it was okay to run cases because the state Bar looks the other way and nothing happens, then they took it to the next level. You give an inch, they take a foot. It's human nature. That's the way it's always been—until someone raised the bar further and came up with the idea to create a plaintiff. So somebody had to ask, why waste a perfectly good case with a good set of facts, with horrible damages, only because no one knows where the Plaintiff is? Let's make one!"

"I see you feel strongly about rogue lawyers. Is that an accurate statement?"

"My grandfather was a lawyer. But not just any lawyer—he was an honorable lawyer. That's all I ever wanted to be. An honorable attorney. I get out of law school and come to find out that I'm working with worms. You can understand my disappointment."

"Yes, I understand. Is there anything else?" April was getting impatient. She couldn't wait to go and hear the tape, which promised the biggest story of her career.

"No. That's it. Thank you for coming."

April Wingate got up from her chair and started packing her things. She scribbled something on the back of her business card and slipped it to Alex. It had her phone number scribbled on it and read, *Call Me.*

Alex felt flattered, and with good reason. He was now the most eligible bachelor in town.

As he sat at his desk in his well-appointed office, Alex realized that he had arrived. Just a year earlier, he'd been scraping by without an inkling as to how to run a law office, much less make any money at it, and now he had people, businesses, and governments calling and wanting his firm to represent them. The *Texas Monthly*, the *Bar Journal,* and others were all seeking interviews. As he was savoring the moment, Romeo walked in with a copy of the Lifestyle pages of the *Rio Grand Post*, the local newspaper.

"Have you seen this?" the assistant asked.

"What is it?"

"An article on Paloma Yarrington's wedding," Romeo explained. "Wasn't she the ex-girlfriend you had me send the box of photos to?"

"Yes, that was her," said Alex.

"Well then, you might want to look at it." He handed Alex a section of the paper and quickly made his way out of the boss's office. Alex grabbed the paper and saw the first of two full pages describing the Yarrington-Macallan wedding as the event of the decade.

The front page of the Lifestyle section featured photos of the wedding and the reception at Rancho del Cielo Country Club. It was a "who's who" affair. Photos splashed across the front page revealed the presence of friends of the Yarrington family. There were senators, governors, former governors, county judges, lesser known politicos, and even one or two past presidential nominees. On the Macallans' side, guests included the state's Republican leadership and the heads of some very important oil companies. It had been a star-studded affair, including a special appearance by Luis Miguel, a crooner and Mexican pop star.

Alex wanted to throw up.

On the second page, there were more pictures of the bride and her bridesmaids. Even the menu was reproduced on the bottom of the page. After the religious ceremony, the guests had all participated in a fabulous five-course meal. The first course had been boneless breasts of Texas white wing dove, sprinkled with sesame seed oil and rice wine vinaigrette with baby greens. Then the bride had served her guests a creamy seafood bisque made with jumbo Texas gulf shrimp and bay scallops. The third course had consisted of a choice of free-range Cornish game hens in jalapeno mango relish, slow-roasted, herb-infused baby *cabrito*, pan sautéed red fish in a creamy *veracruzano beurre blanc*, or Argentinean beef tenderloin *a la pampa* with rosemary potatoes.

The paper went on and on about what was served, who drank what, and the hundreds of thousands of dollars a wedding for a thousand guests must have cost. The Valley would probably never see a wedding like that again in a thousand years.

The bride and her geeky groom, Calvin Macallan, son of the Honorable Walter Macallan, district judge for Cameron County, Texas, would honeymoon in Europe for six weeks. After their honeymoon, the couple would reside in their newly built, two-million dollar home at Laguna Bella Estates, an exclusive gated community built right on the shores of the Laguna Madre and the Gulf of Mexico.

But Alex would have the last laugh. It was just a matter of days before April Wingate figured out who was on the tape. Once she broke the story, all hell would break loose. In a few days, the Valley's focus would shift from the joyous wedding to a scandalous criminal investigation involving well-known public figures. The wedding would soon be history.

Romeo could be heard in the break room down the hall from Alex's office, calling Jim's Pier out at Port Mansfield and requesting information about water temperatures, the latest catches, and the times for high and low tides. Alex was still in his office digesting the news from the morning, now more than ever looking forward to the fishing trip, when Betty interrupted his thoughts.

"Mr. del Fuerte?" she called.

"What is it, Betty?"

"There's a young lady out her to see you. She doesn't have an appointment. Her name is Naivi García—at least, I think that's what she said. Says it's important."

"Give me a minute," he said. He had a problem with people who didn't make appointments, but it was part of the business. After all, that's how he'd come to meet Pilo. He had been a walk-in, pretty much.

"Betty?" the young attorney called out over the speaker phone.

"Yes, Mr. del Fuerte."

"Show Ms. García to my office. Thanks."

Alex had just thrown the newspaper into the basket when Betty knocked on his door.

"Here's Ms. García," she announced as she opened the door. "Will you be needing anything?"

"Ms. García," Alex asked, "can we offer you something to drink?" The attorney figured she was another groupie who was after the most eligible bachelor in town. Funny how news of the multimillion dollar settlement recovered on behalf of his clients had made him such an object of female attention.

"No, I'm okay. This won't take long," she said as she placed a shoe box on Alex's desk.

"Thanks, Betty," Alex said, "please close the door behind you and hold all my calls."

"Will do."

"Please have a seat," Alex told the young lady in his office. "Let me ask you, what kind of name is Naivi?"

"It's Nahuatl for 'autumn breeze,'" she replied. "My mother, I'm told, was very proud of her heritage. So that's what she named me."

"That's original. I've never heard that name before, although I must admit it is very pretty."

"Thanks," Naivi said.

"So, anyway," he asked, "what can I do for you?"

"I just wanted to stop by and congratulate you," she said, "or rather, meet you in person."

"Why would you want to do that?"

"A few years ago, I worked down at the courthouse, in the district clerk's office. After I quit my job, I would read the daily paper, trying to keep up with all the comings and goings down there. Then, recently, I started reading about your case and started following it. Just got curious, I guess."

"So you used to work down at the courthouse?"

"Yes."

"And you've been following the trial?" Alex asked.

"Yes, you could say that," she said. "I'm glad to finally meet an attorney who doesn't mind socking it to the bad guys."

"That's a compliment, right?"

"Yes," she said. "After witnessing the atrocities some attorneys would commit and get away with, I always wondered how come nobody took them to task. You know what I mean?"

"Yes, I guess. You hear some horror stories. There are bad apples in every barrel," he said.

"It's refreshing to see somebody taking on the big and the powerful."

"I did it because I didn't know better. I don't know that I would do it again," Alex said uncomfortably.

"Well, I just wanted to come by and say hi. You gave me hope, and in a roundabout kind of way, you motivated me to go to law school. I start next week." Naivi said.

"I did that?" asked Alex, not knowing what to believe.

"Yes, Mr. del Fuerte, you did that, believe it or not! Let me ask you. What do you know about the Macallan family?"

"Not much, really."

"Certainly you must have heard something. Did you grow up in this area?" she asked.

"Yes, I grew up in Matamoros but attended school here in Brownsville."

"So, you know people on both sides of the border. You've heard of the Guerras, the Abregos, the Cárdenas, the Garzas, and the Macallans, right?" she asked.

"Yes. I'm familiar with the names."

"What exactly have you heard about the Macallan family?" she asked.

"Truthfully, I wasn't very familiar with the Macallan clan until recently. Judge Sanchez told me some stories about them. Nothing, really. Stuff like they were politically connected. Staunch Republicans. Old money. You know . . . that's about it."

"Did Judge Sanchez happen to mention anything about the worker who was killed by Walter Macallan as a young man?"

"I think he might have mentioned it. Something about a young woman who worked for the family and rejected his advances. Why do you ask?" Alex was wondering where this conversation was heading to.

"I was wondering how much you knew. You see, that worker was my mother, Mercedes."

His heart skipped a beat. "I'm sorry," he said, blushing while at the same time feeling shocked.

"It's okay, not too many people know that I'm her daughter. When my uncle, who was a foreman for old man Macallan, adopted me, he gave me his last name. So no one knows that. Except for a few members of my family."

"Anyway . . . " Alex said, checking the time on his watch. He was looking forward to his fishing trip. "Why are you telling me all this?"

"Well," she started, "because, like I said, not too many people take a stance. And I admire the fact that you went up against one of the most corrupt firms in Texas. You exposed them. They had it coming."

"How do you know so much?" he asked. "Don't tell me that you pick all that up just from reading the newspaper."

"I know that and more," she said. "Harrow is just the tip of the iceberg. The judges . . . they're worse than some of the lawyers. Macallan included!"

"Is that so?" Alex asked. "Can you back it up?"

"Sure! Do you still have the tape?"

"So it was you!" Alex said in disbelief. "I was wondering how long it was going to take for you to come out and show your face. But to answer your question, no, I don't have the tape. I leaked it to the press. I did keep a copy, though. Anyway, how did you get it?"

"After working two years in the district clerk's office, I got promoted to deputy clerk, and my assignment was in Judge Macallan's chambers. I was his deputy clerk for a few years. During that time, I witnessed all kinds of shady deals—money changing hands and stuff. Anyway, one thing led to another, and I started tape-recording his conversations. I figured one day the tapes might be useful. It was easy. I kept a voice-activated micro recorder behind a painting on the wall. On Fridays, when the judge left early to go golfing with his buddies, I'd replace the tape and the batteries."

"That was slic," said Alex sounding amazed.

"Don't forget, he murdered my mother," she said in a serious tone.

"Now . . . you said tapes," Alex said, eyebrows arched and peering at the shoe box on his desk. "Eh . . . you mean there are more tapes?"

"Yes, this box is full."

"What are you going to do with them? Are they as compromising as the one you gave me?" he demanded to know.

"Yes, maybe even more so," she said. "Anyway, Macallan's days are numbered. He had it coming."

"Wow!" exclaimed the attorney, his head spinning. "You mean business, eh?"

"I had no mother, remember?" she said as she looked intently into the attorney's eyes. "Anyway, I'd like you to listen to the other tapes. Interested?"

"Sure, maybe something else will develop," he volunteered. "We'll see." His plan was already in motion, since he had pitched Wingate a copy. Even Chordelli would become a target, especially since Chordelli had lied to him and had put Alex's professional career at risk.

"Aren't you afraid they'll figure out who made the recordings?"

"Yes, some. That's another reason I came to see you. Who can I trust?"

"Tell you what," Alex said, "you should leave the box here. Let me talk to my partner and see if we can get you immunity before we turn them over to the authorities. That way you won't get in trouble for illegally recording the judge and others."

"You think it will work?" she asked, worried.

"Sure, if it brings down a lot of people. Let me ask you . . . Are there any recordings between Macallan and Yarrington?"

"Who?"

"Lieutenant Governor Yarrington? Does that name ring a bell?"

"I don't know," she said. "I haven't listened to all the tapes. Maybe. Who knows?" She was biting her nails and looking somewhat preoccupied.

"Very well. Where can I reach you with information? I'll need to discuss your situation with my partner first, okay?"

"As I said, I start law school next week. How about this . . . What if I call you from Austin, once I'm all settled in and stuff?"

"That'll work. Call the office and leave your phone number and address. Also, take my card." He reached for his business card on the desk and was about to give it to her when he surprised her by saying, "Here, let me write my cell and my home phone number on the back. Call if you need anything. And I mean anything."

"Thanks, I hope I'm not too much trouble," she said, cracking a smile.

"No trouble at all," said Alex, smiling. He liked what he saw. Not only was Naivi beautiful, but obviously she had brains, ambition, and guts. She was definitely law firm material.

"Okay, then, I'll leave the box of tapes with your receptionist up front," she said as she got up from the desk.

"Sounds good. We'll be in touch," Alex said as he extended his hand to his new client.

"*Hasta pronto*," Naivi said as she let herself out of his office.

"*Adiós*," answered Alex, sad to see her go.

He stood in the dead silence of his office going over the details of the meeting. He wondered what was in that boxful of incriminating tapes and whether Naivi really would call back. What if she didn't and her story about going to law school was just that, a story? Would Yarrington surface among the tapes?

He decided that right after the fishing trip, he would make time and go through the tapes. He needed to know what was on them.

Chapter 38

ALEJANDRO DEL FUERTE WAS AT HOME at the Contesse di Mare, sitting on the couch with the sliding doors to his balcony open. The early morning breeze was flowing gently, and in the distance, down by the jetties, he could make out hundreds of swimmers splashing about as they competed in the SPI's Extreme Macho Man Triathlon.

As he sat there in the quiet of his villa, wrapped in a beach towel and nothing else, feet on the coffee table and drinking a *licuado de plátano*, he fiddled with the box of tapes given to him by Naivi. He fumbled with the micro-cassette player and installed a set of fresh AAs. He felt his heart rate quicken as he plopped the first tape into the player.

"My law practice is failing," said the voice, sounding worried, "so I'm begging you, Judge . . . see if you could shoot a juicy *ad litem* appointment my way?"

"What's in it for me, Galindo?" Macallan replied.

"You set the terms," the lawyer answered. "Whatever you think is fair."

"I don't think I have any appointments to give right now."

"Please, Judge," cried the attorney, "I'll split it fifty-fifty with you. Help me out, throw me a bone. Both my kids are in medical school . . . they're about to bankrupt me."

"All right, Galindo," Macallan agreed, "but only if you do sixty-forty. Sixty for the house and forty for you."

"Thanks, thanks," said the voice, "I'll make sure that the forty percent goes back to your reelection campaign."

"All right," Macallan instructed, "talk to my clerk and tell her that I said to appoint you to represent the children in the dismemberment case at the port's grain elevator. It's the Ostos Grain Company case. There's a settlement hearing in three weeks. Should be pretty easy money. A quick hundred thousand."

"Thanks, Judge . . . thanks. I'll never forget it, I promise."

"Just remember, not a word."

"Not a word."

The next tape began with an attorney and Judge Macallan discussing the attorney's last divorce.

"I never thanked you," said the voice, "for helping me in my last divorce. You made all the difference."

"I always help my buddies, you know that, Sergio," Macallan said.

"I'm just glad you paid no mind to my ex-wife's exaggerated claims of infidelity. I mean, sure I cheated on her once or twice with Cindy, my secretary, but not one hundred times as she claimed."

"Ha, ha," laughed the judge, "cheating means nothing to me. I would be a hypocrite if I'd let that affect me . . . you know what I mean?"

"Yes, but you were very lucky," the lawyer said. "No one ever found out you dabbled on the side."

"Well," the judge said, "thanks to you, I was able to get rid of that pesky and bothersome threat. I mean, you were brilliant when you called your *compadre* at the lab and asked him to manipulate the DNA so there would be no match. Pure genius."

"We pulled it off," said the voice. "I'm glad only you and I knew, and no one else ever found out, especially Mrs. Macallan."

"Me too," said the judge. "I wonder, where in Mexico does Aracely live?"

"Who knows, who cares?"

"Can you imagine?" asked the judge. "What would have happened if I had gotten busted having an affair and I had a bastard child?"

"No, I don't even want to think about it. I sure as hell don't want to go there," the lawyer said.

One after the other, the tapes contained incriminating and telling conversations. There were hundreds of hours of conversations, and most, if not all, showed the parties scheming, conspiring, or attempting to commit all kinds of criminal acts and ethical violations.

Alex started playing another tape. The attorney was discussing a criminal case with the judge.

"I'll be the first to admit that I screwed up big, Judge," said the attorney. "I told my client that he wasn't going to have to register as a sex offender, but I didn't realize registration was mandatory for this type of offense. Now I don't know what to do."

"How can we fix it?" asked the judge.

"I was thinking I could contribute to your reelection campaign," explained the attorney. "Anything to avoid the client filing a grievance."

"Anything?" asked the judge.

"Anything."

"All right, write a check to my campaign for ten thousand," instructed Macallan. "I'll bust the plea and allow you and your client to renegotiate with the D.A. and plead to something else."

After five hours of listening to taped conversations, it appeared that many a prominent lawyer in Cameron County was in bed with Judge Macallan. Hundreds of deals flying back and forth for five thousand here, ten thousand there, a percentage here and a kickback there. Alex was shocked.

"What do you need?" asked the judge. Alex had switched tapes and was starting the twentieth one of the day.

"I just wanted to make sure I understood your instructions," the voice said.

"What's there to explain, Jesse?" demanded Macallan. "I want you to take a bat to Ramón, my gardener, and rough him up. Are you in or out?"

"Well," answered the voice, "I just wanted to make sure you know. When your bailiff told me you wanted to talk to me about a job, I didn't know what to believe . . . with you being a judge and all."

"Look," said the judge softly, as if trying to ensure no one was listening, "I just need you to roughen him up a bit. Teach him a lesson. He's been getting too close to Rosario, my live-in maid. If I can't have her, then nobody can."

"Okay, but it's going to cost you."

"How much?"

"Five hundred for a rough up. Anything more, we'll have to renegotiate."

"No," the judge said, "I just need you to rough him up some. That's all."

"I'll see that it gets done."

By the end of the day, Alex had heard all kinds of conversations dealing with all sorts of things, and he doubted it could get any worse. Boy, was he wrong.

"What happened, Jesse?" demanded the judge.

"We took Ramón out to the shrimp basin pier, outside the city limits," Jesse explained. "It was dark, deserted, and colder than hell."

"What's this 'we' business?" shouted the judge, and Alex could hear the sound of his fist pounding the desk.

"Uhm," Jesse cleared his throat, "I needed backup, just in case . . . you know."

"Backup? Backup? I didn't hire you to go and hire backup! You were supposed to act alone. Who did you take with you?"

"Raul, your bailiff . . . We were going to split the five hundred."

"Idiots!" Macallan cursed. "Did you screw it up?"

"That's what I was getting to," Jesse explained. "You see, we blindfolded Ramón and threw him in the trunk of the car. When we got there, we got him out and had him kneel down on the pier."

"And then?"

"I tell Raul to take off the blindfold. I want Ramón to see. Then the strangest thing happens. I guess he figures he's about to get the ass-kicking from hell, and he wants to negotiate. He offers us one thousand dollars. He says he might be able to come up with more. Before you know it, he's rambling. Not making much sense. Then Raul says, 'Shut him up.'

"'Do it, do it, *Chingalo, chingalo*,' Raul is screaming. I didn't mean to hurt him so much. I just wanted to get him on the side of the arm, rough him up just like you said. So, I pull the bat, and he comes at me, and I miss and end up whacking him on the head. And down he goes, like a sack of potatoes into the water. He never came up again. I guess . . . I guess . . ."

"Say it!" the judge screamed.

"He must have drowned."

"You sure?"

"I'm pretty sure. His body never came up."

"I can't believe it! Leave it to an amateur," Judge Macallan complained. "Leave, get out!"

Going through the tapes took the whole day. Alex finally had managed to understand the magnitude of the corruption in the halls of justice of Cameron County. He left his villa and took his time driving to Manny's Bayside Paradise. He needed a drink. He was immediately met at the door by a tanned "beach bunny" who wasn't a day past twenty. "One for dinner?" she asked.

"No," replied the attorney, "just drinks at the bar upstairs."

"Go ahead," said the hostess, "there's a drink special on Zooming Torpedoes. They're two dollars."

"I'm not touching that stuff," said Alex, smiling. "I learned my lesson in high school. Thanks, but no thanks."

The alcoholic beverage the hostess was referring to was served in a cup the size of a six-inch flowerpot and had ten different types of liquor in it. Then to top it off, the bartender floated it with a half-ounce of 151 rum. It was lethal. And Manny's Bayside Paradise was famous for it.

Alex sat at the bar and ordered a Shiner Bock beer on tap. He looked up at the TV, which was showing a game between the Spurs and the Detroit Pistons in game four of the NBA finals. The game was tied. Suddenly there was a tap on his shoulder.

"Alex?"

Alex turned quickly and did a double take. "Paloma?" he mumbled. "What a surprise. I didn't expect to see you here."

"We live across the bay," she said. "The island is our play-ground. How are you?" Paloma Yarrington Macallan was not only smiling, she was glowing. Calvin Macallan was standing next to her, and they were holding hands.

"I'm fine, thanks," Alex said. "How's married life?"

"Fabulous. This is my husband, Calvin. Have you two met?" she asked, obviously enjoying making Alejandro del Fuerte squirm.

"Hi," Alex said, stretching his hand, "we may have met years ago at Rancho del Cielo Country Club, I think."

"How's it going?" Calvin replied and shook Alex's hand. He was also struggling with the situation.

Alex looked the happy couple over. He was at a loss for words and struggled to say anything else. There was a moment of silence, which felt like an eternity.

"How's the law practice?" Paloma finally asked. "I hear you settled a big one?"

"Oh," said Alex, with modesty, "it was nothing, really. But I guess you could say the days of cheese and crackers are over."

"Well," she said, "I'm glad to see you're doing okay. Anyway, Daddy's throwing his hat in the governor's race. I hope we can count on your support."

"Sure," the attorney said, taking a swig of beer, "you can count on me. Whatever I can do to help, just let me know."

"Thanks," said Paloma, the fundraiser queen. "Maybe later this month we can have you come out to the house for a fish fry and soft shell crab fundraiser we're having, drink a few beers. Right, Calvin?"

"Sure," said the husband, not looking very enthusiastic.

"All right," Alex said, "let me know."

"Bye, take care," Paloma said as she reached over to hug Alex and plant a soft kiss on his cheek. Calvin's eyeballs almost jumped out of his eye sockets.

Alex reached again for his beer, took a swig, and could barely mumble, "See ya later."

Chapter 39

THE RECEPTIONIST WHO TOOK ALEX'S CALL put him on hold at first. After coming back on the line, she apologized for the wait and quickly said she would transfer him to Jeff Chordelli's office. Another few minutes went by, during which he continued to listen to Muzak, until a pleasant female voice came on the line.

"Happy holidays. Mr. Chordelli's office. This is Mary, how can I help you?" she asked without missing a beat.

"I need to speak with Mr. Chordelli," demanded Alex.

"Mr. Chordelli is on a conference call," she said, feeding him the standard law office reply in order to screen the call or caller. "Can I take a message and have him call you back?"

"It's a personal matter. Just tell him Alejandro del Fuerte needs to speak with him. It's important."

"Very well," she replied. "Does he have a number where he can reach you?"

"Yes, he's got my number."

"Very well," she said and hung up.

Alejandro del Fuerte picked up the phone and prepared to call the lieutenant governor's office in Austin. In the many years he had known Paloma's father, he had never had the need to call his state office. Nor had he ever felt the desire to talk business with him. But now, Alex needed to place a call. This time it was he who was looking for Yarrington; a year ago, it had been the other way around. There were some old scores he needed to settle.

Besides, he needed to call him and congratulate him on the passage of the AMEGO legislation. Yarrington had finally managed to get a bill passed. Rumor had it that in his many years of public service—first as speaker of the house, then as secretary of agriculture, and finally as lieutenant governor—Yarrington had had a poor record of sponsoring original legislation, much less getting any of it passed. To his constituents, however, Yarrington was a man of action. He called himself a "full-time public servant," proud to serve the State of Texas and the Republican Party. For him and his staff, the moniker meant being at all the right political functions—little *pachangas*, fundraisers, rallies, parades, wherever, whenever, it didn't matter. Yarrington would be there "working" for the cause.

Truth be told, the AMEGO had not affected the outcome of the Harrow litigation. The case had settled prior to the jury reaching a verdict and prior to AMEGO becoming law. Besides, since the case had been settled, no post-trial motions had been filed, and there were no appeals or other time-consuming legal maneuvers. Alex had barely squeaked by. Thousands of other attorneys across Texas had not been so lucky. Those with pending legal malpractice cases against other attorneys or law firms had seen the potential damages in those cases capped at twenty-five thousand dollars by the act. Since the legislature had made the application of the AMEGO retroactive, the claims were now almost worthless. The plaintiffs' Bar was up in arms over the matter.

To Alex, "barely squeaking by" had meant about nine million for Pilo's estate and the heirs and another six million in fees for his firm. Some would call this working capital. Now his call to Yarrington was to get himself a healthy dose of political capital. It couldn't hurt to have both.

The legislative aide who answered the telephone in the lieutenant governor's office informed him that Yarrington was down at the governor's office welcoming a group of Taiwanese businessmen. That was staff code that really meant that Yarrington was unavailable because he was playing golf.

"Can I have his cell?" Alex asked.

"He's not taking any calls right now. But I'll make sure he gets your message."

"Tell him to call Alejandro del Fuerte," the young attorney said and left his cell number.

Two hours later, Yarrington was on the phone returning del Fuerte's call. The background noise was that of the Texas senate floor. It was not unusual for the legislators to take or make calls down from the senate floor, particularly when it involved urgent matters such as golf tee times, lobbyists' receptions, or the discussion of dinner invitations at Jeffrey's, Louis 106, or Ruth's Chris Steakhouse.

"Counselor, how the hell are you?" asked Yarrington.

"Great!" replied the attorney. "And yourself? How are you doing, Lieutenant Governor?"

"Fine, fine, son," the busiest public servant in Texas replied. "Thanks for asking. What can I do for you?"

"I know you're still working on school finance reform, but I was wondering if we could meet in the next few days. I could either fly to Austin, or if you happened to be down here in your old district, maybe we could go to breakfast or something."

"I'm heading back on the direct flight at 1:00 p.m. I had a meeting with some big contributors," Yarrington said with a grin that Alex could hear over the phone line. "A fundraiser, if you will, along with other meetings. But I'm done. Do you want to meet this afternoon?"

"That would be great," Alex replied.

"What's the meeting about?" Yarrington asked.

"Del Fuerte & Fetzer want to make a contribution to your arsenal," Alex said. "Is that okay?"

"Sure!" Yarrington cried out. If the man he had expected to become his son-in-law wanted to buy the peace by making a generous campaign contribution, who was he to decline? Especially with an election year looming fast on the horizon. It was time to fill the war chest and let bygones be bygones. Who really cared where the money came from? Money was money. It didn't matter if it came from PACs, Republican or Democratic donors, detractors, opponents, friends, or foes. A war chest overflowing with millions was the best weapon to intimidate opponents in an election year.

"I tell you what," the lieutenant governor said, fast to jump on the money. "I'll just drive directly from the airport to your office and pick up the check. We'll do some catching up. All right?"

"I'll expect you then around two-thirty?" asked the attorney. "Is that about right?"

"Yes, two-thirty is fine. Is your office still inside Artemis Square?"

"Yes."

"All right then, I'll find it. See you then."

"Good enough."

Alejandro del Fuerte sat patiently in his office waiting for this 2:30 appointment. He reached across his desk, and out of a small stack of micro-cassettes, he picked out the one with the name Macallan/ Yarrington. He loaded it in the cassette player and found the exact place where the conversation started. The rest of the cassettes he packed away in the original shoe box, put a rubber band around it, and put it away in a drawer. At 2:30 exactly, Betty buzzed him.

"Mr. del Fuerte," she said, "Lieutenant Governor Yarrington is here to see you."

"Send him right in," said the attorney, "and hold all my calls, please."

Seconds later, Yarrington was letting himself into Alex's office and greeting the young attorney.

"Come here, son," said Yarrington, "let me look at you. How the hell are you?" He shook Alex's hand and grinned from cheek to cheek in anticipation of the size of the check.

"Good, Lieutenant Governor," Alex said, "keeping busy. Screening cases, you know."

"I hear your name in all kinds of circles, even Austin," Yarrington said. "You know what they say. All publicity is good publicity."

"Thanks."

"Anyway, I certainly appreciate your call. Offering a contribution couldn't have come at a better time, you know. Since the passage of AMEGO, I've heard that the plaintiffs' Bar has tapped Tommy Burnham, from McAllen, to run against me in the next election. So, your money is a godsend."

"That's what I wanted to talk to you about," del Fuerte explained. "I have something better than money to give you. I hope that you appreciate it."

"What is it?" asked Yarrington, looking somewhat confused. "You don't have a check for me?" He seemed disappointed and was almost pouting.

"No, not really. Listen to this. I think it will interest you," Alex said as he hit the play button.

Yarrington stared at him in astonishment as he heard his own voice on the tape:

"When can I expect another ad litem *appointment? You know how much I love them!"*

Judge Macallan's voice came in reply. *"There's a case against a pharmaceutical company that's getting ready to settle. In the next week or so you should be receiving the order appointing you."*

"I really appreciate it, Walter. Do you have any idea what we're looking at?"

"I'd say about one hundred thousand in ad litem *fees for you."*

"Great! A few more of those, and the mortgage for my penthouse at Isla Towers will be paid."

"Not so fast!" said Macallan. *"Aren't you forgetting something?"*

"Of course not. You think I'd forget our arrangement? When have I forgotten? I've always kicked you back fifty percent. You and Humphrey from the 203rd in Houston and Earl from the 270th in Austin. They've always been part of my circle of trust. Always!"

"And I do appreciate it. That way I too can have campaign money. It's easier than going out there and hitting the pavement, that's for sure! Of course, it helps to tilt the scales of justice, too, in favor of your lawyer friends. That way all their cases land in my court and thus a win is almost guaranteed."

"Hey! If they win, I win and you win, too. Nothing wrong with a nice juicy campaign contribution, right?"

"I hear you. Besides, I hate to campaign and pretend that I still care about the administration of justice. Let the insurance companies pay your ad litem fees! They've got money. Like plucking a hair from a cat. Ha! Ha!"

"You know, what's funny is that on the one hand I've advocated enacting legislation to cap damages in lawsuits, but on the other hand, folks like me are making a killing on ad litem fees."

Macallan could be heard chuckling in the background. "If the public only knew . . ."

"Let's keep it under the radar. Ad litem fees are easier to get; there's minimal work involved. It's the gift that keeps on giving. It's beautiful."

Alex hit the stop button. A silence came over the room. The most powerful person in Texas stared at Alejandro del Fuerte as if the wind had just been knocked out of him. Alejandro pulled the tape out and tossed it to Yarrington.

"Please don't say a word. No need," said Alex. "I don't want you to try to explain it. It would be useless. I do want you to listen to me, however. What I have to say is important."

"All right," said Yarrington. He was barely able to mumble. His cheeks had turned red, and beads of sweat had formed on his forehead. He was embarrassed. This had all the makings of the end of his political career. What other surprise did the attorney have under his sleeve?

"I want you to keep the tape," said Alex. "It's yours, do whatever you want with it."

"Where did you get it?"

"Let's just say there was a source who had in her possession a few compromising recordings," explained Alex. "I pulled this one from the box before the recordings were turned over to the feds. And let's be clear, I did that not as a favor to you but as a favor to Paloma and your family. Spare them the embarrassment."

"Did you keep a copy?" Yarrington asked nervously.

"No. You can count on it. As far as I can tell, that was the only tape that you're on," said Alex. "Now, I don't know if the source has more tapes. If that's the case, I don't know what's on them."

"I can explain," started Yarrington. "It sounds worse than it really is."

"Save it," Alex said interrupting. "It is what it is, bribery. But that's your business. You know how to run your life. Besides, I didn't invite you over to lecture you. I just wanted you to have the tape. I don't care what you do with it. I'm not going to say anything."

"Oh, thanks," said Yarrington, "thanks, thanks for the heads up. Thanks a million. I could never repay you."

"Like I said," the attorney replied, "it's better than a contribution."

"I hate to admit it, but you're right. A scandal like this would kill all hopes of reelection."

"Just remember," replied Alex, "I've got your number. Now leave!"

"Yes," said Yarrington, fumbling with his chair as he tried to get up. "I won't forget. Whatever you need, and I mean whatever, anything, really . . . here or in Austin."

"And stay away from your *compadre*, Judge Macallan. The feds are onto him," Alex said as he sent Yarrington on his merry way. "They have tapes, too. If I were you, I wouldn't even call him."

"Yes . . . yes, I'll do that, thanks."

"Chordelli, too," Alex added. "Stay away from him and his firm."

"Them too?"

"Yes."

Astrid walked into his office and announced that some attorney named Chordelli was on line two. "He sounds pissed off," she said and left the room. The thought of Chordelli fuming amused Alex. In a few minutes, the powerful and influential lawyer would have difficulty breathing.

"This is Mr. del Fuerte," said Alex into the phone, pretending not to know who was calling.

"I told you not to ever call!" screamed the San Antonio lawyer at the end of the line. "Why didn't you use my email?"

"Because," Alex replied as he let out a lion-sized yawn into the speaker phone, "if I emailed you, you wouldn't be able to hear something I want you to hear."

"I don't have time for these games!" Chordelli said. "Especially after you screwed up the Harrow lawsuit."

"How so?" asked Alex.

"You weren't supposed to settle for fifteen million!" Chordelli cried. "It was policy limits, the twenty-five million, or a jury verdict! Maybe even a huge punitive award. That's what we wanted. Big headlines! Not a crappy settlement and no admission of liability. What was that? You were supposed to expose the bastards in every newspaper in the country, on every news channel. I wanted Tod's picture on CNN, MSNBC, the networks! You were supposed to make the rounds on TV. Be on Larry King!"

"Hey!" Alex explained, "talk to Judge Robles. He forced the settlement. Besides, the AMEGO legislation, which, I might add, was drafted by your point man Yarrington, would have reduced any award to just twenty-five thousand. How do you explain that to the client? That we could have walked away with fifteen million, but we gambled it away for a paper verdict? Ha! Give me a break! Do you think I'm an idiot?"

"You were paid up front. Who cares about the client? We had a deal!" shouted Chordelli into the phone.

"You forget," started Alex slowly, "you are not my client. I owe no duty to you. Pilo Medina, his estate, and the heirs are my clients. There is no disciplinary committee in the entire United States that will find fault with what I did. You wanted to finance the litigation, that's your problem."

"I'll sue you to recover the millions we gave you, del Fuerte!" Chordelli threatened. "It will be you looking at the end of a barrel as we ask a jury to order you to repay the firm!"

"Whatever," Alex shot back. "And just how do you propose to explain to the same jury that you received close to eighteen million dollars from a fraudulent scheme you yourself concocted?" Alex asked matter-of-factly.

"You son of a bitch!" screamed Chordelli. "I'll have your license, you wait!"

"Yeah, yeah. Why don't we talk about you losing *your* license? Have you thought about disgorging the eighteen million that the fake pitched to you? Have you considered tendering the monies to my client's estate? Have you given it any thought? Or will I have to sue you as well and parade you and your firm in front of Joe Public?" Alex was almost sounding cocky.

"You can't prove anything. There's no paper trail. I'll deny that I or my firm ever received anything from anybody."

"How do you explain that your firm handled all the other wrongful death cases from that rollover accident, except Rosario and the boy's?" asked Alex. "Too much of a coincidence, don't you think? Could it be that maybe you set up another firm to take the fall?"

"That doesn't mean anything! And I wouldn't be so cocky if I were you. I'm calling my buddies at the state Bar right now. You're done, del Fuerte!"

"The state Bar is the least of my worries," declared Alex. "Why don't you listen to this? Figure out how you're going to explain this to the feds." He hit the play button of the tape recorder on his desk and placed the receiver near the small speaker.

"Here, take a seat," came Judge Macallan's voice. *"We can talk in complete safety here in chambers. So, how do you propose we make the case work?"*

"It's easy, Judge," said another voice. *"Willy Hankins tells me the girl and the boy worked for you. Is that right?"*

"Yes, but I don't want my name connected to them in any way. They were working for me but were here illegally. Any scandal, and I mean anything, would mean I would have to step down. No one knows I hire mojados. I want to keep it that way. I'm close to retiring; I'd hate to screw that up."

"This is what you do," said the voice, sounding confident. *"You call Tod Harrow and tell him that you have a wrongful death case involving a mother and child, worth millions. You want a million dollar finder's fee in order for you to deliver the case. That way, you're covered. Have them wire your money to your offshore account."*

"What if his firm isn't interested?"

"Shit, are you kidding? Those guys never met a wrongful death case they didn't like. They'll jump on it, trust me. Besides, I've checked the case out. There's liability on the manufacturers, so they'll take the bait. And you have damages, serious damages. It's a laid down. They'll take it!"

"And then?"

"I'll have Willy come up with a substitute plaintiff and have him send the decoy to Harrow as soon as you've made the deal."

"Why, there are no relatives out there that can sue?" asked Judge Macallan.

"We've searched here and in Mexico, everywhere, but haven't been able to find anyone. We need to get in there while this thing is hot. There's no time to waste!"

"So, you're creating the plaintiff, is that how it works?"

"Yes, Willy will take care of it. He's good. He'll get someone from Mexico to play the part. He'll come up with the fake marriage license, IDs, voter registration cards. That stuff is easy to get in Mexico. Before you know it, we'll have created your maid's spouse and the child's father. No one will question it. Besides, this isn't the first time we've manufactured evidence . . . you know that."

"I'd rather not go there," said Macallan. "I never liked the idea of making evidence up."

"Hey, somebody has got to make Corporate America pay," the man boasted. "I'm not going to let them get away with maiming people because the case is missing one key piece of evidence or because I can't find a plaintiff. Remember Parker Ditlow?"

"Who?"

"Ditlow, the guy who testified in Congress that Ford kept a double set of books to fool federal regulators."

"Oh, you mean on the exposed rear tanks and the Pinto investigation?"

"Exactly. Ford was also playing dirty . . . and the car manufacturers were purposefully concealing defects as far back as the early seventies."

"And don't forget GM," Macallan added. "They flooded the markets with pickup trucks armed with saddle gas tanks that exploded if the truck got T-boned."

"And Erin Brockovich," the voice reminded the judge. *"She busted corporate polluters that contaminated the water supply in California. No, I don't have a problem manufacturing evidence or even a plaintiff if it means sticking it to pharmaceutical companies selling bullshit 'miracle' drugs or the asbestos manufacturers. Not if it means socking it to companies like Enron, WorldCom, and the Tycos of the world."*

"I guess I can see the justice in what you do."

"Sure! Who's going to keep corporate America in check? Congress? The Consumer Safety Commission? The FDA? Ha! That'll be the day."

"So," Macallan said, changing the subject, *"you're still working with Hankins?"*

"Yes, he's connected. I mean, he's not cheap, but with him it's guaranteed that we'll make the case. He can tweak it just right, although lately he's told me he wants to get out of the racket."

"And do what?"

"Something about a llama operation . . . or raising llamas, something like that. Go figure!"

"Wasn't he in hot water with the state Bar?"

"I made some calls," said the voice, *"and took care of it. The problems started when the ex-wife called the Bar to turn him in. The whole thing was motivated by the divorce. I made sure the Bar understood that. End of story."*

"I see you're still able to pull strings at the state capitol," replied Macallan.

"Well, it also helped that the Bar was coming up for sunset review. I made sure Yarrington advised the sunset review committee chairman to leave my investigator alone."

"Well, sounds good," the judge said, *"but you trust Willy will pull it off?"*

"Yeah, Harrow will be blinded by greed. They won't suspect a thing."

"So, I'll pitch them the case, negotiate my finder's fee. When they ask for the case info, I'll tell them that in the next few weeks I'll deliver the husband with a guarantee that he will sign up with the firm. Willy delivers the guy. But the plaintiff is under contract with you guys. Right?"

"Yes. Do you know how many unemployed actors are out there willing to make a hundred K to be on call for a couple of meetings while the case is pending? They're a dime a dozen."

"Do you think it'll work?"

"We've done it dozens of times. Remember the Peña case? The Ortiz case up in Hogg County? We bring somebody in, he plays the part, one deposition, maybe two max. Bam! Done. These cases always settle without going to trial, you know that."

"So, the decoy has limited involvement?" asked Macallan.

"Look, the defense is always busy fighting our experts, shooting discovery, taking depositions, challenging our experts, but they rarely focus on the plaintiff. Besides, no one really knows what the mother and child looked like. After the autopsy, they were buried. So, we can recreate the family pictures, just like that! So our guy at most answers some discovery and gives a two-hour deposition. Gives the defense some sob story about how good they were and how much he misses them."

"So, it's kind of like using just a warm body, somebody with a face to claim the millions? That's pretty ingenious. I had no clue you guys had carried it that far."

"You have to get creative if you want to survive in this business or get to the big money."

"I'm not so sure," the judge said, sounding worried. "I wouldn't say my hands are clean, but I've never been involved in something of this magnitude."

"Look. Leave the small details to me. I'll pay the guy good money, and my firm will keep the rest. The beauty of it all is that we have another firm do all the work. And after the guy collects, he just pitches us the lion's share. We're happy, and the decoy is happy because he made the easiest, quickest one hundred thousand of his life. When we're done, we send him back to Mexico, never to be found again. It's beautiful!"

"What do you mean, never to be found again? Are you saying what I think you're saying?"

"Hey, we have to have assurances. Something like this, you can't have any loose ends . . . you know what I mean?"

"I don't know,"

"It's not a crime in Texas if it happens in Mexico, right?"

"There's one thing I don't understand, Jeff. Why do you hate Harrow so much?"

"Remember the two kids who were electrocuted at the Port of Brownsville, about ten years ago?"

"How could I forget? The settlement made headlines. Harrow got the plaintiffs about forty million. Twenty million to each kid's family. If I remember correctly, most of the money was for pain and suffering . . . I mean, having to bury a child cooked to a crisp can't possibly be a pretty sight."

"We got wind that a relative of the family was talking to an immigration lawyer, seeking help. So Willy immediately went to work, tracking down the families. We snatched it from the lawyer, but the families later on fired us. I couldn't believe it. I mean, we paid each family twenty-five thousand dollars for the case. We then find out that Harrow talked to them behind the scenes and had them fire us. They paid one hundred thousand dollars to the parents of each boy!"

"So, that's it?"

"That was the first time. Then there were others. After that, they just got bolder and gutsier, to the point that they became a threat to my firm."

Alejandro del Fuerte hit the stop button on the recorder.

"You son of a bitch!" screamed Chordelli on the other end. "You listen to me! Where did you get that tape?"

"I don't have to tell you shit!" Alex screamed back. "I suggest you call a good criminal defense attorney. You're going to need it!"

"Wait! Don't hang up, maybe we can patch things up," cried Chordelli, changing his tune right away. "Be reasonable."

"Does two to twenty sound reasonable?" asked Alex. "That's the penalty for conspiring to commit murder in Texas, you know."

"Please!" Chordelli begged. "Let's cut a deal. I can pitch another two or three million. Listen to me!"

"I tell you what," began Alex, "you come clean and tell me if you had something to do with Pilo's murder, and then we can deal."

"Who?" Chordelli asked, pretending not to understand.

Alex hit the record button, slowly, trying to make minimal noise. "Porfirio Medina. My client," he clarified. "You know who I'm talking about. Did you have anything to do with his death?"

There was silence. Chordelli was breathing heavily at the other end of the line. Alejandro waited for an explanation.

"That was never the plan," a remorseful Chordelli explained. "Willy was to tip a friend of his at border patrol to raid his hotel room and simply deport the old man to old Mexico. Away from here. Away from the courthouse and his family's case. Far, far away . . . you never know what might turn up when somebody starts digging. With him snooping around, we didn't know what was going to happen. We couldn't take any chances."

"So, what happened?"

"Well, things got rough and there was a struggle, and your client got killed. I'm sorry. The plan was just to send him back to Mexico. Later on, we realized the guy had already hired you, and when you kept digging and digging, we had to act."

"I don't believe you!" screamed Alex. "The guy couldn't kill a fly! He was thin and frail. He almost died on his trip up here. And you expect me to believe that story?"

"I swear that's what happened. Hear me out. We can work this thing out, please!" begged Chordelli.

"Why don't you tell your lawyer to give that explanation to the prosecutor in charge of your case?" replied Alex. "See ya around."

"Wait! *Por favor*, Alex."

Chapter 40

THE SENATE COMMITTEE on Criminal Justice was called to order by the presiding chairman, Senator Mark "the Hammer" Cromwell. Ever since he had first run for the Texas senate a decade ago, he'd been very interested in issues regulating the legal profession, including tort reform, referral fee reform, workmen's compensation reform, medical malpractice reform, class action reform, and asbestos reform. This of course had created a lot of enemies with the plaintiffs' bar. As a result, the plaintiffs' bar had, unsuccessfully, attempted many times to finance opponents in an effort to vote him out of office. He'd managed to survive all the challenges.

The committee had begun taking testimony regarding the effects of a new proposed bill—now making the rounds in both houses and various legal circles—that attempted to end case running once and for all.

"This hearing is called to order. All of those testifying here today please raise your hands," announced Senator Cromwell.

"All right," the committee chairman continued, "please announce your names for the record."

"Verónica Ameel."

"John Snyder."

"Alejandro del Fuerte."

"Robert Gomez."

"Jimmy Fitzpatrick."

"Patrick Colvin."

"Mike Roerig."

"María Muñoz."

"Very well," Cromwell said. "Anybody else? No? Okay then. Ms. Ameel, please come up. The other committee members, Senator Judy Massini, Senator Steve Brody, Senator Mark Mullins and Senator Tyrone Ellis want to know what you have to say."

And with that, the hearing was open for public comment. Ms. Ameel testified about the horrors and the humiliation she and her family had suffered at the hands of funeral directors who shoved contracts down her throat so that the Margoux law firm from San Antonio, Texas, could sue on their behalf for the death of her husband as a result of a horrific work accident. The funeral directors had been so brash as to suggest that she and her family were a bunch of retards if they didn't sign up with Mr. Margoux, since no other lawyer in Texas knew as much as he did. Not only was having a loved one die a tragedy in itself, but dealing with Margoux had been a hellish experience. Neither he nor his office would return the family's phone calls. When they did, after three weeks of calling every day, the employees couldn't remember the clients' names, and they were treated as third-class citizens. In the end, the attorney had settled their case for two million dollars but kept $1.2 million in fees and expenses, and the family had received eight hundred thousand dollars. The family had never approved the settlement.

Roberto Gomez, a Mexican national, testified that he had been involved in a fender bender in Matamoros, Mexico. The responsible party that hit him had been an American driver, driving an American car and insured by the Hughston American Insurance Group. He'd suffered soft tissue injuries and a minimal amount of property damage to his vehicle. The Mexican cop investigating the accident had put him in touch with a Mexican attorney, who said she would handle everything for him, leaving him free to get his life back in order.

The alleged Mexican attorney had taken him to her house, where she had received, via fax, a retainer contract from a Corpus Christi firm. She had told Mr. Gomez that his signature was needed to authorize the body shop to start repairing the damage to his vehicle and to get him to see an American doctor. The client had no clue that he was signing a retainer contract. By the time he had arrived at home that evening, someone from a Brownsville medical office had already called his house to confirm his first office visit. He was treated by the doctor for a period of two months. And after two months of haggling with the Mexican lawyer, the firm in Corpus Christi, and the body shop, he'd finally gotten his car back. Six months later he was called to Harlingen, Texas, to get his money from the accident. In some shady back office, next to a Greyhound bus station, he'd been given a check for five hundred dollars. When he'd asked for a copy of the disbursal statement, he'd been told that it was confidential and he was not entitled to it. He was then ordered to leave. He'd never met his lawyer, never authorized a settlement of the case, and never approved the disbursement.

In the end it transpired that the doctor was not an M.D. but a chiropractor, and the Mexican attorney was not an attorney but a Texas notary public moonlighting for a law firm. The five hundred dollars that he received he'd had to sink back into his car to replace all the junk parts that had been used to fix it. It was no wonder lawyers got a bad name!

And so the horror stories continued. By mid-morning, the legal profession in Texas had gotten one big black eye. A female victim of a collision with an eighteen-wheeler testified as to how an investigator for the law offices of Israel Cantu, a Valley attorney who controlled a stretch of highway, had visited her in the intensive care unit at Mission Memorial Hospital. The investigator had been wearing scrubs while posing as a male nurse. While the victim was slipping in and out of consciousness, he had grabbed her hand, which was in a cast, and had affixed her name to Cantu's contingency fee contract. She never knew what she had signed and was surprised, eighteen months later, to hear that there was a check waiting for her at Mr. Cantu's monumental office. She was surprised to hear she had retained an attorney, since she couldn't remember when that had happened, and was upset at not being able to talk with her alleged attorney.

She had filed a grievance with the Texas State Bar Grievance Committee against the attorney and demanded some answers. But the state Bar had ruled that she had failed to state "with particularity" a violation in her complaint, and thus her grievance had been thrown out. Since she was not an attorney and didn't know what exactly constituted a violation of the rules of ethics, she was not allowed to participate in the grievance process. She later found out that the investigator for the state Bar was friends with Cantu, and the investigator pulled some strings to get the case dismissed.

Another individual testified about Everardo Ayala, a shyster out of Robstown, near Corpus Christi, and how this guy controlled the stretch of highway from Corpus Christi all the way down to the Sarita checkpoint deep in South Texas. Ayala had tow truck drivers, sheriff's deputies, EMS personnel, and even Border Patrol agents on his payroll. If they signed up a case, no matter how big or small, they would get a five-hundred-dollar consulting fee. So in order to sign up the case on the spot, these individuals would carry Ayalas' contracts and business cards. They were ruthless.

The parade of witnesses continued. Some of them were sponsored by the Civil Justice Reform Group, an anti-frivolous lawsuit group with tremendous influence in Texas politics. And so the damaging revelations continued. There were stories about characters like Roger O'Sheen, Oziel Abrego, Tom Sanchez, Cuco García, and other lesser-known case runners. All millionaires. All known to run cases. All scot-free, laughing all the way to the bank. While the state Bar in Austin pounded its chest and screamed that such conduct wouldn't be tolerated, the truth was that the state Bar had done a poor job of eliminating the problem. In fact, the state Bar became part of the problem when its members decided to protect their colleagues and throw out complaints rightfully asserted by the victims. The Bar was no different from the Board of Dental Examiners or the Board of Medical Examiners. It was colleagues protecting colleagues. Now it was time for the legislature to act. The lawyers had the AMEGO legislation to protect them from each other, and now it was time to protect the clients and victims.

"Mr. del Fuerte," committee chairman Cromwell said, "are you ready to proceed?"

"Yes, Mr. Chairman," Alex said. He took a swig of water out of a Styrofoam cup, collected his thoughts, and proceeded to relive his story.

He told the committee of how he had grown up in Mexico, and how, having been raised along the border, it was impossible not to compare Mexico with the United States. In Mexico corruption was rampant, but not in the United States. In Mexico opportunity was limited, but not so in America. In Mexico you had to be born into a wealthy family or be well connected to make your mark, but not so in the land of the free. So, at a young age he'd decided to be a lawyer. But not a Mexican lawyer, something better. He'd decided to be part of the noble profession and become an American lawyer.

He'd worked hard to pay his way through college and then law school. He'd struggled to graduate and decided to come back to the Rio Grande Valley because that was where his talents could be best applied. This was where he could make a difference and help the poor, the disenfranchised, and the downtrodden. And when he tried to do just that, he uncovered a conspiracy and corruption, and he realized that America was no different from Mexico. But the worst part was not the fact that he'd discovered people snatching cases left and right; the real tragedy was that everyone in the legal profession knew this went on. And yet no one did anything about it. The Bar knew the players involved. The Texas Supreme Court knew who ran cases. Sure, the court had tried to clean up by tinkering with the referral fee system. But that was just a front. Even the justices were known to accept large campaign contributions from firms running cases. But no one said a word. When somebody finally turned somebody in, the Bar protected them and gave the offenders a mere slap on the wrist. The Bar wasn't any different from a Mexican judge helping out a *compadre* lawyer.

"What was your client's name?" Cromwell asked.

"Porfirio Medina," Alex took a deep breath. He was having a difficult time containing himself. His eyes started getting watery. "He'd come into the United States in search of his wife and only son, Juan José."

"Was he here legally or illegally?" asked Cromwell.

"Illegally. He risked life and limb to find his family."

Alex told the committee about Pilo's difficult trek to the border. He told of the beatings and the highway robbers, the *federales*, and about Pilo's unrelenting resolve to find his family. And how he never had the chance to find out what had happened to them.

Alex pulled photos of Pilo's wedding from an envelope, his family and the *actas*. He approached the chairman and handed him the envelope for all the committee members to see.

"When did you first discover," Senator Ellis asked, "that somebody else was pretending to be your client and suing on behalf of the wife and child?"

"About three weeks after my client had hired me, Senator."

"And that the whole thing had been allegedly set up by Harrow & Amaro?" asked Senator Massini.

"A few months after that."

"Do you really think that this new proposed bill will stop individuals like Harrow, Cantu, Ayala, Margoux, and their cronies from engaging in similar conduct, Mr. del Fuerte?" asked Senator Brody.

"It's a start, Senator. It's a step toward restoring trust, honor, and confidence to this noble profession," Alex said without missing a beat. "And I think that some firms will think twice before engaging in this type of conduct. You won't be able to stop it completely from happening. But for those who were considering engaging in it, this new law might just deter them. It will counteract the effects of the AMEGO legislation. No one wants to lose their license and go to prison for two to ten years. It's not a perfect solution, but right now it's the only feasible solution. The way things have been in the past, no one is afraid of getting caught running cases. It's not a crime, just a violation of the rules of ethics. So you're labeled unethical—big deal! There are lawyers down in the Valley who have been found to have engaged in running cases repeatedly. They get reprimanded, put on probation, pay a small fine, and are allowed to continue to practice law. It's a joke!"

Massini, Brody, and Ellis continued to ask questions and write notes on their pads.

"Do you have any suggestions," asked Cromwell, "or thoughts or comments as to whether instead of criminalizing such conduct, it would be, perhaps, more appropriate that an attorney should lose his license for a period of, say, two years and to disgorge all fees earned from running cases or dirty cases?"

"I think there is considerable support for such a bill. Its proponents argue that running cases is a victimless crime. They argue that ultimately the cases go to the better lawyers who will get the client the best result, that the market takes care of the client. It's a valid argument. No harm, no foul. I would think a bill that would automatically trigger punitive damages upon a finding that barratry—parties conspired to engage in 'case running,' or paid others to bring in cases—was committed would make people notice and think twice. Make it a per se fraud violation that entitles the plaintiff to punitive damages. A bill like that, with teeth, might work, without criminalizing such conduct. I'm not opposed to such a measure."

"Do you have anything else to add before we open the floor to somebody else?" Cromwell asked.

"Yes. If you're really serious about fixing the problem, it's simple. It will take guts, but it can be done. First, you educate the public that it's wrong and illegal to be solicited. Secondly, prohibit the attorneys from lending any money to the client; make it illegal. The attorney may foot medical expenses or court costs, but that's it. The medical expenses need to be paid directly to the provider. Now notice I said court costs. I did not say litigation costs. If you give attorneys the opportunity to lend money, they will disguise the loan as litigation costs. Make it impossible for the attorney to advance money directly to the client, thinking the client will reimburse the provider. An attorney should not be allowed to give the money to the client who then gives it to the provider. That right there is half the problem. A victim finds it very hard to say no to a lawyer or somebody working for the lawyer who shows up with fifteen thousand dollars in exchange for a signature along the dotted line. Most states already prohibit lawyers and law firms from lending money to clients. Texas is the exception.

"Finally, have the profession monitor itself, but with incentives. For example, the lawyer who files a lawsuit against another for case running gets assistance from the attorney general's office with financial and litigation support. If he prevails, the AG and the attorney split the disgorged fee. This will put money back into the state's coffers. Secondly, the losing party surrenders his or her license for five years and must also pay the prevailing parties' litigation costs and court costs. No ifs, ands, or buts."

"What about if the losing party appeals?" the chairman asked.

"They have to post a bond for the entire amount, just like any other losing party," Alex said.

The committee continued to listen to testimony in favor and against such a measure. The two proposed bills would have far-reaching implications not only in Texas, but in other parts of the country as well. It was the beginning of the end.

Fetzer and Alex drove together to Austin's Bergstrom International Airport. Over the P.A. system, a woman announced that Alex's flight was now boarding at gate 21-A. Fetzer walked his former student to the gate. It had been a long week of meetings with senators, the governor's office, house representatives, and their staff, as well as hearings and testimonials.

Fetzer was needed in Houston to close on the sale of his house. The beach was calling. Alex was needed back at the office. The trial's publicity had made him a hot commodity. He was now the talk of the town and the lawyer everyone wanted. Clients were waiting in droves. There was a one-month waiting list to get in to see him. Everyone wanted to have del Fuerte & Fetzer, attorneys at law, as their counsel.

Even the Mexican government had come calling. Mexican officials wanted to launch an inquiry in connection with similar cases involving Mexican families that may have suffered the same fate as the Medinas. They wanted the firm to investigate several other wrongful death actions all along the U.S. and Mexico border.

To Fetzer, the short week at the state capitol was a symbol that sometimes even the little people can bring about great changes. He was proud of his student and of the changes that were forthcoming. He truly wished that either of the proposed bills would pass and become law, although he knew how politics was played.

In the end, justice was for sale in Austin. That's the way it was. That's the way it had always been. At that very moment, the trial lawyers and their lobbyists, the insurance industry and their lobbyists, product manufacturers and their lobbyists, car makers and their lobbyists, powerful players and law firms and their lobbyists, even those firms that had no desire to stop running cases, and others were cutting deals in the state capitol behind closed doors. It was a process that had no room for victims and the little people. Instead, it catered to big interests, big business, big lawyers, and big money.

Alex was anxious to get back to his firm and start helping people. This time, he would pick the cases that he wanted, the cases where he could make a real difference. The pressures to take a case because he needed money to pay the bills were gone. He could be the lawyer he wanted to be. Everything else was of no consequence or significance.

"They were in on it," Alex said, breaking the silence as he thought back on the series of events in his life during the past year.

"Who?" asked Fetzer. "What are you talking about?"

"Chordelli and his firm," replied Alex, looking at his old professor.

"Why are you saying that? Why now?" Fetzer asked.

"If you're going to be my partner, I can't keep this from you. Chordelli set this whole thing up—and set me up, too. By the time I realized it, it was too late. The jury was close to reaching a verdict."

"Who was financing the deal?" demanded the professor.

"Chordelli."

"I figured that much. I suspected they were somehow involved. I never trusted Jeff. Not in law school when he was my student, and definitely not now. He was always a shyster."

"The good news is that we can now have a little fun with him and his firm," Alex said.

"How so?"

Alex pulled a micro-cassette out of his pocket and held it up for the professor to see. "Let's just say a source turned me on to this tape where Jeff C. and Judge Macallan are discussing the perfect case, the kind of case where they both stand to reap millions in fees. There's only one slight problem."

"They're missing a plaintiff, right?" Fetzer guessed, eyes wide open.

"You got it. I want to see them try to explain that one to the feds," Alex said, smiling. "But wait, there's more."

"What do you mean, there's more?"

"All they're missing is an unsuspecting firm to accept the case so they won't have to touch it."

"Ouch!" Fetzer exclaimed. "You know what that means?"

"I can guess."

"Chordelli's days are numbered," Fetzer explained.

"You're right. It's payback time. And we'll be watching from the sidelines."

"Just when you thought things couldn't get any stranger," the professor said. "No wonder the legal profession gets a bad name. Are you sure it's Chordelli and Macallan on the tape?"

"Positive."

"Well, I'll be dammed!" exclaimed Fetzer. "We are going to have fun with this one!"

"You better believe it! Fun is my middle name. You still have friends in the justice department, right?"

"*Tú estás correcto*," Fetzer said in broken Spanish, smiling.

The student and his professor started laughing. They laughed louder and louder until it was time to board the plane. The Texas-Mexico border was calling.

Chapter 41

GARCÍA'S IN MATAMOROS was the meeting place. Schlaeter wanted to talk, and since García's also happened to have the best frog legs in all of northern Mexico, not to mention spicy *micheladas*, he'd picked the place. The special agent had discovered the hole in the wall while conducting surveillance on Gonzalo Armendáriz, the new head of the Gulf cartel.

"So, what did the U.S. attorney's office say?" Alex asked pleasantly as he removed his sunglasses. Negotiations for a deal on behalf of Naivi had now been going on for several months.

"They've offered immunity," the FBI agent said, "but we had to call Houston, and Houston had to call Washington and get authority. You know how those government lawyers operate. They always have to check with the heads up there. Always punting. Anyway, it took a while, but it looks good for your girl."

"When can you get me something in writing?" the attorney asked.

"The U.S. attorney is preparing a cooperation and immunity agreement as we speak. I'll fax it to your office this afternoon so that you and your client can review it."

"So, they're okay with her not having to testify?"

"Yes," the agent said, "but only if the tapes are as good as you say. If that's the case, then I doubt any knucklehead will want to take his chances at trial."

"Well, from the portions you and I have heard, I think you'll agree the main targets are done. The guys you were after, anyway," Alejandro del Fuerte said with confidence as he sipped on his ice-cold *michelada*. He reached for a Cohiba and proceeded to light it up.

"After all those years," marveled the special agent, "I finally get to put these jerks away. Just the kind of evidence I've been looking for. Are you sure there's nothing on Yarrington? I want that jerk more than anything else!"

"As much as you and I hate the *sanababiche*," said Alex, "I hate to say it, but there's nothing on him."

"Too bad."

"Who would have guessed, right?" the young attorney said, sounding surprised, and switched from the Yarrington topic. "A worker at the clerk's office cracks the case! Unbelievable!"

"Pretty amazing!" exclaimed Schlaeter as he chomped on his *ancas de rana al ajillo,* garlic butter dripping down his chin. "At least now, two of the biggest law firms running cases are gone. And after news of the indictments hit the airwaves, if there are others out there thinking of doing it, they'll have second thoughts about getting their hands dirty."

"Well, I'm glad the feds are picking up the prosecution," said Alex, "especially since the Bar can't swat a fly and the Texas Rangers have no interest in prosecuting these cases."

"You forget the legislature," Schlaeter said, sounding pissed off. "They don't want to clean up. And no wonder, ninety percent of all members are lawyers themselves!"

"It would be like taking food off the table," responded Alex, as images of Yarrington popped into his head. If it hadn't been for him, right now Lieutenant Governor Yarrington would be getting intimately familiar with the federal sentencing guidelines.

"That's exactly right!"

"Well, I was glad to help. I'll call my client and give her the good news," the attorney said as he finished his drink.

"Just one thing before you go," said the agent. "How did you manage not to get caught up in the mess, since Chordelli pitched you all that money?"

"What I did was not illegal or unethical. My client was Pilo, his estate, and the heirs. I owed no duty to Chordelli."

"Yes, but you haven't paid taxes on the money Chordelli sent you," the agent reminded him.

"You know damn well," countered the attorney, "that you would have never cracked this case without my effort! Besides, two of the most corrupt law firms in Texas are gone . . . and, if I remember correctly, we had a deal, no?"

"Yes, I took care of everything with the IRS."

"All right, then," Alex answered, "we're even."

"I just can't believe they wanted Harrow so bad. It never made sense to me."

"Well, they had to have clean hands. Especially since they had been involved from the get-go."

"But," said the agent, "to try to set somebody up like that? That level of involvement? They must have really, really disliked the Corpus Christi boys."

"You're right. I never understood it myself, but whatever happened between those two firms doesn't concern me."

"I see. Is the state also going after your girl?" asked the agent. "Do you know?"

"I think I've got that covered already."

"Really?" replied the agent, "who are you talking to over there at the D.A.'s office?"

"Assistant D.A. Montemayor," replied the attorney.

"She agreed to help you? I'm surprised. I hear she's tough to the point that the feds offered her a job handling portions of the Enron prosecution."

"Well," said Alex smiling, "you're right, she's tough. But she's not going anywhere. At least, not with the feds in Houston."

"Is that so?"

"*Pa'que veas*," Alex said as he tugged on his lapels, radiant and grinning. "There you have it. Speaking of, I have a lunch engagement at Café Latino in ten minutes with a colleague."

"Let me guess—Gigi, right?"

"You're good," Alex answered and started laughing.

"No wonder I noticed something different when you walked in," exclaimed the agent. "I just couldn't put my finger on it."

"What can I say?" the attorney replied.

"All right, counselor," said the agent, extending his greasy hand to shake the attorney's. "I won't keep you from your date."

"See ya around," Alex said as he threw a twenty on the table and started to walk away. "Good luck taking them down."

"*Adiós, compadre,*" the agent said. "Oh, say hello to Ms. Montemayor. . . . Too bad I won't get to work with her over here, with us on this side."

"Don't fret," the attorney said. "*Ya veremos qué pasa.* You never know."

"We'll be in touch."

"*Órale,* bye."

"YOU WANT ME TO DO WHAT?" Gigi asked, eyes wide open, cheeks blushing. They were having dinner at Café Latino, waiting for their entrees to arrive.

"Come with me to Mexico," Alex explained.

"*¿Estás seguro?* Are you serious?" she asked, again.

"*Estoy segurísimo.*"

"So, you want me to take a week off during Charro Days and go traveling with you in Mexico?"

"Yes."

"And miss out on prosecuting the leader of the Texas mafia for the murder of an undercover narcotics agent? Is that what you're asking?" She was looking straight into Alejandro del Fuerte's green eyes, as they sat across from each other. Her stomach was tied up in knots; she could not believe what she'd just heard.

"Well," Alex said clearing his throat, while reaching across the table and grabbing her hands in his, "I've thought about taking a week off in the next couple of months . . . and maybe do a bit of traveling, some celebrating too, I guess. After the Harrow trial, I've felt pretty spent, emotionally and physically."

"I know what you mean," Gigi replied, "trials do that, they can be pretty exhausting."

"I don't know how you do it, week after week, in and out of trial. And now that you've been promoted to felony prosecutor, I guess it is even more daunting."

"It is," said Gigi, "especially since I haven't taken time off in over two years. I got two or three weeks of accumulated vacation time, not to mention all my sick days."

"So, what do you say? C'mon, let's do it. It'll be fun."

"I need another glass of wine," Gigi said nervously, obviously still trying to digest the meaning of Alejandro's invitation. She was now looking down on the table, the cozy dining room had started to spin, slowly. She blurted out, "I'll have to think about it. When is Charro Days?"

"Three months from now."

"I guess I could use my vacation time. Could we go to San Miguel de Allende? I've heard it's beautiful. Would you take me?"

"I'd love to."

"I'll tell you what," Gigi sighed, "if the Texas mafia trial washes out, or the defendant decides to cop a plea, then I'll go. Otherwise, I'll have to stay and get the case ready for trial."

"*Bien,*" said Alex, "I'll keep my fingers crossed."

"*Changuitos,*" Gigi replied smiling, as she crossed her fingers too.

Alex grabbed his wine glass, took a sip and said, "you know, I had not heard that expression in a million years. But I'll keep my fingers crossed so that you say yes. To *changuitos. Salud.*"

"*Changuitos.*" Gigi countered.

They raised their wine glasses and together toasted their good fortunes.

Chapter 42

THE WOODEN CROSSES WERE MADE OF CEDAR and were painted bright white. Alex had asked Romeo to make three of them—two large ones and one small—with the names Porfirio Medina, Rosario Medina, and Juan José Medina inscribed on them.

Now, almost two years later, Alex, Aurora, and María Luisa stood on the deserted stretch of South Texas highway near the scene of the rollover accident. Alex carried the crosses, a shovel, and a hammer while Pilo's daughter held a small teddy bear.

"We'll set them there, near that cattle fence," Alex said in Spanish as he pointed to a clearing under a large *huisache* tree with twisted branches hanging over the barbed wire. He started digging holes in the ground. "People driving north will see the three markers. It'll be a reminder for everyone to see. I only wish they could have been given a proper burial."

"You've done enough for our family," Aurora said.

"*Jamás nos olvidaremos*," María Luisa added.

"I wish I could have done more," Alex replied with a sad smile as he positioned the crosses in a small cluster and began driving the pointed ends further into the ground with the hammer. "I wish Pilo was still alive. I'll never forget him, my first client."

"It was better this way," Aurora interjected. "Had he found out the truth, he would have died a broken man."

"And to think he only wanted to make sure they were okay," said Alex. He used the shovel again to fill in the holes, then tamped down the dirt.

"*Eran todo para él*," María Luisa said as she hung the brown teddy bear on her half brother's cross. Aurora decorated the other two crosses with colorful bows and ribbons. Then María Luisa knelt down on a little patch of grass and started praying quietly as her aunt looked on.

Alex walked back to the truck parked on the road's shoulder. He sat in the cab, lit up a cigarette, and waited for María Luisa and Aurora as traffic whooshed by. He turned on the satellite radio and listened to "Seasons in the Sun."

Twenty minutes later, María Luisa and Aurora walked back to the truck and climbed in. Alex turned the key, and a moment later they were driving south on Highway 77 back to Brownsville. The burnt orange sun was setting gently over the horizon, looking as if it were about to land on the famous Divisadero Ranch. Sheets of blue bonnets, Mexican hats, and daisies dotted the landscape.

Alex broke the silence at last. Turning to María Luisa, he asked, "Are you ready to get back to Mexico City?"

María Luisa looked out the window and thought for a while. Then she smiled and with a nod of her head said she missed her people: "*Extraño a mi familia. Mi gente.*"

Alex reached for another cigarette, lit it, and exhaled slowly. He understood what she meant.

"*Te entiendo perfectamente,*" he said. *Not a day goes by that I don't think of Mamá and Papá*, he thought, smiling. *I miss them too.*